"LET ME WELCOME YOU TO IRELAND."

Meaghan felt more than heard the collective intake of breath from the cluster of girls across the room. Drawn from scandal or envy? He was an extraordinarily handsome man. Before she could back down, she stretched up and kissed him, square on the mouth.

From the instant they touched she was lost. This was not going to be the polite peck or the brief salute she'd hoped would satisfy the foolish challenge she'd accepted. This kiss flamed to life a portion of herself she had given up as fantasy many years ago.

The Blessing, with all the trappings she'd heard her brothers deny and then extol. As she experienced herself once before. This time the Blessing reverberated richer . . . deeper, reaching through her from across centuries of Reillys.

She'd told her brothers that the Blessing was in the blood of all the Reillys—even girls. But she'd never expected to find her heritage—and her destiny—in a stranger's kiss. An *Englishman's* kiss.

As she tried to pull away, still dizzy, his arms slid around her waist. "This is not how I remember being greeted the last time I visited your island."

Dear Romance Reader,

Last year, we launched the Ballad line with four new series, and each month we'll present both new and continuing stories set everywhere from medieval England to the American West—the kind of passionate, romantic stories you love best, written by the most gifted authors. At the back of each book, we'll tell you when you can find subsequent books in the series that have captured your heart.

This month, rising star Martha Schroeder returns with the final book in her *Angels of Mercy* series. In **A Rose for Julian**, a young nurse with a painful past agrees to care for a nobleman's wounded son—but never imagines she will come to love him, too. Next, Linda Devlin offers the next installment of *The Rock Creek Six* with **Jed**. What happens when an independent man and a stubborn woman must work together to solve a crime? Teamwork, of course—the married kind!

In the last entry of RITA-nominated author Elizabeth Keys's atmospheric *Irish Blessing* series, the youngest Reilly sibling believes she's immune to the family Blessing because she's a woman. But one kiss from a certain man changes that immediately—and she vows to show him the power of *this* **Reilly's Heart**. Finally, Kathryn Fox concludes her adventurous *Mounties* series with **The Third Daughter**, as a new mounted officer makes a business arrangement with a local ranch, and finds that he wants something far more personal from the rancher's oldest daughter—her love. Enjoy!

Kate Duffy
Editorial Director

Irish Blessing

REILLY'S HEART

Elizabeth Keys

ZEBRA BOOKS
Kensington Publishing Corp.
http://www.kensingtonbooks.com

For Roberta, who asked
"Can you give the boys a sister?"
And for Gwen, who cried. . . .

PROLOGUE

Limerick, Ireland
1847

"It's not fair." Meaghan Reilly stamped her foot, aggravated beyond the limits of her formidable five-year-old restraint.

The older boys' chuckles only grew louder in answer to her grievance. Even her own brothers—Devin, who was closest to her in age and usually understood her, and Quin, just home from his first long sea voyage, had joined with the others as they toasted their prowess on the cricket field and shut her out of the fun.

Fury flooded her bruised heart. She would have liked nothing better than to kick each one of them with her little black dress boots. She'd bet they wouldn't laugh then. But Mama was forever telling her such actions weren't ladylike. And Da wanted her to be a lady he could be proud of, not a hoyden romping through the shipyard. That was why she had to practice her stitching and her music, even though she hated it, and why she restrained herself now despite the depths of her fury.

What she really wanted to do was join the boys

on the pitch for the next round of cricket, not get stuck listening to the governess drone on with all the enthusiasm of a funeral service. How else was she going to learn to be a batsman or a bowler fit to play with her brothers when they all returned home to Beannacht Island?

"I don't like any of you," she told the teammates finally, meaning each word, as she stared particularly hard at her brothers. If Bryan were here he would let her play. He understood unfair behavior.

"Not one little bit," she stated again, anger burning inside her.

She turned and fled from them then, through the throngs of party goers, not stopping even when Quin called after her. She dodged the elbows and legs of the gentlemen in attendance and the wide rustling skirts of the ladies, searching for a quiet spot where she could fume in peace and release the angry torrent churning deep within her.

She reached a wide set of French doors, beyond which freedom beckoned in the form of open gardens and wide blue sky. Without hesitation she reached for the doorknob, her breath hitching in her chest as she escaped.

Her cousin Sheila's birthday party brimmed with laughter, as everyone celebrated on, heedless of Meaghan's unhappiness. With a mutinous sniff, she muffled them all by closing the door behind her.

Tears stung her eyes, dripping down her cheeks and chin despite her best efforts to hold them back. How dare they tell her girls would never be able to play cricket as well as boys? Wherever did they get the idea men were so superior? It was just like being told she would never receive The Blessing just because she'd been born a girl! She would. She just knew she would. It didn't matter how many times Quin or Devin or even Bryan tried to tell her otherwise.

Gnawing her lip, she swiped at her tears as she marched some distance away from the house and plopped herself down on a stone bench at the edge of a hedgerow filled with the soothing scent of honeysuckle. Warmed by the sun, the bench seemed much more welcoming than the hateful party had been.

"I *will* have The Blessing."

"Indeed?" The one-word question made her jump and startled away her tears.

"Who said that?" She looked around her, wondering what fey fairy folk might be inhabiting the hedge.

"I did." The tall, handsome boy she'd noticed talking with Uncle Gill earlier came from behind the hedge. He smiled down at her, his clear blue eyes crinkling at the corners. He had a nice face.

She couldn't help smiling back at him. He looked to be older than Devin, but not nearly as old as Quin, who was now turning into a terrible grouch, since he fancied himself grown.

The boy motioned to the other side of the bench. "Is this seat taken?"

"No." She shook her head vigorously and scooted over to make room for him.

"What is this Blessing?" he asked her in a tone holding none of the derision her brothers offered when she spoke of their family heritage.

She considered her answer for a moment. " 'Tis in the blood of all Reillys."

His eyebrows arched together over his clear

blue gaze. "Indeed, sounds interesting. And you are a Reilly I suppose?"

She nodded and carefully recited the words she'd learned describing The Blessing. " 'Tis a sound once heard that lingers on. A sight once seen and never forgotten. A feeling once felt, always remembered."

That's what she'd heard Quin tell Bryan more than once before Bryan had left their island to study the law.

"Sounds quite wonderful," her new companion said.

"Yes, and I will have it. I *will.*" She clenched her fists for emphasis and frowned up into the most beautiful blue eyes she'd ever seen. Eyes that smiled understanding and acceptance of her declarations despite her being a lowly girl.

The boy brushed her cheek with his fingers, catching her last tear as it fell.

She blinked, surprised by the gentleness of his touch, so different from her rough-and-tumble brothers. They might have grown up on the docks and decks of Reilly Ship Works, with a seaman's discipline and their mother's strictures, but this boy had obviously learned his manners elsewhere.

"And do you think you'll know when it happens?"

"Aye, I'll know." She sought the words her brothers spoke, echoes from the granny she couldn't remember. "We must be ready for The Blessing at any time. And we must take heed, 'cause a Blessing missed is a Curse, indeed."

"Then I hope you get everything you are looking for, sweeting." He squeezed her hand.

"Thank you." Without thinking, she scooted

to her knees and looped her hands around his neck. "You're very nice."

She stretched up and kissed him, square on the mouth.

Her own boldness surprised a gasp from her as she pulled back. But she didn't pull back soon enough to stop the wild spiral of dizziness sweeping through her, stronger than anything she'd ever felt before. Better even than when Da twirled her around and around. It was the best feeling in the whole world and deep inside her, her soul sighed with satisfied recognition.

She clutched his collar and rested her chin on his shoulder to keep herself from spinning completely away like a leaf tossed in the wind.

The handsome boy's arm slid around her shoulders as if he too needed to hold on. She was glad it was not just she who felt these wondrous things. Feelings were so much better when shared.

She felt lighter than air and heavier than stone, and she could only close her eyes and hold on to her handsome new friend, certain she would fall if she didn't. She took a deep breath and the scents of oranges and mint filled her.

If that was what kissing felt like, no wonder her parents did it so often. The sound of laughter, pure and joyous, echoed through her, as though chased by a rainbow of colored stars.

"Nick!" a voice called from the house.

Meaghan opened her eyes, leaned back to look up at him, and smiled. He smiled too, but he seemed almost as if he didn't really see her at all.

"Nick, are you out here?" Closer now.

The tall boy blinked and released her. "That's my father, I have to go."

"I wish you didn't." The strength of that wish echoed to her toes.

"Me, too." He ruffled her hair, his blue eyes narrowing as he scrutinized her. "How old are you?"

"Five." She sighed, still feeling the wild dizziness deep inside her.

He laughed, but it was not a nasty laugh like the other boys had laughed earlier. She liked the tickle of his laughter as it rumbled through her.

"Nick!" His father sounded more urgent.

"I'm coming." Nick shouted and got to his feet. He bent toward her and touched her lips with his finger. "If you kiss like that at five, I'd be interested to see what you're like when you get older."

With that he was gone, and she could only watch his easy stride as he walked away. Sunlight glinted on his dusty blond hair. He waved once before disappearing into the house.

She waved back, still feeling the touch of his finger against her mouth. And quite certain kissing was her new favorite thing.

Better than birthday cake and lemonade put together.

One

"It is not too late to stop this, Nick."

Nicholas Mansfield, Lord Ashton, accepted his bowler from Randall, his new valet, and straightened his cuffs as he eyed his ward without comment. They both knew it was far too late to stop what had been set in motion by hands other than theirs. They'd discussed all the ramifications before undertaking the voyage. Their very lives could depend on what they discovered when they disembarked.

"We could leave this to the authorities and return to London before May Day with none the wiser." Jamie's normally merry features quieted into serious lines eerily reminiscent of his late father's as he pushed away from the cabin wall and settled his own hat atop his short blond curls.

Nick shook his head. He understood Jamie's reluctance all too well, but he couldn't escape the inner certainty that they had delayed their investigation too long already. A deep sense of foreboding had shrouded his thoughts as they'd

sailed toward the land of myths and mists. He'd
not set foot in Ireland in nearly fifteen years, not
since escorting the caskets bearing his parents
home to England.

Old guilt shuddered through him. He'd
thought the worst of it was spent when they
passed those godforsaken rocks. But the burden
of survival seemed to grow heavier with each
breath he took as they traversed the River Shannon and neared Limerick—just as his instinct for
survival sharpened with his anticipation of the
confrontations and maneuvers yet to come.

"We can no longer ignore the coincidences.
There are too many signs pointing to our associate here. Yet nothing substantial enough for the
authorities to take action." Their facts were as
murky as the Irish fog, like the river currents
swirling in ever deeper and darker eddies, ready
to snatch the unwary.

"Yes." Jamie sighed. "I suppose we've had this
discussion often enough for me to recognize
when we reach the end. At least you brought me
with you rather than keeping me under lock and
key at home in Suffolk."

"Given the dangers there of late, I feel better
having you where I can see you, pup."

A resounding jolt and the rapid tattoo of footsteps on the deck overhead heralded the ship's
docking. The time for discussion was indeed at
an end. Nick's gut tightened. What would the
Honorable Gill O'Brien have to say for himself
when confronted face-to-face with his partners?

"Come along, my lord." Jamie offered an ex-
aggerated bow and gestured toward the stateroom door, his normally jovial spirits reasserting
themselves.

"Stay with the baggage, Randall." Nick fished some coins from his pocket and handed them to his valet. "I'll make arrangements for a cart to follow us once we secure suitable lodgings."

"Very good, sir." Randall nodded as he shut the last case. He was a bit burly for a valet, but then his size was something to be prized, along with his solid credentials. Nick felt better for having the former soldier at his back and looking out for Jamie. Randall should also prove invaluable in helping uncover any connection between O'Brien and the alarming number of accidents Nick had escaped of late.

"Watch your head, boy," Nick warned as he ducked through the stateroom hatch.

"You must cease acting as if you are my nursery maid while we're here. I am no longer in need of leading strings." Jamie's grumbles held more humor than spleen.

"Barely."

They emerged onto a deck swallowed almost completely by fog. Thick, cloying, all too familiar. Ireland and danger rolled into one ominous cloud. An uncomfortable lump formed in Nick's throat, sank like an icy ball to his stomach, and sent corresponding shivers over his arms. He fought the urge to grab Jamie and drag him back to the quiet safety of the cabin.

His stomach tightened. Ship cabins were no havens of safety. Not in a fog like this. A fog like the one that stole his parents. He jumped as a crate dropped from a hoist on the aft deck. The percussion as it hit the planks echoed like the explosion of a hull on granite. The creaking of this ship's timbers brought back the groans of another vessel as it tore apart in the waves, splintered on rocks hidden in the gloom. The distant calls from the rigging and dock became screams for help that gradually faded until all that was left was the relentless lap of water and the cursed fog.

He pulled his thoughts together with an effort and forced his attention forward. This was not that long ago night, but a bustling wharf. Any danger lying within this fog came not from rocks or timber, but from human intent.

"Heave to, Nick, or we'll never get there." Jamie nudged the back of Nick's shoulder.

Heave to, indeed. He'd solve nothing if he allowed himself to be mired in past despair and regrets. Jamie's future, and his own, required his complete concentration.

Captain McManus, the *Caithream II*'s officer, emerged from the mists. "Good day to you, Lord Ashton. Ye'll need to have a care. There's quite a crush on the docks, but with the fog clinging to the wharf line, ye can barely see in front of yer face." He led them toward the gangplank.

"You have a fine vessel, McManus." Nick shook the captain's hand. "Every bit as well built and smooth sailing as you promised."

"Thank ye, Lord Ashton." The Irishman's face crinkled into a smile. "She's Reilly born and Reilly built. Ye can't ask for better."

"Thank you, too, for that wonderful restorative you supplied our man." Jamie shook the captain's hand as well. "For a big fellow he certainly was done in by the smallest of motion once we got underway."

The image of Randall, collapsed against the bulkhead and clutching a chamber pot for dear life as they departed Bristol, swam forward. Nick and Jamie had both been flummoxed by what to do to ease the big man's suffering. And his embarrassment. The tea McManus had sent down to the valet had alleviated Randall's suffering almost immediately.

Captain McManus chuckled. "Another Reilly trademark. No Reilly vessel sails without a bountiful supply of Granny Reilly's special ginger tea."

"Well, it certainly did the trick," Nick said. "These Reillys must be a remarkable lot."

"They are at that, my lord. None finer," Captain McManus agreed. "I hope ye have a successful trip here in Limerick, sirs. Good luck to ye both."

Crowds swirled on the docks below as ghostly passengers streamed past from the invisible ships anchored nearby. The hum of excited voices rose from the throng, swallowing anything else the captain might have said. Because they hadn't wished to tip O'Brien off to their visit in advance, they'd need to make arrangements for lodgings and transportation now that they'd arrived.

Nick craned his head before stepping into the masses, wishing he could ascertain the direction of the custom house where McManus had told them they would most readily find a hackney. The jostling of elbows and shoulders forced him to work his way toward the edge of the crowd.

"Follow me," he barked over his shoulder, praying Jamie could hear him.

Concern needled him as he reached the wharf's edge. Nick turned to check on Jamie through the surging masses swirling past in the whitewall of fog. As he strained to see, an unseen hand thrust hard into the small of his back. The force of the shove threw him off balance. He stepped to the side and met only air. For an eternal second he teetered on the edge of the dock.

The descent toward the black, scum-encrusted water took an age. His fingers scrambled for purchase on the dock or on the side of the *Caithream II*. Both were well out of reach. Somewhere above he heard shouting and a high-pitched scream.

He gulped for air, swallowing a lungful of the foul stench rising from the harbor before he hit the water with a stunning force. His last breath whooshed out of him and he fought to keep from filling his lungs with the murky water as it closed over him.

Cold. The living embodiment of his worst nightmare. A cloying death he had escaped once before.

The pitch-black water swallowed him in icy sludge. He kicked for what he prayed was the surface, as his sodden clothes and twisted memory fought to keep him under. Trying to swim in the cold muck of Limerick Harbor was all too much like struggling to escape the unyielding clutches of his nightmare.

Nick pushed harder. He'd be damned if he'd traveled all this way to drown or be crushed between pilings in such an ignominious manner before he'd gotten the answers he sought.

"Nick! Nick!" he heard his name repeated, muffled and distant.

He broke to the surface and gulped a breath. Relief pushed through him when he saw Jamie bending over the edge of the dock with an audience of curious onlookers behind him. At least the lad hadn't followed him into the drink or suffered some other dire consequence during the scuffle.

"I'm all right," Nick wheezed, then sputtered as backwash from his efforts to stay afloat slapped his chin. Gads, this stuff was rank. It would be a wonder if he wasn't felled by typhus or some other disease—provided he wasn't pulverized first.

The *Caithream II* creaked dangerously near.

He swabbed the water streaming from his hair out of his eyes and searched for a means to climb back up to the pier. His bowler bobbed pristinely a few feet away, as if mocking his sodden condition. The effort to retrieve it wasn't worth the trouble. He'd buy a dozen like it at the nearest haberdashery, once he was dry.

"Hold on, Lord Ashton. We'll throw ye a rope."

He looked behind him to see Captain McManus peering down at him from the deck of the *Caithream II*. The captain held a long gaffer's pike, which was thrust into the pier to keep his ship from shifting in her berth and knocking Nick to pieces against the wharf. Several of his sailors joined him with their own pikes to stave off such disaster.

Nick struggled out of his coat as the garment tried to pull him back under. His rapidly depleting stores of energy needed all the help he could muster to fight the cold and the current.

"Here you go, Nick," Jamie called as he heard a slap on the water beside him. "Wrap it around you and we'll haul you up."

He didn't need to be told twice. His fingers were numb from the cold as he grabbed his lifeline. He clung to the rope with leaden arms as the men pulled him back up to the docks.

Randall was there with several of the *Caithream II*'s crew, hauling him up. The crowd of onlookers cheered as Jamie helped him to his feet. So much for slipping quietly into town.

"Are you all right?" The anxiety in Jamie's voice promised the rest of the day would be spent with an endless stream of such inquiries. This was neither the time nor the place to discuss the deliberate nature of the blow that sent him over the edge.

"I'm fine, pup. A clumsy accident is all." Nick spoke loud enough for all in the crowd to hear as he locked a meaningful gaze with Randall. The valet nodded, taking his point without the need for him to explain.

Nick leaned closer to Jamie's ear. "This sort of incident is precisely the reason I was so adamant about the need to proceed with care whilst we are here," he hissed, despite the chattering of his teeth.

Jamie had the sense to clamp his mouth into a grim line and say nothing further. Randall scanned the assemblage for a few seconds, then scooped up a thick blanket and put it around Nick's shoulders. "Will you come back on board and change, sir?"

"No. Everything is packed, and after soaking in that filth, I want a real bath. I will change once we arrive at our associate's. We'll go there first after all. Mr. O'Brien must accept me as I am."

"Very good, sir." Randall scanned the crowd again as it began to disperse. The police inspector who had recommended him had spoken highly of his abilities, especially at remembering faces.

With a salute to Captain McManus on the deck behind him, Nick shook the sailors' hands and thanked them. "Tell your captain I am in his debt."

The show over, the crowd dispersed. Nick and Jamie made their way down the pier with Randall keeping a watchful eye over them. After hailing a hackney, the former soldier gave the O'Brien's address to the driver and opened the door.

"You should be all right until I arrive, sir. I'll arrange for suitable lodgings and bring a small bag with a change of clothes for you with me in the hackney to the O'Brien's."

Nick merely nodded his agreement to this plan. His jaw was clenched tight, trying to prevent the shivers of cold that were threatening to overtake him. Randall used the opportunity of a last handshake to unobtrusively slip a small hand pistol into his employer's fingers. Nick clutched the small weapon fiercely. The sooner they could prove or eliminate Gill O'Brien as a suspect in these accidents the better.

"Truth or hazard, Eloise? Have you ever allowed your betrothed liberties beyond a kiss on the hand or cheek?" Sheila O'Brien challenged her guest while refilling her teacup.

The question drew Meaghan Reilly's gaze from the edition of the *London Times* Uncle Gill had given her earlier in the day.

A blush and a giggle confirmed Eloise Farrell's answer before the slender blonde even opened her mouth. "Well, I'll only tell you"—she spoke with husky excitement, and the arch of her delicate brows invited the whole assemblage to listen—"because you may all soon find yourselves in the same situation."

The rest of the girls crowding the O'Brien salon gasped and clustered closer as the soon-to-be bride strove to describe in hushed tones the ecstasies of the courtship liberties her swain attempted to cajole from her during their moments of stolen privacy.

The cream of Limerick society had gathered ostensibly for tea and embroidery this afternoon, but their needles and hoops were quickly cast aside, replaced by cozy gossip and boisterous parlor games.

Meaghan rolled her eyes, imagining her three brothers' reactions to such a gathering. Now that they were all married and settled with families, however, they were no doubt learning to cope with such social occasions in their own homes.

The image of her three handsome brothers balancing teacups and struggling with pithy conversations not involving ships or shipbuilding elicited a soft giggle and she returned to perusing her periodical. She might have no interest in exchanging fashion tips or recipes for spiced beef, let alone disclosing to her cousin's friends intimacies best kept private, but she would surely survive this afternoon with little harm to show and perhaps an ally or two gained for a project that truly mattered. If only she could find the right opportunity to introduce the subject.

She shifted uncomfortably on the gold satin-tufted settee. Every one of the nine hoops on her new crinoline seemed determined to raise her peridot tea dress to ungainly and uncomfortable angles. How she longed for the simple skirts and blouses she'd worn during her travels with her parents in Italy and Switzerland or at home on Beannacht.

"Oh, no!" Sheila squealed good-naturedly as she snatched the pages from Meaghan's hands. "You're not going to hide in some moldy old tome today, Meggy. You're supposed to be enjoying your visit here. I invited my closest and dearest friends for tea today just so you could meet them without the crush of a party or theater outing to distract them from getting to know you."

"Closest and dearest? All fifteen of them?" Meaghan raised a skeptical brow as she looked past her cousin to the gaggle still squawking over Eloise's beau's attempted kiss during a turn in the garden the evening before.

Sheila laughed, and set the small brown ringlets fringing her face to dancing. "One can never have too many friends, dearest. If your parents hadn't made you practically a vagabond, traipsing through the Continent these past few years, you'd realize how much you missed in not making your bow to society."

"You're so right, Cousin," Meaghan agreed in a mock serious tone. "What could Da and Mama have been thinking to force me into touring all those magnificent art collections and ancient architectural structures, or by introducing me to some of the greatest medical minds of the modern age?"

"Exactly." As usual, Sheila missed the sarcasm. "Now, come join the others. I imagine you have a tale or two worth hazarding."

She pulled Meaghan to a stand with a smile that lit the depths of her soft brown eyes. "Especially about the handsome and titled gentlemen you must have met during your tours."

Meaghan shook her head, but allowed her cousin to lead her toward the rest of the party.

How naive. And Sheila thought *she* was the one who needed to be brought up to snuff. "Not much to tell. I had a far better time talking to the patients or the clinic workers. I had very little tolerance for the spoiled dilettantes we occasionally met, who had too little to do beyond seeing to their own selfish entertainments."

Having listened to the most titillating tidbits of Eloise's courtship, the rest of the girls shifted their attention to Sheila as she returned.

"I believe it's Meaghan's turn," Sheila announced without a comment on Meaghan's remarks.

Eloise's perfect bow mouth puffed downward for a moment into a small pout. She was obviously not quite ready to relinquish being the center of attention. Meaghan noticed a dangerous light leap to life in the blonde's eyes as a sly smile quickly replaced her frown. "Well, as the last player, I get to challenge her."

Meaghan heaved an inner sigh. If only Mama and Da had taken her with them to America rather than sentenced her to this duration in society.

"Very well," she agreed with a casual shrug. "What would you like to know?"

"Have you ever kissed a man not of your family? And how many times? Truth or hazard." Eloise wore a smug smile as she leaned forward slightly to hear the reply.

A fleeting memory of a casual gratitude turned to magic on a sun-warmed bench not fifty yards from this very room flew into Meaghan's thoughts, accompanied by the years she had spent trying to repeat the wondrous experience with any boy she could persuade to pucker up.

Disappointment had long ago led her to the certainty she'd imagined the whole experience— that it had seemed larger and grander from of a child's viewpoint. The romance and high-flung emotions novels spoke of, that these girls craved, did not exist. Not for her. She far preferred her studies and her plans to make the world a better place.

She hesitated in answering. Disclosing all of this was not the way to make friends and win converts to her cause. And she'd promised Mama and Da not to stir up any controversy while they were away in America. Lying and dissemblance were not among her talents. Yet she was not about to let honesty over childhood indiscretions jeopardize her visit or her plans. The glimmer of sly satisfaction in Eloise Farrell's wide eyes and the expectant silence from the rest told her she was teetering on some unforseen brink. Neat trap and she'd sailed right into it.

"That's two questions. And besides, they are not fit questions to ask someone who is not attached," Sheila protested as Meaghan's silence stretched on.

"I'll take the hazard," Meaghan said at last. How bad could it be—balancing a teacup on her head or showing them her lack of talent as a singer?

The collective gasp told her she might have spoken too soon.

"The same as always—" Eloise began with a galling look of triumph.

"You must kiss the first man to walk through the door," one of the two flame-haired Carlson twins blurted out.

"No one's ever taken the challenge," her sister exclaimed.

Kiss the first man? With none of Sheila's brothers in residence, that would either be her Uncle Gill or Jacobs, the O'Brien's butler, Meaghan guessed. A quick kiss on the cheek would suffice. Either one would be startled at the warmth of such a greeting, but nothing scandalous would occur.

"Very well." She shrugged again, ignoring the sympathetic looks from several of the other girls as she tried to swallow her anger at being forced into this situation. She should have claimed a headache earlier and retired to her room with the latest article detailing the progress at Miss Nightingale's newest venture.

"It must be a true kiss, not a mere brush of the lip." Eloise clearly wanted full measure for her victory. Resentment flared in Meaghan. What had she ever done to this girl?

Stifling her qualms, she turned to Sheila. "May I pour myself a fresh cup of tea? Mine has grown stale, I'm afraid."

Sheila nodded. "Of course. Help yourself. Who would like to look through the latest issue of *Belle Assemblee*? I saw the most charming riding hat in there when Mama brought it to me, and I want all your opinions."

Bless Sheila for changing the subject. Meaghan added a bit more cream to her cup as she delayed returning to the group now clustered about the fashion magazine, giggling and exclaiming over the illustrations.

What on earth had she been thinking to accept Eloise's challenge once she knew its true depth? She shook her head, acknowledging the painful truth. She hadn't thought at all. Perhaps Da had been right not to let her stay with Quin and Siannon on the island or to go to Bryan and Emilynne. She could surely benefit from a few weeks' experience in polite society. Her glance slid to Eloise as she exclaimed over a design she found especially enticing. Meaghan certainly could learn a thing or two about cunning that might come in handy if she was going to be of any use to the local Nightingale Society.

She could almost hear her mother's sigh. *That's your father's temper, Meaghan—reacting before all the consequences have been thought through. Difficult at best for a businessman, and not at all suitable for a young lady.*

With any luck it would be another half hour or more before Jacobs came to collect the tray, and by that time surely the company would either be thinning or would have forgotten their challenge.

Stalwart footsteps just outside the salon's entrance sank her hopes. Her gaze flew to the polished-oak double doors. The conversation over which milliner could best match the hats in the magazine ceased as the doorknob turned. She swore she could feel every pair of eyes in the room boring into her back.

Meaghan put down her cup and saucer with a chink and swallowed. She'd accepted the challenge and she'd live through this. Kissing Jacobs's wrinkled cheek would cause him far less consternation than would the damage to her integrity should she quibble.

She advanced toward the door as it opened partway. Anticipation thickened in the salon like clotted cream. Was that her heartbeat racing or the stampeding echo from everyone else's?

"Mr. O'Brien?" A deep but unfamiliar voice called into the room as the door continued its inward swing.

"Diabhal." She whispered her brothers' favorite curse. Devil, indeed. The clipped voice was decidedly not Jacobs's. Not even Irish. It was an English voice.

The tall gentleman who entered the room wore an expensive brown brushed-wool suit that hugged his broad shoulders and fell smoothly past his trim hips. His dusty brown hair was a trifle long for the first order of fashion, but it suited his chiseled features and softened the jut of his chin. The bluest eyes she had ever seen scanned the salon's interior in confusion for a second. He was quite clearly the most handsome man Sheila's company had ever encountered, given the mooncalf looks of surprised adoration they all cast in his direction.

"I beg your pardon, ladies." He nodded his head at the assemblage clustered by Sheila and smiled thinly. "I have clearly taken a wrong turn. Could someone direct me to Mr. O'Brien's study?"

Practically gap mouthed, the girls remained frozen as they drank in the unexpected appearance of this god in their midst. He was younger than the men she'd expected to face in this challenge, but clearly he was old enough to handle the resulting awkwardness and view it as the prank it was clearly meant to be.

"I'd be happy to direct you to the study." Meaghan stepped forward as he turned to face her. Something familiar about the blazing blue

of the gaze that locked with hers tugged at her
memory, but she could not place it. Heat burned
her cheeks and she swallowed hard. "But first,
let me welcome you to Ireland."

She felt more than heard the collective intake
of breath from the cluster across the room.
Drawn from scandal or envy? He was an extraordinarily handsome man. Before she could back
down, she stretched up and kissed him, square
on the mouth.

From the instant they touched she was lost.
This was not going to be the polite peck given
a relative or the brief salute she'd hoped would
satisfy the foolish challenge she'd accepted. Vivid
images of broad, muscled chests, of warriors'
fierce pride, and men who knew how to claim
women's hearts exploded inside her. A maiden's
wish—a devil's curse. This kiss flamed to life a
portion of herself she had given up as fantasy
many years ago. The certainty shook her as much
as her own boldness.

"Mo laoch grian," she whispered against his
mouth. A sun warrior.

Despite the avid crowd watching them as their
lips brushed, it seemed as if the two of them
stood alone in an Alpine meadow surrounded by
majestic peaks. Instead of cool mountain breezes
though, a wave of heat, stronger than the sun
on a Mediterranean beach, streaked through her
to undulate low in her belly. The high-pitched
sound of unseen children's laughter, pure and
joyous, echoed through her, chased by a rainbow
of colored stars.

The Blessing, with all the trappings she'd
heard her brothers deny and then extol, as she'd
experienced herself once before. This time The

Blessing reverberated richer . . . deeper, reaching through her from across centuries of Reillys.

'Tis a sound once heard that lingers on. A sight once seen and never forgotten. A feeling once felt, always remembered. . . . Granny Reilly's words, oft repeated by her brothers, echoed through her.

At first, stiff with surprise at her assault, the man growled softly in his throat and met the touch of her lips with a stronger pressure from his own. Heartbeats drummed in her ears—her own? His? His lips drank from hers like a man parched. His hands slid over her back, molding her to him in an intimate embrace the like of which she'd never experienced.

The tingling intensity of her response surprised her, rending both her defenses and the stiff strictures of polite society. Sunlight and breezes skipping over sand dunes, the exhilaration of cutting across the waves with a stiff wind filling the sails, moonlight glistening on snow-covered peaks—all tumbled through her.

Overwhelmed, she pulled away, but not soon enough to stop the wild spiral of dizziness sweeping through her. Had the kiss lasted for the briefest of seconds or for an eternity? She'd lost all track. All reason.

Her knees trembled, refusing her silent command to step back.

Clutching his lapels, she rested her forehead against the cool worsted wool of his jacket. A tantalizing mixture of oranges and mint seemed to rise from her memory of a long time ago.

His arms slid around her waist as if he too needed to hold something. He gulped several deep breaths. Her skin burned from the contact of his hands on her dress as if chemise, stays, and silk had melted away. She felt lighter than air and heavier than stone, and she could only close her eyes and hold on to him, certain she would fall if she didn't.

This was what kissing should feel like. This was what she had been waiting for practically her whole life. This could not be happening. She'd told Quin that even girls could have The Blessing. She'd told them all. *'Tis in the blood of all Reillys.* But she'd never expected to find her heritage in a stranger's kiss. An Englishman's kiss.

Her Blessing. Her Curse? Uncertainty stole the remainder of her breath. What fearsome choice was she being asked to make? *Accept The Blessing or suffer The Curse . . . fer a blessing missed is a curse indeed.* So Devin had been wont to tease.

"This is not how I remember being greeted the last time I visited your island." The Englishman still clutched her waist, but icy disapproval frosted his tone. "But then, I was only a boy."

"You have been to Beannacht?" Surely, if he'd come to visit her father at Reilly Ship Works she'd remember. Worse, if he proved to be a friend of any of her brothers she'd be sunk once they heard of her shocking behavior.

He frowned at her as if she were a half-wit. "I referred to Ireland. Miss—?"

"I beg your pardon?" She drew back and blinked in confusion, uncomfortably aware of the watchful silence provided by Sheila and her friends.

"Your name, my dear? I generally like to know whom I am . . . addressing." He quirked a brow at her and allowed his gaze to drop from her face.

Fresh heat stung Meaghan's cheeks. As his hands dropped away from her sides, relief flowed through her, followed by a disconcerting sense of loss. She stepped back and offered him her hand. "Reilly. Meaghan Reilly."

He stared at her fingers as if they had suddenly sprouted talons and kept his clenched by his side. "Of the ship-building Reillys?"

It was Meaghan's turn to be surprised. Her hopes for a quiet passing of this debacle sank even lower. He must know one of her brothers. Quin perhaps? Or Bryan. Either one would be sure to lecture her quite forcefully on this brazen behavior. She could almost hear Bryan's advice. Best to meet things straight on. Her chin came up.

Regret for her impulsive acceptance of the challenge, and embarrassment over the intimacy she had just experienced, flooded her as her gaze locked with his. This Englishman was a victim far more than she. His obvious disdain scoured her, and the continued silence from the room's other occupants made matters all the worse.

She didn't trust her voice, especially with his pointed refusal to meet her verbal greeting halfway. She nodded her acknowledgment of her family ties and dropped her hand.

He looked her up and down for what seemed a breathless eternity as she waited for him to spill the scathing remarks crackling behind the icy condemnation in his eyes. "I'd heard you were a remarkable family—"

"My lord?" A familiar voice called from far down the hall, interrupting the rest of his observation. Meaghan's heart seized with new panic. Aunt Edna! She must be seeking this very man. What would she have to say about what had just transpired in her home? Had she truly called him "my lord?"

"The footman said he thought you might have taken a wrong turn." Aunt Edna closed in on her quarry. Meaghan wished for all her life she could sink into the very carpet.

"Ah." The visitor smiled, but little humor touched his eyes. "It would appear my hostess has set out to find me and guide me to the study herself. I will not be needing your . . . services after all."

Abruptly, he turned on his heel with a polite nod of farewell toward the group. "Ladies, pardon my interruption."

The last arrogant look he cast in her direction so clearly dismissed whatever he was going to say previously, dismissed what just rocked her very foundation as trivial, she couldn't stifle the spark of indignation that flared. He hadn't even afforded her the chance to explain, to apologize.

Still stunned by it all, Meaghan watched his easy gait as he walked away, terminating their encounter as no more than an annoyance and leaving her to deal with the consequences of her actions.

He had the stride of a man who knew his place in the world and was comfortable with it. The door clicked shut behind him, leaving no doubt his place was definitely not in that room.

The girls exploded with a volley of comments and exclamations as they streamed toward Meaghan. She couldn't sort through all their questions as she struggled to quell both mortification and the lingering echoes from the sudden uncontrolled longing rippling on inside her.

Two

"A nip of brandy should chase away any lingering chill from your dunking, Lord Ashton. And it will keep you occupied until my husband arrives."

Edna O'Brien shooed Nick into a wing chair in her husband's study and gestured to her butler. The wizened fellow offered Nick a tumbler from the silver tray he carried. Since exiting the drawing room, the plump matron had fluttered behind Nick, alternating between maternal concern and worry over her husband's continued absence. Now that they had arrived, perhaps her well-meaning agitation could be mollified.

Nick tried to settle his thoughts by taking a deep breath of the study's comfortably masculine wood-and-tobacco scents, to no avail. Who would have believed a wayward scrap of muslin could create such havoc? "The warmth of your hospitality overshadows the incident already, Mrs. O'Brien."

Striving to burn away the perverse appeal of Meaghan Reilly's furious green eyes, Nick took a healthy swallow of the fiery liquor in the cut-crystal glass. The spirits did little to extinguish the desire ignited by a less-than-innocent young lady reaching up to kiss him so unexpectedly.

Let me welcome you to Ireland, the hoyden had whispered, stealing the last vestiges of his self-control. Snared by a perverse wisp of remembrance he couldn't place, he'd lost all reason and gathered her into his arms.

Mrs. O'Brien prattled on. "I cannot imagine anyone being so manhandled . . ."

Her remark pulled Nick away from the embarrassment still churning through his gut over his lack of control. Could Mrs. O'Brien have any notion of what had just occurred in her drawing room? In front of the very shocked faces of her young guests? Impossible.

He dismissed the guilty notion before it could fully bloom. He had no culpability in the little drama just foisted on him. Forcing himself to push aside the all-too-fetching impression of Meaghan Reilly pressed so thoroughly against his chest while he kissed her back in full measure, he strove to concentrate on his hostess.

". . . As I told your cousin prior to your coming downstairs, you did absolutely the right thing in coming straight to us. I'm sure Mr. O'Brien will have a word with the harbormaster as soon as he hears of the incident." Mrs. O'Brien's strawberry curls bounced under her lace cap as she nodded her head, emphasizing her faith in her husband's ability to set things aright.

Nick eyed Jamie, who was ensconced in a matching burgundy leather chair at the other side of the plush hearth rug. Jamie raised the glass he'd just accepted from the butler and shrugged, a look of baffled amusement edging his slight grin. Obviously, their hostess had been jabbering away to him since he'd left Nick alone with Randall to finish his toilet. This impromptu confrontation fell far short of the surprise they'd intended when they'd hailed the hackney and demanded to be brought immediately to the Honorable Gill O'Brien's residence.

After the shove, Nick had been too furious to think of his suspected adversary's professional duties as a barrister and head to O'Brien's office—a miscalculation born in the heat of the moment, something he usually prided himself in avoiding. Instead of coming face-to-face with his adversary, they'd found themselves welcomed with open arms and feminine fuss. Not to mention the scorching salute he'd just escaped.

"Arriving as you did, you've caused quite a stir with my Ladies Guild, my lord. You are the talk of my salon, I must tell you. And the drawing room, no doubt. I do think I've quelled any scandal over the state of your dress upon your arrival. I explained how very right you were to call on old friends of both your parents in your hour of need."

Mrs. O'Brien barely paused for breath as she favored both Mansfield men with her motherly eye and reassuring smile. "You've both grown into such handsome men since we last saw you. Your mothers would be so proud—"

Mercifully, the crunch of carriage wheels on the drive outside interrupted Mrs. O'Brien. She swiveled her attention toward the window. "That must be Mr. O'Brien, now. I'll bring him to you directly. Pray excuse me."

With that, she sailed out of the room, the expanse of turquoise silk over her petticoats and hoops whooshing as she passed through the double oak doors.

Jamie exhaled a long breath. "Do you think she lets *him* get a word in edgewise?" He chuckled and took a sip from his glass. "I only vaguely remember O'Brien from my last visit to Ireland with my father. But Mrs. O'Brien I remember right enough—cheerful and well-meaning in her way."

Nick also remembered her from his last visit. How she had wept over him, following the disaster that had cost him his parents. He shuttered the black memory before his thoughts could scatter any further.

Mrs. O'Brien seemed plumper and her face carried a few more cheery laugh lines, but he knew his mother had treasured this woman's friendship just as his father respected her husband. Could his father's judgment have been so misplaced as to trust the very man who may have been responsible for his death? Add to that the deaths of his wife and brother and the attempts on his son. Sentiment might lean in one direction, but logic told Nick to look very carefully at the one man who had the most to gain from the decimation of the Mansfield family.

"Mrs. O'Brien would not necessarily know her husband's business or intentions. She makes a perfect foil for the shrewd man of business he comes across as in his correspondence." Nick tensed, anticipating O'Brien's entrance. Edna O'Brien's words haunted him.

Your mothers would have been so proud.

He doubted that. Not after the way he'd reacted to the little spitfire in the drawing room. *Mo layosh greeun,* she'd whispered as their lips first brushed. He wondered what the phrase could possibly mean and if it had any bearing on her inexplicable breach of etiquette.

"You look a tad flushed, Nick. Are you sure you haven't taken a fever?" Jamie leaned in for a closer look. He cocked his head and raised an eyebrow, reminding Nick for all the world of the ancient nanny Jamie's mother had employed one summer at Brighton. What a frightful harridan she'd been, always wanting to dose Nick with cod-liver oil even though he was sixteen and well out of the nursery.

"I'm fine, stripling."

Flushed was he? Nick laid his heightened color squarely at the feet of a brazen young woman with lush black hair, haunting green eyes, and pale skin. Or more aptly, in the beckoning appeal of her impish mouth. Meaghan Reilly, she'd answered him when he asked, extending her hand as if they hadn't just shared the sort of introduction more appropriate for an expensive bordello.

He hadn't trusted himself to touch her again and not draw her back into his embrace. So her fingers had dangled for a dozen heartbeats, until she dropped them to her side. Had she deserved such a public humiliation despite her forward behavior? His chair squeaked a low protest as he shifted his position. He'd enough on his plate without worrying over the social gaffes of one impertinent debutante.

"You seem very preoccupied. Did you remember any further details from this morning's incident while I was dancing attendance on our hostess? Are you certain you are not suffering

some lingering injury?" Jamie continued his
scrutiny with a wary air.

"Just who is treating whom as if he is in leading strings?" Nick lifted a brow and fixed a quell-
ing look on Jamie before taking another swig
from his glass.

The brandy scorched a trail down his gullet,
but the effect was naught compared to the smol-
dering response Meaghan Reilly's kiss still fired
inside him. The softness of her lips, the smell of
wild meadowsweet and honeysuckle wafting from
her skin, the all-too-perfect feel of her in his
arms with her breasts and hips crushed against
him, combined to produce the most powerful
lure any female had cast his way in a long time.

He gave himself a mental shake. He could
not spare the attention such an appealing package presented even if he were inclined to dally
with untried virgins. Wayward misses, no matter
their charms, were not his preferred prowling
grounds. He could only hope the spectacle she
had raised would not send some earnest father
or brother scurrying forward demanding satisfaction, or worse yet, a declaration.

His frigid departure should have dashed any
scheme to that effect. He'd enough trouble on
his hands. Another swallow of brandy failed to
obliterate his twinge of guilt over the dazed dismay on Meaghan Reilly's refined features at his
calculated disdain in front of her friends. The
gleam of temper lighting the depths of her eyes
immediately afterward failed to lessen their appeal or his culpability in the awkward situation
he'd left her to face alone.

Still snared, despite himself, in the tantalizing
memory of a wanton in peridot silk, it took Nick

a moment to realize Jamie was speaking to him again.

"You are a bit distracted, Nick. Are you sure you're up to this? Perhaps we should just thank Mrs. O'Brien and be on our way for today—"

Footsteps against the hall's marble floor forestalled the rest of Jamie's concern. Was Nick ready? He had to be. He shoved aside the lingering reverberations of meeting Miss Reilly and concentrated on the confrontation at hand.

The oak portal thrust open with a decisive motion as a slender man in an expertly tailored suit strode into the room. Like his wife, Gill O'Brien had a few more lines on his face and his hair and neat mustache were a bit grayer than Nick recalled from their last meeting half his lifetime ago. Despite the intervening years, keen intelligence shone in his blue eyes as he offered his hand in greeting. Just as Nick remembered.

"Lord Ashton. Mr. Mansfield." O'Brien's grip was firm as he shook their hands. He perused them quickly with a barrister's appraising acumen as he gestured for both men to retake their seats. "My wife has told me of your accident on the docks today. I will arrange to have the matter investigated at once. Are you certain you have no need of a physician, my lord?"

Nick sensed no malice lingering in his host's thoughtful regard. He admired the man's cool demeanor—just the right mix of courteous concern and wary curiosity. He waved away both suggestions. "No need for either, sir. Why investigate what was surely an accident caused by overcrowding and my own inattention? As you can see, I am none the worse for my unintentional swim, thanks to your wife's generous hospitality."

"Offering a place to dry off and clean up is the least we could do for the son of an old friend. I am more than glad to see you both." O'Brien smiled warmly enough as his glance swept over Jamie and back to Nick. "You've grown into men so like your fathers. Men I was proud to call my friends."

The older man pressed his lips into a serious line as if he were considering what to say next. His stance relaxed a little and he stepped back to pour himself some spirits from the decanter the butler had placed on a table near the hearth. Awkward silence stretched across the study.

"Mrs. O'Brien said much the same thing just a moment ago. I know my father enjoyed his correspondence with you over the years," Jamie offered. "He always chuckled over the stories you wrote about your family. I trust they are all well."

"Yes, thank you. My eldest is your age, I believe. He has finished his studies in Dublin and is clerking in my office there." O'Brien leaned one shoulder against the mantel and took a sip from his glass. "The next two boys are hard at work at university. The younger four are still in England at school. The only one still home with us is our Sheila. She keeps her mother busier than the other seven put together. And my pockets much thinner, with her gowns and shoes and other fripperies."

And a healthy dowry to provide as well. Nick kept his posture casual, but his ears perked up at this small admission. Eight children in all—a large number to provide with a living, let alone a legacy. The luxurious lifestyle the O'Briens enjoyed in their home and the number of dependents the barrister supported had raised red flags

for Nick long ago. Especially knowing Gill
O'Brien had attended Eton on a stipend from a
rich client of the Irish barrister's father.

The bonds of shared misery for first-year
schoolmates had forged a friendship between
Nick's father and Gill across normally forbidding
class lines, a friendship that had lasted into adult-
hood. Had those bonds been severed by greed
when the men formed a business partnership in
later years? The question neatly distilled the sole
purpose for this crossing of the Irish Sea.

"I have been thinking of James and Jonathan
a great deal of late, what with the trust we
formed so long ago due to pay out within the
year." O'Brien's keen gaze centered on Nick
once again. Nick had the fleeting notion he was
in a witness box having his testimony analyzed,
as the barrister continued.

"Not that I am anything but pleased to see
you—and young Mansfield here as well," O'Brien
continued. "But I admit to being a trifle surprised
to see you, my lord. I received a packet of papers
from your man of business just this morning, and
he gave me no indication you intended to favor
us with a visit."

"Oh, it was a lark, really," Jamie interjected at
just the right moment. "Nick was kind enough
to indulge me when I told him I had a desire
to take a look at some bloodstock recommended
to me."

"I decided to accompany him and attend to
some other matters of business," Nick added,
pleased Jamie had hit just the note they had discussed. Horse-mad since he was a lad, they had
decided his interest would provide them with a
reasonable explanation for their travel.

Their host set down his glass and turned his attention to Jamie. "So you are still interested in horses?" A smile touched his lips and he stroked his mustache. "Your father told many a tale of having to drag you out of the stables since before you were old enough to ride."

The spark of excitement lighting Jamie's eyes was genuine as he replied. "I have high hopes of expanding the stables at High Meadows now that I have completed my stint at university. I've already acquired a few studs I find promising for producing hunters. I am hoping to acquire some solid brood mares during our sojourn here. I have several recommendations for stock in Kildare worth perusing."

"How refreshingly enterprising for a man of your age and background." O'Brien nodded his head and quirked one of his eyebrows as he perused Jamie with a practiced eye. He looked surprised and satisfied at one and the same time. "If you wouldn't mind another suggestion, I could give you the direction of a former associate in my firm who might be able to assist your inquiries. He and his family are in residence at their stud farm for the season."

"That would be most kind," Nick answered for Jamie as his cousin hesitated and looked his way for direction.

O'Brien strode over to the massive desk that stood before the front windows and proceeded to scribble a brief note on a piece of paper he abstracted from a desk drawer. "Have you no plans to tour the Continent or kick up your heels in London for a few years before settling down?"

Jamie cast a quick glance over to Nick, then shrugged. "Haven't felt the need. Nick's been shouldering all the responsibilities for Mansfield holdings since he was much the same age as I am. And looking out for me, too. I'd like to free him up a bit."

"Admirable." O'Brien stepped back around his desk and extended the note to Nick. "And have you any plans for your newfound time once this young man relieves you of some of your burdens, my lord?"

"I am quite sure the matters I currently attend will continue to occupy the majority of my attention, even with Jamie's assistance," Nick said as he accepted the scrap of paper from the older man. "I find the intricacies of finance quite fascinating."

Now to get to the true heart of their visit. Nick leaned forward. "Since you brought up the matter earlier, perhaps we will be able to find some time to discuss the final disbursement of the trust face-to-face."

Nothing flickered in O'Brien's face. Neither alarm nor denial. He certainly earned his reputation in the courtroom. "A very reasonable suggestion." The barrister nodded. "That should facilitate several pending matters. We will have to schedule something as soon as you have the time."

The doors to the study pushed inward at that moment.

"Pardon me for interrupting, gentlemen." Mrs. O'Brien bustled into the room with a cheery smile belying the apology. "One of the Guild members would like to have a word with you, Mr. O'Brien, before they all depart. You will have plenty of time to catch up with Lord Ashton and Mr. Mansfield over dinner this evening. I'm certain the gentlemen are all done in from their travels and would appreciate a few quiet hours to collect themselves."

"Thank you for your kind invitation, Mrs. O'Brien." Nick and Jamie stood as she advanced toward them. "But perhaps we could arrange to come at a different time. We really should seek the accommodations our man attained for us."

"Oh, posh. You have already arrived at them." She waved one plump hand as she twinkled a smile at him. "When he told me where you were staying, I sent him off to bring all your luggage straight here. I would never forgive myself if I let you stay in some vermin-infested lodgings or impersonal hotel after your horrifying arrival. Suppose you were yet to take a chill? It's the least we can do given the old ties we have to your parents. Isn't that right, Mr. O'Brien?"

Gill O'Brien looked nearly as perplexed as Nick felt over this turn of events.

"Now, Edna." O'Brien glanced over to Nick as if trying to gauge his guest's reaction to this peremptory action. His shoulders stiffened and he took a deep breath as he turned his attention back to his wife. "The Mansfields are grown men, not the lads who once frolicked on the lawns here—"

"Well, it's not as if we do not have the room. With the boys gone, all we have are Sheila and her cousin with us at the moment." Mrs. O'Brien took her husband's arm and tried to look contrite. "But if you would prefer to stay in a hotel, I'm sure Gill can give you the direction of a suitable one. Oh, I do hope I have not offended you by being too forward."

Their escape dangled in the air for a moment

as Nick considered the options. On the one hand there was the old adage about walking into the viper's den. On the other, there was the one about keeping your friends close and your enemies closer. O'Brien's mouth under his mustache formed an expectant line, but his expression remained inscrutable. Damn all the suspicion and subterfuge, this seemed the perfect opportunity to bring the very crux of their trip to a head. What better way to observe their adversary than in his home?

"Thank you for your kindness. If you are sure it will be no imposition, we'd be delighted to accept your hospitality." Nick returned Edna O'Brien's beaming approval with a slight bow.

"Splendid," she enthused. "You finish your refreshments while we bid our other guests good day, and then I will send our butler to show you the way to your rooms."

Nick couldn't help admiring Edna's cool efficiency as she shot her husband a triumphant look.

"That's settled, then." The older man patted his wife's hand. "Until dinner, my lord. Please consider yourselves welcome for as long as you might wish."

O'Brien's smile remained polite but failed to add a spark of the warmth in his tone to his eyes. He nodded to Jamie. "Mansfield."

The O'Briens exited the room into the hum of voices reverberating in the foyer when Jamie exploded. "Is staying here safe, Nick?"

"It is no more unsafe than elsewhere at this point, stripling. And it should make things a trifle more awkward for O'Brien to explain away should anything untoward befall us." Pray God he was right. If anything happened to Jamie because of this choice . . . Not for the first time, Nick wished he'd left his ward under lock and key in England or that they really were in Ireland to replenish the breeding stock for their stables.

He looked at the crumpled paper in his fist.

> *Bryan Reilly*
> *Blue Hills Stud,*
> *County Kildare*

Reilly.

A tantalizing whiff of meadowsweet and honeysuckle teased him. First the boat they'd arrived on— Reilly born and Reilly built, Captain McManus had boasted. Now this. And in between a scandalous introduction to one Meaghan Reilly. Was the whole cursed island peopled with no one save Reillys? He stifled a groan and tried to suppress the irrational longing for another glimpse of the sparkle in a certain pair of green eyes.

"It's not fair, I tell you." Meaghan groaned and flung herself down on the satin counterpane topping her cousin's four-poster bed.

The smooth fabric cooled her overheated cheeks, but could not freeze the image of a blond warrior-god turning on his heel and striding from the room with disdain in the set of his shoulders. "If I were one of my brothers and had kissed a stranger like that, there would never have been such a furor raised."

Sheila laughed as she turned so her maid could loosen her stays after she shed the bodice of her afternoon tea dress. "Ahh, but if you were one of your brothers you would have created even more of a stir if you'd kissed that Englishman." She heaved a dramatic sigh. "Don't you just love their accents?"

The amusement in her eyes dimmed when her gaze rested on Meaghan. She glanced at the maid. "That will be all for now, Triona. I can manage the skirt, if you'll hang these up."

She handed the embroidered peach bodice and bleached muslin undersleeves to the maid and snatched up a shawl from her dressing table. "Perhaps you could convince Cook to spare a small pot of tea and a scone or two for us. It will be hours before dinner. I was so busy taking care of my guests I barely got a nibble."

"Aye, miss." Triona nodded and moved off to the dressing room connecting Meaghan's and Sheila's bedchambers while Sheila wrapped the green plaid wool around her shoulders and settled herself onto the edge of the bed.

As they waited for the door to click shut so they could talk in private, Meaghan tried without success to douse all thoughts of the powerful feel of firm, masculine lips on hers, lighting a fire that still smoldered in her depths. A fire totally separate from the indignation that burned in her over the injustice of the consequences she stood to face from her impulsive action and the all-too-enthusiastic cooperation it had elicited.

The spite behind Eloise Farrell's challenge paled in comparison to the blame Meaghan heaped on her erstwhile victim's shoulders. Why had he pulled her to him? Why had he deepened their dry brush of lips into a salvo that shot clear through her and heralded a life-shattering outcome? And having made clear his willingness to share such unexpected intimacies, why had he pulled away and proceeded to give her all but the cut direct?

Her conscience twinged. Why should she hold Uncle Gill's English visitor accountable for taking advantage of what she so freely offered? Unreasonable as it seemed, the fact that this stranger's kiss seemed to invoke her family's Blessing chafed her raw. Surely she was mistaken, or at the very least, his touch served as a dire warning, far more likely heralding the dreaded Curse.

She hated all the questions stinging her. "Sheila, who was that man? What will your mother say once she hears of this? She called him *my lord.*"

"He must be one of Papa's clients or business associates, but I've never met him before." Sheila's eyes took on a dreamy cast. "Believe me, I'd remember if I had."

Memorable. That definitely provided a fit description for his mysterious lordship. The clarity of his blue eyes and the sweep of his dusty blond hair snaked a curl of familiarity through the pit of Meaghan's stomach. The scent of oranges and mint lent an odd comfort to the unnameable sensations swirling through her as she had clung to him then and as she thought of him now. How could that be?

"What if he is one of Quin's or Bryan's associates, as well? They'll blister my ears good over this. That's if there's anything left once your mother gets done with me. They'll likely hear her and your father on Beannacht when word of the incident gets out." She groaned and buried her face in the satin again. "What if he's married?"

"He wasn't wearing a ring," Sheila offered

and patted her shoulder. The comforting gesture did little to ease Meaghan's agitation. What a fool. As if her age and gender were not barrier enough. She'd never be able to convince people to donate to the Limerick Nightingale Society's building fund if they considered her to be a brazen upstart.

"You know each of the girls promised not to breathe a word," Sheila soothed. "And Mama never raises her voice. She considers that very unladylike."

"As does my own. My mother's quiet scolds are ten times worse than Da's blusters." For once Meaghan was glad her parents were an ocean away. "But what if he lodges a complaint with your father?"

"I'm sure this will all blow over without further comment, Meggy." If only the confidence in Sheila's words matched her tone. "A man as handsome as that looks to have kissed hundreds of women in his life. If he is here seeking my father's counsel, he surely has more important things on his mind than a few girls and a simple tea. Most likely we'll have no occasion to ever see, let alone speak with, his lordship again."

Mo laoch grian, she had whispered. Sun warrior? What had she been thinking?

Snap description notwithstanding, the arrogant ice in the final dismissive glance he'd cast Meaghan's way as he exited made the suggestion more than a possibility. "Why doesn't that make me feel relieved?" she sighed.

"Because for all your talk about wanting an independent life and marriage not being for you, you liked his kiss." Sheila leaned forward with a definite twinkle in her wide brown gaze. "I saw the dazed look on your face, even after he let go of you. It was as if you'd just gotten back from another time or another place. I always knew kissing a gentleman would be every bit as wonderful as they say in those novels Mama forbids me to read. Deny it if you will for others, Meaghan Reilly, but you enjoyed kissing that man."

The twin truths in Sheila's observations streaked through Meaghan as undeniable as the beauty of a sunrise over Beannacht Harbor and as jagged as sunset on the western cliffs of her home island. She had liked his kiss very much. If all kisses were like that, it would be her favorite thing of all time. Trouble was, nothing that perfect could be real or lasting. She knew better than to trust a kiss— hadn't she proved the matter many years before, with a tall young man she could barely remember? What might come disguised as a tantalizing blessing was truly the hollow shell of a curse.

A man as handsome as that looks to have kissed hundreds of women. Isn't that what Sheila had just said? The bitter truth of that judgment raked her. Meaghan's lips still tingled from his, her sides still felt scorched from the pressure of his hands, and her insides yearned for something more than she could describe. To him she had been an annoyance, a pesty child to be pushed away and reprimanded, the latest in a long line of women no doubt throwing themselves at him for his looks and title. His kiss might burn on in her, but he'd most likely forgotten her as soon as the door clicked shut. That should provide some relief, but it failed miserably.

She sat up and pounded the pillows. *"Diabhal!"* What a devilish mess.

A soft rap sounded from the hall door. "Oh, good. There is our tea." Sheila bounced off the side of the bed and leaped for the door. "We'll have a bite and you can tell me everything you experienced while in passion's embrace. I want all the details."

"Tea will have to wait, my dears."

Sheila jumped back with a guilty start as her mother sailed into the room. Aunt Edna looked from one of the young women to the other with a practiced gaze that did not bode well. Heat crept across Meaghan's cheeks even as her fingers turned to ice while she laced them together.

"Meaghan, would you be so kind as to excuse us?" Aunt Edna favored her with what looked to be a genuine smile. "I'd like to have a word alone with Sheila. I'll come chat with you in your own chamber in a moment or two. That's all the time I have to spare. This has been a most unexpected day."

As she exited to her room via the dressing room, Meaghan overheard enough of the low conversation behind her to make the next few minutes some of the longest she had ever endured.

"I have just received a most distressing note from Mrs. Farrell, Eloise's mother" was all she caught before the door closing shut off the rest of Aunt Edna's sentence.

Sheila's assurances to the contrary, not much later a very unladylike volume from her aunt pushed through both doors and the dressing room between as Meaghan awaited her doom.

"I do not care if it was but a prank. She may not have known better, but you certainly did,"

Aunt Edna thoroughly chastised her only daughter.

Meaghan bit her lip. So much for her Blessing. She was cursed, indeed.

Three

"The carriage will be here at any moment, my dear." Aunt Edna put down the basket of violets she had just gathered in the garden and slipped into her house shoes before crossing the foyer toward Meaghan.

Sunlight from the leaded glass panels framing the front door dappled the marble floor and skipped over her gray muslin skirt and white apron as she approached with an appreciative gleam in her eye. "I must say, you look absolutely charming in your new walking dress. Turn about in the light so I can admire the full effect."

Meaghan finished tying the satin bow on her bonnet and then pirouetted as requested. The click of her wood clogs echoed in the entryway. She hated traipsing about in the heavy things all morning, but they would protect the hem of her new dress from the grime of Limerick's streets.

"Russet becomes you." The older woman's eyes crinkled at the corners as she beamed her approval.

"Thank you." Meaghan smiled at the compliment. Naturally, Aunt Edna would approve of her attire; it was she who had insisted they purchase the garment during the first of several forays to the modiste's after Da and Mama departed to visit Devin and Maggie in America. "As soon as the carriage is brought around, Triona and I will be off to the city. She has the lists, and I have Uncle Gill's letter of introduction."

Meaghan was anxious to leave this morning and evade any possible encounters with the O'Briens' other guests. She wanted to concentrate on her work for the Nightingale Society. Having survived her relative's quiet lecture over her impulsive behavior the previous day and composed the note of apology to his lordship Aunt Edna had insisted be written on the spot, Meaghan was more than ready to escape any possibility of his company for at least the next few hours.

She caught back a sigh. She'd endured what was surely the most awkward dinner of her life last night. Nicholas Mansfield, Lord Ashton of Suffolk, had at least seemed as mercifully set on avoiding her as she was him. Not that either one of them had much opportunity for conversation. Seated at the farthest reaches of the table from the last man she ever wanted to see again, she had barely spoken nor dared even look up from her plate. Not so Sheila, who had spent the evening talking horses and gaits with his lordship's own cousin.

As soon as possible, Meaghan had excused herself and fled to the solace of her room, only to be tormented by fragments of dreams involving the tantalizing wisp of her Blessing blocked by warrior princes and conquering marauders—all tall and blond, with arrogant strides and disdainful airs and the ability to kiss her senseless.

She gave herself a mental shake. Lord Ashton's fine blond hair and piercing blue eyes had taken up entirely too many of her thoughts over the past day and night. She needed more than a few minutes in a carriage to compose her thoughts for her appointment, but that was all she was going to get. Today's trip to solicit a potential subscription for her project required all her concentration. Capricious emotions and unnamed longings had no place in the life she had planned for herself.

"I must say again how I admire the serious work you are undertaking, my dear." Aunt Edna stripped off her garden gloves and put them in her apron pocket. "Too many young girls have nothing more on their minds than parties and gowns. You have as much intelligence and sense of purpose as any of your brothers. I know they are all proud of you and your efforts. But just remember that undertakings aside, you need to become more comfortable in society. Without that, you have nothing."

The endorsement, even laced with a touch of reprimand as it was, warmed Meaghan, as Aunt Edna reached up to adjust the lace on her bonnet, then patted her cheek. "I also know I was a trifle harsh with you yesterday. But I promised your dear mama to look after you as if you were my own. Such spontaneous behavior might be acceptable on Beannacht, where everyone knows and loves you, but here in the city, and in the London social circles Lord Ashton moves through, it most certainly is not."

Meaghan wished for what was surely the hundredth time she'd never agreed to join the foolish parlor game yesterday. Although being distant cousins and not truly her aunt and uncle, her family had always viewed Edna and Gill O'Brien as such out of genuine affection and respect. She truly regretted any embarrassment her behavior had caused them.

"I'm sorry to have distressed you and Uncle Gill, Aunt Edna. I will strive not to tread on your good graces again during my stay here."

She shied away from the rebellious curl of resentment over the blame for the entire incident being placed at her feet. Eloise's jibes and Lord Ashton's not-so-innocent role did not negate the fact she had gotten herself into this situation and only she could extricate herself from it.

"All we are concerned about is your welfare. You must endeavor to keep your behavior completely circumspect from now on, especially during Lord Ashton's stay with us."

Despite the earnest tone, kindness shone in the depths of Aunt Edna's eyes and a sympathetic smile creased her softly rounded features. "Don't fret overmuch on the matter. In a few days the tattle-mongers will have another juicy scrap to chew over."

"Excuse me, mum." Ready for her errands, Triona entered the sunlit foyer from the darkened back hall with a market basket in one hand and her cloak and bonnet in the other. "Cook asked if she might have a word with you over the luncheon menu. She's in a stew, trying to make sure her recipes are up ta royal standards."

Aunt Edna raised an amused brow. "Royal standards, is it? While we want to make a good impression on our guests, I hardly think the queen, let alone one of her barons, could fail to be impressed with Mrs. Kelly's usual fare. Still I'd best go unruffle her feathers."

She patted Meaghan's hand. "Good luck with that old harridan, Elmira Sullivan." Gesturing to her abandoned basket of violets she added, "Would you like a nosegay for your chamber, my dear? I picked them thinking the gentlemen might like something to brighten up their rooms, but there were such an abundance I'm sure I have enough to spare."

"Thank you, Aunt Edna. That would be lovely." Meaghan pulled on her gloves and scooped up her Spanish-lace shawl as her aunt exited to the kitchen.

"Don't thank me. Sheila promised to take care of the arrangements." Aunt Edna's voice carried back from the hall. "Provided she ever returns from her ride with Mr. Mansfield. Seems he's as horse-mad as she is. All he spoke of last night in the drawing room after you left us was his impending expedition to County Kildare."

The Mansfields were leaving for Kildare? With any luck it would be soon. She quashed the biting edge of disappointment that surprised her at the thought of never seeing Nicholas Mansfield again. The realization that Bryan and his family were in residence at their stud farm in that vicinity for the spring foaling squelched Meaghan's simultaneous blossom of relief. Should Lord Ashton meet up with her brother, surely he would relay news of her shocking behavior to her staid brother.

"I believe that's Seamus with the carriage, miss." Triona hastily donned her outer garments and opened the door. "The whole household's in an uproar over our English visitors. Cook and Mrs. McKeever kept addin' things ta me list. It will be a wonder if I can arrange it all and still have ye back fer luncheon."

"At least it's a nice day. I wouldn't mind at all if we missed the meal entirely," Meaghan assured the maid as they emerged from the house, blinking in the bright morning sun. The fewer meals she had to share with the O'Briens' English guests the better.

A soft grass-scented breeze ruffled the hem of her dress and tickled her nose. It was a fine day indeed, welcome after nearly a week of drizzle. Sheila must be enjoying the time spent on her beloved mare. Meaghan could spend the whole day in Limerick, haggling with greengrocers or helping Triona at the dry-goods emporiums on a day like this. That much less time spent avoiding Lord Ashton.

There he was stealing into her thoughts again. She groaned. "You get in first, Triona. I could use a few breaths of this fresh air to clear my thoughts."

Meaghan filled her lungs while Seamus, the coachman, tipped his hat and winked at Triona, then helped her into the O'Briens' carriage.

"Excuse me, sir. I . . . I failed ta see ye there in the dark," Triona squeaked in surprise. "I do hope me basket didn't hurt ye. I can ask Seamus ta put it up top if it is crowding ye."

Sir?

The maid's stumbled apology froze Meaghan's breath for a heartbeat. She peered into the dark recesses and nearly groaned again. There in the corner, bowler hat on his knee, sat the very individual she was trying to erase from her thoughts and avoid at all costs.

"Nonsense. There is plenty of room in here

for your basket. And any other . . . baggage you might be bringing with you."

His last barb was obviously meant to sting her. She'd not give him the satisfaction. She might deserve whatever set downs he saw fit to mete out after the trick served him yesterday, however, having three older brothers had certain advantages. It would take more than a few jibes to rattle her.

She had hoped he would be gentleman enough to let their initial meeting go unremarked in the future, especially given the pretty apology Aunt Edna had practically dictated to her yesterday. But if he chose to deal with her from his vaunted position in English society, so be it. She'd mind her promise to Aunt Edna or choke in the process.

Taking a final breath, she allowed the coachman to assist her into the carriage's suddenly too tiny interior. The elusive scents of mint and oranges that lanced her dreamed-tossed night assailed her as she settled herself on the same crushed-velvet seat as Triona—at the far opposite corner from the coach's other occupant.

"Good day, Lord Ashton." Her voice sounded unnatural to her ears as she strove to keep it cool and remote. *Let me welcome you to Ireland*, had been her first greeting to him. Thankfully, the vehicle's dark interior hid the hot blush stealing over her cheeks.

"Good day to you, Miss Reilly. I hope you do not mind my taking advantage of your sojourn into Limerick to accomplish some of my own business there."

She could have sworn his rich baritone held just an edge of amusement, as if he realized just

how discomforted she felt at being confronted
by him. And in such close quarters.

"If you feel the carriage is too . . . crowded,
I can return to the stable and send for a hackney
to convey me to town," he offered sincerely
enough, his wry tone still scouring her. She'd like
nothing better at the moment.

"That won't be necessary. I have an appointment around the corner from Uncle Gill's office.
We can alight there. I'm sure we can accomplish
most of Triona's errands on foot afterward." The
carriage lurched forward as Seamus whistled to
the team of bays to get started down the drive.

"And what of your return? I would hate to
leave you stranded in the city with no means to
convey you safely home. In my experience, Limerick is filled with any number of unexpected
hazards."

He truly must be making sport of her. She was
quite certain she saw the corners of his mouth
quirking up despite the gloom. Perhaps he was
not so stiff-necked after all. She let out her
breath. "I'm quite certain we can manage.
Triona's lived here all her life and I'll wager
nothing untoward has ever happened to her."

"Still—"

"Don't fret yerself, sir." Triona spoke up.
"We're ta meet Mr. O'Brien at his office by the
time St. Mary's is through sounding the noon-
time bells. Seamus always brings the master
home for luncheon, except on court days. If
ye're through with your business he can fetch ye
back with us then."

"Very well." The sun burst through the window as they turned onto the road and revealed
his lordship smiling at the blushing maid as if to

assure her he did not mind her bursting in with her information. "Noon at O'Brien and Mallory. If I am through."

They rode in silence for the next few moments. Meaghan attempted to fix her attention on the passing scenery. The green of Ireland never ceased to catch her eye. Especially after spending those years in Italy and Switzerland during Da's recuperation. On a hilltop in the distance a small graystone church stood sentinel over a pasture filled with sheep.

"That is the church my Da and Ma were married in." Triona leaned over to point out the very structure. "It has the sweetest stained-glass window with the baby Jesus in it. Nothing so grand as the Italian cathedrals ye described from yer travels, miss. But he has the nicest smile."

"It looks very similar to St. Bridgid's on our island." A pang of homesickness struck Meaghan. She'd always loved the stone church perched on the edge of Beannacht Harbor.

"I don't think I'd like ta live on an island." The little maid shuddered. "Too much water, I'd surely drown."

Meaghan laughed as the church on the hill passed from view, replaced by the beginnings of the city. "Not if you had my three older brothers instead of your five little ones. I learned to sail and to swim almost before I could read. Beannacht is the most beautiful spot on this earth. My Da says that's why it is set in the ocean; to keep it safe."

"If I may be bold enough to intrude, where is this island you extol? If you don't mind sharing something so personal with a virtual stranger."

Meaghan turned and met Lord Ashton's appraising gaze. *A virtual stranger with whom she had been quite intimate.* Why did everything he said to her seem armed with a hidden lance?

She squared her shoulders and faced him more fully. "My family lives on an island off the entrance to the River Shannon. Beannacht Island has been home to Reillys for many generations." Succinct without being overly personal. Even Aunt Edna would approve.

"Beannacht is a most unusual name. . . ."

He was not going to let the conversation die. She prayed they would reach their destination quickly so she could avoid any potential gaffes.

". . . Do you know its origins?"

Although Lord Ashton's pose remained relaxed enough across the carriage, Meaghan sensed he was a man who rarely made casual conversation or asked questions for no reason—much like her brother Bryan. The comparison did little to reassure her.

"Beannacht means blessing." She attempted a light, yet impersonal tone as she tried to mirror his relaxed pose. "When I was little, my brother Quin, a sea captain, said the island got its name because it is an unexpected harbor in a wild ocean. Bryan, who studied law, said it was named so for the sanctuary and protection offered weary travelers over the centuries. But Devin, who views things with an artist's eye, swears the bold green and purple of our hills against the setting sun show it was once a piece of rainbow left behind in the water."

"And which brother's explanation do you find correct?"

She smiled. "They are all correct, because it is how they view their home."

"Three brothers, three unique perspectives—and you to validate them all. You are fortunate to have such a family, Miss Reilly. And such an island to claim for a home."

The carriage jolted around a corner and a burst of sunlight streamed through the window to halo him as he fixed her with an intense look. "I hope you appreciate them."

He looked so serious, every bit as fierce as the marauders in her dreams last night. She swallowed hard and nodded. *Laoch grian*—sun warrior, indeed. She needed to cease viewing him as larger than life. He was but a man. If only she could see him as such. "And what of your family, my lord? Do you appreciate their unique qualities? How would you describe your home?"

"My family is almost nonexistent." He shifted in his seat and turned his gaze from hers. "Jamie is the last. And I am seldom at home."

"That is too bad. In the end, all people have are the memories of the places they love and the people who love them."

He leaned his head back and shut his eyes, cutting off further conversation. Clearly, after he had satisfied his curiosity, he found her own simple question too impertinent. And most likely her reply as well. The feeling of doom crowded her again even as she mulled over his odd answer.

The occupants of the carriage rode in uncomfortable silence for the remainder of the journey.

The jostling of the crowds and the noxious odors of city life in Limerick's commercial district barely registered for Nick as he made his

way toward the offices of O'Brien and Mallory.
He concentrated on sorting through the information he had managed to gather both at the
courthouse and from the banker he had visited
that morning.

The man Randall had hired to shadow him
walked a discreet distance behind, lost in the
late-morning stream of passersby. It was his job
to make sure nothing like the *accidental* shove on
the wharfs yesterday occurred during Nick's forays into the city. Another man was set to keep
watch on Jamie wherever he went.

Randall had assured Nick both men, former
soldiers from his brigade, could be trusted. This
one seemed good at what he did; that much was
certain. After meeting them both at the courthouse steps as appointed, Nick had not been
aware of his new shadow save for the occasional
feeling he was being watched.

The other man should have relieved Randall
from his post observing Jamie, freeing him to
continue the inquiries Nick had begun. Perhaps
he would have more luck.

Despite his humble origins, the Honorable Gill
O'Brien seemed more than capable of sustaining
the financial demands of his large brood and
household. By all accounts, the barrister was as
he appeared—a man of sterling reputation and
keen business sense.

The preliminary information gleaned this
morning should have relieved Nick; instead it left
him more disturbed. He sidestepped a puddle at
the street corner as he made the turn onto the
street where O'Brien's carriage had deposited
him. If O'Brien·was not at the root of these attempts, who stood to gain from the demise of

the Mansfield family? If the culprit still resided in England while they chased their tails here, this whole trip to Ireland might be for naught.

Nick sighed and stopped, rubbing the back of his neck in frustration. Brick-fronted buildings faced the street, exuding wealth and confidence, as clerks and shop assistants scurried in and out of doorways carrying goods or stacks of documents. The block was rife with discreet signs announcing the various firms and business offices where Limerick's highest commerce was conducted. He could almost smell the ink and profits flowing down the street.

How would you describe your home, Lord Ashton? Meaghan Reilly had asked without guile this morning. He'd refused to answer, refused to even acknowledge the answer he should have given if he'd been ruthlessly honest with Miss Reilly. Or himself. Establishments like these were the places he'd felt most at home over the past decade. Orderly transactions and tidy returns organized through solid contracts into neat columns gave him peace.

Family and home might mean more to some men, but to him they represented unnecessary risk. Jamie made all the family he needed—the only weakness he allowed himself. He would see him safe at all costs. When this latest crisis passed he would be glad to return to his orderly life.

"Fresh goods! Strawberries, ripe melon, the finest winter apples!" A greengrocer touting his wares rumbled past with his cart, on his way to homes lying further down the road, no doubt.

Nick glanced across the street as the passersby parted further down the block. A flash of russet and black caught his eye. Miss Reilly strolled toward O'Brien and Mallory from the opposite direction, lost in an animated discussion with her maid. She tilted her head back with what was surely a laugh to go with her broad smile, revealing the slender white column of her throat.

She moved with an easy grace despite the weighty basket she carried, which was filled with a number of brown-paper packages and a long loaf of bread. Even at a distance, her natural beauty appealed to him. She seemed to light up the street, looking as fresh as the bouquets of lilies, roses, and irises in the flower girl's wagon by the edge of the walkway just ahead.

Miss Reilly's maid carried several large white boxes tied with string. Obviously their shopping had been successful. All traces of the difference in the pair's social status seemed lost as they chattered their way to their destination.

What an intriguing mix made up Miss Reilly. She kissed with enough passion to stir a man for days, then begged his forgiveness for indulging in a childish prank. Last night at dinner, and this morning in the carriage, she'd been cool and withdrawn for the most part, warming only when she spoke of her brothers and their home. He shouldn't have reacted so affronted when she asked about his own life. She was very young and innocent, at least to all appearances.

"Stop, thief!" A high-pitched cry from around the corner halted the pair and they turned to look around. A scurvy-looking youth with dark, matted hair and a tattered brown coat pushed between them, clutching a lady's fringed reticule. The boxes flew out of the maid's grasp as she staggered back and lost her balance when he shoved her. She sprawled backward in the street with a cry. Miss Reilly's attempt to grab her met only empty air.

The thief continued his headlong flight down the block. The level of noise on the street seemed to triple in volume as any number of on-lookers called out and pointed to the purse snatcher. No one seemed wont to interfere to the point of apprehending the fellow.

Nick stepped out onto the cobblestones to cross and help the ladies, but paused to turn and catch the eye of his shadow. He inclined his head and with a brisk nod of affirmation, the man turned in the opposite direction to pursue the young larcenist.

With one hand around the little maid's waist and another on her arm as she assisted Triona to her feet, Miss Reilly looked up at that moment and must have realized who rode to their rescue.

A look of absolute horror exploded over her refined features, and she shook her head and yelled something he could not distinguish above the din on the street. She released her compan-ion so quickly the maid nearly went down again.

She dropped her basket. Her purchases scat-tered unheeded. Her reaction startled him. Pick-ing up her skirts far enough to reveal her delicate calves, she kicked off her wooden clogs and ran toward him full tilt in a blur of russet worsted and white petticoats.

"Look out!" Her cry of warning came just as he perceived the rumble of steel on stone com-ing fast and furious. Launching herself at him, Miss Reilly knocked them both to the cobble-stones. The air whooshed out of Nick as the stones bit into his shoulders and back. Together they rolled in the street as the flower wagon crashed by, far too close.

For a moment, Nick couldn't think. He couldn't see and he couldn't breathe. He just lay on the damp stones cradling the woman he had attempted to assist, but who had saved him instead.

When he did regain enough composure to gulp air, it came in a cloud of Meaghan Reilly's soft meadowsweet-and-honeysuckle scent, oddly comforting in this harried circumstance. Would the blackguard behind all this take advantage of the moment further before he could get her to safety?

"Are you hurt?" he gasped into her hair. He very quickly moved his fingers up her arms and over her back to assess any possible injury even before she could answer.

"My lord! Meaghan? What is going on?" Gill O'Brien's voice cut sternly across the street.

"Diabhal." She exhaled against his collar.

"Indeed," he agreed, recognizing at least the tone of the curse if not the meaning. He released his hold enough so he could push against the cobblestones and sit up with her. "But are you all right?"

Her bonnet was lost and her hair tumbled down. A long streak of dirt cut her right cheek, and the promise of a bruise rode her left. At that moment, she was quite the most beautiful girl he'd ever seen. The oddness of that observation struck him as his heart pounded.

She looked around at the circle of gawkers they had gathered and then over at the ramshackle wagon now tilted on the street a few feet away. And shivered. "As right as any girl who has just sprawled herself in the street for all to see."

"Where is the owner? How did this vehicle get left unattended?" Gill O'Brien blustered in the distance.

"I'm sorry, sir. Our horse went lame on our way to market. My brother took him off to get his shoe fixed." Genuine distress wrung in the flower girl's voice as she answered him. She most likely could ill afford the loss of the flowers scattered over the street. "I don't know how it slipped back like that. I only stepped away for a moment."

Miss Reilly's gaze lingered on the overturned vehicle. A hint of tears trembled at the edge of her green eyes and tugged at Nick's conscience. The nearness of the accident that had almost befallen them both must be shaking her as well. He might know it was most likely not an accident at all. No need to burden her with that knowledge.

"Meaghan, are you injured? What on earth were you doing? And on a public street, no less." Gill O'Brien's voice sounded harsh as he pushed through the crowd, but his face was racked with concern.

A distant part of Nick wondered coldly if a guilty conscience had anything to do with the barrister's reaction to what had nearly befallen his ward.

"Oh, miss. Sir. Ye near frightened me ta death." Triona rushed up to them, wringing her hands. "All the candles are strewn in the street, and the cheeses and spices spilled from the basket. Mrs. Kelly will be ever so vexed."

"Mrs. Kelly will make do, Triona. I'll have a word with her myself if need be. At least none of you were hurt. Such a fuss, and right outside my own establishment." O'Brien managed to sound concerned and annoyed all at the same time.

He first helped Meaghan to her feet and offered a hand to Nick, who stood and brushed his jacket while his host escorted Miss Reilly toward the steps of his office.

"I have invited someone to luncheon I wanted you to have a chance to meet and explain your quest to. He is a noted philanthropist, but quite a high-stickler," Nick heard the flustered man say to her.

Nick rescued his hat and her bonnet from a puddle. Both were ruined. Perhaps he should forego hats while in Ireland. He shook his head and joined the small party, which included several of O'Brien's clerks and a tall, white-haired gentleman whose face was an alarming shade of red.

"I was distracted by the flight of a thief down the street, Mr. O'Brien. Miss Reilly was kind enough to put herself at risk in order to rescue me from my folly. I hope you will not censure her too harshly for her method of doing so."

Neville Chase stood in the shadows at the far corner of the street, struggling to keep his outrage at bay lest he draw unnecessary attention to himself. Chance had brought him an opportunity to accomplish his ends and then snatched victory away at the last moment.

"This Mansfield cur has more lives than a cat," he grumbled and then tipped his hat at a gaunt matron who glanced around to see whom he addressed.

"I say, have a care in crossing, madam. There's hazards aplenty for the unwary. That's a fact nearly cost yon gentleman his life." He inclined his head toward the commotion in front of O'Brien and Mallory's offices.

"Only too true." She sniffed and glanced over her shoulder. "He's a fortunate man. That girl saw what was about even if she did make quite a display of herself shouting and showing her petticoats like a true hoyden. With that and the robbery, a body's hardly safe these days."

"Indeed." Chase tipped his hat again and made as if to continue on his own way. *Hardly safe at all.* Fortune would not continue to smile on Lord Ashton, not if he had any say in the matter.

"Keep a sharp watch, Harry, Kevin." The matron looked hard in both directions before continuing across to the far corner, a hand clamped on each of her boys' shoulders. She did not look back again, and Chase returned to his study of the party gathered on the street.

The flower merchant's wagon, with its colorful bounty now spreading across the cobbles like so much spilled paint, had carried a narrow margin for success when he'd indulged in impulse and sent his assistant to push it toward Ashton. Impulse was a luxury he seldom afforded himself.

Mother had never approved of rash behavior.

The ploy had nearly worked. The arrogant fool had been so absorbed in his thoughts and the minor panic caused by the thief he'd taken no notice of the vehicle crashing toward him.

Frustration rifled Chase. To be foiled by a slip of a girl made matters all the worse. By first racing across the Irish Sea and then racketing cross-

country from Dublin, he'd managed to make it
to Limerick before his quarry only to have him
continue to slip through his fingers almost as
neatly as he'd managed to in England. Ashton
truly held the luck of the devil.

Chase noted the solicitous concern Ashton
showed his rescuer, shielding her from most curious onlookers as he retrieved his hat from the
street and handed a few pound notes to the hysterical flower girl. Ashton engaged in a brief conversation with the Honorable Gill O'Brien,
looking quite vexed, and another gentleman who
had emerged from O'Brien's door just as the dis-
turbance reached its disastrous conclusion with
Ashton and the girl actually rolling in the street
as they escaped the cart's iron-banded wheels.

The twinge of a headache nudged Neville. He
was relieved the girl was not hurt. No matter her
interference, as an innocent, she was not the object of his justice.

Ashton shepherded the girl into the carriage
that had pulled up moments before the incident.
So he knew her. Could it be she was not so innocent after all? A mistress perhaps? Fast work
even for the devil, given he'd just arrived in the
city yesterday. She seemed comely enough, with
her long black hair tumbling around a trim figure made for a man's pleasure.

"I nearly had him that time, sir." Rory Muldoon
slid up beside Chase with an absurd gleam of triumph lighting his dark features. His was a typical
Irish face and scrawny build—a face to blend into
a crowd, which was why he'd been hired, but his
wits were not all they could be. That much had
become quite clear during the morning they'd

spent shadowing Ashton to determine the reasoning behind this very impromptu journey.

"*Nearly* places Ashton no closer to his grave than that shove on the docks the other day. He'll simply be more alert. I'm surprised he doesn't have a platoon of guards about him because of your blunders. I'll have to formulate a better plan."

And hire more competent help.

Muldoon looked ready to argue, but apparently thought better of it. His features settled into a sullen, but silent, glower.

"Meet me back at the inn. And bring those cousins you mentioned." Chase dismissed him before anyone took note of the two of them in conversation. Surely the man's entire family could not be so unskilled.

No one had seen Muldoon make the actual shove that nearly cost Ashton his life, not even the flower girl who had stepped away to purchase an apple from the greengrocer. Still, Chase did not wish to be openly associated with the culprit should a hue and cry be raised once the Honorable Gill O'Brien started nosing about the incident.

Now that the Mansfields had so neatly delivered themselves into the household of his remaining enemy, Chase intended to savor his impending victory. The investment trust had been his idea. He'd put the most effort into it. He'd earned the right to dip into it from time to time. Gerald Mansfield acted completely outside his authority to charge Neville with embezzlement.

Little had his lordship known he'd signed his own death warrant, and that of his family, when he'd had O'Brien draw up the charges and then brought them to court so his son might see him triumphant.

It had taken Neville a long time and nearly every groat he could lay his hands on through the years to destroy all records of Mansfield's family perfidy. Soon he would be able reclaim his good name and place in society. Just as soon as the final two witnesses were expunged. O'Brien and Mansfield.

The carriage pulled away bearing his prey.

"The devil's luck can only last so long, my lord. Then you will get your due."

Four

Boom. Thwack.

A shudder ripped through Nick, tossing him awake. The ship beneath him shook as though gripped by pain-racked contortions.

Nick struggled upright to the edge of his bunk, torn awake, yet certain he tarried in the grasp of some strange nightmare. He rubbed his eyes and shook his head, hoping to clear any lingering traces of sleep.

Fierce reverberations quaked around and through him. Again and again the ship lurched from side to side. The very timbers screeched in protest at this rough treatment. Unnatural groaning and splintering from deep in the bowels of the ship echoed with deadly finality.

Gooseflesh quaked over his arms.

He pushed from the mattress. Fog coated the inside of his cabin. His fault for sleeping with the porthole open, despite his mother's warning. Like acrid cotton, the misty taste slid bitter against his tongue. He pushed through, groping for the hatchway, as the thick haze draped a blanket of unreality around him.

Crack.

Another gyration. The door wrenched from his hand. He struggled into the narrow passage. "Father!

Mother!" His shouts were muffled by the thick air. He could barely see his hand as he felt his way along the passage.

Screams rent the darkness. A piercing chorus of commands from the crew joined inhuman outcries of ruptured seams and tearing planks.

A sailor carrying a length of rope rushed past him, nearly knocking Nick flat.

"Best get on deck, lad. Look sharp, now." The man called over his shoulder and moved on in the opposite direction.

Nick swallowed his panic and counted his steps forward. His heartbeat boomed in his ears. Relief surged through him when his fist closed over the latch to his parents' cabin. He drew in a deep breath.

"Father?" He pushed open the door. "Mother?"

"Nicholas!" his mother answered from within the cabin.

The low glow of an oil lamp burned on the wall. Fog swirled past his feet, an eery specter joining the murk within. He could just make out the shapes of his parents standing together. His mother's pale face beckoned through the mist and smoke.

"Over here, son. See to your mother." The calm command in his father's voice offered reassurance. Whatever was occurring, his father would sort things out.

The ship shuddered again, harder and longer than before. Nick fell back into the passage. Chaos clamored all around. He struggled forward again in sudden darkness. The oil lamp had gone out in his parents' cabin.

"Have we run aground? Are we sinking?" he shouted.

A thunderous roar belched from below. Dark smoke seeped through as the wood beneath Nick creaked. The boards heaved and began to separate. He clutched the planking of the door frame. Shafts of light flickered upward.

Fire in the hold. Not fog, but smoke. The smell unmistakable now.

"No." His father's voice, bound with anger and futility, heavy with fear, drove through Nick, magnifying his own terror.

"Nicholas!" His mother screamed his name with a despairing sob.

The ship lurched sideways, first to port, then starboard. The vessel moved as though executing some ungainly ballet orchestrated by giddy demons straight from hell.

The gap widened beneath his feet. His fingers slipped.

Nick clawed for purchase against the cabin doorway. His hands grasped air as he slid down. He thumped hard against something solid behind him. The air whooshed out of his lungs. His head rocked back and connected with the planking of the passage floor. Waves of color and pain ravaged his skull.

Another rumbling shudder seized the ship. His fall changed direction, pitching him headlong into utter darkness.

"Nicholas!" His mother's scream, high and desperate, accompanied him downward.

He fought past the pain in his head and the panic. He spiraled below as the drop continued and the very world slowed to a snail's pace. His thoughts spun, waiting for the embrace of black river from beneath the ship or the solid thwack of plank and beam to break his fall.

And break him in the process.

His stomach rolled.

Then the cold surrounded him. He was in the water. Under the water. Icy. Stinging. Yanking all vestiges of disbelief from his mind. Panic pushed his limbs into action. He kicked for what he prayed was the surface.

His nightclothes twisted about him, holding him submerged. His lungs burned.

Flickering light in the distance beckoned. He kicked desperately. Bitter cold slashed him. What remained of his strength dwindled with each motion. Breaking to the surface at last, he gulped precious air.

Around him in the black water other passengers and crew splashed, battling for life. Numbed by the water and still dizzy from the blow to his head, Nick gasped for breath. Mouthfuls of river water slapped his chin.

The current tugged him away from the flaming wreckage. Had his parents escaped? They had to be here in the water. They had to be.

"Mother! Father!" Fear narrowed his throat. His call came more as a croak between gulps of the bitter river.

He fought to stay afloat. He scraped against rocks, jostled by arms and legs and people he could barely see. Thick fog sliding along the surface of the river obscured all but the nearest objects and the flames. Pain sliced his shoulder, ravaging down his arm as he swallowed more water and choked.

Disjointed commands echoed around him in the fog.

"Swim for the shore."

"This way! I see a light."

"Grab whatever floats."

"Mother! Father!" His calls went nowhere as he sucked in mist with each breath.

"Swim, Nicky. Swim hard." His father's hoarse command shot out of the darkness. Pure terror sliced down Nick's spine as the ship tore apart in front of him.

"No!" Nick struggled up in the bed, denial pulling him from the depths of the nightmare and the icy waters of the Shannon so many years ago.

As it always did.

The screaming. The awful suction of the ship

going under. The slap of wood against flesh. The horrible night of destruction and death lived on in the dark recesses of his dreams. Inescapable and accusing.

His heart pounded. He tried to pull in deep breaths and shove the memories, the guilt, away.

Thrusting the covers and bed curtains aside, Nick planted his feet on the cool hardwood floor. His stomach rolled. Dizzying waves of pain poured through his skull. He gripped the edge of the mattress and waited for the world to right itself—a slow and all too familiar process. His shoulder ached.

"Damnation." He rubbed the scar, a token of the three-inch wood shard they'd pulled from him following the disaster. The pain of the injury stung afresh, although the wound had healed long ago. His hand came away wet with sweat, not river water.

The loss of his family tore at him again, as jagged and raw now as it had been that bleak night fourteen years ago. And more. If only he'd gotten to his mother as his father had asked. If only he'd found them in the water. He should have gone back instead of heading for shore.

He blew out a long breath, trying to loosen the tightness gripping his throat and chest. The fear etched on his mother's face still twisted his heart. He thrust the memory away and swallowed around the awful lump in his throat.

The enduring nightmare, as familiar to him over the intervening years as his own name, seemed exacerbated by the increasing number of *accidents* befalling him of late. His dunking in the dank river water of Limerick Harbor had been the worst.

The darkness in the room seemed stifling despite the chill now that the fire in the grate had died. He considered opening the window to let in some fresh night air but dismissed the thought outright. He never slept with an open window. Not anymore.

He sighed and raked a hand through his hair. The worst of the nightmare's tangible effects seeped away. If only he could disburse the abiding ache in his conscience.

How many times over the years had he questioned the sequence of events that night? If he hadn't stayed up so late reading . . . If he'd woken sooner . . . If he hadn't left the porthole open . . . Would he have reached his parents faster? Did his disappearance from their doorway delay their own escape as they sought for him? If he'd made it inside could they have escaped the doomed ship before it sucked them down into the watery darkness?

No answers to these questions ever came. Survivors from the crew swore they had not run afoul of hidden rocks at the mouth of the Shannon. They said that there had been a series of explosions in the cargo hold, and that if they had not been delayed in launching they would have been so far out in the deep water no one would have survived.

No one knew what triggered the initial detonation, although a fire was suspected. The captain perished in the incident, along with the purser. The harbormaster's cargo records proved incomplete. The board of inquiry that convened to look into the matter had been unable to establish a cause. Even when the hulk of the ship was raised, no firm facts could be discovered.

"No more." Nick pushed himself out of the bed. Now was not the time to wallow in a past that could not be changed. Better to turn his thoughts to contemporary problems and the situation he might yet bring to a more satisfactory conclusion.

He paced the room's interior in his agitation, his feet alternately slapping the polished floors or digging into the plush comfort of the thick rugs adorning his host's guest bedroom. Could such a considerate host also be responsible for the extremely uncomfortable incident played out yesterday in front of his own office? Was it possible O'Brien orchestrated the entire event? Had he hoped to view Nick's demise from close quarters?

Meaghan Reilly's interference had saved him from disaster; that much was certain. Saved by a wisp of a girl and the glimmer of luck that seemed to pull him through all the disasters in his life.

"If you could call it luck." His lips twisted at the thought. Too well he remembered the siren call of the Shannon as he struggled to shore, racked by cold and despair, his injured arm nearly useless and the weight of his weary legs dragging him down. How much easier it would have been to cease his efforts and drift downward into the beckoning numbness of the cold.

Nights like this he could almost swear death would have been more merciful. Almost.

Swim, Nicky. Swim hard. His father's final exhortation had been the only thing that prevented him from giving up.

He rubbed his hand over the tense muscles knotted at the back of his neck. A stiff swallow or two of O'Brien's whiskey should clear his head. He grabbed his discarded trousers and thrust his legs into them, eager to quit the bed-chamber and the harrowing memories.

The hallway was empty and the house quiet as Nick padded barefoot to the stairs. Good. He hadn't wakened Jamie this time. Relief cloaked his shoulders as cool air shivered over his skin. He welcomed the sensation as it sharpened his mind and helped contain the fiery guilt burning in his heart. Too often he'd been unable to wake from the nightmare of his own accord and his uncle or aunt had to waken him.

When they died the task had become Jamie's.

He reached the bottom of the steps and turned to the study, the marble floor cold against his feet. Feeling even more in need of the whis-key than before, he opened the first set of doors he came to, praying they would yield the libation he sought.

The whiskey glittered darkly in a decanter by the hearth on the far side of the room. A low fire burned in the grate. A quick glance assured him the room stood empty. Who would have left a fire to burn unattended?

With a low growl of irritation he crossed the room, intent on helping himself to a healthy por-tion of O'Brien's whiskey before extinguishing the flames and formulating the polite rebuke he would offer his host for servants who showed such little regard for the safety of the entire household.

Let O'Brien chew on that in the morning. It should prove interesting to watch his face, inscrutable though it might be, at the mention of his guests' safety.

The chink of crystal against crystal proved as gratifying as the rye-laden aroma of the whiskey. He swirled the liquid for a moment, lost in the dark amber glow. But somehow he saw the image of Meaghan Reilly swimming in the depths. Silky dark hair and eyes as green as grass. What had her cousin called them? Reilly-green eyes. And lips the color of a newly opened rose.

He knocked back the entire contents in one long swallow. The path the whiskey blazed down his throat and deep into his belly was faint compared to the burn of desire ignited by a certain Irish lass.

What would be proper thanks for the greatest distraction of his trip? And for his savior? Surely not a kiss, although the idea held certain appeal.

He didn't know what to make of Miss Meaghan Reilly, that much was sure. The soul of impropriety before they were even introduced, as she thrust herself into his embrace, later the same evening she presented the picture of demure young womanhood in the presence of her aunt and uncle.

Today she'd been cool and almost businesslike in the privacy of the carriage, then sauntered down the open street with her maid as carefree as a shop girl, at ease before all the world. She'd been a blur of decisive action, knocking him out of harm's way, then wilted under the censure she'd received for the stir created by her quick action.

The inequity of the situation from her viewpoint struck him. He could imagine the lecture that had sent her up to her room with a head-

ache for the rest of the day following luncheon—
*Save a man's life, but for heaven's sake, do it in a
more ladylike manner next time.*

Which was the true impetus for O'Brien's talk
with the girl once his client had departed? Concern for his ward's already bruised reputation or
frustration at another plan thwarted?

He poured himself a second glass of whiskey
and tried to divert his thoughts by perusing his
host's inner sanctum. Shelves lined the walls of
Gill O'Brien's study from floor to ceiling. Shelves
packed with leather-bound volumes of every sort.
Moonlight spilled in through the windows on the
opposite wall, flooding over the desk and across
the floor. He rested a hand on the back of the
chair beside him. The leather was warm from the
careless fire.

With a sigh, he placed the tumbler back on
the tray with a rattling clink. Here was one detail
he could attend. He crouched before the hearth
and reached for the small spade he could use to
cover the paltry blaze with cool ashes. Behind
him there was a soft rustle of fabric punctuated
by a gasp.

"Oh, my."

The words froze him in place as he recognized
Meaghan Reilly's soft tones, almost as if by thinking of her, he had drawn her forth. He bit back
a curse and closed his eyes for a moment. Caught
unawares and raw from the nightmare, he felt
naked in more ways than one. Why hadn't he
taken the time to at least don a shirt?

He cast a look back over his shoulder and bit
back a second, more vehement curse. Enveloped
in pale white cotton batiste, Meaghan sat curled
in a chair in the back corner of the room. There

were papers scattered on a small writing table by her elbow. Her hair tumbled loose about her shoulders as she blinked herself awake. Her lips were parted in an *o* of surprise.

The desire his earlier thoughts of her stirred in him roused still further. Her gaze traveled the length of his bared back. He could almost feel her startled regard as a physical touch.

"Lord Ashton." She breathed his title as if she were not quite certain of it. Her teeth tugged at her lip. "I wasn't expecting to see anyone at this late hour."

"Indeed. Neither was I." He pulled in a calming breath and forced his attention back to the hearth. Far safer for a man to concentrate on glowing embers than a young woman dressed so seductively in her own innocence. He heaped cold ashes on the pathetic blaze until there was no possibility of it coming back to life. If only his own passions were as easily dealt with.

Anger sliced him. Between random attempts on his life, harrowing memories, chronic nightmares, and now willful lust, was there to be no peace for him in Ireland? Not even in the dead of night? He pushed to his feet.

She stood also, as though that were the proper etiquette at an hour such as this, alone with a half-naked man while the rest of the household slept. Still chewing her lip she regarded him in silence, her fists gripped tight around several slender volumes. Soft batiste whispered about her body, drawing his thoughts to what lay beneath. Satin-smooth skin in soft curves and hidden recesses awaiting exploration.

Back away, Nick. Common sense warned him to quit the room with as much haste and dignity as he could muster. Heaven knew he was no stranger to a woman's charms, but he had never before considered himself a ravisher of innocent young ladies.

Hot images of the one kiss he'd shared with this innocent stung him. The taste of her mouth—sweet honey and honest passion, the feel of her slender form pressed tight against him, the fresh-cut meadowsweet-and-honeysuckle scent of her skin filling his senses. An intoxicating mix of minx and novice hiding in the shadows. Distraction and salvation. And certain damnation.

He caught back a groan and heartily wished her, wished himself, elsewhere. *Separately,* he scolded his mutinous wish when the flickering image of dark silken tresses fanning his pillows filled him.

A frown crossed her brow as she tightened her grasp on the books she held in her arms. "Are you all right?"

"I'm quite all right." *I always run around half dressed in the midst of the night.* The sarcasm of his own thoughts tightened his jaw. "I'm sorry I disturbed you. I honestly did not expect to see anyone."

Her gaze traveled his chest, an odd mixture of bold curiosity and hesitant interest. "I . . . can see that."

She turned away from him as though she couldn't bear the sight of him a moment longer. Silence reigned for the space of several heartbeats as she gathered the papers on the table. He could not help himself as he followed her every move.

The alluring whisper of smooth cotton against silken skin screamed for him to fill the room with a less distracting sound. Anything, even idle conversation—no matter how absurd the hour— would be better than the images the seductive whisper of her nightgown evoked.

"I hope you are recovered from your headache." There was nothing like a conversation about one's health to divert wayward impulses. "Or is that what has you up at this time of night?"

"A headache? Is that the excuse they gave?" She shook her head and picked up an ink pot. She walked over to the desk and placed the jar in a drawer. "I often stay up late. Ever since we left Beannacht. When I cannot sleep, I read or write, either in my journals or to my family."

Moonlight from the windows behind the desk spilled around her in a soft halo to sparkle in the ebony depths of her hair. Her face was in shadows, but the light outlined her womanly shape through the voluminous gatherings of her nightgown and matching robe.

A gentleman would have looked away. Or suggested she move out of such insidious illumination. Nick never felt less of a gentleman than he did at that moment. The ripeness of her body was more than he had imagined within the seductive confines of her diaphanous clothing.

Against his better judgment, he followed her to the windows. "So it was not a headache keeping you from joining us for tonight's dinner?"

She offered him a slight smile and shook her head. The light caught her cheek, and he saw that the early promise of a bruise from their tumble in the street had indeed bloomed. "Aunt Edna thought it best I rest today after . . . after the excitement in Limerick. She did not wish me to be overwrought."

He traced his thumb along her jawline. "And I suppose a mark such as this, even though gained in the midst of battle, might have needed a great deal of explaining to the other guests."

She shrugged, but did not back away from his touch. "Another day of two with Mrs. McKeever's poultice and the mark will fade enough to hide with rice flour."

A mischievous smile quirked the corners of her mouth. "Besides, one does not receive commendations for battling inattentiveness. Spending an evening or two reading is hardly punishment. I am unused to the pace of entertaining in this household."

Standing as they were, she in her nightclothes and he in trousers alone, this small admission showed him yet another side to the mysterious Meaghan Reilly. Innocent temptress, beguiling rescuer, and bluestocking. That she stated her preference so matter-of-factly, with naught but moonlight to observe them made her all the more intriguing.

She focused her attention on the window. The scent of wild honeysuckle and meadowsweet— her unique appeal—teased him.

"Extraordinary."

"Aye, it is lovely out there," she agreed, having no idea he was not referring to the moonlit landscape beyond the windows. "I've always liked this view in the moonlight. It is the closest I can get to the beauty of Beannacht."

"If you miss your island so much, why are you here?"

She sighed, a lonely wisp of sound. "I wanted

to go home or with them, but Da insisted . . ." She trailed away and offered him a smile mixed with embarrassment. "I'm sure you don't need to hear about my parents' decision to introduce me into proper society."

She tilted her head against the glass to look up him. Her eyes sparkled deep green-gray in the silver light. Shadows planed her face, marking the slender column of her throat and dipping into the neckline of her gown.

Again the fire inside him licked at the fraying edges of his control. He cleared his throat. "What do you recommend from your reading to settle a person for the night, Meaghan?"

"I do not think you would find much of interest in Miss Nightingale's *Notes On Nursing*, my lord."

"You are an admirer of the Lady of the Lamp?"

She shrugged and the shoulder of her gown slipped a fraction, baring the tiniest bit more of the hollow of her neck. He ground his teeth together. She slid her fingers over the offending collar, displacing it still further as she struggled to adjust her gown and keep hold of the journals she still clutched.

"Aye. But I don't know that I find her teachings especially settling." There was such earnest enthusiasm in her tone, he bit his tongue rather than reveal how startling her choice seemed. "Her theories are fascinating. If one is to be awake when the rest of the world is sleeping, why not put the time to good use? Are you familiar with her work?"

"I followed the reports of her campaign in the *London Times* and actually met her once," he admitted.

"Really? You must tell me about it someday."
Excitement gleamed in her eyes and in the smile
she flashed him. She hugged the volumes closer
as she attempted to adjust her gown again, un-
consciously pressing her breasts up in the process. One of the papers slid from atop the
journals and floated to the floor.

"Diabhal." She bent to catch it and his mouth
dropped open at the sight she unwittingly offered him. The crest of her rounded breasts
shimmered in the light, awaiting his caress. He
wouldn't survive the torment of watching her
stoop to retrieve the papers.

"I'll get that." He gritted out the words and
knelt to snatch the offending pages from the
floor.

"No. Please. I—"

More sheets of paper followed him downward,
a veritable shower of vellum. He was grateful for
the excuse to stay crouched down. His desire for
her had swollen painfully, straining the front of
his trousers. A blatant display he had no wish to
share with her.

No, that wasn't quite right. A display he wished
far too much to share with her. He ground his
teeth together again and willed himself to think
of something else.

"Stay still, Miss Reilly, before you end up
knocking me in the head with your books."

He scooped her papers into a pile. His gaze
drifted over the words, lit by the moon's bright
glow. A letter. An unwanted flash of jealousy had
him wondering if she wrote to some unknown
lover.

He studied the pages under the guise of or-
ganizing them for her.

"Please, Lord Ashton. I can straighten those."

He didn't answer her, reading quickly through the text. She knelt in a whisper of fabric. Fresh honeysuckle and meadowsweet enveloped him. Soft skin and warm woman. All too appealing coupled with the description of himself he'd just found in her letter, detailing their meeting and today's carriage debacle.

"May I please have my letter?" Her cheeks glowed a becoming pink in the wash of moonlight. She held out her hand and lifted her chin slightly despite her obvious embarrassment.

"Indeed." He smiled and handed the pages back to her. "To whom do you write this lengthy tome?"

She licked her lips before answering him and put the pages in a book. "My sister-in-law, Siannon. She understands what it is like to deal with difficult . . . situations."

"Situations?"

"Aye." The delicate bloom on her cheeks darkened further and a pang of conscience pinched him for teasing her.

"Then I hope she is of help to you, Meaghan."

"Thank you." Her answer came with a touch of surprise.

He stood and reached out his hand. "Actually, I have not properly thanked you. If you had not acted when you did today, I might not be standing here."

She slipped her cool fingers into his. "Oh, I doubt . . ."

A strange glow suffused her gaze. Distant. Cool. Distracted by something he could neither hear nor see, and yet, her face seemed filled with a banked fire and latent sensuality that took his

breath away. He recognized the expression. She'd
worn the same one after kissing him the day he'd
arrived.

"Meaghan?" Her name whispered out of him,
intimate in the darkness, stark in the light of the
moon.

"Aye."

Her gaze traced over his face—his brows, his
cheeks, before coming to rest on his mouth. He
could feel her touch against his mouth though
her fingers were still held fast in his. The effect
on his self-control blazed like lighting a cinder
to dry kindling.

He slid his fingers over her wrist. Her pulse
beat wildly. He pulled her closer. She flowed forward, her gaze fixed on him. His hands moved
up over her arms, gripping her shoulders. Soft
flesh and tempting lace.

He bent his head, taking her parted lips in a
kiss that arced a wild mixture of pure lust and
undaunted need straight through his soul. Her
mouth trembled against his, soft and yielding as
she clung to him and demanded more.

He slid his tongue along the tender line of
her lips. She parted for him. Satisfaction blazed
within him as her tongue darted against his own.
Tasting him, even as he tasted her.

She moaned softly into his mouth. The warmth
of her breath washed over his cheeks in tiny
whorls.

Her journals clattered to the floor. Unencum-
bered, her hands slid up over his back, pulling
him closer as she clung to his shoulders. Feeling
her fingers on his skin showered sparks of pure
desire down the length of him. He pressed her

against him. Her breasts pushed against his bared chest, inviting through her nightclothes.

"Meaghan, sweet, Meaghan," he groaned, needing to taste every inch of her, needing to feel her flesh against his. He tangled his fingers in her dark hair, arching her neck, and tasted a trail over her cheek, her throat, and into the warm hollow just above her breasts.

His breath rasped his throat. The tie of her robe came undone and he pushed the fabric aside. Need swelled deep inside him, threatening every bit of control he might lay claim to. And then he kissed the tender upper swells of her breasts. Soft. Resilient. Enough to drive any man out of his mind.

She shivered in his arms. "Nicholas."

The sound of his name, husky with her own needs and innocent confusion, near unmanned him where he stood. She could be his. He knew from the arch of her body, the quickened cadence of her breathing, and the haze of desire on her face. She was his.

Triumph surged through him, hot and demanding. He took her lips again, plunging his tongue deep into her recesses as he laid claim to her. She kissed him back measure for measure, meeting his tongue, exploring his depths.

He had only to divest the two of them of the meager scraps of clothing they sported and there would be nothing to stop him from sheathing himself deep within the tempting confines of her tender body. Over and over again. To find and take surcease from the desire she raised in him so easily. Yet making love to Meaghan Reilly would be more than a physical joining. The strange mixture of sultry heat and wild innocence in her and the last shreds of any decency he still held, screamed as much to him.

He pulled away. Despite the desire thrumming through every straining inch of his body, he was not a despoiler of young virgins. Instead, he bent and kissed her brow. Chaste and circumspect, despite the rigid evidence of his arousal and the drooping shoulder of her now rumpled robe and nightgown.

"How do you do this to me?" His question rasped, husky and hesitant. He hadn't meant to voice his consternation.

"I don't know." She sounded breathless and equally confused.

"I think we've taken this about as far as we dare, Miss Reilly." He strove for a light tone, but hunger rasped his tone as desire burned on inside him. He sounded harsh. Condemning.

Flames lit her soft cheeks as he set her from him.

"I . . . Oh. I . . ." Words failed her.

Did she realize how close she had come to being seduced? He hoped so. The pain of passion denied settled deep in his groin. It was going to be a very long night.

"Perhaps we would be wise to keep a safe distance from each other in the future? I am not a despoiler of young virgins."

Gathering the remnants of her dignity like a regal robe around her scantily clad figure, Meaghan Reilly nodded and quit the room in a swirl of luminous cotton batiste and honeysuckle.

"Good night, Lord Ashton." Her farewell echoed back to him from the foyer.

He bent to retrieve her fallen letter and the journals she so prized and placed them on a small table by the door. He raked his hand through his hair and exhaled a long breath.

Leaning against the doorway, he looked out across the dark and empty expanse of marble to the steps. It was for the best that he let her go, despite the clamoring of his body. They were damned lucky they had roused none of the other inhabitants of the household. Moonlit encounters and virgins did not mix—a lesson for them both.

He turned back to seek the whiskey he had poured earlier. Still, the passionate sound of his name on Meaghan's lips would haunt him for a long time.

Five

"Diabhal."

More aptly, Nicholas Mansfield. The devil himself come to torment her in the flesh. As Meaghan reached the landing, her attempt at cool composure evaporated like meadow mist in summer sunshine.

Words failed her. She leaned against the wall and caught her breath. The cool plaster drew some of the heat from her cheek. Balling her hands into fists, she fought for the mangled shreds of her control.

"I . . . will . . . not . . . cry," she gasped.

A rebellious tear dripped down her cheek. Anger, regret, and shame flamed through her. She had kissed him. Again. And he had kissed her. He had touched her as only a lover would. As only a husband should.

And she had wanted more. A long sigh shuddered out of her.

The last few minutes whirled by in a blur of confusion. At what point did the entire encounter in the secluded study turn from innocent conversation to swift passion? Passion that took her breath and stole her common sense.

Could she blame the silver magic of the moonlight for breaking the ordinary world's conventions and luring a woman in her nightclothes to even dare speak to a half-dressed man she barely knew?

Or had her troubles begun earlier? She had arrived first. Seeking the seclusion of the study to pour out her troubles to Siannon in case Sheila came into her room for a cozy chat. Siannon would understand—she always did. After all, she lived with Quin, the moodiest of her brothers.

And she had not lied when she told Nicholas she had been studying. She had read Miss Nightingale's book until the lamp and the fire burned low. Familiarity with the principles espoused aided Meaghan in soliciting subscriptions for the local society. She'd only closed her eyes for a moment.

The clink of crystal had startled her from her drowsy slumber. She'd turned in the chair enough to see Nicholas crouched by the hearth, firelight gleaming on the chiseled curves and planes of his naked torso.

Caught between the fire and the dark of night, he looked very much the *laoch grian*—sun warrior—she'd dubbed him. She'd been spellbound. The play of light from the meager flames added a glow to his tousled blond hair while shadows cut across his naked muscles, bringing out a ferocity usually hidden by civilized clothing.

She'd seen men in her father's shipyard working without their shirts. Her brothers and the other boys on Beannacht frequently swam in their breeches, or in even less on the far side of the island. But having three brothers and growing up on an island teeming with friends and family busy with work and life had still not prepared her for the effect of waking and seeing Nicholas Mansfield in that state.

Like a moth to a lamp, she had been drawn close. When she should have gathered her books and papers and fled, she lingered, allowing herself to draw close enough to the flame to be singed.

She shivered, recalling the onset of seduction. He'd touched her. He had simply taken her hand. And she had lost command of herself. Lost herself to him and to a family birthright she had once longed to claim.

The Blessing had roared through her like laughter rolling down a hillside. With colored stars and hornpipe music that whistled and drew her far away from all she knew as proper and decent.

Their lips touched. Their tongues parried. His scent, oranges and mint, still lingered on her skin from their intimate embrace.

She'd allowed a man to kiss her breasts and instead of being horrified, she'd been disappointed when he'd pushed her away.

The memory stung like a slap, propelling her forward. Her feet flew up the rest of the stairs. If only she truly could outrun her wantonness and the wild unnameable things Nicholas flamed to life within her.

Her ears drummed with thundering heartbeats and the chastening echoes of her aunt's and uncle's warnings. Nothing they had cautioned her about held the slightest weight when confronted with the magnetism of Nicholas Mansfield. Especially when combined with her Reilly heritage.

The Blessing. More like a Curse disguised in shining raiment. All the tales her brothers told her as a child dogged her heels as she reached the head of the stairs.

'Tis a feeling once felt, always remembered.

She stopped and looked back at the silent foyer. She could certainly account for that part of the legend now, couldn't she? The taste of Lord Ashton's lips, winter apples laced with whiskey, lingered warm and vivid against her own. She doubted she would ever forget the way Nicholas Mansfield made her feel. Not if she lived to be one hundred and twenty or dwelt a thousand lifetimes in the pits of hell.

'Tis in the blood of all Reillys.

More tears stung the backs of her eyes. She bit her lip as hysteria threatened. Wouldn't her brothers have a good laugh to see her running in the dead of night as though she could outdistance the very family legacy she'd vowed she'd claim one day, no matter their denials.

Once given, The Blessing could not be escaped. She knew that as well as she knew her own name. Knew the awesome power of the boon in a bone-deep way no fanciful tales could shake. But why did it have to be now? Why him? She groaned aloud, the sound echoing softly down the hall. What possible use could it be to have her discover The Blessing with a man who doubtless thought her loose and most certainly in severe want of character?

Reillys take heed and Reillys beware.

Perhaps if she had paid attention to the darker portions of the old legend, she wouldn't find herself in her current predicament. In her childhood's fancy, the man she'd imagined as the catalyst for her Blessing had been kind and handsome, embodying all the noblest ideals of men. How naive she'd been to expect a knight on a charger. Nicholas Mansfield did not seem to possess a kind bone in his body.

He was kind enough to release you and send you on your way just now. Her conscience pricked her without remorse.

"Aye, after kissing the stuffing out of me." The admission came out in a husky tone she barely recognized as her own.

Embarrassment scorched her cheeks, a painful mix with the lingering echo of ungoverned yearning experienced in his arms. She groaned again.

The slap of bare feet on marble echoed in the darkness, and her heartbeat drummed louder. Fear and anticipation tasted sharp against her tongue. After a moment, Nicholas appeared at the bottom of the steps. Had he changed his mind? Had he come in search of her? To claim what she had so freely offered only minutes ago?

Moonlight highlighted his tall frame and spilled an enticing pathway across his bare chest. Her fingers itched—feeling again the rough, heated-velvet of his skin, tracing the edges of the scar that slashed his shoulder. How had such an injury occurred? In a duel perhaps? Waged after he'd kissed and seduced another woman? Her stomach rebelled at the thought.

He looked up, halting as his gaze met hers. He didn't look at all surprised to see her there. Everything that had passed between them wavered in the air for a moment—a mirage, something more than a kiss and less than a seduction.

Pure heat sluiced through her body, white-hot

and insistent, melting her resistance and her attempts to gainsay the passion this man fanned to life in her. He didn't even have to touch her to spark such a response. Knowing she would not have stopped him had he demanded more of her, shimmered at the heart of the bald acknowledgment. Everything inside her exhorted her to run back down the stairs and fling herself into his arms.

Madness.

The proprieties her parents instilled, the church-taught strictures voiced by Father Dunnavan at St. Bridgid's, and her own common sense recoiled, struggling to still this insidious desire throbbing in her very bones.

The sound of his name, tumbling wild and husky from her own lips while he caressed and kissed her body, echoed mockingly in her heart. "Nicholas," she'd cried, and he had pushed her away.

Lord Ashton—wedging his title into the mix might help drive some distance between them—stood at the bottom of the stairs in steadfast silence as the conflict raged inside her.

She clutched the newel post with both hands, needing to anchor herself in place. Cool wood dug into her palms. She dredged up the certainty that she had already made a big enough fool of herself. Surely The Blessing could not intend for her to throw away her pride, her principles, and shame herself to the depths of her soul.

A token of esteem, a gift, a fearsome gratitude.

Fearsome. That description of The Blessing never seemed more apt.

She blew out a quick breath and pleaded for

strength—from herself and from the heritage she couldn't fully accept.

She straightened her shoulders and lifted her chin.

Below her, cloaked in deep gray shadows and silvery light, Lord Nicholas Ashton inclined his head in a polite nod. Or was it a mocking nod?

His last words ripped through her. *I am not a despoiler of young virgins.*

Despite her own all-too-obvious willingness to be spoiled.

How mortifying. Embarrassment scalded every inch of her skin. Again. She almost wished it were possible for her own mortification to incinerate her on the spot.

Gritting her teeth, she held back a wave of despair burgeoning within her and released her talonlike grip of the newel post.

Stiff with the effort to keep her pace steady, she walked down the darkened hallway, stifling the blind need to run. She was Reilly born and Reilly bred, despite her recent behavior. Generations of Reilly pride and honor pulsed through her with every beat of her heart.

Something she feared might be lust churned through her middle, followed in a wicked circle by shame and remorse. She gripped the brass doorknob of her bedroom and gave it a vicious twist, venting some of her tangled emotions.

She closed the door behind her and leaned her head back against it, releasing a shaky sigh.

"Meaghan, is that you?" Sheila's whisper shot out of the darkness.

Meaghan jumped. The door behind her rattled. She swallowed, blew out another quick breath, and forced herself forward.

"Aye," she managed to whisper back. She couldn't face a midnight visit. Not after . . . She faked an overlarge yawn, hoping Sheila would take the hint and leave her to seek her bed in peace.

But Sheila O'Brien was not her mother's daughter for nothing. Her feet thudded to the floor next door. In moments she padded quickly through their connecting dressing room and hurried over to plop herself on the end of Meaghan's bed with a slight bounce and aura of lilies—her favorite scent.

The satin comforter slid toward the floor, hissing like gossip in the back pew of St. Bridgid's during Sunday mass. Meaghan caught the coverlet, but restrained herself from cooling her cheek against the slippery fabric.

"I've been waiting for you." Sheila hugged her knees and wiggled her toes beneath the lacy hem of her nightgown, oblivious to the disarray she had caused. "I left both dressing room doors open so I'd be sure to hear you when you came to bed."

"I was . . . reading." And so much more. Meaghan gnawed her lip again. Lying had never been among her talents. Why couldn't Sheila have been asleep? For that matter, if she herself had only stayed in her bedroom tonight she'd have nothing on her conscience to hide. Touché.

"Oh." Sheila made a face and shrugged. "How can you devote yourself to reading those musty old tomes you cart around? They would bore me inside of a minute. And you know how I love to read."

Meaghan held silent. The only things she'd

ever seen Sheila read were fashion magazines and romance novels.

"I thought you would never come up," Sheila continued, before releasing a suffering sigh.

Meaghan smoothed the comforter back into place. Her cheeks burned yet again. Good thing it was dark on this side of the house. Nicholas Mansfield's warm muscles and strong arms had held her fast in the study while Sheila waited innocently upstairs. Under the moonlight, he'd explored her thoroughly with his hands and lips, while Sheila listened for her return.

Sheila was not known for her excessive patience. Suppose she had come downstairs to hurry Meaghan along? The idea made Meaghan's knees weak. She abruptly sat on the edge of the bed.

After several deep breaths to regain some of her equilibrium, she ventured a question. "Why were you waiting for me?"

Sheila smiled. "I wanted to talk with you, silly goose. About the Mansfields. Well, one Mansfield in particular."

"Oh?" Meaghan gripped her hands together. With her thoughts scattered to the wind like so much sea spume, she wasn't sure just how much discussion she might be up to. Especially regarding the Mansfields. Especially one Mansfield in particular.

"Aye. He isn't at all like most of the potential suitors my father brings home to me."

Having no idea what type of men Uncle Gill considered as possible husbands for Sheila, Meaghan chose not to comment.

"Oh?" she prompted when Sheila did not continue.

"Isn't he just the most handsome man you've ever met?" Sheila sighed dramatically.

"He is very pleasant looking," Meaghan offered cautiously. That seemed mild enough. She definitely did not want to discuss Nicholas Mansfield's many charms. Not now, or ever—if she had any spine in her.

"Pleasant is too tame." Sheila dropped back against the mattress. The bounce nearly jolted Meaghan off the bed.

"Dashing. Witty. Thoughtful." Sheila sighed again. "And his laugh, Meggy. I swear when he laughs I get the funniest little ripples in my stomach and then I'm all out of breath."

"His laugh?" For the life of her, Meaghan couldn't remember Lord Ashton finding anything amusing during their brief acquaintance. Let alone laughing. Not once. He'd been too busy turning all she knew about herself to mush.

Perhaps Sheila had heard him laughing over his easy conquest of her? Impossible, but the stab of pain accompanying the thought churned hot in her stomach.

"Aye, his laugh does the most incredible things to me. But that's not the half of it. He makes me feel so wonderful just by walking into a room," Sheila waxed on. "I swear, sometimes I just freeze. It's as if the mere sight of him holds me spellbound. He just radiates."

A sun warrior, crouched by the hearth with firelight and shadows playing over chiseled muscles. The sight that had greeted Meaghan when she awoke from her doze in the study.

"I've never felt anything like this before." Sheila laughed softly and flopped onto her belly as though she could not be still. "And who would believe one of Father's guests could make me feel this way? There are people staying here or coming for luncheon and dinner nearly every day. The idea I might fall in love with a man my father does business with is just ludicrous . . . and wonderful at the same time."

Another long, dramatic sigh burst out of Sheila, followed by a giggle. "Now you see why I just had to talk to you."

Love? Upon two days acquaintance? Nicholas Mansfield was a busy man, indeed. Courting one girl and seducing the other. Would Uncle Gill view such a situation in the same wondrous light his daughter did, titled English lineage or no?

The idea of Lord Ashton kissing Meaghan and pursuing Sheila at the same time was appalling, harrowing to both her sense of pride and her concerns for her cousin. Not a despoiler of young virgins, indeed.

"What do you think, Meggy? Would my father entertain his suit?" This last came out of the darkness in an excited whisper.

Meaghan's heart wrenched and then sank to her toes. "His suit? Oh, Sheila. Has he asked you?"

Giddy laughter precipitated Sheila's answer. "No. No. Not yet. Oh, wouldn't it be wonderful if he did? You must help me convince my parents he would be the perfect match for me."

Nicholas and Sheila? Lord and Lady Ashton? Was this why Uncle Gill had insisted she keep as far away from his guest as possible after the incident outside his office? He wanted Sheila to gain Lord Ashton's notice?

Jealousy surged deep in Meaghan, cold and unwanted. She pressed her hands over her abdomen and clenched her fingers together trying to push the ugly thoughts away. A whiff of oranges and mint tormented her.

She inhaled a deep breath and strove to sound uncommitted and unconcerned. "Don't you think it would be better to wait until the occasion arises, before I offer my opinion? Especially to your parents?"

Not that the O'Briens were likely to pay much attention to what she had to say anyway. She dwelt on the wrong end of the cane with her aunt and uncle at the moment.

"Perhaps you are right and I am letting my imagination get the better of me." Sheila sighed again. "When he looks at me, Meggy, I feel like I am the only woman in the world. As if I am special and he thinks I am beautiful."

"Hmm." Meaghan had been on the receiving end of the way Nicholas Mansfield could make a woman feel just a few moments ago. Heat, passion and a strange spiraling kind of longing. Aye, he did make her feel beautiful. But the fact that he could make her feel this way and court Sheila at the same time rang all kinds of alarm bells for her. But what to tell Sheila?

"Sheila, you hardly know Nicholas Mansfield. Don't you think it would be better to hold yourself back a bit?"

"Nicholas? You mean Lord Ashton?" Sheila laughed and sat up. She wrapped her arms around Meaghan and gave her a quick squeeze. "You are being a goose tonight. He is Jamie's guardian. But that ends soon. Jamie will be free to make his own decisions. To marry whom he chooses.

"Unless . . ." Sheila flopped back onto her

back again and stared at the ceiling, sounding suddenly very strained. "Oh, Meaghan. You can't think Lord Ashton would not approve of me for his cousin."

"Jamie?" Meaghan's mind spun in a muddle.

"Lord Ashton." Sheila sat up. "But if he loved me, no objection would be enough to stand in the way. Not Father's. Not his cousin's."

"Jamie?" This time Meaghan sighed. The whole conversation flowed beyond her.

"Yes. I believe I could be very happy married to James Mansfield. *Married*, Meggy. The very word sounds magical, doesn't it?"

"Jamie?" Meaghan repeated again, stupidly.

Sheila put an arm around Meaghan's shoulders. "I told you no good came from reading those dull books so late in the night. You are not listening. Of course, Jamie. Who do you think I've been talking about for the past ten minutes?"

Heat crept over Meaghan's cheeks again. "Nicholas."

"Nicholas?" Sheila's incredulity whooped out of her. She clutched her stomach and rolled on the bed for a minute. "You mean Lord Ashton?"

"Aye." Meaghan's reply came with a tart edge to it. She could not appreciate her cousin's humor after her increasing distress over the past few minutes. Everything in her felt rubbed raw. First Nicholas's embrace and the fiery things he made her feel, and then her fears for Sheila, coupled with the most awful sensation of jealousy she had ever experienced.

Sheila covered her mouth with her hand to still her laughter. "Meaghan, I'm sorry. It's just that . . . well . . . Lord Ashton is a nice-looking

man, certainly. But he's a bit stodgy and he's so
old."

She dissolved into giggles again. Relief sluiced
through Meaghan, making her light-headed. It
had not been Nicholas Sheila was prosing on
about. It was Jamie.

Meaghan stretched across the bed and got
caught up in Sheila's high-pitched cackle. Off-key
as it seemed, her own laughter felt good after
her fears.

Sweet, pleasant Jamie. She sighed. He seemed
to hold none of the same tensions and drive as
his cousin. He probably could be a good match
for Sheila, provided Uncle Gill and Nicholas re-
solved whatever problem seemed to lie between
them. They acted friendly enough on the surface, but a certain underlying restiveness underscored their conversations.

"Nicholas," Sheila whispered, laughter edging
her tone.

"Aye," Meaghan whispered back, earning a
half-hearted pinch for her efforts.

"Will you think about what we could say to my
father to make Jamie sound like a good match?
He respects you, Meaghan, and so does Mother."

Meaghan looked up at the ceiling, doubting
Gill and Edna O'Brien would listen to her account of what was suitable and what wasn't. "I
don't think—"

"Oh, please, think about it. You're so much
cleverer about changing people's minds than I
am."

"Me?" Meaghan managed not to squeak. "Why
on earth—"

"Just last week you made Mrs. Dalrymple say
she would support your nurses school, didn't

you? That was quite a sizable subscription she took once you'd told her all about Miss Nightingale's success during the war. After she said she wasn't interested at all. You told me so. If you can change her opinions, Meggy, you can change anyone's."

Well, maybe not anyone's. Not Nicholas Mansfield. Not after she granted him far too much liberty to ever reclaim her good name. The clash of her emotions over him—anger, jealousy, regret, and longing in a vicious cycle—exhausted her reserves.

"All right. I'll consider it." Meaghan earned a quick squeeze for her support. "If you really like him that much."

"I do." Sheila's tone went soft and wondering, as if she'd been wrapped in velvet and fur. "Thank you."

Sheila hugged her again. Silence held for a peaceful moment, and then Sheila's voice whispered again. "Meaghan, isn't it grand that love feels like this?"

"Like what? Whispers in the dark?" Meaghan tried for a light note.

"Of course not." Sheila shook her head, obviously taking her own question very seriously. "As though you cannot get enough of being with someone. As though he is the only person you miss if he is not in the room. As though . . . As though the world is not big enough to hold how much you care for him."

"I wouldn't know."

Sheila rose to her elbows and peered down at Meaghan. "Meggy, you've been abroad. You've met lots of men. Haven't you fallen in love with any of them?"

Sheila made it sound as if falling in love should be an everyday occurrence. If that were so, just how deep could her feelings truly be for Jamie Mansfield? Especially on such short acquaintance. The realization he would most likely prove the object of a passing fancy, like last week's new bonnet, relieved Meaghan. The sooner he and his cousin departed the better, especially if it did not leave Sheila broken-hearted and moping over him for weeks.

"No, She, I told you we didn't socialize very much. That's the reason I'm staying with you instead of visiting Devin in America."

"But—"

"It's the truth."

"Then why did you take the hazard when Eloise challenged you? You could have gotten by unscathed."

"What?"

"I saw your face when Eloise asked you about kissing a man. Why did you take the hazard if you had nothing to hide with your answer?"

"Oh, for heaven's sake. Were you expecting a deep dark secret hidden in my past all this time?" Meaghan laughed.

"Aye." Sheila inched closer to peer again at Meaghan in the darkness.

"Well, there wasn't one." Meaghan carefully shoved aside the knowledge that there was one now.

"Then why?"

"If you must know, it is because of a misunderstanding I had when I was very small."

"What misunderstanding?"

"When I was five, my family visited your family

here. You were still a baby and hogging all the attention, if I remember correctly."

Sheila laughed.

"My brothers teased me. They have always been very good about that. And I had had enough. So I went outside to sulk, which *I* was very good at. While I sat in the garden I met the nicest boy. He was about Bryan's age. Tall, handsome. He talked to me and treated me as though I were special. Not just the youngest and a girl to boot, but someone he wanted to be with. So I kissed him to say thank you."

Sheila gasped and playfully tapped her on the shoulder. "You were a bold thing!"

"Aye." Meaghan smiled, lingering over the old memory and a nagging sensation that somehow reminded her of Nicholas Mansfield's oranges-and-mint scent. "And I believed kissing seemed the very best thing that could ever happen to me in my entire life. All five years of it, which seemed extremely old and mature to me at the time. I spent the next year or two kissing any boy who would hold still long enough, trying to repeat the feeling."

"Oh." Sheila dissolved into giggles.

"That was not a story I cared to share with Eloise Farrell and the Carlson twins. Or almost anybody else for that matter. My brothers teased me unmercifully for years, calling me the Kissing Buccaneer. Most of the boys on Beannacht ran when they saw me coming."

She sighed, the shame and frustration still scoured her when she thought of how foolish she'd been. "I believed the hazard would prove far safer than relating all my childish shame."

I was surely mistaken in that respect, she added silently.

Sheila laughed, hugging her stomach until her breath ran out.

"Oh, I had no idea." She gasped finally. "No wonder you risked the hazard. I don't blame you."

"Thank you."

"So was kissing Lord Ashton anything like kissing your young man so long ago?" Sheila dissolved into laughter again, barely getting the question out.

Meaghan sighed. So much for getting some understanding from Sheila, but at least she had managed to lighten the mood and distract her cousin from the depth of her feelings for Jamie.

"I'm glad you find me so humorous. If we don't get some sleep we'll be next to useless tomorrow."

"I know," Sheila sobered enough to reply. She hugged Meaghan again and kissed her on the cheek, enveloping her in the comfortingly sweet scent of lilies and true innocence. "I hope I dream of Jamie."

She bounced off the edge of the bed and disappeared into the dressing room. "Sleep well, Meaghan. I'm so glad you're here and not in America. Who else could I talk to about all this? You are so sensible and prudent."

Sensible and *prudent?* If only Sheila knew about the tryst earlier between her sensible cousin and Jamie's stodgy guardian. Meaghan didn't dare enlighten her.

"Good night, Sheila." For her part, she hoped the Mansfields stayed far from her dreams. Both waking and asleep.

Six

"What in the name of St. Bridgid are you two doing?"

Edna O'Brien's shocked tones cut straight through Meaghan as Nicholas trailed kisses down her throat. She jumped, guilt prickling her skin.

It took a moment for her to realize she lay safe in her bed. Alone. Not locked in Nicholas Mansfield's scandalous embrace as she had dreamed every night for the past week.

"I sent Triona for you long ago." Aunt Edna's scolding voice continued from Sheila's room.

"Why so early?" Sheila's sleep-muffled complaint drifted through the dressing room toward Meaghan, along with a stream of sunlight as her mother shoved Sheila's curtains open.

"You know very well." Aunt Edna sounded harassed.

"Meaghan?" Her aunt's determined footsteps proceeded through the dressing room and Meaghan pushed herself up in the bed to greet her.

"Yes, Aunt?" She swiped her hair out of her eyes, wishing she felt less groggy. Her dreams of Lord Ashton always left her exhausted and edgy.

Aunt Edna shook her head, her sharp gaze taking in Meaghan's disheveled hair and rumpled bedclothes. She quirked one disapproving eyebrow. "We've so much to do this morning, and you look like you've been wrestling demons all night. Heaven forgive me. You girls have both forgotten the Lough Gur picnic is today."

Meaghan's heart sank. The picnic. She had forgotten completely. Between throwing herself into her work with the Nightingale Society and doing her best to avoid Lord Ashton, she had forgotten all about her aunt's annual party.

One look at Meaghan's face raised both her aunt's eyebrows. "Have you also forgotten your promise to help with the preparations? We've any number of guests due here in just a few hours. Even with the extra people we hired, the staff cannot be expected to handle everything."

With an impatient swish of her skirts, Aunt Edna proceeded to Meaghan's window and flung open the curtains. Bright sunshine flooded the chamber. "Do hurry, Sheila," she called. "We are behind enough already."

Every spring Aunt Edna and Uncle Gill invited their acquaintances—friends, clients, and other business associates to partake in a day of feasting and games. This year they had chosen to lead an expedition to Lough Gur, to allow their guests to stroll the ancient ruins between footraces and cricket matches.

All week the servants had been packing tables and chairs, china and linens onto carts under Aunt Edna's and Mrs. McKeever's watchful eyes.

Meaghan doubted either the housekeeper or her mistress had neglected any detail in planning for their guests' comfort and entertainment.

That certainty did not negate the guilt scouring her for adding to Aunt Edna's distress. She flung back her covers.

"Meggy and I stayed up late talking." Sheila came up behind her mother and gave her a hug. "We'll be ready as quick as you please."

Edna's impatient gleam softened beneath her daughter's affection. "Don't try to placate me, Sheila O'Brien." Her words held no sting as she patted Sheila's check. "Quick as you please would have pleased me an hour ago."

"Quicker than you please," Sheila offered with an engaging smile. Her brown curls bounced over her shoulders as she spun back to the dressing room.

Edna sighed. "I supposed that will have to do. Mrs. Kelly's in a stew down in the kitchen, and they cannot clear off breakfast until you have eaten. Where can that Triona have gotten herself?"

She glanced at the watch pinned to her bodice. "I need you both, and I needed you about half an hour ago. Dress in old clothes for now. We'll all change before the guests arrive."

She turned toward the door. "Come along quickly now. I'll expect you in the dining room."

"We'll be there," Meaghan promised as she stood up from her bed and stepped into the sunlight.

Edna's gaze shot back to her. "Are you well, Meaghan? You look flushed."

In two short steps, her aunt's cool palm graced Meaghan's cheek. "You've got dark circles under your eyes, too. Aren't you feeling well? It would be a shame for you to miss the picnic."

Her escape beckoned. She could avoid the Mansfields yet again. "I—"

"She just feels guilty for oversleeping," Sheila called from the other room. "You know how responsible Meaghan usually is. I should not have kept her up all night."

"Mmm." Edna frowned and then patted Meaghan's cheek. "You'll feel more the thing as soon as the two of you are downstairs and about the tasks I have set for you. Social occasions come with their own collection of responsibilities, Meaghan. Everything important in life is not confined to the realm of books, no matter how interesting you find them."

Meaghan strove for a humble tone. "Yes, Aunt."

"Quickly, then." Edna released Meaghan from her perusal and then whisked out the door in a swirl of efficiency and rustling petticoats.

Meaghan and Sheila made it downstairs within fifteen minutes of Aunt Edna's summons. She met them at the bottom of the steps, her cool gray-eyed gaze evaluating them carefully.

"That was very prompt, my dears. Thank you." She handed them both aprons and a list of items for them to check. "Eat quickly. There is much to be done if we are going to be finished in time to dress and fix your hair."

Sheila took her list and apron and dashed into the dining room. She'd been talking nonstop since her mother left them alone. Did Meaghan think she should wear her blue habit or her green one? Which hat should she choose? Would Jamie sit with her when they dined? She prattled on, insisting she could hardly wait to spend the entire day with Jamie Mansfield.

Although from the number of rides and walks the pair had taken in recent days, Meaghan wondered how today could be any different than all the others, save for several dozen other guests accompanying them rather than a solitary groom. She'd bitten her tongue over that one, her own thoughts trying to devise the means to avoid any proximity to Lord Ashton for the day without being obvious.

"Meaghan, if you could spare a moment." Aunt Edna put her hand on Meaghan's sleeve and halted her before she followed her cousin.

"Your uncle and I wanted to tell you how pleased we have been with your behavior this past week. You have been most circumspect, especially where Lord Ashton and Mr. Mansfield are concerned. Almost too circumspect . . ."

They'd hardly think that if they knew what had happened, what had nearly happened in their very study. Not if they knew the direction of her dreams. She'd kept her distance at the few meals she had been unable to escape and then fled to her room to read each night, mostly for her own safety.

". . . We invited you to stay because your parents wanted you to have some fun after traipsing through Europe while your father convalesced."

"I appreciate that, Aunt. I am having a lovely stay."

"Well, we don't want you to think we are so strict you must be serious all the time. Enjoy today with the other young people. Have Triona do a little something different with your hair. Try to put aside your passion for Florence Nightingale and her reforms for one day, at least."

Meaghan put her hand over her aunt's and

quickly squeezed her fingers. "I'll try. Now, I'd best have tea and a bite of toast before Sheila claims it all."

"Yes, and I must go and see where Triona has gotten off to this time. Your uncle diverted her when she should have woken you, sending her to scour the boys' rooms for fishing rods to offer the gentlemen first. Fishing rods."

Aunt Edna turned and headed toward the kitchen. "He might have her out digging for worms with Seamus for all I know. Men and their fishing."

Meaghan chuckled. Do something with my hair. As if something that simple could change anything. The modest bun she'd adopted helped her look older than her nineteen years and thus, people listened more readily to her when she spoke about the need for modern, trained nurses. Still, it was something to consider, and anything that provided a diversion from her mooning over Nicholas Mansfield proved gratifying after a week of guilt and unwelcome longing.

The household bustled merrily for the next two hours providing almost enough distraction to suit even Meaghan. Great hampers of food and drink of every description were packed and checked. Hired carriages for the elder set and mounts for those inclined to ride were polished and brushed in anticipation of the ride to the lake. Most of the furniture and table settings were sent ahead so all could be in readiness when the picnickers arrived at Lough Gur.

Even Jamie and his cousin were pressed into service, much to Sheila's delight, carrying items out to be stowed in the provision wagons. Meaghan found it almost as easy to locate tasks

that kept her as far away from Lord Ashton as
Sheila found ones that placed herself working
very near the younger Mansfield.

As Meaghan watched Sheila giggle at some remark from her beau, she hoped again that Jamie
Mansfield proved just what he appeared to be—a
kind young man who respected her cousin. From
the late-night confessions Sheila whispered to
her, he had made no untoward gestures to date.
But given his own guardian's nocturnal behavior,
Meaghan couldn't help but worry.

To his credit, Lord Ashton had been most
helpful this morning, carrying and sorting whatever Aunt Edna requested of him without the
slightest hint of impatience.

At last, approval beamed from Aunt Edna as
Meaghan and Sheila settled the last ribbon-
trimmed basket in with the rest. "You two go
in and change now. I would appreciate you being prompt in your attendance in the drawing
room. I would like you to greet our guests as
they arrive. I've much to oversee still in the
preparations and you need to perfect your skills
as hostesses."

"Yes, General." Sheila affected a meek pose,
but the twinkle in her eyes gave her away.

Aunt Edna's eyebrow quirked at the teasing,
but she held her peace.

"Couldn't I help you, Aunt?" Meaghan offered. Anything to avoid spending time in close
quarters with Lord Ashton. Uncle Gill had just
invited the Mansfields to join him there for some
early refreshment.

"Bless you, Meaghan. But you've done enough
for now. You may assist Sheila. The charity you

are so determined to champion will not be hurt through honing your social skills, either."

Meaghan sighed. Probably so, especially if she truly wanted to raise as much funding for the Nightingale Society as possible. Sheila sailed through these long drawn-out outings as though she lived for them. Meaghan couldn't imagine that ever being the case for herself, no matter how many she attended.

"Mother is so pleased. This picnic is an even bigger success than last year's," Sheila enthused a short while later. Most of the guests had arrived, making the O'Briens's more than adequately appointed drawing room feel cramped. Sheila and her mother were in their element, but between Eloise Farrell and the Carlson twins, Meaghan felt suffocated. Despite hanging on her betrothed's arm, Eloise seemed determined to engage Lord Ashton in conversation, and the Carlson twins were atwitter like brightly colored birds, flitting between the Mansfields and any other eligible man they spotted.

Dressed in her hunter green riding habit with its gold buttons and trim, Sheila looked every bit as excited as her mother, speaking at great length with the wife of Limerick's chief magistrate. The simple braid hanging down Sheila's back tamed her hair and looked quite fetching with the small bowler perched at the crown.

"You look so pretty today," Sheila leaned in to say in Meaghan's ear. "Triona's suggestion to leave your hair long gives you quite the fresh-country-girl look. Perfect for a day outdoors exploring cairns and old ruins by a lake. Eloise will be lucky if her ringlets make it through the ride there."

The other girl's muted blue ensemble trimmed with black braid and jet beading highlighted her fair coloring and delicate features. Near her, Meaghan felt very much the gauche island girl, no matter how many times Sheila assured her Eloise envied Meaghan for her years in Europe and the aura of mystery and adventure surrounding her. The notion seemed absurd.

She smoothed the skirt of her burgundy serge riding skirt and tugged at the sleeves of the matching jacket. The shade was a bit brighter than she normally preferred, but even Uncle Gill had unbent enough to tell her how delightful she looked when she'd come downstairs with Sheila. She hadn't dared assess Lord Ashton's reaction to her appearance, although she had caught him looking her way on more than one occasion as the picnickers arrived and began to fill the room.

After an extended conversation with Miss Eleanor Carlson, the twins' maiden aunt, Meaghan finally slipped away from the crowd awaiting the last few arrivals. The woman had obviously thought Meaghan's efforts to improve health care in Ireland extended to an intense fascination over the symptoms of every ache and illness she suffered. Relief surged as the voices retreated to a low hum behind her when she stepped into the foyer.

Outside, through the open front door, the saddled horses stood tethered for the group who would ride to their destination. Freedom beckoned. She chewed her lip and tried to suppress the urge to run out the door and just keep going. She really shouldn't leave her aunt's guests quite so blatantly, but the promise of fresh air and the sun on her back drew her onward.

A breeze, cool and bracing, ruffled her hair as she walked to the mare Sheila had designated for her. Because she had never done much riding on Beannacht and almost none in Italy and Switzerland, Sheila had assured her the little sorrell held a gentle disposition and an easy gait.

One of the grooms hired for the day stepped into her path, startling her. He tipped his hat, but did not move out of her way. "Can I help you, miss?"

She shook her head and shaded her eyes to look at him in the bright sunshine. His face still seemed to be in the shadows. "I believe the rest of the party will be coming out soon."

"Very good, miss. If you need any assistance, just ask for Cullen Muldoon."

She thanked him and watched him saunter off. Something about the man bothered her, but she couldn't put her finger on just what it was. At least he would only be there for the one day. She continued on to the mare and brushed her sleek white mane.

"*Anseao mo cara*. Here my friend," Meaghan whispered to the horse the way Siannon's grandda had taught her. She reached into her pocket for a lump of the sugar she'd hidden in its depths.

She turned her face back to the sun. How good it felt to be away, not only from the company of the picnic goers, but from Lord Ashton's discerning eye. More than once in the drawing room she had caught his gaze on her. Each time, heat rippled through her stomach as an echo of the sensations he'd provoked with his touch.

The low hum of conversation and laughter increased in decibel as several of the picnickers spilled through the doorway. Lord Ashton edged away from the crowd. He tugged on his collar and sighed. Laughter gathered inside her. At least she was not the only reveler looking for some air.

The Englishman claimed the roan gelding set aside for him from the head groomsman and drew the animal a little to the side without looking over and spying her with her own horse. Or perhaps he chose not to speak to her. She ran her fingers through the mare's mane and watched him as he made his way carefully around the horse.

A flick of his eyes caught her observing him. He nodded. She lifted a brow in question, but he merely continued his perusal of the saddle, cinch, and fittings. This was not the first time she had observed him checking details so thoroughly.

"Why do you do that?" She couldn't hold back the question.

It was his turn to lift a brow at her. The blue of his eyes as he looked at her fully made her breath catch in her chest. Why had she spoken up?

"Accidents happen to the unwary, Miss Reilly." He took a moment before answering. "A lesson you so clearly delivered to me just the other day . . ."

Was that what he called what had happened, what had nearly happened between them in the study? An accident?

". . . near your uncle's office."

A spark of relief streaked through her as his

gaze remained fastened on hers. She managed to not look away, even when he so easily reduced her from haughtily dressed young lady to hoyden in nightclothes by looking at her that way.

En masse, the group of Sheila's friends emerged from the house in boisterous spirits, with Jamie and Sheila leading the way. All opportunity for further conversation with Lord Ashton was lost. Meaghan felt torn between relief and a disturbing ripple of disappointment. Hadn't she learned her lesson about being alone with or too close to this man?

Eloise Farrell, with her arm still holding fast to her fiancé, spied Meaghan and Lord Ashton together and offered her a triumphant little smile. Drawing on immaculate white gloves, she proceeded to pull her long-suffering swain toward Meaghan.

Meaghan groaned inwardly, well aware of everything Eloise thought of her behind her carefully executed pleasantries. Her gaze plainly said she remembered the kiss Meaghan had bestowed on Nicholas that very first day, and relished the idea that they had been outside talking—alone.

She had probably taken great delight in regaling everyone in earshot with the details of Lord Ashton and Miss Reilly's first meeting.

"Hello again, Miss Reilly. Lord Ashton." Eloise smiled and moved her head in a manner that cast her sleek curls dancing and set Meaghan's teeth on edge. "Have you been introduced to my betrothed, Meaghan? Mr. Horatio Mann, Miss Reilly from Beannacht Island. She is new to Limerick, but fast becoming my bosom companion."

"Hello." Meaghan smiled at the slender man,

who looked quite bewildered. Bosom companion, indeed. What was Eloise fishing for?

"Miss Farrell. Mr. Mann. Good to see you again, so soon." Lord Ashton tipped his hat.

"It's so nice to see you out in company again, Meaghan. Everyone has remarked on your absences from our teas and little get-togethers of late." Eloise's tone seemed friendly enough. Too friendly. "Did you know, Lord Ashton, that Meaghan has practically shunned us all since you arrived in town?"

Indignation flared. Meaghan detested being spoken about as if she were not standing right there. She bit her tongue. Eloise's goading had gotten her into enough trouble the last time she'd succumbed.

Eloise batted her baby blue eyes at Lord Ashton and simpered a smile. "Her cousin claims she does not enjoy social engagements. Quite awkward for someone badgering everyone she meets for money. She does not even like simple parlor games."

Lord Ashton raised a brow, as though he were well used to the kinds of games Eloise played. A spark of pleasure at his less-than-cordial reaction shot through Meaghan.

"Neither of those are favorite pastimes of mine, either, Miss Farrell," he said.

"I see." Eloise's perfect rosebud mouth gave a small twist of displeasure. Mr. Mann looked as if he were struggling not to smile. "What is your favorite pastime, Lord Ashton?" Eloise asked, undeterred.

"Late-night reading in the study has become my favorite for the moment."

Heat stole over Meaghan's cheeks and bolted

down her spine at his reply. Her gaze darted to
his. His devastating blue eyes held teasing light
and something she couldn't define sparkling in
their depths. No man had the right to have eyes
that color blue.

A longing to kick him in the back of his well-
tailored riding breeches welled, in complete dis-
regard for her mature years or the training her
mother had so diligently applied. With three
brothers, she'd learned to give as good as she got
to survive. Knowing Aunt Edna would never coun-
tenance such behavior kept her boot planted on
the drive.

He grinned at her, apparently not the least bit
repentant for teasing her so blatantly. The urge
grew stronger. She wondered what the look on
Eloise's face would be when Meaghan hiked up
her skirts and delivered the blow.

"If you'll excuse me, ladies, I need to speak
with my cousin a moment." His lordship tipped
his hat to both ladies.

"Care to join me, Mann?" He walked away
with Eloise's fiancé, neatly avoiding his punishment.

"He is certainly handsome, Meaghan." Eloise
sighed almost as dramatically as Sheila was wont
to do. "How do you stand being near him after
sharing such a shatteringly intimate kiss? Everyone is wondering."

Everyone? Meaghan's heart sank. Here she
was, doing her best to put the incident behind
her—Nick's teasing aside—and Eloise seemed intent on keeping the tale alive, if not colorfully
embellished. Her stomach tightened.

"Who is wondering, Eloise?"

"Why the other girls, of course." Eloise

laughed, her tone high and jubilant, anticipation gleaming in her eyes. "We never did wheedle all the details from you after you kissed him at tea. You were so eager. Why, it was almost as if you knew he would be the one to walk through those doors. As if you knew him already . . ."

Meaghan wished she had an excuse to be anyplace except there, undergoing this interrogation. She tried to spot Sheila over the sea of heads and faces. The older set were ascending into the carriages set to convey them along Bruff Road to Lough Gur. Many of the young gentlemen were helping the young ladies to mount for the cross-country ride. But there was no sign of Sheila.

"So which is it—were you just blessed or were you previously acquainted with Lord Ashton?" Eloise spoke louder and regained Meaghan's attention. She prayed no one else had heard.

"I guess I was just lucky. Blessed as you say." Meaghan chewed her lip. Winter apples, the overwhelming sensations exploding when their lips touched . . . Familiar, but certainly not from a previous acquaintance. Only those things had presaged disaster, not happiness.

Eloise leaned closer. "So, now, tell me all about it."

"You were there, Eloise. I shouldn't think there was much more to tell. I took the hazard. I carried through on my debt. End of discussion."

Eloise pouted. "Don't be so coy. Were his lips dry or moist? Was his breath fetid or sweet? Did he touch you with his tongue? And did you enjoy it? You certainly looked as if you did. I've never seen anything so scandalous. The Carlsons both nearly swooned."

Meaghan's cheeks heated. How could she ask such questions? There were so many other people swarming around. With an effort her mother would have been proud of, Meaghan controlled herself.

"You make the episode sound repugnant," she managed, trying to sound unconcerned. "I really must find Sheila—"

"Oh, no. Not repugnant at all. Your kiss was so romantic and thrilling." Eloise reached out and squeezed Meaghan's hand, halting her.

"It's just, well, I've had a few beaus try to kiss me. And sometimes Horatio uses his tongue. I thought you might understand. I find I wouldn't mind if Lord Ashton kissed me—" Eloise's porcelain cheeks actually blushed, her gaze widening as she broke off in midconfession.

The girl obviously hadn't meant to spill quite so much of her own history in the quest for Meaghan's secrets. "I mean, I know there is more to things than a simple kiss and . . . and . . ."

"It's all right." Meaghan returned the pressure of Eloise's clasp and strove to sound reassuring. "I won't breathe a word to anyone."

"Oh." Gratitude and embarrassment warred across Eloise's lovely features, making her look distinctly out-of-sorts. The conversation had not gone as she intended. "I . . . I . . . thank you, I'm sure. I think . . . I am in need of Sheila. Pray excuse me."

She hurried away as Meaghan choked back a laugh. Besting Eloise came almost as much of a shock to her as to Eloise. Maybe she had learned a little bit about how to handle herself in society.

"You neatly dispatched Miss Farrell, I see." Lord Ashton appeared at her elbow. His mouth

quirked in a smile as he watched Eloise stride
away through the crowd with unusual haste.

"Aye." Meaghan giggled, unrepentant.

He cocked his head to one side. His gaze slid
over her face, from her hair and down over her
eyes, pausing at her lips. Her laughter died away,
though her small triumph continued to glow inside her.

"Her conversation was interesting . . . to say
the least."

She held his gaze. "You were eavesdropping?"

He inclined his head, looking not the least repentant. "Guilty. Though not on purpose, I assure you. I returned to collect my horse. I was
seeking a means of rescue for you that would
not sharpen her tongue any further, when the
tide turned in your favor. Well done."

Meaghan's heartbeat drummed in her ears at
his praise. The seconds ticked by. She should
mumble something polite and back away from
this man. She hadn't spent almost an entire week
in her room or staying as far from him as possible to break now. Especially with so many witnesses.

*Better in a throng of thousands than alone in the
dead of night.* Despite herself, she remained
caught in the sparkling depths of Nicholas Mansfield's gaze, although all the censoring eyes in
the world might fix on them. Caught by a look
promising both heaven and hell in his arms. On
his lips. She could almost taste those lips against
hers. His unique oranges-and-mint scent puffed
past on the breeze.

"The carriages are loaded. Looks like we're
ready to go, Nick." Jamie appeared at Ashton's

side pulling a roan gelding that was twin to the
one his cousin was set to ride.

"Hullo, Miss Reilly. Fine weather we are having."

"Indeed, Mr. Mansfield," she managed in a
normal tone. "Although like all islands, the
weather in Ireland can change quite suddenly."

"Well, I like to count my blessings whenever I
can. Today's sun and clear skies are definitely
boons for which we can be grateful, eh, Nick?"

Jamie Mansfield's eyes were a shade lighter
than his guardian's, Meaghan observed, but they
had the same way of looking at a person as if
they could see right into their thoughts. He'd
looked straight at her when she'd jumped at his
mention of blessings.

How much did he know of the intimacies she
had granted his cousin? Her cheeks burned. Still
very aware of the man she'd been staring at before Jamie's interruption, she turned her attention to the mare, digging out another sugar
lump. Perhaps she had escaped The Curse this
time.

Lord Ashton did not appear interested in the
weather. Instead of answering, he eyed Jamie's
saddle and bridal. "Did you check—"

"Yes, I checked everything," Jamie said, cutting off his guardian's question, his face lit with
teasing humor. "Cease with the leading strings.
No worries for today. The sun is shining, the ladies are fair, and we've a grand ride ahead of
us."

"If I don't worry, who will, stripling?" Nick
smiled, but his unease keened on inside him.
This damned picnic came at a most inopportune
time. After a frustrating week that left him with

more questions than explanations, he had no desire to be horse-bound anywhere, let alone traipsing the Irish countryside with a gaggle of strangers on a pleasure jaunt.

Jamie smiled and shook his head after a quick glance at both Nick and Meaghan. He took himself and his horse off to the steps where Sheila waited to mount her black mare. Nick tried not to begrudge his cousin's ability to set aside their concerns and just enjoy the sun and the company of the fair ladies.

At least there had been no more *accidents*, not since he'd escaped being crushed to death by a wagon of posies. Were the incidents unbounded ill fortune or had he only achieved an ominous reprieve?

Guilt twinged afresh. No matter how it came about, he enjoyed this respite thanks to Meaghan Reilly. She'd very likely saved his life, and instead of gratitude, he had responded by nearly making love to her on her uncle's desk, as though she were a strumpet. Hardly the honorable behavior in keeping with the image he carried of himself. Sending her away that night and being careful to keep his distance did little to alleviate his guilt.

He glanced around at her as she stroked a little sorrel mare's nose and whispered in her ear. How could anyone so contrary reach so far inside him and tear all his cautions to shreds? Her hair flowed like a black waterfall over her slender back as she moved. The seductive play of light in the silken ebony depths belied the innocent style. Although her riding habit was not nearly as form-revealing as the Farrell chit's, his thoughts conjured the tender flesh and lithe limbs he had held in his arms.

How do you do this to me? His question whispered in the midst of passion and a deserted study surfaced again. Still with no answer.

"Can I help you up, miss?" One of the grooms inquired as he passed.

An ordinary enough question given the number of ladies seeking assistance. Meaghan's reaction surprised Nick. She shook her head and clutched the mare's bridle, taking a half step backward, almost as if the man frightened her.

"I will help the young lady." Nick reached her side in two strides.

"Very good, sir." The groom touched his hat and moved on.

"Do you know him? Has he done something to offend you?" The sharpness of his tone startled them both. Her gaze flew to his.

"No. There is just something about him that rubs me wrong. My brother Quin's wife, Siannon, says people should listen to their inner voices when they send a warning."

"And what does your inner voice tell you about me?"

Surely it must scream at her to run as far and as fast as possible, but deep inside, a perverse corner of his soul hoped this was not the case. *I am not a despoiler of young virgins,* he'd declared. After the sensual dreams of Meaghan Reilly haunting him this week, he'd begun to wonder.

"Nothing," she declared with a defiant lift of her chin. She had the temerity to look him in the eye and raise her eyebrows. "I feel nothing where you are concerned."

"Indeed?" He frowned at her.

"Indeed." She nodded. A breeze drifted through her dark hair, and ruffled the lace at her throat. She had felt something when he'd kissed that throat. His name had shivered out of her on a husky whisper that tightened his groin just to think of it.

With a low growl he reached for her waist and settled his fingers about the tiny circumference. Soft beneath the very proper layers of her clothing, his fingers defiantly itched to feel the satin texture of her skin. Honeysuckle and skin-warmed meadowsweet filled him.

As he caught her to him, her breathed hitched and then quickened. Her lips parted. Around them a flurry of activity continued as other picnickers gained their mounts, but all he could concentrate on was the feel of Meaghan Reilly within his hands.

Meaghan's dark green gaze sought his. Banked passion glowed in the depths of her eyes. Satisfaction poured through him, accompanied by his own memories. Heat surged low in his belly. The urge to kiss her senseless raked him.

"Damnation." He bit off the curse. He couldn't manage to bait her without baiting himself in the process.

"—Hurry up, will you?" Her cousin Sheila's encouragement caught Nick's attention.

The uncomfortable awareness grew that the entire company awaited only him and Meaghan. The Farrells, the Carlson twins, the O'Briens, and all of their guests waited at varied intervals, watching them as he stood with his hands clasped to Meaghan's waist.

"Lord Ashton?" Meaghan's breathless prompt included a soft plea for him to pull himself together for both their sakes.

He gritted his teeth yet again and swung her up to the saddle in silence.

"Thank you."

He turned from her without comment and snatched his horse's reins from the waiting groomsman as Edna O'Brien called out directions to her guests.

Seven

"Ready, Nick?"

Jamie cut into Nick's surreptitious perusal of Meaghan Reilly as the company of riders made their way slowly down the drive behind the carriages and gigs.

He was anything but ready for the day ahead, despite his hold on the roan gelding currently sampling one of Mrs. O'Brien's front flower beds.

How could one slender girl prove such a powerful draw for disaster? The increasing distraction provided by the mixture of decorum and impropriety that made up the attractive package of Miss Meaghan Reilly disturbed him. Whenever he came near her, social strictures seemed to wash away.

They had just created a very public demonstration of that fact. Again. The smell of honeysuckle and meadowsweet still teased his senses.

Her rigid posture as she sat atop her little mare, her shoulders straight, chin held high, reminded him all too clearly of the night she had fled the study. The mare danced a little as riders and mounts jostled about and Meaghan tugged at the reins trying to bring the little sorrel into line as she joined Sheila and some of the other young women in attendance. The dark hue of her riding habit and her long hair swaying seductively down her slender back made her stand out even from a distance—a vixen in burgundy.

"Nick." Jamie spoke sharper this time.

"I'm fine." His terse answer came rife with the unwanted longing and irritation that seemed to come hand in hand whenever Meaghan Reilly came into in view.

"She's not much of a horsewoman." Jamie's observation gained Nick's attention.

"What?" He shaded his eyes and looked up at his cousin seated on a massive bay gelding. "Who?"

Jamie laughed. "You know perfectly well who. Sheila says Miss Reilly spent most of her time as a child sailing a little skiff or trying any number of other daring occupations, trying to prove she was as good as her brothers. She says her mother worries about all the freedom they indulged her with as she was growing up, reasoning that is why she is having such a difficult time conforming to expectations."

"Who?" Jamie's tangled tale annoyed him with its criticism of Miss Reilly for the very things he had just been thinking. He swung up into his saddle. "There are entirely too many females involved in this conversation to follow you, stripling."

Jamie laughed again, obviously taking the picnic spirit to heart. Nick wished he could so easily put aside the prickly feeling at the back of his neck. Although their inquiries had yet to yield anything of substance pointing to their host—in fact, quite the opposite—and there had been no more *accidents* since the disaster outside O'Brien's office last week, that knowledge did not lessen the feeling of danger lurking in this sunny expedition.

"Damnation." Nick grimaced. He'd meant to check the roan's harness one more time before they left. He moved to dismount.

"You checked twice already, Nick. Give over. We're already bringing up the rear." Jamie nodded his head toward the gate at the end of the O'Brien drive. Nick could see Miss O'Brien in her green habit just turning out onto the street, accompanied by a bevy of other young people, including Miss Reilly.

"What about yourself?" He stayed put, but remained unresolved over whether to let extra caution rule. He looked about to make sure none of the servants left behind tarried nearby listening. "We must look to ourselves today, Jamie. This damned picnic ride is going to make it near impossible for Randall's men to be of any use. Two strangers lurking at the fringes of an outdoor party would stand out like peacocks among the pigeons."

He grimaced again, still hesitating. "Are you sure you—"

"Yes, for the sixth bloody time," Jamie said, cutting him off. "I checked the saddle, the cinching, the reins. I asked the horse how he felt today and if he'd noticed anything untoward in his feed lately."

Jamie shook his head. "Honestly, Nick, I can look after myself. You're getting worse about this rather than better. Can you think of nothing else?"

Nothing else? Ire crackled through Nick. He

bit his tongue to keep from spewing the length
and breadth of his thoughts. In his view, thanks
to a certain Irish lass, he wasn't spending nearly
enough time concentrating on the true reason
behind their sojourn in Ireland. She encroached
too often on his thoughts.

Myriad images flooded him—a veritable rainbow of Meaghans—a wanton in peridot silk,
blindsiding him with her sizzling greeting, a
heroine in russet, tumbling with him in the
street with too little regard for her own safety,
a virgin in gossamer white, tempting him with
her soft skin and sighs, and today, today she was
a vixen in burgundy.

He shook his head. He'd just proven his own
point. He acted almost as moonstruck as Jamie
did over the impertinent Miss O'Brien. Instead
of gallivanting across the green Irish countryside
on some abysmal picnic, he should be accompanying Randall on their latest round of discreet
inquiries.

"I could as easily say your interest in Sheila
O'Brien seems to have drained all your concern
for resolving the issues that brought us here in
the first place. Can you think of nothing beyond
her opinion on the cut of your jacket?" he managed through gritted teeth.

"Nick." Jamie's eyebrows shot up to his hairline. "We've discussed this. Going about with
Sheila provides me the opportunity to meet the
people in her father's social and business circles
informally. They all seem to hold the highest
opinion of him. But I am keeping my eyes and
ears open."

"Reputations can be deceiving." Guilt touched
Nick. He was being unfair, allowing his own in-

attention to color his view of Jamie's role. He'd
hired Randall specifically to limit his cousin's
need for involvement. "I'm sorry I sounded
harsh. Tension."

Jamie nodded, the anger draining from his
face. "Are you sleeping well? You haven't woken
me with one of your nightmares since our first
night here, but you look a trifle haggard."

He hadn't slept well for the past week, but he
wasn't about to admit to anyone, even Jamie, that
the vision haunting his nights over the past week
was Meaghan Reilly highlighted by moonlight as
he kissed her senseless.

The last of the riders disappeared around the
gate. "Come on, lad, we'd best catch up before
your Sheila sends a search party back for us."

He kicked the roan and set off at a brisk walk.
Jamie and his bay caught up with them halfway
to the gate. Nick tried to force himself to relax
and let the spirit of the day take over. It had
been too long since he had done anything just
for fun, but the prickle of imminent danger still
scoured his spine.

"Slow down a minute, Nick. Sheila showed me
the direction we'd be heading in yesterday,"
Jamie shouted over the sounds of the horses. "I
wanted to know how I could perhaps steer some
of today's conversations in directions of interest
to us. There are any number of people who have
come up today and professed knowing our parents."

Nick slowed as they gained the road. The picnickers were far ahead, but he trusted Jamie's
sense of direction. And if they got legitimately
lost so much the better. "Everything appears in
order right up to the time my parents last came

to Ireland. It's time we delve further back. Randall is set to visit with one of the clerks employed at the time our parents set up the trust with O'Brien and that other fellow. Perhaps he can add a new perspective."

"I'd forgotten there was another partner besides our fathers and Sheila's." Jamie tugged his horse to a halt. "Hasn't he been dead for some time?"

Nick halted, too. "Aye. Before my parents even. His participation in the venture had been severed by then. Embezzlement, I think. I remember my father taking me to court with my mother when I was younger. To watch the wheels of justice grind, he said."

"What was the man's name?"

"Chase." Nick searched his memory. "Newton . . . Neville . . . Ned. Something like that." He shrugged.

"What does O'Brien have to say on the matter?" Jamie squinted into the distance.

"I have managed to avoid any serious discussions with him regarding the investment trust. I haven't wanted to tip him yet. As far as he is concerned, we are still here to check on a few other investments and to look into acquiring horseflesh for you. That's all."

Jamie nodded. "We'd best be off in earnest then, if we want to blend in with the rest of the guests."

He kicked his horse into a brisk canter and Nick joined him. His thoughts churned as they rode past several well-tended estates belonging to Limerick's wealthiest citizens and out into the true countryside.

Rounding a bend a few minutes later, they spied their party, considerably thinned, waiting for them under a tree. A surprising edge of relief rippled through Nick when he glimpsed a slender figure in burgundy among the half-dozen riders lingering beside the oak.

"I believe your Sheila is looking for you, stripling." Nick nodded in Miss O'Brien's direction as they reined in their mounts. She flashed a broad smile at Jamie.

"So she is." Jamie nudged his gelding forward.

"Jamie."

"I know. I'll be careful." The words tossed back to Nick on a laugh as Jamie made his way through the youngest of the party-goers to reach Sheila's side.

"This will be such fun," the Carlson twins twittered to each other as Nick passed them, their tone and inflection as identical as their bland faces and carrot-red curls.

He nodded to them and continued on until he reached the small cluster made up of Jamie, Sheila, Meaghan, and Eloise with her beau, Horatio.

"I still think going out toward the hills would be the fastest way," Eloise said as Nick joined them. "Riding around through the lower grasses is not as picturesque, nor as much fun. We might as well follow the main road with the rest. Wouldn't you agree, Lord Ashton?"

"Oh, Eloise." Impatience tinged Sheila's voice.

"I am not familiar with this countryside, Miss Farrell," Nick offered. "I would have no way of knowing."

"Perhaps we should break off in different directions?" Jamie suggested.

"Indeed?" Sheila tossed him a smile as if he'd said the most amazing thing she'd ever heard.

Nick held back a sigh.

Caught off guard by the suggestion, Eloise Farrell edged a haughty blond brow upward. "Well—"

"Let's see who gets there first." Sheila pounced on the idea with a wide smile. "You go over the hill, Eloise, and take Sarah and Jenna with you." She pointed at the Carlsons, who bobbed their heads in unison. "Mr. Mann can provide you safe escort."

"Lord Ashton, Meaghan, Mr. Mansfield, and I will go around through the lower grasses. We'll see who gets there first."

Eloise pouted for a moment, obviously not happy she was not the instigator for this expedition. "What will be the forfeit?"

"The forfeit?" Meaghan's question held a sharp note of caution.

"You cannot accept a wager without there being consequences, Meaghan. I should think *you* learned that from the last time." Eloise smiled. A triumphant sparkle lit her eyes.

Color washed Meaghan's cheeks, but she held her peace. Nick wondered what lay behind the interchange.

"Very well, Eloise. What do you propose as a forfeit?" Sheila demanded, inching her mount forward to shield Meaghan from the other girl's glee.

"If our party wins, I get to pick the luncheon partners." Eloise beamed at the group as if her scheme was the best thing that could possibly happen to the lot of them.

"And if you arrive last?" Sheila prodded.

"Well, that is not very likely to happen, is it? You know I always win." Eloise frowned, tapped

her chin, and then shrugged. "If you get there
first, you get to pick."

Nick looked across the meadows. The land
opened up here. Sheep dotted the far hillside
within neat rows of stone-etched pastures sloping
upward. Two shepherds watched over them from
the ridge. At least with so much open ground
surrounding them there was little chance they'd
be caught unawares.

"It's settled. Let's be off, then." Sheila urged
her mount forward. Jamie followed after her with
Meaghan close behind. Eloise's group filed away
to the left and thundered toward the hill. Nick
pushed the roan forward, anxious to get the
whole damned day over with.

Meaghan bounced atop the mare she rode,
her hair gleaming dark and shiny in the sunlight
as it cascaded down her back, caressing the slim
curve of her waist. Despite her cousin's summation of her abilities, she appeared able to hold
her own on the ride. He barely noticed the green
of the Irish countryside they traversed, entranced
instead by the view she presented.

A vixen in burgundy, indeed.

Sheila reined in as they approached the lower
slope.

"What is it?" Jamie asked as they all came to
a halt beside her. The horses whickered and
tossed their heads, anxious to continue their run
now that they tasted the freedom.

"She does have a chance of beating us." Sheila
worried her lower lip and looked ahead. "Once
we clear the grasses we've a few miles of rock-
studded terrain to get through. We'll need to
push hard through the grass, so the rocks won't
matter. Are you game?"

"I certainly don't want to sit with Eloise's choice of lunch partners." Jamie shuddered.

Sheila favored him with one of her oh-aren't-you-wonderful smiles. Nick shook his head as Jamie actually puffed out his chest while smiling back at her.

"Let's make a dash, then. I'm sure she intends to stick me with the Carlsons' aunt and I have no wish to discuss her bunions in any further depth." Meaghan glanced at Nick. Light sparkled in the depths of her green eyes. He caught himself smiling.

"Indeed," he agreed, wondering if he'd end up with one or both of the Carlson twins simpering at him over cold fowl. Or even Eloise herself.

"Lead the way, Sheila," Jamie urged.

She kicked her mount into motion and the horse took off with more speed than Nick had anticipated as she rode out through the grass.

"Come on!" Jamie laughed and left Nick and Meaghan behind, galloping out onto the wild-flower-strewn meadow.

"Are you sure you wish to participate in this race?" Meaghan coaxed her mare forward.

"And miss viewing Miss Farrell's comeuppance?" He urged the roan beside her. "Miss Reilly, how could you ask such a question?"

"Put that way, I wouldn't want to miss this either." She clucked her tongue to the mare and started forward. Nick followed suit.

In moments they thundered through the open grass as it hissed and whipped beneath them. Meaghan laughed, leaning low over her horse to increase her speed. Her hair flowed behind her like a black stream. He urged the gelding to keep pace with her. The bigger horse could have easily outdistanced the mare, but the sparkle in her rider's eye caught at him somewhere under his ribs.

He felt free for the first time in far too long, free to ride beside a pretty woman in the sunlight and not worry about the danger lurking in the shadows of his life. The worries that had been his companion for the last twelve months or more loosened as he released his cares to the moment and the maid.

Meaghan's teeth showed white between the rosy redness of her lips as she smiled and urged the mare to an even faster pace. He realized she meant to race him. Anticipation shot through him. He kicked the roan and leaned out over the reins, picking up speed as the wind whipped his face with the scent of deep green earth.

The two of them caught up with Sheila and Jamie and passed them easily.

"Go, Nick. Go!" Jamie's laughter rang out after him as Nick closed in on Meaghan.

Anticipation surged within him as Meaghan glanced over her shoulder and shrieked with laughter. He would catch the sweet vixen in burgundy. And what would be the forfeit then?

In the distance ahead he could see the rocks Sheila had spoken of and he realized they would soon have to slow down. He urged the roan for more speed and easily passed her.

Satisfaction swelled inside him. Who would have expected such from a simple race over the countryside? He almost reached the rocks. He turned the gelding and started to pull on the reins.

A loud crack split the air.

Something whooshed past his face so close he could feel the hot sting of it. He yanked on the reins, pulling the roan up short.

Meaghan's horse screamed and raced past him out, of control.

"Damnation."

He kicked the gelding back into motion and thundered after the runaway horse. Onto the rocks they raced in earnest now as the mare shied and Meaghan nearly lost her seat.

He pulled up next to them and snagged the mare's bridle, forcing the horse to slow and halt. Relief sluiced through him. His vixen was safe.

The roan protested the sudden check in their run. His saddle suddenly slipped. Too loose. All motion slowed to a crawl. The roan bucked again. The world tilted beneath him and he spilled backward toward the rocky ground.

"Nicholas." Meaghan's scream echoed through him as pain crashed against his shoulder and the side of his head.

Blackness shrouded him.

He was dead, and it was all her fault.

Meaghan jumped from the mare's back and ran to the crumpled form on the ground by the roan gelding's feet. Suppose the horse spooked again and trampled Nicholas while he lay helpless? She reached for the reins and pulled the animal away.

Everything had happened so quickly. Too quickly. One minute they were laughing, leaning low, and racing free. Then came the loud report of what could only be gunshots from a careless hunter. The terror of her horse. The terror she'd felt. If it hadn't been for Nicholas she might very well have been the one thrown. Agony ripped

through her at what she had caused to happen
to him.

Jamie's face was pale and frightened as he
pulled up beside her and scrambled to dismount.
"Nick! Nick!"

He rushed to his cousin's side. Nick stretched
out on the turf, lifeless. Her heart turned over
for both of them. For Jamie, who so obviously
loved and admired his elder cousin. And for
Nicholas.

Blood stained the back of Nick's head. Bright
crimson on gold. She swallowed hard. Jamie cradled his head and gently rolled him over.

"He's breathing at least." He spoke in a strangled voice, then proceeded to run his hands
along his cousin's ribs and limbs checking for
other injuries.

Sheila rode up. She dismounted and came to
stand with Meaghan, who still gripped the roan's
reins tight in her fingers. She slipped her arm
around Meaghan's waist.

"Time to wake up, Nick. This is a hell of a
moment to take a nap. We can't let that sly Eloise
Farrell get the best of us now, can we?" Jamie's
voice cracked as he chafed Nick's hand and wrist.

A look, frozen with helpless fear, passed between Sheila and Jamie. The panic that had held
Meaghan stone-still in silence snapped like a twig
beneath a booted foot.

"We'll have to move him. He can't stay out in
the open like this."

Sheila and Jamie both blinked at her in surprise. She ignored the small questioning voice
inside asking who put her in charge. That voice
sounded far too much like Nicholas.

"A storm is blowing in from the sea." She

pointed east, the direction they'd been heading. Dark gray clouds gathered on the horizon. "The picnic may very well be cut short. We have to get help and a wagon of some kind here before everyone scatters."

She knelt by Nick's side. The blood glistened bright red against his scalp. She swayed and then struggled to gather her control again. Now was not the time to succumb to her own weakness.

"Good thinking," Jamie's low tones sounded above her. "We'll move him, then go for help. Are we better off heading back or going on to the lake?"

"Lough Gur is closer. We should head there." Sheila's announcement was subdued compared to her boisterous enthusiasm when they started out. "Dr. Norton is among the guests. He'll know what to do."

A brief struggle ensued as the three of them maneuvered the unconscious Nick the short distance to an outcropping among rock. They reached the natural shelter as thunder rumbled in the distance. Meaghan could only think of the storms on Beannacht and hope this one would be short-lived.

"We've got to leave before the storm gets any nearer." Jamie knelt next to Meaghan after stripping off his jacket and laying it under his cousin. He'd already removed Nicholas's and put it over him. "Keep him warm."

"I will." She nodded.

"I spotted a trickle of water over there." He pointed a few feet beyond the rocks.

"Hurry." She looked him straight in the eye. "Before there is more water than we can handle."

He nodded slowly, reluctance clear in the gesture and in his eyes. His lips were set in a thin line as he looked down at Nicholas, so white even in the shadow of the rocks. Her heart twisted.

"But we can't leave Meaghan here alone," Sheila whispered in a small squeak of protest. She put a reassuring hand on Jamie's shoulder. "If the storm comes soon it may not be as easy to find help as we'd like to think. Who knows where in the ruins the party will find shelter, or how long before we can get back?"

"It will be all right, She. Lord Ashton and I will be dry until you return," Meaghan assured her. "Neither Jamie nor I know the way. You can't go alone. And you are both better horsemen than I. Just hurry."

"She's right, Sheila." Jamie squeezed her hand. "The less time spent dithering, the better. Nick would agree. Could you tether their horses? I'll be right there."

Sheila nodded. "We'll be back as soon as we can, Meaghan. You'll see. It's not much over a half-hour to the lake from here."

Jamie frowned down at Nicholas. "I'm sorry, Nick. I should have listened to you."

His confession confused her. What fault did he lay at his own door? He brought his gaze back to meet hers as he reached into his pocket. "Keep this with you, Miss Reilly . . . Meaghan. In case you have a need."

He handed her a small, flat pistol. The little weapon weighed heavy in her hand for all its small proportions. "Are you saying—"

"It's just a precaution. I could not ride off and leave you completely defenseless. Nick would never forgive me." He closed his hand over hers and squeezed her fingers. "Have you ever used a gun?"

She nodded. "My brother Quin taught me the summer after he took charge of his own ship."

"Good." He gained his feet and strode out to Sheila, waiting with their horses. In moments they had both mounted and disappeared in a clatter of hooves.

"Hurry," she whispered as a stiff breeze lifted her hair. "And be careful."

She checked Nick and headed out to the small spring beside the rocks. The sky to the east was blanketed with rain-heavy clouds. A streak of lightning lit the distance.

She pocketed the pistol and looked around. Suppose that other gun had not gone off accidentally? Suppose whoever had been hunting lurked nearby? She shivered and hugged her arms. She couldn't let her imagination run away with her. Jamie was counting on her. Nicholas was counting on her.

She knelt by the stream and tried to rip her petticoat the way the heroines in the novels Sheila hid under her mattress did. "*Diabhal.* Either these seams are as tight as the ones on Da's ships or those fictional women are extremely strong."

She gave a final tug in frustration and dropped the hem. The water gurgled in its rocky channel. Thunder roared closer. She prayed Sheila and Jamie reached the shelter of the ruins before they were soaked to the skin.

Inspiration struck and she kicked off her boots and unrolled her stockings. She rinsed them in the cool spring and headed back to bathe the blood from Nicholas. Perhaps he would awaken before Jamie and Sheila returned with help.

Hours passed. Long hours of listening to thunder breaking overhead and rain washing in rivulets down granite. Hours of waiting for help delayed by the torrential downpour. Of waiting with increasing worry for Nicholas to wake up.

She cradled his head in her lap. He lay so very still and white against the burgundy of her skirt. She sighed over the fear locked in her breast.

A frown flitted across his forehead. She soothed her fingers over his brow. She'd lost track of how many times she'd done this to chase away his frowns. The contact soothed her at least.

Beyond cradling his head and worrying over him, she hadn't accomplished very much at all. All her study of Miss Nighingale's *Notes*, notwithstanding.

He frowned again and she traced the furrow with her fingertips. If it weren't for the lump at the back of his head and the ache beginning at the base of her spine, she might have enjoyed sitting with him like this. He was handsome, even without the benefit of those blazing blue eyes of his to disconcert a girl. She ran her finger over his eyebrows.

"No man should have eyes your color blue, Nicholas. No matter what he is the lord of."

He frowned again, deeper this time, as though he did not agree with her in the least. He shifted his shoulders. She soothed his brow and bit her lip. She would almost relish his scowling demeanor, if only he would wake up.

He moaned softly, a sound of despairing protest that wrenched her heart. Whatever bothered him in the darkness of his dreams grew more upsetting with each passing moment.

"Nicholas."

"Uhh," he moaned again and thrashed his feet.

Hope rallied within Meaghan at this first response in all the time they'd been waiting. She leaned over him. "Nicholas? Can you hear me?"

"No."

"Nicholas?" She touched his shoulder.

"NO!" His shout echoed against the rain-slick rocks. He groaned. His eyes opened wide and she lost herself in the shadowy despair gleaming in their depths.

Her heart twisted. "Oh, Nicholas."

"Yes." He hissed out the word. Torment clear down to his soul showed in his gaze. He slid his hands up into her hair, anchoring his fingers in her long tresses as he pulled her mouth down to meet his in hot demand.

A gasp shuddered out of her as he kissed her. His tongue thrust into her mouth, bold and commanding. She tried to think of his injury and how she should be checking him for coherence, but the feel of his lips and the audacious taste of his tongue drove her good intentions to dust.

Long and slow and thorough, his tongue slid against hers. Heat swirled low in her belly. Her breasts tingled and ached with a sweet pain she already associated with Nicholas and his touch. She couldn't breathe, but it didn't matter as his hand slid over her back and down her side, brushing the side of her breast in a slow and deliberate caress.

He released her lips to nuzzle the sensitive skin

of her neck and she gasped for air, her thoughts dizzy and disorganized before his onslaught.

"Nicholas." Was that her voice so low and husky?

He brushed her breast again with his fingers and she shuddered. Once, twice, and then his palm moved inside her jacket and closed fully over her breast, claiming her.

"Oh, Nicholas." She should stop him. Surely he couldn't be aware of what he was doing, but the feel of his hand caressing her through her thin blouse and chemise held her spellbound. He brushed the taut tip of her breast and pleasure spiraled through her, hot and tight and undeniable.

She moaned softly, unable to stop herself.

With a low satisfied growl, his lips claimed hers again, melding their mouths together in a kiss that blotted out any sane thought she might hold claim to. Waves of sensation, white-hot and intense, raced through her.

His tongue filled her as it laved and flicked. His fingers strayed from her breast, leaving her achingly alone. Cool air shivered over her skin as he released the buttons of her blouse in rapid succession. He spread the edges and reclaimed her breast with naught but her chemise shielding her bare flesh from his touch.

She shuddered again, alarms ringing clear in her head as he weighed her breast with the hot feel of his hand. He stroked the taut peak, the rough pads of his fingers pulling at the silk as he kissed her breathless.

He released her lips, and next she felt the heat of his breath against her breast.

"Nicholas." She rasped his name, needing to

stop him, to stop them both before anything further happened. He ignored her, nuzzling her breast with his lips. The hot spiral of pleasure swirled through her again, stronger and more enticing.

She moaned and placed both hands on his shoulders while she struggled to maintain what little grasp of her own thoughts she still retained. "Nicholas, stop."

Something in her tone must have reached him. He released her immediately.

"Meaghan?" He frowned at her, obviously perplexed.

Cold reason doused her. Shame followed with an icy wake. She pulled the edges of her blouse together, scrambling to find some explanation for her actions over the last few moments.

Lord Ashton had been beyond himself—obviously—doing what men were driven to do when a willing woman complied. Her brothers had warned her of such hazards on many occasions.

There could be no such excuse for her participation. None, whatsoever. She had indulged herself at an injured man's expense. Guilt and shame shrived her.

"Aye, Lord Ashton."

He groaned and lay back against her lap.

Eight

"What happened?" Nicholas closed his eyes again before he even finished his question.

You mean, before or after you unbuttoned my blouse? Meaghan bit back the tart question and took a deep breath.

"You fell."

He groaned and touched the side of his head. "I remember. There was a shot; then your horse—"

"You saved me. In doing so you were thrown yourself." She tried to button her blouse unobtrusively. Perhaps if she could set herself back to rights he would think the interlude had been part of an injury-related delirium.

She drew a shaky breath. Perhaps she could believe that herself. "I . . . I must thank you. You were very brave and resourceful."

His blue gaze pinned her as she reached for her second button.

She stopped, frozen in place as his gaze took in every element of her dishevelment, from her hair to the disarrangement of her clothing. Heat stung her cheeks as every burning detail of the past few minutes raced through her mind—his hand kneading her breast, the hot sweet taste of his tongue against hers.

Shame washed her again.

"What happened?" He repeated his question, sharper now. And he was not referring to the accident on horseback. The patter of rain on granite echoed through the enclosure.

"I—" Her mouth went dry. What could she tell him? What did he remember?

"I took advantage of you." His bald statement hung in the air like a pennant on a mast racing the wind. He closed his eyes. A long shuddering breath hissed from him.

Her entire body smoldered with embarrassment. "I think it might have been more or less the other way around."

"Tell me the truth, Meaghan." His tone brooked no argument. What on earth had made her think she couldn't wait for him to wake up? At least he kept his eyes closed so she did not have to read the accusation in them.

I am not a despoiler of young virgins. His denial from the night in the study haunted her. She'd taken advantage of an injured man, indulging herself in the forbidden pleasures he offered. She should have stopped. She should have pulled away. And now he was shouldering the blame. How much could she admit to expiate his burgeoning guilt.

"You . . . You were not yourself." Searing kisses notwithstanding.

She struggled not only to say them but to accept the words. She took another deep breath as her fingers went back to the task of refastening her blouse. The top three buttons were missing.

She sighed, knotting her fingers together in

her lap. "You were in pain. You didn't know where you were. You had no idea what you were doing."

"Apparently I knew enough to start undressing you." His retort held equal measure of pain and disgust. He balled and flexed his hands.

She squirmed. She *had* known where they were and what they were doing. "You make it sound so . . . sordid."

"What would you call it, Miss Reilly?" Sarcasm layered his words. A familiar frown creased his brow. With obvious effort he opened his eyes and fixed her with his gaze.

"An accident?" She hoped to end the whole discussion with that offering.

"I seem more than prone to those of late, don't I?" He lifted his head, raised a haughty brow at her, and then groaned.

Hysterical laughter bubbled in Meaghan's throat, laced with worried relief and the lingering passion of Nicholas's kisses.

She couldn't believe they were having this ridiculous discussion sitting on the dirt with his head in her lap. But then she couldn't believe any number of the things that had happened between herself and the arrogant Lord Ashton in little more than a week.

"Are you laughing, Miss Reilly?" Nicholas peered at her through narrowed eyes. His voice, a husky blend of passion and pain, tugged at her heartstrings.

"Nay, I'm not." Dark humor caught at her again. "Why on earth would I laugh? Look at us."

She swept a hand indicating their disheveled state and their crude shelter beneath the rocky outcropping. "You have been thrown from a horse and severely injured. We are miles from anywhere either of us knows. We are damp from the rain. Because of this storm, our rescue is possibly still hours away. And your chief concern since coming to yourself is a few buttons."

His gaze held hers for the span of several heartbeats. The rain dripped on the rocks. Of all the times, her stomach rumbled at that moment, hunger twisting it.

"I see your point." His mouth curved upward in a grin that spiraled through her with a flare of remembered heat.

She sobered, as longing swept through her anew. She shouldn't be sitting here wishing he would kiss her again, wondering what might have happened if he hadn't stopped when he did. Those were not the thoughts of the well-brought-up young lady her mother had struggled to make of her.

But then her behavior with Nicholas Mansfield had been anything but proper from the moment she met him. Thank heaven her parents had no inkling of her current transgressions. She didn't know which she dreaded more—Da's blusters or Mama's pained silence.

Nick's gaze roved her face for a moment before turning outward toward the rain. He pressed his lips into a solemn line and took a shaky breath. "Where are Jamie and your cousin?

He looked back at her. A different, deeper pain haunted his expression. "Are they all right? How is it you came to be left here, unprotected, in the middle of nowhere?"

"They have gone for help. Sheila knows the way. I'm sure it is just the storm blowing in that is delaying their return. It thundered and poured most impressively for quite a while."

"Indeed." A concerned frown twisted his brows. He pushed himself upright and then groaned again.

"Still, the pup should not have left you here with no regard to your safety," he ground out, his eyes lowering to her open blouse.

She put her hand into her jacket pocket and placed the pistol on the ground beside them. "He left me this. We were perfectly safe—"

She paused. "You cannot mean you believe that gunshot was any more than a careless hunter? Most likely boys after rabbits."

He brought his gaze slowly up to meet hers. He was ashen, but he held her gaze steady.

"No," he gritted out and squeezed his eyes shut. "No, I'm sure it is as you say. Careless boys."

He groaned a second time and his hands sought purchase on the ground.

"Not so fast, Lord Ashton." She leaned toward him, placing a hand on his shoulder. "You suffered a terrible blow that should have rattled the very teeth from your head when you fell from your horse. You were gone to the world for quite some time. You should lie still for a while."

"Wisdom garnered from your study of Miss Nightingale's book?" he snapped, but he made no further struggle to rise.

"I may not be a nurse, but I don't think you should be moving about anytime soon. Activity cannot be good for you."

"Especially ravishing lovely young women." His lips contorted over the words. His face was gray. He had to be in pain. And struggling with nausea, most likely.

"You don't look up to taking advantage of me at the moment." Her tart tone belied the warmth rushing over her cheeks as his use of the word lovely to describe her echoed on inside.

"Don't test me," he warned her, but he swayed as he did so, quite ruining his threat. "You said it's been hours. That is too long."

"Nicholas." Worry lashed her afresh and she pushed against his shoulder. "Maybe you'd better lie down again."

"I must go look for Jamie. There's no telling what kind of trouble he might be in." He tried to push up on one knee and ended up slumped back against the rocks with a loud groan.

"See there? You should listen to your nurse." She kept her voice stern despite the concern harrowing her. "You'll not get three feet before you're a heap on the ground. You may do yourself more damage in the process, and then what help will you be to Jamie?"

She reached for his jacket to put around him. Keeping an injured man warm was something she had learned from her life on Beannacht. "Not to mention the fact that I shall have to go out into the rain and drag you back here by myself this time."

"And have you appointed yourself my nursery maid as well as my guardian angel and nurse?" He lifted an aristocratic brow and frowned at her. She hesitated, thinking better of tucking under the blue wool garment just yet.

"Only if you continue to act as if you are in need of one." She lifted her chin, refusing to be intimidated by his lordly manner. She handed him the jacket instead. "There is nothing we can do to hurry Jamie and the rescue party along.

We must wait here, where they expect to find us."

"Indeed." He groaned and leaned his forehead against his arms. "Jamie may be in more trouble than we know. But I haven't enough strength to help myself gain my feet at the moment, let alone find him."

He released a long sigh that echoed against the rocky walls. "I could truly use a drink."

"Ah." She brightened and scrambled to her knees. "I might be able to fix that."

She reached into a hollow in the rocks and scooped a handful of rain that had collected in the spot.

"Here you are." She brought her hands to his lips. "But I think you should drink it slowly, in case . . . well in case it doesn't quite sit well with you."

"In case it makes me quite wretchedly ill, you mean." He carefully took a few swallows from her palms.

"Aye, something like that."

His breath was warm against her wrists. Wayward sparks fanned upward along her arms. She was shameless.

He relaxed back against the rocks with a shuddering sigh. "Not quite the whiskey I hoped for, but thank you just the same."

"You're quite welcome." She shivered and picked up Jamie's jacket from where it had lain under Nicholas. Blood stained the buff wool.

Silence held for a moment, broken only by the raindrops splattering the rocky ground. Nicholas looked at the jacket and then over to the stockings she had rinsed and hung up to dry as best they could in the middle of a storm. Stains still streaked them.

"Mine?" he asked.

She nodded. "I cleaned your wound as best I could. It is not terribly deep, for all the mess. It still seeps a little and should only require a few stitches."

"Your study has certainly benefited me. You make an excellent nurse."

She shook her head. "I'll never make a nurse. I wanted to, at one time. More than anything. But the sight of blood makes me quite ill. So I am reduced to helping others gain the skills."

They fell silent again. The sound of the rain kept up its lulling pace. Meaghan's thoughts twisted. Shame over her behavior, over her failings, wrenched her stomach, but not as much as her concern for Nicholas, who looked so pale against the cold granite. Would help never come?

"Meaghan."

She jumped as he spoke, though the sound was barely more than a whisper. "Aye?"

"I'm sorry."

"About what?"

"About this." He flicked a gentle finger over the open vee of her blouse. "I seem to apologize repeatedly for taking advantage of you. I assure you, despite all evidence to the contrary, it is not my habit."

"I believe you, Lord Ashton." Despite the history between them, she did. And she recognized her equal culpability for everything that transpired between them. Especially that very first kiss in Aunt Edna's drawing room.

"I like it better when you call me Nicholas." His gaze snared hers again for a breathless mo-

ment; then he closed his eyes with another low
groan. He swallowed hard and reached out to
support himself on the ground.

"I really think it would be better if you lay
down again, Lord Ashton."

He pinned her again within that uniquely blazing blue.

"Nicholas," she amended. "Please?"

"Very well." He shuddered as he pushed away
from his rocky support and she scooted closer
beside him.

With a rueful grin that twisted through her
heart, he settled his head back in her lap and
allowed her to put his jacket over his shoulders.
"I promise not to attack you this time."

"I'll hold you to that," she told him, ignoring
the rebellious pang of regret shooting through
her.

She stroked her fingers along his brow. He
started at her initial touch, but did not protest.

"My mother used to do this when I was a
child," she explained. "She said it would chase
away my bad dreams."

"And did it work?"

"Most of the time."

"What makes you think I am prone to bad
dreams as well as accidents?"

She stroked him again. "Something was bothering you just before you woke up. This worked
for a time."

"Indeed?" He closed his eyes, hiding the startled flicker of recognition she saw there.

"Aye. But then you frowned mightily and
shouted out *no*. That's when you woke up."

Tension tightened his neck against her leg. His
eyes opened again. "What else did I say?"

"That was all."

He sighed. "That's all I ever say."

"What do you mean?"

"It is the same nightmare I always have. Have had for the past fifteen years. It never changes." He spoke in a flat and emotionless tone. "I do not care to speak of it."

Something that haunted him for so long must surely be painful. It could not be good for him to dredge up an old memory like that, especially while he was still injured. She needed to distract him. The obvious would not do, she lectured herself and her wayward wanton nature.

Inspiration struck. "Did you not say you would tell me about meeting Miss Nightingale?"

"Now?" His brow quirked at the absurdity, but his frown lightened. "Very well. She is a remarkable woman, very unassuming, but when she enters a room . . ."

He recounted his memory of Miss Nightingale in slower and slower spurts, finally drifting to sleep as she traced her fingers over his forehead with long, soothing strokes, just like her mother used to do.

She closed her eyes and imagined herself at the reception he'd attended where Miss Nightingale had been present. But the part of the fantasy that warmed her most was that she was there on Nicholas Mansfield's arm.

"You dolt." Neville sighed with long-suffering disgust. "Why did you waste the opportunity? How could you waste *any* opportunity that stumbles into your path?"

"But Mr. Chase—"

"Enough." Neville cut the air sharply with his hand, unwilling to listen to the latest laundry list of watery excuses. "I can't stomach another of your self-determined dispensations. When I think of the time and energy devoted to this, and the years of planning."

Years of affliction. The long dark shadow of prison still tainted him. Not to mention the fortunes expended.

He paced away, nibbling the callus at the tip of his thumb. Raucous shouts and laughter from the tap room next door intruded. He hated the stench in this low establishment, but where else was he to find the type of miscreant willing to at least try to do his bidding? If try is what Muldoon, here, could lay stake to.

He turned back to the grungy Irishman shoveling noisily into his mouth between swills of home brew. Which one of the lumbering jackanapes was this? Rory? Cullen? He shook his head. It didn't matter. Each demonstrated incompetence in his own intolerable way. If only they could accomplish the simple chores he gave them.

He sniffed. If only they could begin to understand the scope, the magnitude, of the tasks he entrusted to them. To come so far under the sheer power of his own intellect and then be faced with lack wits and slipshod efforts was maddening.

You get what you pay for. His mother's words of warning echoed across the decades. *Cheaply bought is cheaply used.*

Acid churned in his stomach, an unfortunate side effect of having to wait so very long for the justice he deserved. But soon—very soon—he would right the unbearable wrongs done him.

Inequity ate at him as surely as the Mansfields' lack of integrity. Their vile scheme had placed him at their mercy. For years. The acid churned higher.

He banged his hand on the table. He would only succeed in making himself ill by following this well-worn path of thought, bringing his whole carefully laid restoration to a screeching halt.

Whichever Muldoon graced his company looked up from his bowl and wiped the gravy from his face with his sleeve before grunting, his brows beetling.

"Where is . . . your cousin?" Neville tried a more level tone. Perhaps he would get more from the dolt with sugar. Bluster had gotten him nowhere.

"Rory?" Cullen Muldoon flexed his arm and scowled.

Something about these Muldoons reminded him of too many surly inmates crowded into too small a cell. He shuddered and shoved the putrid memory aside.

"Yes. Yes. Answer the question."

"He stayed to keep watch. I come on here. We figured ye'd want to know what happened."

Imagine that. A tiny bit of independent thought. "And?"

"We'll have ta wait fer Rory ta know the answer to that, Mr. Chase."

Neville narrowed his eyes at the hulk. The man didn't flinch. For just an instant the idea occurred that perhaps these Muldoons were not as stupid as they appeared. If they were not availing themselves of their opportunities in order to pump him for more money, they would find themselves very sadly mistaken.

He nibbled his callus again. It would almost be an improvement to find out the two of them were scheming against him. At least he would have something to work with. In the meantime he would make do with what was available.

"Tell me again all that happened." Neville leaned forward, eager to savor what triumph he could.

Cullen took a swig from his mug. "We waited all morning on the ridge fer the ridin' party, just as ye told us—after I loosened his saddle while he were distracted. The whole lot of 'em was headin' ta Lough Gur. We kept our eyes out fer the blond gentlemen using the spyglass ye give us."

He drained the dregs and peered sadly at the bottom of his mug. "It was right hot work, out in the sun like that, Mr. Chase. Work like that gives a man a powerful thirst."

"Tell me what I ask and I'll buy the next drink."

"They was late joining the main group, but some waited fer them. Then they broke into two groups. The Mansfields and two women headed fer the grass." He shrugged and looked down into the depths of his tankard again. "Then we slipped down ta get ready fer them once we knew which way they'd pass."

"Everything was perfect for you. What happened?"

"Rory took aim—he's the better shot, Mr. Chase. Lord Ashton was chasing a pretty dark-haired lass, the two of them riding fast. Rory squeezed off a shot, but he missed."

No doubt because he was busy watching the *pretty lass* instead of paying attention to what he should have been doing. "And then?"

"Her horse bolted. Ashton saved her, but fell off his horse in the process. He knocked his head on a rock. We could hear the thud."

That part, at least, held a scrap of satisfaction. Neville closed his eyes, savoring the mental images. Proud Lord Ashton falling off his horse while saving a young maiden in distress. How touching. Perhaps he'd knocked himself hard enough to succumb to his injuries. The task might yet be accomplished, however backwardly.

"Very well," he instructed. "Go back to your cousin and continue to keep watch."

He tightened his gaze, trying to bore through the thick Muldoon skull. "If the opportunity arises, while still affording the mask of unattributable accident, you are to seize the moment. Do you understand me?"

"Aye, Mr. Chase. But what about my mug? It's raining powerful hard out there."

"Give me a better report the next time and I'll pay for a whole keg."

The Muldoon turned away and hurried out of Neville's spartan room, his boots ringing over the rough-planked floors. Neville's lips twisted. Between prison and the mines, he'd suffered worse accommodations over the years. But soon, very soon, he would never have to live this way again. His long period of skulking anonymously in the shadows would be over. The necessity of doing so now churned his gut again.

His mind churned back over the story he'd

just heard and the mention of the *pretty dark-haired lass*. He rubbed his chin. Could it be the same vixenish hoyden who foiled his plans in the street the other morning? Her interference in his strategies was becoming habitual. He could almost imagine focusing his energies on dispatching her as well.

The thought of harming an innocent sent a river of ice through his veins in perfect concert with the painful pulse shattering his temples. Dark, dizzying waves pulsed through him. He shuddered with nausea and gripped the edge of the windowsill. Cold sweat popped across his brow. He squinted against the sunlight.

He shuddered again and forced himself to take long, slow breaths of damp Irish air.

In. Out.

In. Out.

Minutes ticked by like hours on the ramshackle clock adorning the crooked mantel. In a slow spiral, the nausea subsided and he breathed a little easier.

This was not the first time such a reaction transpired. In fact, they seemed to occur with more and more frequency. He attributed the phenomena to mounting frustrations with the inordinate amount of time consumed by this mission. But each time the thoughts occurred, they brought with them a frightening abyss, seductive and inviting. A hell he struggled to avoid.

Madness.

He shuddered and gathered his thoughts like so much scattered chaff in the wind, ordering the bits into small, neat folds of information. His goal was retribution and justice, not violence for the sake of violence alone. His was not a criminal's intent. What he did now, he did because it was the right thing to do—because he could not allow the besmirchment of his good name to go unamended.

The one promise he had made to his mother on her deathbed had been to protect his father's good name.

And he had done that.

He had even taken that good name to great heights. Built a reputation for himself beyond reproach, far past what his mother had asked of him. And in doing so he had built wealth both his parents would have been proud of.

Until *they* had seen fit to take everything away from him. His erstwhile partners had not been content merely to take his carefully acquired funds from him. They had taken his name, his life, and his heritage.

Restoring his reputation was a quest of honor, a blessed struggle for righteousness. Only two souls remained between him and his goal. But not for long.

The abyss receded with all its dark allure beneath the persistent hammer of his carefully patterned logic. As it always did. The uneasy feeling that at some point it might become unmanageable haunted him, but he had not yet reached that point.

If he could just complete his task he could turn away from all the violence he was forced to spend so much time plotting and return to the carefully balanced life he had built for himself.

He sighed again and rubbed his stomach to ease the burning. No matter the obstacles, he would succeed because he must.

* * *

"They're over this way." Jamie's shout woke Meaghan from a sound sleep.

She'd been dreaming strange mixed-up dreams with Florence Nightingale and tales of The Blessing. She shook her head, trying unsuccessfully to clear it, and squinted around her through gritty eyes. Daylight spilled over the edges of rock and washed the granite floor beyond.

She rubbed at her eyes. Daylight? The rain had finally ended? Horse hooves thundered nearer, pounding rhythmically against the ground. She struggled to bring her thoughts into order.

She'd fallen asleep. Nicholas still slumbered in her lap. His head nuzzled intimately against her stomach as though he belonged there. Her blouse buttons had opened by two or three beyond the missing ones. Her heart sank.

"Diabhal." They couldn't be seen like this. She scrambled to close the gap.

"Nicholas." She whispered his name urgently and shook his shoulder. "Wake up."

"Meaghan?" He opened his eyes and smiled blearily at her as he blinked.

She sighed as his smile spiraled through her. There was no time for such.

"Lord Ashton, we've company." She shook him harder. He needed to move away from her, at least.

Booted feet rang over the stony ground. She gnawed her lip as awareness of their predicament dawned on Nicholas's face. It was already too late as he finally struggled to rise.

A cluster of concerned faces appeared beneath

the granite boulder that served as their shelter. Varying degrees of shocked dismay registered slowly, like the distant rising of a scorching sun.

Meaghan's heart twisted as she recognized Eloise's father, the magistrate, accompanying Uncle Gill, Jamie, and Dr. Norton. She was going to be violently ill in a moment.

Jaws dropped as their gazes raked her appearance, from her gaping blouse to her discarded stockings. Not to mention her intimate pose with Lord Ashton. They were damned for any number of transgressions.

"Hullo, Uncle," she offered meekly when she could stand the judgmental silence no longer.

"Lord Ashton, this is intolerable—"

"Gentlemen." Nicholas's tone rolled against the rocks, formal and commanding, cutting Uncle Gill's courtroom bluster off in midremonstrance.

"May I take this opportunity to introduce you to my betrothed, Miss Meaghan Reilly of Beannacht Island?"

Nine

"Diabhal."

Meaghan paced the confines of her chamber, doing her best to avoid even looking at the pastel mountain piled on the bed. She fully expected Aunt Edna to come bustling in at any moment, to upbraid her for failing to select the dress for her wedding tomorrow.

After trying on what was surely every offering from both hers and Sheila's wardrobes she'd dismissed Triona to go seek her overdue luncheon, refusing the maid's suggestion that she return afterward with a tray for the bride. Everything Meaghan ate these past few days tasted like dust.

By this time tomorrow she would be Lady Ashton. Her letters to her brothers begging their assistance in avoiding this doom had gone unanswered. How craven of her to try to wedge Bryan and Quin between her and the demands of society, but on her own she would not be able to face down the well-intentioned interference of all and sundry and still explain everything away to Mama and Da when they returned from America.

But what really daunted her was the fact that on her own she would not have the strength to

refuse Lord Ashton outright. She had tried and
failed. He remained determined to do the right
thing even if it proved all wrong. If only she
hadn't kissed him in the parlor that first day. Nor
in the study. Or worst of all when he was injured.
How could she have fallen asleep in his arms like
that. If only she'd heeded the warning of The
Blessing.

She halted at the edge of the delicate rose tap-
estry rug by her bed and glared at the heap of
clothing. The ceremony was scheduled for tomorrow morning and she could arrive at the
courthouse in sackcloth for all she cared at this
point.

Or in the fine lawn petticoats, stays, and chemise she wore at the moment. Why not prove
herself the wanton the whole of Limerick now
presumed her to be? Tempting, but the threat
would prove an empty one. She'd shamed her
family and the O'Briens enough already. She
balled her fists in frustration.

Aunt Edna must be thoroughly disheartened
at the almost indifferent attitudes both parts of
the nuptial pair had adopted to the plans she
had been making all week. The dear soul was
trying to make the event a festive one despite
the circumstances.

How could Meaghan tell her aunt that the very
thought of marrying Lord Ashton made her nau-
seous? He didn't want a wife, despite Aunt
Edna's protest to the contrary.

Caught up in her infatuation with Jamie Mansfield, Sheila was even worse. Her cousin kept
looking for the romance in every meeting or
conversation between the betrothed couple. Not
that there had been many of those in the past

Introducing Ballad,
A LINE OF HISTORICAL ROMANCES

*A*s a lover of historical romance, you'll adore Ballad Romances. Written by today's most popular romance authors, every book in the Ballad line is not only an individual story, but part of a two to six book series as well. You can look forward to 4 new titles each month – each taking place at a different time and place in history.

But don't take our word for how wonderful these stories are! Accept our introductory shipment of 4 Ballad Romance novels – a $23.96 value – ABSOLUTELY FREE – and see for yourself!

*O*nce you've experienced your first 4 Ballad Romances, we're sure you'll want to continue receiving these wonderful historical romance novels each month – without ever having to leave your home – using our convenient and inexpensive home subscription service. Here's what you get for joining:

* *4 BRAND NEW Ballad Romances delivered to your door each month*

* *30% off the cover price with your home subscription.*

* *A FREE monthly newsletter filled with author interviews, book previews, special offers, and more!*

* *No risk or obligation...you're free to cancel whenever you wish... no questions asked.*

*T*o start your membership, simply complete and return the card provided. You'll receive your Introductory Shipment of 4 FREE Ballad Romances. Then, each month, as long as your account is in good standing, you will receive the 4 newest Ballad Romances. Each shipment will be yours to examine for 10 days. If you decide to keep the books, you'll pay the preferred home subscriber's price – a savings of 30% off the cover price! (plus shipping & handling) If you want us to stop sending books, just say the word...it's that simple.

Passion-
Adventure-
Excitement-
Romance-
Ballad!

Get 4 Ballad Historical Romance Novels FREE! ❖

A $23.96 value – **FREE** No obligation to buy anything – ever.
4 FREE BOOKS are waiting for you! Just mail in the certificate below!

BOOK CERTIFICATE

Yes! Please send me 4 Ballad Romances ABSOLUTELY FREE! After my introductory shipment, I will receive 4 new Ballad Romances each month to preview FREE for 10 days (as long as my account is in good standing). If I decide to keep the books, I will pay the money-saving preferred publisher's price plus shipping and handling. That's 30% off the cover price. I may return the shipment within 10 days and owe nothing, and I may cancel my subscription at any time. The 4 FREE books will be mine to keep in any case.

Name _____

Address _____ Apt. _____

City _____ State _____ Zip _____

Telephone (____) _____

Signature _____

(If under 18, parent or guardian must sign)

All orders subject to approval by Zebra Home Subscription Service.
Terms and prices subject to change. Offer valid only in the U.S.

DN121A

If the certificate is
missing below, write to:

**Ballad Romances,
c/o Zebra Home
Subscription Service Inc.**

P.O. Box 5214,
Clifton, New Jersey
07015-5214

OR call TOLL FREE
1-888-345-BOOK (26665)

Passion...
Adventure...
Excitement...
Romance...

Get 4
Ballad
Historical
Romance
Novels
FREE!

ll..l..l.lll...ll.l.l.ll..l.l..ll..l..l

BALLAD ROMANCES
Zebra Home Subscription Service, Inc.
P.O. Box 5214
Clifton NJ 07015-5214

week. And certainly none in private where Meaghan might have tried to dissuade his lordship from this course to destruction.

Aunt Edna kept extolling the virtues of married life and how mutual regard and respect frequently blossomed into abiding affection. Not in Meaghan's limited realm of observation. Her brothers might have been lucky enough to find women they loved and respected from the first, but that did not form the basis for her marriage.

"This is impossible," Meaghan declared to the pile of garments menacing her. How could she spend the rest of her life tied to a man who only offered for her because he would have seemed a veritable cad to do otherwise?

Lord Ashton . . . Nicholas—he'd asked her to call him that three times just yesterday evening at dinner—had no desire to marry at all, and certainly not her. He'd made himself abundantly clear the night they'd shared in the study and in the days since the disastrous picnic. He'd even moved to lodgings outside the O'Brien household.

"The matter has surely been out of our hands since our first kiss." His quiet answer during her one brief opportunity to protest his startling announcement of their betrothal only added to her certainty this was not the right action for either of them to take. He was hardly the doting fiancé or eager bridegroom. On the few occasions they had been in each other's company he'd kept a safe distance between them.

Lord Ashton had even proffered her betrothal present in a detached manner, sending her a

flawless emerald and diamond ring by courier,
with a note that read simply:

> *To match your eyes.*
> *N.*

She paced over and unlatched the windows
that looked out to the back gardens. There was
Aunt Edna, dressed in her apron and broad-
brimmed hat, deep in conversation with the gar-
dener. Discussing wedding flowers, no doubt.
Meaghan's heart plummeted, although if her
aunt was in the garden it meant a few more moments of reprieve before her choice of bridal
gowns must be made.

Leaning out, she gulped a breath of the warm
afternoon air to clear her thoughts. The sky was
a piercing blue, almost the shade of Lord . . .
Nicholas's eyes. She shivered and rubbed her
bare arms. Why did every thought lead back to
him?

All because of a kiss delivered in response to
a parlor game. Her Blessing. All of her brothers
had warned her girls did not receive Blessings.
How could she have been so foolish to think she
would prove them wrong? Her mind flew back
to the waves of heat, the sensations of joy and
freedom tumbling through her when her lips
touched his. How could anything so wondrous
prove a harbinger for a lifetime's worth of regret?

Only ye can direct the course to joy or sorrow, Devin
would say, quoting Granny's warnings to her with
great relish. *Only ye decide if it is Blessing or Curse.*

"Definitely Cursed."

A loud knock on her door pulled her back

from her unwelcome reverie. Who could that be? Aunt Edna was outside, it was a court day for Uncle Gill, and Triona should still be enjoying her meal.

"Not now, Sheila, I'm . . . I'm resting." Meaghan couldn't face another afternoon of Sheila waxing on about how beautifully Jamie sat a horse or how his smile sent flights of butterflies through her every time she thought of it—which would be every half minute or so, from what Meaghan observed.

"I hope you are not so tired you couldn't spare a few moments for a visit after I've come all this way." The deep rumble of a familiar masculine voice sent a shower of relief sluicing through her.

"Quin." She fairly flew to the door. Wrenching it open, she buried herself in her brother's arms before he had a chance to even enter.

"You came. Oh, Quin, you came," she managed between sobs and deep comforting breaths of his fresh ocean breeze and whitewater scent. Everything would be all right now. He'd come to fetch her home and put an end to this nonsense.

Quin gathered her close for what seemed both a timeless moment and too short a span before he set her from him and looked her up and down. "You've landed yourself on the shoals but good this time, lass. That much is certain."

His gaze bore into her as she nodded and swiped at the tears threatening to spill from the corners of her eyes. "How is everyone on Beannacht?"

Her question came out in a husky whisper as a wave of homesickness rushed through her at the sight of her handsome brother standing by the still-open door. He'd come after all. Just when she'd given up hope.

"Timothy has grown another span of my hand since you sailed here. He's getting quite good with his skiff, too. Says to tell you he'll beat you next time you race." Quin's somber features relaxed as he spoke of his son.

He leaned a shoulder against the doorjamb and kept up his careful scrutiny for a few heartbeats. Meaghan felt with uncomfortable certainty that she now knew what one of his seamen must have felt when his work did not quite measure up.

"Siannon is well and keeps busy with her crockery painting. And the babe has her mother's lines and trim." Pride over his thriving family filled his tone and shone in his eyes.

"Good thing, too. Who'd want a daughter who took after an old salt like you?" Another figure loomed in the doorway.

"Bryan! You came, too."

Quin stepped aside so she could be enveloped in their brother's embrace.

"Seems I have a weakness for damsels in distress." Bryan chuckled into her hair. "Emilynne sends her love."

"And how is your son?" Meaghan pulled back so she could look at him.

"He's so fat, it's a wonder he's learned to walk already. Abby and Christian spoil him to the point Emilynne and the nurse practically have to scold them into letting him do things for himself."

Both her brothers chuckled and clapped each other on the shoulders. They looked so alike they could almost be twins, save for the dimple in Bryan's chin and the small scar above Quin's eye. She felt better than she had in weeks.

"How do you suppose Devin's making out with two of them demanding Maggie's attention?" Bryan arched a knowing brow at Quin.

The eldest of the Reillys smiled at the mention of their youngest brother's children. "Maggie seems the sort who will handle it all with style, even her husband's wailing and gnashing of teeth."

"Ahh, the joys of new parenthood." Bryan shook his head. "The midnight feedings."

"The crying," sighed Quin.

"When all you can do is walk the floorboards and pray for morning," Bryan agreed.

"And then there's the smells." Quin grimaced.

"Well, that will all go double for Dev."

Both brothers laughed outright. The sound warmed Meaghan and gave her further hope they were not taking this scandal with undue seriousness.

Bryan sobered first. "But this reverie over the joys of parenthood is not why we are here. Or is it, Meaghan?" His gaze fixed on her in much the same way Uncle Gill sometimes possessed, as if he examined a hostile witness.

Her heart plummeted. Did both her brothers believe she had been ruined? One look at their mirror-imaged expressions told her the jovial part of this reunion had passed. Time to face the matters at hand. And from the frowns fixed on her, they each looked prepared to hear a full litany of her sins. "Must you think the worst, too?"

"We can't think anything until you tell us how

this came about." Bryan's tone softened, but his gaze remained resolute.

She turned from them both and paced back to the window, snatching up her shawl from the back of the chair as she passed. She flung it around her shoulders against the sudden chill and hugged the soft wool tight to her chest.

"Showing your temper will not get you out of answering, not if you want our help." Quin stood back from the door and shut it with a click that held staunch purpose. "Perhaps you would prefer a little privacy, lass?"

She would prefer not to undergo this examination at all. But she knew better. The best way to deal with Reilly men was head-on, Mama always said. A lesson honed over her lifetime. She turned back to glare at them. "There is nothing to tell."

"Then you did not kiss him full and fair in front of a room full of people?" Bryan raised a brow.

"And you did not throw yourself into his arms and sprawl in the streets with your petticoats up to your knees?" Quin waved away the protest she tried to voice. "Good reason or not, we are only reciting events."

"And you were not alone with the man for hours, then discovered half dressed in his arms?" Bryan balled his fists as he baldly stated the worst of her offenses.

The litany of her transgressions stung, especially when outlined by the brothers she had hoped would be her staunchest defenders. At least no one knew of the encounter in the study. Her public behavior had been reckless enough, and certainly scandalous when recited like that.

Marriage with the other participant would soothe the social ripples and eventually allow her to resume her quest to help reform medical care and other causes from an even better social position. But her very spirit rebelled at the thought that she . . . that they . . . were being forced into the union.

"I still think we should be asking this of the Englishman, not her." Quin's fists were also clenched tight. That's all she needed. Her two big brothers coming to her defense with their fists.

"All I want to do is go home." She met Quin's gaze with as much appeal as she could muster. "It's bad enough that I have to distance myself from the Nightingale Society. That I can't help build the nursing school so desperately needed here. I've lost my dearest dream of making a difference in the lives of others. Why do I have to marry him?"

She turned to meet Bryan's stare. "We could just say there is a betrothal and all else is postponed until Mama and Da return. I can go home, and in a few months we can end the agreement quietly. By then everyone here will have forgotten."

"You have yet to answer our questions, Meaghan." Bryan refused to budge.

"Your charges you mean," she countered.

Her brothers exchanged exasperated looks.

"What does your betrothed have to say about your proposal to let him off the hook?" Quin snapped.

"He refused to discuss the matter when I tried to explain it to him." Frustration clenched her again. "He said everything was settled and that I must put aside my fears."

Bryan spoke first. "The marriage settlement is very generous. I reviewed the contracts myself this morning. Gill believes the man will do well by you."

"You went to Uncle Gill before coming here?" She should have known, but finding out still rankled.

"Ashton's a good man by all accounts and reputation," Quin offered in a reasonable tone. He didn't look one bit apologetic for checking into things before seeing her. Neither did Bryan.

"Are you saying you have no feelings for him? Despite all that has passed between you?" he continued. This time his tone held more of an edge. He'd tired of her evasions.

She couldn't look them in the face and lie outright.

"Nothing passed between us save a kiss or two." Rainbows of colored stars and white-hot passion that stole her breath and her common sense, notwithstanding.

"A kiss or two can signify quite a wealth of feeling, Meaghan," Bryan assured her with conviction.

She shook her head and turned away from them. The concern etched in their faces boded poorly for her escape. If either of her brothers guessed the depth of her feelings, she was lost. Seeing Nicholas crumpled on the ground the day of the picnic—deadly still and silent—wrenched her heart with a pain she had never imagined possible. It was then she knew she was in danger of loving him. With equal surety came the knowledge he did not return the sentiment.

"In the dead of night in a moonlit study, or in a dappled glade, Lord Ashton might desire an Irish lass, but he does not love me," she whispered the certainty that had scoured her for days.

She closed her eyes and fought the groan that welled from deep within. She'd watched the color drain from his face when they had been discovered in such disarray. Seen the light in his eyes grow hard when he shielded her from censure by making his peremptory announcement. Known right then she could not punish him for her mistake.

"How could I have ever thought Nicholas's kiss heralded a Blessing?" she whispered for the thousandth time. "I am Cursed."

"Did you say something about The Blessing, lass?" Quin's question startled her. Caught up in her misery and guilt she'd somehow forgotten her brothers were there.

"I think she said Curse," Bryan said.

"More a warning I failed to heed." She turned back to face them. For some reason they both looked far less surprised than she would have thought. And some of the tension had eased from their stances.

"So you proved us wrong." A trace of humor sparked in Bryan's appraising gaze. "Girls can have a Blessing after all."

"Are you sure you felt The Blessing, sweeting?" Quin's first use of the endearment from her childhood clutched her. Perhaps he was on her side after all.

"The knowin' is up to us; the doin's another part." He quoted the legend the way he had throughout her childhood.

"And this happened when you kissed Lord Ashton?" Bryan stepped over to her and touched her cheek.

"Aye," she nodded. "I received plenty of warning that what might pass between us was dangerous. Almost from the start Nicholas caused nothing but confusion and disaster. Now I have lost everything I hoped for."

"But still you kissed him again. And you'd kiss him now if he were standing here." Bryan spoke the statement as fact, not in question. Fact she could not deny. She nodded again, unable to speak through the tightness of her throat.

"That's it, then." He looked over at Quin, who nodded.

"Aye. We'd best go unpack." Quin reached for the doorknob.

"Wait. I failed to heed my Blessing so now I am condemned to a loveless marriage?"

"Mayhap you have not failed to heed it so much as failed to yield to it, Meaghan." Quin was the one who spoke, but Bryan nodded and stroked her cheek with his thumb.

He dropped his hand to her shoulder. *"The choice once made cannot be undone."* He intoned the last of the oft-told tale.

"The decision once made cannot be altered," Quin said, joining in, but leaving out the final words that echoed on in her heart anyway. *Blessing or Curse for all time.*

"We'll see you at dinner, lass."

"I won't be coming down."

"Then we'll see you in the morning." Quin opened the door, then turned back to her.

"Before I forget, I brought you this." He strode over, proffering a slim box. Bending

down, he gave her a kiss on the cheek as he
slipped the box into her hands.

"Things have a way of working out, even if we
don't always understand our Blessings when they
come. Right, boy-o?" He winked at Bryan.

Bryan favored their brother with a wry smile,
then turned his gaze to the mountain of discarded gowns on the bed. He quirked a brow.
"I'd choose the peridot silk, if I were you. It will
bring out the green in your eyes."

He'd chosen the very gown she'd been wearing the day Nicholas Mansfield walked into the
parlor and changed her life. Somehow that
seemed fitting. Now that all hope was gone,
Meaghan felt strangely calm.

"Perhaps the *Sidhe* will come and spirit me
away if I wear it," she said, wistful irony lacing
her words as she thought of the superstitious
warning of such happenings, should an unwary
bride wear green.

"We'll be there to see that doesn't happen,
Meaghan. You must cease your fretting and just
enjoy this new path you've chosen." Quin kissed
her forehead.

"When The Blessing's involved, things have a
way of working out. You'll see, Meaghan," Bryan
added as he fished for something in his pocket.
He handed her a small box. "Emilynne sent you
these. She said they would go with whatever you
chose to wear."

It was as if she viewed the scene from somewhere outside. Tomorrow she would no longer
be Meaghan Reilly of Beannacht. Tomorrow she
would wed Nicholas Mansfield and become Lady
Ashton. No more tears; no more remonstrations.
The choice had been made.

For all time.

"Thank you," she said, looking at the two boxes in her hands and then at her two brothers. "Thank you both for coming."

"I wouldn't have missed your wedding for all the fish in the ocean, sweeting," Quin answered.

"Nor all the stars in the sky," said Bryan.

Just the way they had promised to come home whenever they left. No matter how else her life might change, at least she knew she could count on them.

"Stop pacing, stripling. You are making me dizzy." Nick tugged at his cuffs and watched as Jamie came to a halt for the moment. "You would think it was you about to embark on the voyage to connubial bliss."

Jamie snorted. The sound echoed in the clerk's paper-shrouded office where they awaited the summons to the magistrate's chambers across the hall. "I wish I could convince you to find another way out of this predicament. We have enough matters hanging over us."

"The predicament is one of my own making. I must set things right." Nick stood and clapped a reassuring hand on his cousin's shoulder. "You would not have me try to sneak out the back door, Jamie. I have given my word."

"No." The hard-wrung answer did not lessen the concern glittering in his cousin's eyes. "But the haste of these proceedings will most certainly lend credence to the worst of the gossip."

"Haste is necessary so I can concentrate on the very matters you so shrewdly pointed to a moment ago." And surely marriage would quench the burning desire that roared to life whenever his thoughts turned to his bride. He needed his wits about him. Far too many of his thoughts were haunted by the honeyed taste of Meaghan Reilly's lips and the feel of her in his arms.

"By playing the besotted groom, impatient for the bride of my choosing, I have a far better chance of curtailing unnecessary curiosity into our business here. Once Meaghan and I are a staid married couple the gossip will die away, and you and I can go back to our investigations unremarked."

Jamie scrubbed a hand through his hair. "But surely you are placing Miss Reilly in the midst of our troubles?"

His cousin's question pointed to the crux of the argument Nick had waged with himself over marrying Meaghan immediately or sending her safely home to her island for a long betrothal. He'd had this very debate numerous times each day since the picnic. Each time he found himself snagged by the compassion and worry shining in her eyes as he'd woken and found her leaning over him that day.

"If the worst happens, she can return to her family's home as a wealthy and respectable widow," he assured Jamie and himself. "I have taken steps to apprise her family of the situation should it come to that. Everything I have heard about her brothers tells me they are more than capable of protecting her in the years to come. But until we can ascertain where these threats come from, she is safer with us."

"It's curious there have been no more incidents since the picnic." Jamie shook his head.

"Randall's men have reported nothing unusual either at the O'Brien household or at our new lodgings."

Nick shrugged and paced over to the small office window and looked up at the scrap of sky. Jamie joined him.

"It's possible this marriage has given our opponent pause." Especially if the opponent was Gill O'Brien, although the possibility of that seemed more in doubt with each passing day. There was no need to reiterate the old suspicion. Jamie's favoring the O'Brien girl might color his reaction. "More likely he is just regrouping after three failed attempts here and the others at home."

"All the more reason not to marry the girl right now. It is like putting her up as a target." Trust Jamie not to lose sight of his objective.

"If she is sent home now and I have not made things right for her, she will live in disgrace with no hope of redemption." He couldn't bear the thought of Meaghan's spirit so confined. Jamie slowly nodded his understanding.

Since turning and seeing the shocked expressions from the rescue party at discovering Lord Ashton and Miss Reilly in such a disheveled state, his own choices had narrowed to these two considerations. Surprisingly, for a confirmed bachelor who had never planned to wed, marriage to Meaghan Reilly held unexpected appeal despite the circumstances.

He'd found the time between the picnic and this morning almost unbearable, knowing she would be his completely and yet not able to touch her, to be alone with her. The O'Briens had seen to that.

He, Jamie, and Randall had been settled almost immediately into one of the Reilly brothers'
empty bachelor quarters. The small but comfortable town house had suddenly become vacant.
At least living within the city limits had allowed
Randall more access for his investigations and
made it easier for the guards set to watch over
Jamie and now Meaghan. And it would afford
them a modicum of privacy to begin their married life.

Married to Meaghan. In a few moments she
would be his, bonded to him for all time. His
thoughts snagged on the picture of his bride with
her long black hair falling loose around her
shoulders. There had been desire shining in the
depths of her green eyes, passion on her lips.
The honeysuckle-and-meadowsweet softness of
her skin had yielded to his touch.

And yield she did. Whether she recognized it
or not, she wanted him just as he wanted her.
There was something shared between the two of
them that was rare. That certainty made all the
rest of this possible. He was not distasteful to her.
And God knew she was far from distasteful to
him.

While she might not be happy about the circumstances surrounding this wedding, he firmly
believed she would come around.

There was little romance to satisfy a young
girl's heart in his hasty declaration. He had not
courted her with flowers and pretty phrases of
undying love, and he had stayed away this week
in part to avoid making promises he was not capable of keeping. Love held no place in this
union.

They would build their foundation on shared

passion and, in time, learn to share other interests and hopefully build some common goals. But love was a trap he planned to avoid. Loving too deeply surely meant risking too much loss. He had lost enough to last his lifetime already.

A rap rattled the glass-paneled door. He and Jamie turned as one toward the sound, as the portal cracked open. "They are ready for you, my lord," the clerk announced.

"Fetch our hats, will you, Jamie?" Nick tossed over his shoulder as he strode out into the narrow hall. He surprised himself with his eagerness to get through this day.

"Miss Reilly and her party await within?" he inquired of the mousy clerk.

The clerk hesitated before opening the door to the magistrate's private chamber. "There are two gentlemen who wish to make your acquaintance before your bride is ushered in, Lord Ashton. Two rather large gentlemen."

Nick entered the chamber and saw two very large gentlemen, indeed, standing in hushed conversation with the Honorable Gill O'Brien. From the look of them, with their dark hair and unmistakable green eyes, he knew them to be Meaghan's brothers. According to Randall, Quin and Bryan Reilly had arrived in Limerick yesterday.

Jamie offered a low whistle as he entered. "Called in the troops, I see."

The Reilly brothers looked up, then, and moved forward to greet him. The thought that they might have been called on to make sure he did, indeed, do the right thing by their sister rankled.

"Don't go getting all bristly or hung up in your

rigging, lad," Quintin said, grinning after Gill introduced them. "We're not here to strong-arm you. We're only here . . ."

"What my brother means to say," Bryan interrupted, "is that we came to see to our sister's happiness."

"And to see to it she didn't jump ship on you," Quin added.

Looking at Meaghan's brothers, Nick wondered if he hadn't made the wrong choice regarding her welfare after all. Each of them looked more than capable of protecting her if called upon. Together they would make powerful obstacles in the path of potential harm from his unknown enemy. *Reilly born and Reilly bred.* The catchphrase took on added meaning looking at the two of them. Add in the brother in America and their father, his notion that she would be safer with him than with her family seemed almost ludicrous.

Almost.

The door squeaked behind Nick.

"There she is now," said Bryan.

The brothers moved past Nick, who turned in time to see his bride pale and beautiful in hauntingly familiar peridot silk. Flanking Meaghan stood a beaming Edna O'Brien and her daughter. Sheila favored Jamie with a smile and small wave of her hand before she was lost from view as the Reilly brothers gathered their sister into alternating hugs.

"You look beautiful, lass," said Quin. "It's a wonder the *Sidhe* did not steal you away, indeed."

"Mama will cry to think she missed this day," said Bryan. "But she would be proud to see you so calm and composed."

She did look composed. A trifle pale, but the light shade of green brought out the luster in her skin and accented the lush color of her eyes. Her hair was pulled back in a simple knot with a dusting of ringlets fringing her face. She handed her gloves and a straw bonnet to Sheila.

Moving forward to greet him, a tremulous smile crossed her lips, belying the rest of her demeanor.

He took her hands in his. They were cold and trembled, another sign of the nerves she strove to hide. "And just who is this *she* who threatened to steal my bride?" he teased.

A genuine smile lit her face. "The *Sidhe* is the Irish name given to fairy folk. Legend has it they like to steal unwary brides in green."

"Then I am glad today is so clear and bright. The sun must have blinded them so you could be delivered safely to me."

"The magistrate has arrived." Gill nodded toward the door at the opposite side of the chamber as it opened.

A stout man in the robes and wig of his office huffed over to his large desk and shuffled through the papers there without looking up at the assemblage before him. His clerk cleared his throat.

"My lord, I would like to present Nicholas Mansfield, Lord Ashton of Suffolk, England, and the spinster, Miss Meaghan Reilly of Beannacht Island, matrimonial candidates."

Accepting the paper proffered by the clerk, the magistrate stared over the top of the glasses perched on his nose at the gathering in front of him.

"You Ashton?" he barked, fixing his gaze on Nick.

"Aye."

"Very good." The magistrate then swept the crowd with an appraising glare.

"Good day, O'Brien. Pleasure to see your missus and charming daughter. She's grown into quite a beauty. Good to see you again, too, Reilly." Bryan Reilly returned his nod.

He paused in his greetings to stare hard at Quintin Reilly. "Good to see you, as well, Captain. Didn't I perform your nuptials, too? Hope your pretty wife is well."

"Very well, sir." Quin answered. "Thank you."

The magistrate chuckled. "No need to thank me. Warmest wedding I ever performed.

"Well," he said, putting aside the papers, "let's get this one underway, shall we?"

Nick nodded. Next to him Meaghan also nodded her consent to proceed.

"Join hands," the magistrate intoned.

Ten

Nicholas slid the gold circle onto Meaghan's finger, binding their futures together. He quirked a smile at her when she raised her gaze to meet his; then he gently squeezed her fingers before they turned back to face the magistrate.

". . . God save the Queen." The official's voice boomed the last of the ceremony that changed both their lives forever.

"Ladies and gentlemen, may I present Lord and Lady Ashton?" The magistrate gestured for them to turn around and face their relations.

Quin and Bryan looked solemn, but at least they were not frowning. Bryan winked. Aunt Edna sniffled into a handkerchief while Uncle Gill patted her hand. Sheila and Jamie Mansfield exchanged lingering sideways glances.

"You may kiss your bride, Lord Ashton," the magistrate said.

Nicholas trailed his finger along her jawline and under her chin, turning her face up to his. He bent over her lips. For a moment their gazes locked. The blue of his eyes reached right through her, but she could not read his expres-

sion. The oranges-and-mint smell of him filled
her and then his lips brushed against hers.

Her husband.

As always when he touched her, white heat
sluiced through her middle, insistent and undeniable. His hands rested on her shoulders and
he pulled her closer until her hands brushed the
lapels of his jacket. The wool's rough texture tingled against her fingertips just as his lips sparked
small whorls of sensation on her mouth.

It felt as if time stopped or spun away into the
distance. All that remained was the two of them
locked together. He pulled her closer still and
demanded more from her lips. They parted and
the tip of his tongue traced their outline.

She was molten wax in his hands. All thought
fled and the deep yearning to be nearer, closer
to this man flowed through her. This was her
husband, and for the moment she allowed herself to be swept far away from the certainty that
what passed between them now would burn away
too quickly and leave a lifetime of bitter ashes.

She clutched his jacket and kissed him back
full measure, savoring the strength and warmth
of his lips.

"That's a fine seal you've placed on your vows,
lad." The rumble of humor in Quin's voice
pulled them back to the company surrounding
them.

Nicholas stepped aside, slipping his arm
around her waist when she swayed, still caught
in the magical sensations evoked by his kiss.

"About as fine as I've ever witnessed, Captain
Reilly. Save one." The magistrate's laughter rumbled at his own jest. And while no one else

seemed to get the humor, she could have sworn Quin blushed ever so slightly.

Almost as one, their families surged forward. The exchange of felicitations made a great clamor in the chamber and swept the newlyweds apart. Hands were shaken and Meaghan's cheek kissed by all and sundry. Everything seemed to happen in a blur. Meaghan struggled to sort it all out.

"I only wish your dear mama was here," Aunt Edna whispered.

"I hope I make as beautiful a bride someday." Sheila hugged Meaghan as her gaze slid back to Jamie with a dreamy sigh.

"Welcome to the family. Nicholas is a lucky man." Jamie hugged her as her brothers busied themselves clapping Nicholas on the shoulder.

"Congratulations, my lord. You made a wise choice. We both wish you years of joy," Uncle Gill said, greeting the groom.

"If you will but sign the register, the matter can be concluded, Lord and Lady Ashton." The clerk's high-pitched tone cut through the convivial din.

"Shall we, my dear?" Nicholas offered her his arm. "I for one am most anxious to be done here."

They accomplished the last official act binding her forever to a man she barely knew, and whom, she felt quite certain, did not truly wish to know her.

Emerging minutes later from the darkened marble halls of the courthouse, Meaghan used her hand to shield her eyes from the glare of sunshine. Carriages and horses clattered over the cobblestones on the street below. Vendors called out their wares from curbs and corners. Passersby of every sort hastened past, intent on their business. How was it everything seemed the same out here and yet her whole world had changed since she climbed these steps only a few minutes ago? She chewed her lip and gripped her husband's arm tighter.

Her husband. Even through the wool of his jacket and her gloves, her fingers fairly hummed with the pleasure of touching him. He put his hand over hers as they descended the steps. "We will make this work, Meaghan. You'll see."

The rich timbre of his voice sounded so sure. So reassuring, but now that the deed was done what little peace she had found with their actions blew away on the breeze ruffling her skirt. The certainty that momentary passion could not possibly fuel a lifetime clutched her.

"Happy is the bride the sun shines for, or so Granny used to say—eh, Bryan?" Quin looked at the sky and squinted as they all reached the street.

"I'll leave you with your brothers while I go speak with your uncle." Nick released his hold of her and walked over to Uncle Gill, giving her a little privacy with her family. His consideration left her somewhat bereft.

"Didn't she used to add something about growin' moon and a flowin' tide ensuring happiness and good fortune?" Bryan took a deep breath and looked up at the courthouse and then across to the tavern. His life, his ambitions before he married Emilynne Wellesley.

"Do you miss your work here?" What she really wanted to know was if Bryan was content with giving up his life and practice in Limerick to help his wife manage their niece and nephew's estates in England and Ireland.

The assessing look he shot her told her he knew exactly what she wanted to know. He reached over and squeezed her hand. "The choice once made cannot be broken, Meaghan, but that does not mean we always understand what we have chosen."

"I might wax nostalgic for my days of shuffling papers up there." He pointed in the direction of his old office. "Or the nights wrangling with colleagues over an obscure ruling in there." He nodded toward the tavern across the street. "But I'd not trade my life or my family now to come back to any of it. Not for a single second."

She tried to take comfort in his assurance. She really did.

"Siannon said to tell you to listen to your heart, sweeting. Even if it takes a while to grasp." Quin spoke up, warm understanding shining in his eyes. "You'll see. And if you don't, it won't matter where you go. One of your brothers will always come to set your course straight."

She smiled then as tears welled in her eyes. "I'm counting on that."

She touched the pearl-and-gold cross hanging around her neck. "Thank you for bringing me Granny's cross, Quin. I'll treasure it because it belonged to her and because it's a little piece of home."

She felt grateful for far more, but she knew he understood.

"Well, lass," he said and gathered her into a hug, "your mention of home and this old tar's mention of the flowing tide reminds me I'd best be on my way before I miss it."

"Are you sure you must leave?" Meaghan gave Quin's neck a final squeeze. Homesickness stabbed her along with a twinge of panic. She wished she could sail home with him to Beannacht.

"Aye." He set her from him, though his hands lingered on her elbows. "We're a week away from launching our next bark. I'm needed in the shipyard and at home."

"Besides"—he winked—"you'll find married life suits you much better than you think beforehand. I know I have. Don't give up on your Blessing just yet."

"He's right. You mustn't view events as Cursed until it all unfolds. You may be surprised," Bryan added.

All well and good for them. Look how things had turned out for all her brothers, each deeply in love with the woman of his choice. She stole a glance past them to Nicholas, deep in conversation with his cousin and Sheila. If they had managed to stay awake and escape the glade unscathed by scandal, she doubted her husband would have freely made the choice to cement passion into a permanent union.

"Will you be returning to Kildare immediately, as well?" she asked Bryan. "Or can you visit for a few days?"

"I'll stay long enough to toast you at Gill's, but I'm looking to get as close to the Blue Hills as possible by nightfall," he answered. "I left Emilynne with three mares about to drop foals and two more due in a week or so."

"Please thank her for the lovely earrings. They complemented Granny's cross so nicely. Aunt Edna was most impressed."

"Emilynne wanted you to have something special. She thinks very highly of you, Meggy." He chucked her under the chin as he used to do when she was a child.

Nicholas joined them, and her brothers shook his hand, offering their congratulations again.

"Bring her by for a look-see before you leave for England?" Quin asked, although his question seemed more a command.

"That would be after you come to us in Kildare," Bryan interjected. "I'll be happy to show young Mansfield enough horseflesh to stock three stables."

"I'll take good care of her. You have my word." Nick said, answering the concerns underlying her brothers' invitations.

"We're counting on that, lad." Quin fixed him with a serious look and a nod.

"Aye," Bryan agreed.

The arrival of Seamus and the O'Brien carriage followed by the hackneys hired to carry the day's overflow of passengers forestalled any further unspoken warnings about to be issued to her groom by his new brothers-in-law. This was it. She was about to begin the rest of her life.

The course once set cannot be undone.

She swallowed hard and tried to look happy for all their sakes.

With a quick kiss to her cheek, and a farewell slap on the shoulder for Bryan, Quin sauntered off toward the harbor and his trip home to Beannacht. Meaghan wished again she could go with him. Then her husband took her hand and escorted her to the waiting carriage.

* * *

"Here ye go, sir." The tavern wench clunked the pewter mug on the table beside him and scooped up the coin Neville tossed her. "The stew's mighty fine taday if'n ye decide yer hungry after all."

"I'll keep that in mind while I watch for my friend." He took a sip of the brew. Standing by the pub's window, he watched for the wedding party to descend the steps of Limerick's venerable courthouse.

Favored as an informal gathering place by the city's legal establishment for quick refreshments between court appearances, the well-scrubbed tap hummed with conversation and commerce. He recognized no one and felt certain no one recognized him. The years lost to the Mansfields had not been kind.

At one time, he'd spent many an hour in a shadowed corner of this very establishment, listening for useful tips or information carelessly relayed. The more information you gathered, the fewer things might catch you by surprise down the road, so Mother had cautioned him often enough.

Ashton's marriage today had surprised him. And he did not like surprises. The arrogant pup had shown little inclination toward courtship through the years, preferring discreet alliances with widows or mistresses not likely to seek the security of a wedding band. Gossip had it the fool had taken advantage of a young innocent and been caught in the act. Hence the hasty nuptials.

Curiosity aimed at getting a closer view of the chit he planned to rescue from Mansfield by making her a widow had driven him to keep this vigil in the pub. He'd have finished Mansfield before the ceremony, save for his concern the girl might already be breeding. It would never do to be the cause of another bastard coming into the world. He could still hear Mother admonishing him over the evils sure to befall anyone involved with a babe born on the wrong side of the blanket.

What looked to be the marriage party emerged through the courthouse's massive doors, although it was impossible to discern faces through the thick panes of window glass. "Damnation."

He drained the dregs from the mug. There looked to be sufficient traffic on the street to allow him to retain his anonymity and still get a closer look at the object of his unwilling mercy. He tossed a smaller coin to the barmaid and tipped his hat as he exited.

"Good luck finding your friend, sir," she called after him. If only she knew luck had nothing to do with it. Planning was at the root of any success he would have. Thorough planning and the will to succeed.

Mansfield stood at the bottom of the steps in conversation with his cousin and O'Brien's brat. The slender brunette from the flower cart disaster held herself apart from the cozy group. Dressed in pale green peridot silk that highlighted the fine porcelain luster of her skin and her hair's ebony sheen even at this distance, Lady Ashton hardly looked the joyous bride.

She had been a guest in the O'Brien household. "Did he ravish you right under the Honorable Gill O'Brien's very nose, my dear?"

The images that thought provoked disgusted him.

Already Ashton neglected his bride, keeping his distance just minutes after the ceremony. She would be well rid of him.

Two men bore her company in her groom's stead, both alike enough to be twins and to mark them as her family. Brothers? The tender regard they showered on her showed their concern for their sister. Could they not have protected her better and circumvented the need for this short-lived union? With no parents there to witness the ceremony, she must be orphaned. Virtually alone in the world with a guardian and brothers who had done her no good.

He found himself fascinated with the pale translucence of her skin. So fresh and innocent. "What a cad Mansfield must be, despoiling one such as you. Your suffering will be over soon," he promised through gritted teeth before stepping into the crowd swirling down the street. "I'll see to that."

He allowed himself one final look over his shoulder at her lithe form and delicate features. "Mansfield will not enjoy your bed for long, Lady Ashton."

"Meaghan." Nick rapped on the door to the chamber he now shared with his wife. "I've brought you some champagne."

He stood barefoot in the hall of her brother's town house and waited for her answer. How long was sufficient to allow a new bride to prepare herself for her first night in her husband's bed? He had shed his jacket, boots, and socks below stairs to allow her more privacy.

It could be worse, they could be in a noisy,

anonymous inn or still lodged at the O'Briens' where the household could wait in breathless anticipation of the deed to be done this night.

Balancing the tray in one hand, Nick turned the knob. "I'm coming in."

The door swung open just as the glasses and bottle shifted on the tray with a chink. He fought to save them, but ended up practically stumbling into the darkened room and losing the battle. The bottle thudded to the carpet, followed by the glasses he had carried so carefully up the stairs. So much for sophistication winning out over wedding-night nerves.

Meaghan jumped up from the tapestry-upholstered settee near the fire and rushed to assist him. She had changed into the diaphanous white nightgown and robe he remembered from the night he'd discovered her in the O'Briens' study. It flowed around her like an enticing halo. Desire burst to life inside him.

For the span of a heartbeat their fingers brushed on the edge of the tray as she bent to help him. She rocked back on her heels as if the contact burned her.

"Looks like we'll have to enjoy a private toast at a later time, Lady Ashton." He strove for a jovial note.

"That . . . That was very thoughtful of you, Lord . . . Nicholas. I don't often drink champagne. The bubbles make me sneeze." She twisted the rings he had placed on her slender fingers and tried to smile. "I believe there is a pitcher of water on the sill, if you are thirsty."

She turned her head toward the window. The ebony curtain of her hair flowed over her shoulder. The enticing blend of honeysuckle and meadowsweet filled him. He swallowed hard, suddenly quite thirsty. But not for water or any other libation.

"Let's get this taken care of first," he told himself as much as her. She snagged the glasses where they had rolled while he retrieved the bottle. All were miraculously intact. Taking her elbow, he helped Meaghan regain her feet.

His hand lingered on her arm for a moment as he tried to look into the depths of her gaze and judge how best to proceed from here. The dimness in the room did not help. With only the glow from one lamp on the washstand and the flicker of the fire, her face remained shadowed in uncertainty.

Perhaps a little conversation would help. Releasing her, he walked across the room to the settee, where she had been curled to await him, and placed the tray on a small table. His wife closed the door and followed him.

"This is better," he said. "I can see your eyes over here."

They glittered with questions as she looked up at him, the green intensity almost black in the light. She held herself tense with anticipation, but she returned his regard without comment. Damnation, this was awkward.

"Meaghan." He cupped her face and ran his thumb along her cheek. She closed her eyes as he stroked her. She looked so beautiful. The firelight and shadows highlighted the soft luster of her skin. Her lips, parted ever so slightly as she drew in a long breath, invited his kiss.

Everything in him leaped to claim her. To kiss her senseless and carry her to the velvet-covered bed. To make wild, passionate love to her all night. It was his right. It was his duty as her husband and the one thought that had carried him through this past week—once the ceremony was over, she would be his. She was his.

She was also an innocent. He held back, willing himself to go slow as he initiated her into marital relations. He leaned in and brushed her lips in the briefest of salutes and stepped back.

She appeared puzzled as she opened her eyes and studied his face again. "Yes, Nicholas?"

"Are you nervous?" He glanced at the bed.

She followed his gaze over to the four-poster they would soon share and shook her head. "No. I am not nervous about . . . that. At least not overmuch."

She turned back to face him briefly and then her gaze dropped to her hands. She twisted her rings again. The emerald betrothal ring he had sent her gleamed in the firelight.

"Really?" Her answer seemed so contrary to her appearance. "May I ask why not? You do know what to anticipate, do you not?"

"I grew up on a very small island." The wry smile twisting her lips also added a welcome sparkle to her eyes. "And Aunt Edna felt it her duty to make sure I was prepared since my own mother was not here."

"That must have been an interesting conversation. Would you care to enlighten me by sharing her advice?"

She looked up and this time her smile over his teasing appeared more genuine. "She was very sweet and truly wanted to be helpful. She and Uncle Gill do have eight children, you know."

"I bow to her expertise." He bent his head.

"But if it is not . . . that, what is twisting you into such knots?"

He regretted his question immediately. The humor bled from her face and, if possible, her skin turned even whiter. Her eyes widened as she hesitated answering him. Would she trust him enough to enlighten him? It suddenly seemed very important to him that she would.

"Everything else," she whispered from a throat that seemed to have suddenly closed on her. She sank onto the settee and clasped her hands in her lap. Shaking her head, she repeated, "Everything else."

He sat beside her, perplexed. "What do you mean? What everything?"

He covered her hands with his own. Her fingers trembled, ice-cold, in his grasp, but she did not pull away. Instead she fixed him with a look at once so hopeless and desperate it knotted a chord of sympathy deep within him.

She'd been surprised by his betrothal announcement, without even speaking to her first. High-handed for sure, but the only honorable path open to him, to them both. Even she had acknowledged that, according to her aunt. Had she been more reluctant than he'd been led to believe? Did she have a beau back on her island? One she had pledged herself to or given herself to and thus her lack of fear for the marriage bed?

His conscience twinged. He had no proof she was not the innocent she appeared. Neither could he claim his own past spotless. He pushed aside the injustice of his doubts and searched for other reasons for Meaghan's distress.

Perhaps her brothers or O'Brien had resorted

to some Draconian measure to ensure she went through with what they surely viewed as an excellent match—if only for his lands and title. Her drawn-out silence stretched his forbearance almost to the breaking. He struggled not to make things worse for her by showing his impatience.

"Everything. Everything," she said finally, as if that summation explained all her troubles.

She took a deep breath and exhaled. The sound shuddered over his taut nerves.

"I like your kisses very much, my lord," she managed with a gulp. "And your . . . other attentions, as well. I believe we will be most companionable in that regard."

She stopped and looked beyond him toward the fire. Her teeth flashed white as she worried her lip for a moment. Nick tensed further, trying not to rush her.

"But aside from that aspect, we are strangers forced into one another's company with no idea of each other." She looked directly into his eyes. Beneath her determination to tell him what he wanted to know, uncertainty and melancholy lurked in her eyes. "I know almost nothing about you and you know very little about me. How are we to spend the rest of our lives together?"

"Is *that* what all this is about?" He could scarcely credit it. He would have laughed out loud from relief alone, except for the very serious look on his bride's delicate face.

"Is that not enough, my lord?" One slender brow edged up. A hint of color appeared at the top of her cheeks. "How do you propose we spend our waking hours? The whole of our married life? What do you know about me that makes you think I will make a suitable companion at the breakfast table? Or a fit mother for your heirs?"

Her voice rose and she leaned forward. "What sort of sauce do you prefer with a roast? What dessert do you find revoltingly sweet? Where will we live when we leave Ireland? What business brought you here in the first place? What customs does your family keep during the Christmas holidays?"

He put a finger to her lips, silencing her before she became too wrapped up in her sharp queries. "I concede your point, my lady. You would like us to be better acquainted."

She nodded. A wary look edged her beautiful eyes. "I realize we cannot cram our entire histories into one night, but I would like us to at least begin to be friends. To be able to trust each other."

She could have confessed a past indiscretion or disclosed a hidden malady. Relief sluiced down his spine. She wanted to get to know him. To be his friend. He'd brought her champagne to help alleviate the tension. But if a few minutes of conversation would make things easier, how could he refuse?

They had all night.

And the rest of their lives once he got to the basis of his accidents. Something he very much wished to put paid to, now more than ever.

"Very well, Wife." He put his arm about her and turned her so her back rested against his side and her head against his shoulder. She relaxed into him without resistance. "Let's begin with you telling me more about your family and that remarkable island you all come from."

She told him about her island and Reilly Ship

Works, which provided the bulk of the employment for her neighbors either as shipwrights or sailors. What stood out was the respect given the islanders. She spoke of them all as friends, not her father's employees or dependents, even if he couldn't untangle all the names.

She talked about her sisters-in-law and how strong and independent they were in their own unique ways. How they had to be to make any headway with their willful husbands. It seemed amazing that one wife was a scholar, another ran a lumber mill, and the third a prosperous business painting china. No wonder his bride expected so much of herself and her involvement with the Nightingale Society. He viewed his new brothers-in-law with increased respect as well for their abilities to handle such accomplished wives. A benchmark for himself to meet.

The fire burned low as nearly an hour ticked by on the small mantel clock. The time seemed immaterial. He laughed when she told him some of the trouble she had gotten into trying to compete with her brothers and he understood why she clung to her books and her admiration of Florence Nightingale through the loneliness and fright of her father's illness and recovery so far from the home and friends she loved.

She turned, nestling closer against his chest and running her finger absently along his arm while she talked. He could feel the steady beating of her heart and the pleasure weaving through her answers to the questions he posed. When she finished her tale she grew quiet for a moment. It struck him that he was more than content to sit in silence beside her. How odd. The silence drifted on for a moment as he traced a gentle finger over her brow.

Soft laughter drifted upward toward him and then she turned a twinkling gaze up at him.

"I stayed here with the O'Briens because Mama said it was too wild in America. Between the political tension and the fact that Devin was attacked the moment he walked down the gangplank, she was having none of my accompanying them. She wanted to keep me out of trouble. I offered to stay on Beannacht or to visit with Bryan and Emilynne, but Mama believed a stay with Sheila would be more fun. I don't think she expected that fun to lead to marriage, however."

Acceptance laced her humor. For that he was grateful.

"And what of you? You know far more about my life than you can possibly keep straight until you meet everyone. Yet you've told me nothing of yourself."

Tension tightened along the back of his neck as her attention shifted to him. Her finger ceased its travels on his arm as she waited for him to begin. He missed the intimacy of the gesture.

"I like hunter sauce with roast. I find fruited honey too sweet for my taste. I never thought to marry, so I never considered how I'd spend my time in this state. Jamie and I are here to deal with some financial matters and to buy horses. And he and I usually go off to visit friends at Christmas and adopt the customs of the household."

He answered the questions that began the conversation, quite pleased he remembered so many of them. "Anything more?"

She sighed. "That is a start."

She remained quiet for a moment. The cadence of her heart had not changed. Tension drained from him. He had come out of this conversation relatively easily.

"Tell me about your family. About Jamie's parents and your own. What were they like? What was your last happy memory of them? Then tell me about your nightmares."

"I never speak of those things." He nearly jumped from the settee. Somehow, the warmth of her body pressed against his, his arms encircling her, kept him anchored.

She shifted her head so she could look up at him. The intense green of her eyes bore right through him. "If we are going to trust each other, we must share the darkness as well as the light, Nicholas. We must always tell each other the truth."

Trust? Truth?

He'd narrowly escaped more than a few attempts on his life. He had even less idea who the culprit was after all this time than when he arrived. The last *accident* left him leg-shackled to an Irish temptress who had taken his orderly world and turned it inside out. All those truths tumbled through him.

Trust. She wanted him to trust her. She had placed the rest of her life in his hands, trusting him, and now she wanted a little in return.

He remembered the quiet conversations he had frequently caught his parents having. The small gestures and gentle glances seemed to say so much. They had trusted each other. Before being cut off prematurely, they had built a lifetime based on the intimacy that came with trust. Could he give less to his own wife?

As deeply as he wished to have done with all this talk, he could not fail her so soon after their vows. A quick recitation of the facts should satisfy Meaghan's curiosity and allow him to skim by unscathed from the darkest of the memories.

He took a deep breath. "Jamie has been my ward for these past six years. His parents perished in a fire while he was away at school. They were my guardians after my own parents' deaths. He was fourteen when they died, the same age I had been when I lost mine. We understand each other."

She nodded, but held her peace. Her hand rested on his chest, her soft gaze urging him to continue.

He forced himself to go on. "The last happy memory I have of my parents was a garden party at the O'Briens' nearly fifteen years ago. Afterward we left Limerick for home, sailing on the evening tide. They died later that night, when the ship sank."

"You were on board the ship that sank?" Concern filled her eyes. He turned away as guilt washed through him. Resentment flared. The last thing he needed was her, or anyone, dredging the past for his mistakes. He tamped his annoyance back with an effort. He had dragged her into this marriage. He owed her the answers to her questions, at the very least. Closing his eyes, he nodded. "Aye. I was there."

"Your nightmares." A statement, not a question. She stiffened against him as he dropped his arm from her on one side.

He balled his hand tight, trying to squeeze back the painful tide of his memories. "Yes, that night is the source of my nightmares. I relive my failure over and over."

"*Your* failure?" she whispered.

He opened his eyes. Her gaze held steady with his.

"Yes." He did not soften the fierceness in his answer. "I erased all claims I had to a future, to happiness, that night. I let my parents die. I didn't even try to save them. I only saved myself."

Pain tore through him afresh as his regrets and inadequacies rushed to the surface, pouring out in a long torrent of events from the first explosion to reaching the rocks by the banks of the Shannon. His bride never moved. She didn't say a word. She just listened.

And did not back away from the terror and disgrace he confessed. There was that at least. Something to cling to amidst the darkness from his past. A long breath shuddered out of him as he finished.

She put her hand up to first cup his cheek and then to stroke his head the way she had when he'd been injured. "Everyone deserves to be happy, Nicholas."

Her eyes were luminous in the firelight. "Even you. Especially you."

He would have shaken his head in denial, but her fingers caught his chin. "Your parents' deaths had nothing to do with what you did or did not do. There was a terrible accident—an explosion. You were thrown free. You were injured. And your father told you to swim. *To live.*"

She edged closer in his arms, arms suddenly holding on to her as if she were a piece of timber floating on the river so long ago, buoyant enough to carry him to shore. The painful clash of guilt and hope surging in his chest held him silent.

"Do you honestly think after giving you life, after raising you with all the care and advantages they could, your parents could begrudge the fact you lived? You gave them the satisfaction of knowing their only son lives on. Each breath you take reaffirms their life together."

Meaghan's unique honeysuckle-and-fresh-cut-meadowsweet scent filled him, carrying the promise of tomorrow. Their tomorrows. "Of course they would want your happiness today, just as they did every day of your life when they were alive."

She stretched up and kissed him then, brushing her lips against his. The warmth of her breath whispered over his cheeks and reached straight into his heart.

He gathered her against him and pulled her into a deeper kiss, basking in the light she brought into his darkness. Finding solace in the quickening of her pulse and the eager response of her mouth against his.

Everyone deserves to be happy. Her comforting words raced through him again. He'd do his damnedest to make it true for her, at least.

Eleven

Meaghan sighed against her husband's mouth as his lips claimed hers for a deeper kiss. Her declaration echoed through her. *Everyone deserves to be happy.* She prayed the promise would prove true for both of them.

What began as a comforting gesture intensified, sending familiar waves of white-hot heat rushing through her. She slid her fingers through the hair at the nape of Nicholas's neck and curled closer on his lap. His hands clung to her, sending whorls of pleasure down her spine.

He alternately took her lower lip between his, suckling and releasing, then applying his attentions to her full mouth again. The effect proved mesmerizing. All she could feel was Nicholas. All she could see was Nicholas. All thoughts were of Nicholas. Oranges and mint, colors and laughter. Everything inside her seemed to reach out to accept and return his embrace.

His hand released her shoulder and stroked her hair away from her cheek. He cupped her face, the pad of his thumb stroking her as he pulled away with a shuddering breath. He looked at her, for the span of several heartbeats—his expression fathomless, his eyes glittering in the dying flicker of the fire. She placed her hand over his.

"You are so beautiful," he whispered. He leaned forward and kissed her brow. She felt beautiful. And cherished.

Capturing her lips again, he pulled her higher against his shoulder. He traced the outline of her mouth with his tongue and then ran it over her lips until they parted on her sigh. Her tongue met and matched his stroke for stroke in a dizzying dance that left her breathless but begging for more. Like being spun in circles as a child.

Her hand rested on his chest, clutching the fabric of his shirt between her fingers. She wished it would melt away and allow her to explore the promise of warm flesh and muscle beneath. Scandalous thoughts for a maid, but she was a maid no more. Or soon she would not be.

Freedom flared, catching her unawares. Lying in her husband's arms, the bonds of marriage unshackled her from the strictures of polite behavior. At this moment, she could happily remain locked in his embrace—his lips on hers, their tongues caressing—and no one could gainsay them. The thought was surely more intoxicating than the champagne he'd intended to offer her.

His hand laced through her hair and he tugged her head back, gently arching her neck. His breath brushed warm across her skin as he kissed a path down her throat. Each brush of his lips or tongue seemed to make the room fade farther away.

All that remained in the world was Nicholas. And he was more than enough for her.

He stopped his leisurely progress to lavish attention on the pulse point at the base of her neck, drawing her into his mouth and grazing her with his teeth. Great waves of color coursed through her and she heard herself moan somewhere far in the distance. She clutched his shirt tighter, the soft linen anchoring her to the moment and the man.

He untied her robe and flicked it open. She shivered as his fingers skimmed her tender breasts exposed by the gesture. He traced his lips along the ridge of her nightgown, lingering in the same spot where he had frozen the last time they had been alone in the dark.

This time, instead of pushing her away, he pulled her closer, his breath fanning heat across her skin and deep into her core.

"Nicholas." She exhaled his name on a wondrous sigh, tangling her fingers in his hair as she arched her back.

He shifted and sought her lips, plunging his tongue deep into her mouth. He tasted of winter apples and raw passion—a heady combination that filled her but left her wanting more. She met and matched each thrust of his tongue with her own, wanting to give him some measure of the amazing joy pouring through her with his every touch.

He cupped her breast through the thin cotton of her nightgown, circling and teasing the taut nipple with his palm. Pleasure rushed through her and she strained against his caress, seeking more. She wished the barrier of her nightgown gone, flamed away by the fire raging inside her. He wrestled the buttons on her nightgown and finally bared her skin to the cool night air and his hot fingers.

Releasing her lips, he shifted her in his arms until he cradled her full on his lap. The evidence of his desire for her jutted hard against the softness of her hip. He kissed her throat again and again, traveling downward until he captured her nipple with his lips.

He sucked her into his mouth and teased her tender tip with his tongue, circling and flicking and sending showers of sparks through her to light flames deep within her very soul. She clutched his shoulders and strained against him, trying to get nearer, closer. She was pliant as wax in his hands, under his lips.

He explored her, teasing, fondling, and caressing her with his fingers and tongue while she gave herself over to the spirals of desire he drew from her. He turned her slightly in his arms and gathered her other breast deep into his mouth, suckling her with a pressure that fanned the flames higher.

She fumbled with the buttons on his shirt, wanting, needing to touch him. To give back to him some measure of the passion pouring through her with each tantalizing stroke of his hands on her flesh. He tugged open the last of the buttons and pulled her up for another soul-searing kiss while her hand finally found purchase on the smooth plane of his chest.

She trailed her fingers along the line of his collar while his tongue traced the edge of her teeth. His skin felt hot and he growled low in his throat as her thumb caressed the pulse she found beating at its base. Her breast brushed against his hard muscles. The thrill of the contact made her gasp.

He pulled back, releasing her lips. There was

enough light from the lamp on the washstand to
form a halo through his blond hair. *Laoch grian,*
her sun warrior come to claim his prize. He
smoothed a stray lock of her hair away from her
cheek and breast and looked down at her for a
breathless moment.

"So incredibly beautiful. I am a lucky man,
Meaghan."

His husky admission tumbled through her.
He'd trusted her with his past. He called her
beautiful. That he wanted her was plain. It was
a start.

"I am ready to be your wife, Nicholas."

"Soon, my lady. Very soon." He smiled, an intimate gesture that added sparkle to his eyes and
touched her heart.

He bent again to catch her lips, stealing her
breath with the gentle thoroughness of his lips
on hers, stealing all thought save the sensuous
blaze he ignited and fanned with his every touch.
The arm and hand he used to cradle her to him
both supported and freed her, as if she were a
ship anchoring in safe harbor, but still free to
float with the ebb and flow of the tide.

He turned his attention back to her breasts,
supping from first one, then the other. Beneath
his open shirt, she spiraled her fingers over his
muscles and stroked his shoulder and upper arm,
reveling in the rugged strength she discovered.

His free hand moved along her side to capture
her leg. Her skin burned through the nightgown
before he swept it from his path. With excruci-
ating slowness, he stroked up her inner calf, pulling a response from farther up and far deeper
inside.

He parted her knees and continued his slow

caressing journey up her leg, all the while lavishing his attention on her breasts as he teased and suckled them. She kissed the top of his head where he bent over her. The scent of oranges, mint, and man filled her.

When his hand finally reached the curls at the joining of her legs she gasped into his ear, surprised not by the contact, but by how eagerly she had been anticipating it. He kissed a path to the base of her neck and centered his attentions there once again, laving and nibbling on her throat while his hand remained still.

Slowly his thumb began to circle, finding a hidden pleasure spot in his quest. Heat and lightning jolted through her, white and intense, as he rubbed and caressed her so intimately.

He slid further down, slipping his fingers through the moist folds of her flesh. Never before had she felt so incredibly treasured. Never before had she felt anything like the feverish desire her husband blazed to life in her.

He took her lips again in another long, drugging kiss. His breath blew hot on her cheeks. She was pliant in his arms, open to his every touch. He slipped one finger inside her and swallowed her gasp with his mouth, intense pleasure flowing at his intimate invasion.

His rigid flesh pulsed against her side as she tensed, branding her with its heat even through their remaining clothes. His tongue teased her mouth, flicking lightly and retreating while his hand remained still and allowed her to adjust to his invasion.

Gradually she relaxed and found herself parrying her husband's tongue with her own. She kissed him back full measure, and his hand picked up the rhythm of their tongues—in and out, in and out. She moved her hips to better meet each thrust.

A second of his fingers joined the first, stretching her further. The new fullness added more urgency to her response. She wanted, needed more.

She moved her hips against his hand, gaining the rhythm as he stroked her faster and deeper, in and out. His thumb still teased her pleasure spot. She pushed against his shoulder, urging him to continue, demanding he persist, although she did not understand what or why.

She only knew that in this one moment she was his—body and soul—and she prayed the moment would last an eternity.

With a shattering force well beyond the power of a full gale, colored lights seemed to burst through her, at once spiraling up and carrying her with them.

She broke free of his kisses long enough to gulp a breath.

"Nicholas," she managed; then she disappeared, lost in the undulating waves flowing over and through her.

Cradled in her husband's arms, listening to the steady beat of his heart while he pressed kisses into her hair, Meaghan drifted back to herself. To a new, more aware self. Her entire being hummed with fresh magic and wonder. She edged her fingers up to rub along the soft bristles of his chin. She exhaled a long sigh of contentment and pulled away enough to look at him.

He smiled at her. His lips spread wide beneath her fingers. Nicholas Mansfield, Lord Ashton,

her husband, sat half dressed with a disheveled
Irish lass in his lap, grinning in the dark. She
wanted to thank him for what he had just shared
with her. Would that be considered proper? She
giggled, here in his arms what was proper did
not seem to matter in the least. "So which is—"

"Only the beginning," he finished for her. "I
believe it is time we retire to bed, Lady Ashton."

He kissed her temple one more time and then
rose to his feet, keeping her cradled close in his
arms. She wrapped her arms around his neck
while he carried her the short distance to the
bed. She was quite sure the air was cool now that
the fire had died, but all she could feel was the
heat of her husband's body.

He released her knees to let her legs slide
down to the floor. His hands rested on her waist.
She turned to face him, wondering what she
should do next. Hopping onto the bed and bur-
rowing under the quilt the way Sheila would do
late at night when she came to share confidences
did not seem quite right.

Nicholas gazed into his bride's glittering green
eyes still wide and dewy with the passion he had
wrung from her. Meaghan's incredibly sensual re-
sponses to his lovemaking had nearly unmanned
him as she shivered her release there in his arms.
Desire raged through him, but he had deliber-
ately held himself back, wanting to ensure her
pleasure, her readiness.

Now, with Meaghan's arms wrapped around
his neck and her fresh honeysuckle-and-meadowsweet scent filling him, doubt touched him.
He'd no desire to add hurting one so young and
innocent to his failures. The flame from the
lamp on the washstand cast shadows that loomed

around them, like the guilt and horror that usually haunted his nights.

What was it she had said? *Everyone deserves to be happy. Even you.*

The light reflecting in her eyes as she looked up at him with patient expectation told him she still believed that to be true. And for tonight he would accept her faith and make it his own. He prayed she was right. For this night, and for many more to come.

He pulled her close and bent, taking her lips in a kiss meant to seal this unspoken contract with himself. She flowed into him, pressing herself against his length. Her tongue teased the lower rim of his lip and he drank deep from the promises he tasted on her mouth.

The edges of her nightgown gaped open against his unbuttoned shirt pressing folds of cool cotton and warm supple flesh against his chest. His fingers tangled in her robe as it flowed off her shoulders.

He pulled away and released her. "There is more than enough to come between us, Meaghan. Past and future. I would see all of you now."

She nodded. The edge of her tongue peeked out, moistening her lips still full from being thoroughly kissed. She kept her eyes focused on his. Her chin rose a notch and she stepped back, shrugging out of the robe at the same time. The gossamer cotton whispered to the floor and exposed the alabaster skin of her delicate shoulders and lithe arms. He sucked in a slow breath as everything in him tightened in anticipation and appreciation.

A hesitant smile edged her mouth as she

reached up her hands to part the open gown. Her rings flashed in the light. She stretched the opening wide to pass over her shoulders, and exposed her breasts to him, rosy tipped and enticing.

His breath froze in his chest as the garment sighed down the length of his bride.

She was incredible—more so than he had even imagined possible. The light gleamed on her skin. The flushed hue of his recent attentions blended with the ivory-white glow of her complexion. Her ebony hair flowed down her back, contrasting and highlighting her color as it wisped dark curls around her trim waist and dainty elbows. Her hips flared gently atop long, graceful legs. Her stomach was flat, right down to the dark curls at the juncture of her thighs.

She stood silent, but not disconcerted, accepting his perusal without comment. Shadows caressed her curves and delved into hidden recesses he longed to explore.

"You are beautiful." He could think of nothing more apt to tell her, nothing more eloquent. The usual flowery phrases of courtship, of seduction, seemed unfit to even utter at this moment. To this woman. "I am a lucky man, indeed. Blessed, even."

At this last admission, a wry smile quirked the corners of her mouth, reaching up to add more sparkle to her eyes. He held out his hands. She took them and stepped into his embrace.

The kiss they shared stayed tender, filled with the sweet taste of expectation. Her lips were soft and inviting. Her breasts pressed against him with tantalizing resilience. His fingers laced tight with hers as the tips of their tongues frisked together at the union of their mouths. He growled low in his throat, a primal sound of possession welling from deep within him to claim her.

He released her fingers to run his hands through her hair. She slid her hands up his chest, sending arcs of lightning—white-hot and searing—through him with the contact. Sucking her tongue deep into his mouth, he sifted his fingers through her silken tresses. Her skin was warm and yielding. He pulled her closer to him and skimmed his hands down her spine and back up her sides. She pressed intimately against his erection. The wool of his trousers rasped hard between them.

Her fingers edged up to claim both sides of his jaw. She pulled back from the kiss. "I would see all of you, too, Nicholas."

Her whisper fanned across his cheeks and set the fire already burning in him to a blazing roar. She skimmed her hands across his collar and tugged his shirt down his arms. Cool air streamed over his back as his wife planted hot kisses on his jawline and down his throat while she gripped his shoulders. Her nipples teased his chest.

He drew in a sharp breath as she tormented the soft spot by his collarbone with her teeth, sucking on the flesh there as he had done to her. He moved his hands in circles up her waist to fondle her breasts. Her nipples were tight as he circled them with his thumbs. He kneaded the pliant softness with his palms and then slid his hands down her satiny skin to cup her bottom and pull her even tighter against him.

She moved her torturing pleasure to the other side of his neck and massaged her way down his sides until her hands delved into his waistband at his hips. The heat of her fingers so close to his engorged flesh sent tremors of fierce passion through him. He felt quite certain he would burst at any moment, like some untried lad about to taste his first woman.

"Enough waiting," he rasped and scooped her back into his arms. With a quick kiss to her startled lips, he deposited her gently on the bed and stood back.

His breath caught for a second as he looked at her stretched across the coverings, naked and awaiting him. The dark velvet made her skin almost luminous. He ached to be one with her.

She kept her gaze fixed on him expectantly and smiled, a soft, trusting expression that shot pure desire right through him. This amazingly beautiful woman was his. He desperately wanted to be worthy of her trust. To be worthy of her.

He loosened the fastenings on his trousers and stepped out of them. His flesh jutted forward, brazenly eager to claim his bride with no doubts or uncertainty. He allowed her a few seconds before he sought her gaze. She studied him in silence and then looked up. Her expression betrayed no fear, but he read hesitation in the stiff line of her shoulders and the stilling of her breath.

He looked down. "Don't tell me," he teased. "You have three brothers and—"

"I never saw my brothers thus," she interrupted. The spark of humor relaxed her shoulders, though.

He joined her on the velvet counterpane, lying beside her and cupping her face in his hand. Their gazes locked, and he stroked her face with his thumb for a moment, granting them both the increasing power of anticipation soon to be satisfied.

She reached her hand over to twine around his shoulder, then drew herself up to kiss him. Her lips were soft and sweet, tasting of stars and laughter and warm desire. He moved his hand down to her breast and cupped it, feeling her expectant quiver with his whole body.

He left her lips, to press kisses down her slender throat and along her shoulder. Her breath rippled hot on his temple as he squeezed her breast and teased the nipple by rubbing and pinching it between his thumb and finger. She arched her back and drew in a quick breath when he took her in his mouth and suckled hard. He grazed her tip with his teeth and kissed a trail from one peak to the other, repeating his treatment.

Her hand stroked down his side, pulling him closer. Her fingers sent whorls of white heat through him as they moved over his skin. Her breath quickened as he transferred his attention from one breast to the other and back until her nipples were swollen and tight with passion.

His arousal pressed hard against her outer thigh. He fought the urge to move too quickly. He wanted to bring her back to the edge, so this first time would be as satisfying as possible for her.

He kissed his way back to her face and took her lips again, demanding and hard. Her mouth clung to his in urgent response. He skimmed his hand over her smooth abdomen and dipped his fingers between her thighs, stroking her.

She was hot and slick. Her lips trembled

against his lips and her hips rose up to greet his
invasion. He could take her now, but he wanted
her at fever pitch when he entered her for the
first time.

He slipped two fingers inside her and
thumbed her sensitive nub. She moaned her
greeting as her hips rose again to urge him further in. Her legs spread apart to better accommodate his hand. He plunged his tongue deep
into her mouth, caressing hers as he dipped into
her core.

He pushed his fingers in and out of her and
circled her sensitive nether flesh with increasing
intensity. Her body moved in cadence with his
attentions—a sinuous and sensual dance carrying
the carnal rhythm straight back to his soul.

Her lips worked on his, while her tongue laved
his own. Her fingers dug into his back as she
clung to him and urged him on. He could feel
her response building from deep within her and
knew he was near to bursting himself. But still
he held back.

She twisted her head and broke free of his
mouth, gasping for air, for release. Her neck and
back arched up, thrusting her breasts toward
him.

"Nicholas. Nicholas," she breathed.

It was time.

Panting, he kissed her neck where her jaw met
her ear. She trembled beneath him, more than
ready. He slid his fingers out of her wet center
and captured her breast with his hand. The scent
of meadowsweet and honeysuckle melded with
pure Meaghan poured through him in an erotic
torrent.

He thumbed her swollen tip and moved himself between her legs. His arousal eagerly nudged her damp curls while her hands slipped to his waist. She looked up at him, desire blazing in her eyes.

"Make me your wife, Nicholas," she whispered fiercely, her voice husky with the passion he had wrought in her.

The effort of holding himself back for so long, of fighting his lust for this woman both tonight and for the past weeks, held him speechless. She sprawled voluptuously beneath him, primed and eager. He was more than ready to take her, to make her his wife. The sheer majesty of the moment and the beauty of this woman took his breath away.

He spread her legs further as he guided himself into her center. She was slick and hot. Incredibly tight. He put his hands on her hips and pulled her forward as he pushed. She drew in a deep breath and tensed as he moved in, feeling her delicate barrier with his tip.

"Don't fight it, sweetheart," he rasped. Satisfaction beckoned after all this time, like a feast to a starving man. He might be able to slow the process, to ease it for her, but he would not be able to stop now.

With a speed that propelled a gasp from him she rose up to capture his lips and impaled herself deeply on his shaft with the same motion. He swallowed her cry and held her close, waiting for the shock and pain to subside. She held him close and eased back onto the coverlet, keeping her lips pressed to his as he followed her down, supporting them both with his arms.

Her fingers clung to his shoulders; then gradually she relaxed their hold. Her breathing deep-

ened and her lips parted beneath his. His flesh
pulsed deep within her and she edged her
tongue out to run its tip over his mouth in a
tingling circle.

Slowly he began to move, unable to hold back
any longer, unable to do anything but surrender
to the primal beat of his need for release. His
need for all of this woman.

He shifted position and tilted her hips to better fit him. Her breasts rubbed against him as
he moved faster now—pulling out a little, then
going forward. He kissed her neck and withdrew,
then drove farther into her still. She was tight
around him, gripping him with her hot, moist
core.

Her back arched slowly, thrusting her breasts
higher, closer. He captured her in his mouth and
suckled her, laving her succulent nipple with his
tongue and pulling her back into the dance joining their bodies.

A few more thrusts and she picked up the
rhythm, meeting him again and again. Pulling
him deeper into her very center. All he could
feel was Meaghan below him, surrounding him.
Within his very soul.

He sank himself into her, mindless of anything
except his need for her. Her hands dug into him
as she urged him on and strained against him.
In and out, in and out—a dance as old as time
and as new as their union.

She was soft and hot and wet as she moved
under him. He was hard and straining as he
drove into her. He could not get close enough,
could not move deep enough. He released her
breast and pulled her knees up to get closer to

her still. Her head moved from side to side and her back arched higher.

"Nicholas. Oh Nicholas." She cried out his name as her body undulated beneath him and honey poured from her womb in a rush.

Everyone deserves to be happy. Especially you.

With a shout of triumphant relief, he poured his seed into her, shuddering over and over, his hips pumping against hers. Then he collapsed against her, following her into a night filled with shooting stars.

It was still dark when Meaghan awoke. The even rise and fall of her husband's chest against her back and the tickle of his breath on her neck told her he still slept. One of his arms circled her waist, holding her securely against him.

Outside, the sounds of a city beginning its day stirred with the clop of horse hoofs and rattle of wheels on the cobblestones echoing up from the street with increasing frequency. The oil in the lamp was nearly gone, its flames reduced to an edge of light.

How different she felt this morning, compared to only yesterday. Today she felt wonderfully languid and content. Her body thrummed with new awareness, a satisfaction running deeper than physical gratification. Truth be told, she was a little sore from stretching in unaccustomed ways. Sore, and a trifle sticky.

She shifted against him, solid and warm behind her. He did not stir. There was something else. She felt strangely whole, complete in a way she had never before imagined possible. All because of her husband. She exhaled with unfettered appreciation.

Nicholas thought her beautiful. Perhaps he did not wholly regret the hasty declaration that had brought them to this point. He had certainly been tender in his affections and generous with his concern for her pleasure last night.

When he'd told her he felt lucky—Blessed even—her heart had melted and at least for that moment, in this room, she believed they were both Blessed. Her heritage had been prodding her to a future with this man.

She eased out from under his arm and left the bed long enough to wash herself. Before turning the wick down and extinguishing the lamp, she looked over to the bed and the man sleeping there.

He was beautiful. His blond hair was tousled and his sculpted cheek buried in the pillow. Bristles studded his chiseled chin and the hands that had caressed and fondled her with such care rested on the bed linens. He slept with the relaxed breathing of a child. There were no nightmares, so far this night, to startle him from his slumber. And if they came, she would be there to soothe them from his brow.

She lowered the wick, plunging the room into darkness, then slid back into bed with her husband.

"What were you doing?" he asked her sleepily as she settled the velvet coverlet back over them both. The scent of oranges and mint mixed with his manly musk greeted her.

"Watching you sleep," she answered as he drew her into his arms again and settled her atop his chest. The steady thump of his heart filled her.

"You should sleep, too," he said, his breath tickling her scalp. His hand softly stroked the back of her shoulder. "This has been an exceptional night."

"Indeed." She nodded, rubbing her cheek on the warm, muscled hollow just under his shoulder. They lay entwined in the dark for several minutes, still and content. She couldn't sleep, too aware of the power and passion coursing just beneath her fingertips to rest.

"Well, my lady," he said, breaking the silence, "did our night measure up to the expectations raised by your Aunt Edna's enlightenments on marital relations?" Quiet humor laced his question as he settled his arms closer around her and pressed a kiss into her hair.

"Well, my lord . . ." she edged her fingers through the soft curls on his chest. "We *are* only just wed. You'll have years to perfect your craft before all hope is lost."

He laughed then, with a rumble rolling straight through him to shake his shoulders. The first genuine laugh she had ever heard from this man.

He lifted her chin in the dark. "Well, then, if practice makes perfect, I believe I have some studies to pursue."

Twelve

Pa-ping. Pa-ping. Pa-ping.

The small china clock on the mantelpiece chimed the next quarter hour, breaking the pervasive silence in the dining room.

A quiet dinner at home—Jamie's suggestion for the two newlyweds before he left to dine with Sheila and her parents.

That is, if her husband ever returned home to join her.

Meaghan released a sigh as she awaited Nicholas's appearance in the small dining room at Bryan's town house. It was certainly quiet. She would almost welcome Jamie's return. At least his presence at the dinner table might fill up any empty spaces between hers and Nicholas's conversation.

She shifted on the buff-colored silk settee she occupied. What on earth would they find to discuss at every meal for a lifetime? Surely they would find a time, and probably not too far from now, where they'd said everything they had to say and all their meals would be as silent as the room at this moment.

Silver polished to a pristine glow lay on snowy

linen napkins. The candelabra was lit. Bryan's plain white china decorated the table along with some fresh-cut flowers the housekeeper had brought home with her marketing to *brighten up the place*, as she put it.

Mrs. McFee was right about that. The place could use some brightening. Bryan's spartan furnishings befit his former bachelor's existence and had most likely dovetailed with the preferences of the young solicitor who rented from him until recently. But the rooms of the tidy house were rather more functional than decorative.

Like the settees Bryan had in nearly every room. Heat stole over her cheeks as she remembered how handy the one in the master chamber had proved only last night.

She'd asked her brother about them during one of her stays here with Mama. He'd shrugged and explained that he liked to stretch out to read his briefs and contracts, but he didn't like to discommode the McFees into keeping fires in every room. He would just settle himself in whichever location seemed most convenient based on his plans for the evening—dining room, bedroom, study.

She chuckled. Her mirth echoed hollow in the room. No one wanted to discomfit the McFees. The housekeeper and her butler husband had come with the house when Bryan acquired it. The couple's routines were the household routines, or so Bryan used to warn their mother when she suggested modifications.

Mrs. McFee had always gone out of her way to indulge Master Bryan's sister, and she had welcomed her in the kitchen when she had gone down to visit. But she had solicited no advice regarding the assigning of rooms to Jamie and the valet when they arrived after luncheon. Nor had she consulted Meaghan on tonight's dinner menu.

Meaghan picked at the lace on her sleeve and smoothed the flounce of the hunter green taffeta dress she had chosen to wear. With time weighing heavy on her hands, she'd spent a great deal of it choosing this dress and arranging her hair before deciding to pull it into a soft, matronly knot at the base of her skull. What did other new brides do to fill their days?

She'd been left to her own devices most of the day. Nicholas had left her in the bed to sleep this morning, leaving with only the barest kiss to her cheek before he disappeared. Meeting with some horse traders, according to Randall. Or off to visit an investment banker, as Jamie had offered. It was evidently none of her business how her husband occupied himself. The progress she thought they were making last night wilted in the light of day.

She couldn't even spend her day as she had at Aunt Edna's, going on calls or visiting the lending library. Not until after the reception the O'Briens were planning to introduce Lord and Lady Ashton to society.

Meaghan tightened her fingers together and paced over to the windows. Tears stung the backs of her eyes and burned in her throat as she twisted her rings. So much for a happily-ever-after heralded by the fabled Reilly Blessing. She'd never felt so miserable in her life. The truth was, she had snared the Curse for herself.

And for Nicholas, too.

Nothing about this marriage proved to be the way it was supposed to be. She swiped a wayward tear away from her cheek and blew out another long sigh. Questions she didn't have answers for churned through her.

Why had he married her?

Surely there would have been some other way out of the debacle they found themselves in. The look on Uncle Gill's face when he'd found her and Nick together, locked in a seeming embrace, shuddered through her.

"Meaghan."

She started at the sound of Nick's voice and turned to find him standing in the doorway. He'd removed the jacket to his suit and unbuttoned the top button on his shirt, revealing the strong column of his throat.

She swallowed as the previous night flashed through her mind. She could almost taste his warm skin, feel the tender pressure of his lips against her mouth, her breast, and . . . other places. Heat washed over her cheeks and pooled low in her belly.

Whatever else lay between them there was that. But could passion be enough to last them in the years to come?

"Hullo, Nicholas."

He strode toward her, his face shadowed as the sun began its lazy dip toward the horizon. She wished she had lit the lamps on the wall.

"I didn't intend to be this long. I apologize." He reached for her hand. She slid her cold fingers into his. Flesh against flesh. Desire rippled through her. The longing to ask him to make love to her again welled from deep inside her.

"I understand." No, she didn't. Or at least she

wished she didn't. He seemed willing to make
room for her in his bed, but the rest of his
life . . . ?

"Do you?" He captured her chin with his fingers and tipped her face up to his. "You look
vexed, as well you ought, Meaghan."

"I—" What could she say? I don't think you
should have married me? Make love to me because I ache for your touch? Her thoughts
clashed in chaotic disharmony.

"What?" Annoyance tinged his question. She
couldn't blame him. She was acting like a vapid
fool.

"Nothing is wrong. Shall we eat?" She stepped
around him. "I've had them keep our food
warm, although Mrs. McFee mentioned she
hoped we would be more prompt for meals."
She tugged at the bellpull.

"Meaghan." He started to round the table and
she moved over to the doorway, opening the
door in time to greet Bryan's housekeeper.

"Here ye are, Lord Ashton. Mr. McFee said
you had come straight here without even changing fer dinner." Mrs. McFee bustled in followed
in quick succession by her daughters, Dora and
Darla. They set the food on the table with quiet
efficiency.

Nick watched in silence, merely lifting an eyebrow when Meaghan met his gaze. She glanced
away. Mrs. McFee was outspoken, but a kinder
woman she'd never met. Bryan said that's why
everyone tolerated her commanding ways.

"I've made yer favorites, mistress. I do hope
ye still like them. Just let us know if there is anything else we can bring ye. And pull when ye're

ready fer dessert." The housekeeper bustled around the table.

"Lady Ashton and I would appreciate a little privacy. Will you excuse us?" Nick told Mrs. McFee in what Meaghan had begun to think of as his aristocratic tone.

Lady Ashton. The title still didn't seem to fit, especially in relation to herself. If there was anyone in the entire history of her family less suited to being a *lady* surely it would be her.

"Certainly, yer lordship." The housekeeper bobbed her head. "Come along now, Dora, Darla."

The housekeeper bustled out with her minions, closing the door behind her and closeting Nick and Meaghan alone once more.

The clock *pa-pinged* on the mantelpiece, chiming the hour.

"Shall we?" Nick moved close. His unique orange-mint scent filled the air. He held out his hand and she was forced to place her own into it again. The touch of his skin against hers proved maddening, like having a hundred tiny little flames dancing through her blood.

She fanned herself. It was much too warm in here.

He drew her to the table and seated her politely before taking his own chair. The McFees had broken with proper decorum and seated them beside each other instead of at opposite ends of the table. More of Jamie's romantic machinations?

The scent of roasted chicken and browned potatoes seasoned with rosemary wafted up from the plates Dora and Darla had fixed for them.

Her stomach growled audibly. She winced. Lady Ashton, indeed.

Nick poured her a glass of wine and she sipped it gratefully. The fruity bouquet teased her nose and slipped down her throat.

"Meaghan, we need to continue our conversation from last night."

She almost spit out her mouthful of wine. She swallowed and coughed. "Our conversation?"

The substance of their chat last night had burned away in the flames he'd ignited in her with his lovemaking. They smoldered still in his presence. A half hour ago she could have related the matters verbatim, but half an hour ago he had not been in the room.

"Yes." He topped her glass again before sipping his own.

She took a bite of chicken so she wouldn't have to answer. Mrs. McFee was right. It was one of her favorites.

"This marriage was not what either one of us expected. But I have thought about it a great deal this day."

Her stomach twisted and she wished she hadn't eaten the chicken. "Really?"

"I see no reason we should not deal well with each other, even given the circumstances."

"The circumstances?"

"Yes. Once I finish my business here in Ireland, it was my intention to go home to Suffolk. There is much to be tended there, including seeing to a good match for Jamie. . . ."

What a stilted conversation they were having. She wanted to weep. This was not what she had seen of marriage. Her parents were the best of friends, filling whatever room they occupied with love and laughter. As for her brothers' marriages—Quin and Siannon, Bryan and Emilynne, Devin and Maggie—there could be no question of the love they shared. It was plain in each couples' eyes when they looked at each other.

But then she and Nick had not married for love. For lust perhaps, but not for love.

Cursed, indeed.

". . . I know you are used to traveling. Perhaps you would like to go abroad?" His words cut through her. Did he propose they go their separate ways? And if so, could she stop him from seeing how devastated that would make her? Surely that future was not what he proposed.

"Whatever you would like to do is fine with me," she managed as pain twisted through her. Why did it hurt so much to face the distances still between them despite last night's intimacies? The chicken and potatoes blurred as tears stung again.

She swallowed more wine and tried to quash the desire to weep until there were no more tears left inside her.

"Meaghan, come here." Nick pushed back from the table and held out his hand to her.

She pushed out of her chair and crossed the short distance between them. He settled his hands at her waist and pulled her down into his lap. The feel of his thighs against her own rushed the memory of him settled between them and . . .

"Meaghan?"

She yanked her wayward thoughts back from the path they were wont to travel. "Aye?"

"What is wrong?" He enunciated each word, and his tone demanded an answer.

Heat rushed through her entire body in a hot mingling of embarrassment and desire. "I . . . can't seem to stop thinking about it."

He blinked. "About what? Where we are going to live?"

"No." She shook her head and wished she could sink straight through the floor.

"Then what?"

"Last night."

Last night. Two little words, but they poured a rush of heat through Nick so fast it left him dizzy.

He remembered every burning second of his bride in his arms last night. The memories had distracted him nearly all day. Meaghan squirmed in his lap, her sweet little bottom rubbing over his almost instant erection. The impulse to raise her skirts and satisfy them both right there taunted him. He caught back a groan and stilled her movements by grasping her hips.

She gasped.

"Is *that* what is bothering you?"

"Aye." She spoke so softly he almost couldn't hear her admission.

"Why?" Had he been too demanding? Was she trying to entreat him to be more circumspect?

She squirmed again. Such actions would not gain her that particular wish. His breath hissed out of him and she stopped, concern knitting her dark brows as she glanced at him.

"Because I . . ." Color washed her fair cheeks. Her green gaze traveled his face. "I want . . ."

He slid his fingers up over her back and watched her eyelids drop closed as she arched her back beneath his touch. Satisfaction lanced him. She wanted him. Even if she did not yet possess the courage to say the words aloud.

"You want what, Meaghan?" His fingers inched up against the back of her neck. He stroked her skin and she shivered. Then he urged her face toward his until he could taste her wine-fruited breath against his tongue.

"What do you want, my sweet wife?"

"This," she told him softly and then her lips were against his, tentative and questing as if at any moment she might shy away from him.

He released the growl building inside him and slid his fingers into her dark hair, tilting her mouth against his and forcing a deeper pressure. She moaned as he traced her lips with his tongue. So soft.

Her lips parted for him and he slid his tongue inside, tasting the welcome she hid in her depths. The promise of new delights laced the lingering echo of the passion they had already shared. She sighed and looped her arms around his neck, curving her body against his chest.

A far better greeting than the stiff politeness she had faced him with upon his arrival. Far, far better.

"Meaghan." He released her lips to taste her throat, his hand questing over the buttons at her bodice. "Perhaps the meal can wait a bit longer."

"Aye." Her breath fanned his cheeks while her ready agreement sent new waves of desire racing through him.

Her buttons popped open for him, revealing the tempting bounty beneath. He pressed his lips against the fresh soft skin of her breasts above the low neckline of her chemise and corset. Desire tightened painfully inside him.

Hot blood thundered in his veins as she shivered under his touch. He laved her softness, suckling the flesh he'd laid bare.

"Nicholas." His name on her lips, in a husky tone of arousal, was one of the most erotic things he had ever heard. The taste of her he'd indulged last night only deepened the lust he had for this woman. His wife.

A bell rang frantically in the distance, but all he could think of was her. On his lap, in his mouth, and very soon beneath him.

"Lord Ashton? Lord Ashton? You'd best come at once. There is someone here," a voice called through the hall door. Meaghan started in his arms.

Damnation. At least McFee had taken the hint and was being as discreet as possible.

"Open the damned door, man. Can't you see he's hurt?" Randall's voice sounded from the stoop.

"Set yourself to rights, Lady Ashton. It appears we have company." Nicholas set Meaghan on her feet with a quick kiss to her pert nose. A deep feeling of unease settled in his gut.

Her hair had come loose from its matronly knot and her eyes glowed a deep green. Would there ever be a time he could ravish his wife in peace? He caught back a sigh of regret and turned toward the door as she buttoned the top button of her bodice and smoothed the dishevelment from her long dark hair.

Tonight. Nick wrenched the door open as the decibel level in the hallway reached new heights. "What is going on out here, Randall?"

"Sir." Randall looked like a man in need of a lifeline. He stood inches from the doorway with

Gill O'Brien more than half slumped against his shoulder. O'Brien was pale, and there was blood seeping down his fingers.

"Bring him in here." Nick opened the door wider. "Meaghan, I need your help. What the devil happened?"

"Uncle Gill." Dismay sounded in her cry as she reached Nick's side. "He's bleeding."

"Yes, mum." Randall nodded at her and then his gaze met Nick's. Nick could read the unspoken question. Was he free to speak in front of her?

He shook his head. "Keep it brief."

"Oh, Uncle Gill." Meaghan pulled Nick out of the doorway. "Over here on the settee, Randall, please." She moved ahead of the ex-sergeant-turned-valet.

"Have Mrs. McFee fetch me hot water and several clean cloths. Oh, and I may need a sewing kit." She nibbled her lip as the valet bobbed his head and disappeared back down the hallway. Gill collapsed onto the settee with a moan.

"Are you sure you can handle this, Meaghan? I thought you said blood—"

"I seem to have gotten over that weakness," she cut him off. "At least when I am concerned for someone I love. What happened?"

She looked first at Gill, then Randall who had just returned. Gill closed his eyes. He looked extremely pale and drawn.

"An accident, my lady," Randall supplied.

An accident. Not very likely. The wariness in Randall's gaze confirmed his suspicion. This had been no accident. Thank heaven the man could think fast on his feet. The more of this he could keep from Meaghan, the better.

"What kind of accident?" She tossed the question over her shoulder as she bent down to examine O'Brien. "Uncle Gill, can you hear me?"

He groaned in response.

"Oh, where is Mrs. McFee?" She looked back at Nick. "Could you take off his coat?"

"Aye, my lady." Randall stepped to the task.

She rose from her stance by the settee to give the large man room to accomplish what she'd asked. Her worried gaze collided with Nick's. She searched his eyes for a moment.

"I'll go see what is keeping Mrs. McFee. See if you can get him to drink some of the wine." Her words were soft. He sensed it was not what she had intended to say. There were questions lurking in his wife's lovely green eyes. Inquiries he had no doubt she would make before the night ran its course. The only question in his mind is how much he dared answer.

"Go then." He nodded.

She disappeared out the door, leaving him alone with Randall and the semiconscious Gill. Best not to waste this precious privacy they'd been granted.

"What happened?"

"Sir." Randall grunted as he lifted Gill high enough to pull the barrister's jacket and waistcoat out from under him. O'Brien moaned. "I was watching the office, as we had discussed. Nothing untoward had happened. Just Mr. O'Brien in his office tidying up paperwork. He turned out the lamps, getting ready to leave. I'd about decided it was time to leave myself. I'm not sure what made me stay the extra few moments I did."

"Instinct," Nick offered, gratified for at least

the dozenth time in as many days that he had happened upon the ex-soldier when he did.

"Aye, my lord, most likely." Randall offered a slight grin. "I watched him turn out the last lamp. The office plunged into darkness. I found myself wondering just how he would manage to exit the office with no light. Then there was a scuffle from the darkness. I couldn't see a blasted thing. But I could hear. There was shouting and then a shot."

The jacket slipped to the floor, revealing a stain of blood spreading over O'Brien's shoulder.

Nick glanced over his shoulder, expecting Meaghan's return at any moment. "And?"

"I went in. In the dark I could barely see. I stumbled into someone who cursed me roundly and shoved me." Randall deftly stripped the Irish barrister of his gray-and-yellow waistcoat as he talked. "I've no idea who did this. Whoever it was must have entered the office and lain in wait. Footsteps rang behind me. The devil disappeared back the way I had come. But I'd a feeling he'd already done what he set out to do. I expected to find this gentleman dead."

He balled the striped vest and pressed it to the wound to staunch any possible recurrence of the flow of blood from all the undressing. "The ball seems to have passed right through his shoulder. He was lucky."

"Damned lucky. You were right to bring him here. We can keep the whole incident quieter this way."

Randall straightened from his crouch at O'Brien's side. "My lord, it was not I who decided to come to you."

"It wasn't?"

"No. It was—"

"Me." O'Brien rasped the word, ending on a loud groan.

"O'Brien—"

"Figured if you were going to do me in I might as well shorten the wait." Sarcasm edged the barrister's pain-racked tone.

"I see." Nick arched an eyebrow. He didn't. Or did the man believe his squabs had come home to roost and he was being paid in kind for his own assassination attempts?

"You don't appear to be in a large hurry to do that. Despite setting your man to watch me." He winced and closed his eyes.

"You don't appear to be in any shape to do me in, either."

"What?" The barrister's eyes snapped open and the demand came in a ghost of his regular bluster. "What do you mean?"

"Perhaps we have been speaking at cross-purposes, O'Brien. Have you had many of these . . . accidents?"

"Aye, enough to have me looking over my shoulder at shadows." O'Brien's gaze narrowed. "You?"

"The same."

"Mayhap your enemy is a common one, my lord," Randall offered into the silence as Nick digested the information.

"Mayhap." He nodded. "How long, O'Brien. When did you first start having unexplained incidents?"

"Six months, possibly nine. A man in my position sometimes makes enemies along the way. There have been any number of . . . accidents over the past several years, but they didn't start with any regularity until more recently." O'Brien closed his eyes for a moment. "I must admit with the trust payout looming on the horizon and then your sudden appearance here, I'd a strong suspicion you were involved."

Nick laughed. "And I have been busy suspecting you."

"Suspecting him of what?" Meaghan bustled into the room with a basin of steaming water, followed by Mrs. McFee laden with a mountain of clean linen napkins and a sewing box.

Randall scooted a small table closer to the settee and Meaghan placed the basin on top of it. She knelt next to her uncle. "Oh, Uncle Gill, I'm glad you're awake. What on earth happened to you?"

Gill caught Nick's gaze above his niece's shoulder and Nick shook his head. "An accident, my dear, nothing more."

"Indeed." She glanced back at Nick. "Randall, can you remove his shirt? I'm sorry, Uncle, but I'll need to dress your wound. This looks like an attack to me, not an accident. You must tell me what happened."

"You sound just like my Edna when she is determined to get information. If only I could employ her in my practice. The staunchest witnesses would pale." O'Brien blanched to an alarming shade of gray by the time Randall loosened his cravat, and removed his studs.

"Don't soothe me, Uncle. What happened?"

He groaned and closed his eyes as Randall eased his arms out of his sleeves. "Well, now perhaps it's your brother you remind me of." He chewed his lip as she wiped the water over his wound. "Bryan never could accept what's offered without plunging ahead and seeking his own answers."

"Mr. O'Brien, 'tis a good thing Master Bryan isn't here to hear you malign him," Mrs. McFee tisked as she stood ready to offer Meaghan assistance.

Nick admired the way the barrister kept the conversation going to distract Meaghan from the fright she must be feeling.

"Aye, Mrs. McFee, no doubt you're right." He groaned again and seemed to shrink back against the settee as Randall peeled the stained linen back from his chest.

"My lady, I daren't take it back any more, lest I start the bleeding afresh."

"I'll soak the rest off, Randall. Thank you." She favored him with a fleeting smile and then her troubled gaze sought Nick's.

He gave her a nod of encouragement.

"Uncle?" Meaghan took a linen square from Mrs. McFee's pile, dipped it in the basin, and applied it to the dried blood caked around the hole in his shirt.

O'Brien sucked in a breath. "Gads, lass, can you not be a little more careful with an injured man? Like as not, it is just as well you decided to leave the healing arts to gentler hands."

"Perhaps if you give her an answer?" Nick suggested, hoping for a little help as to what he should tell Meaghan.

"Ah, yes." O'Brien hesitated for only a moment before continuing, but the barrister's mask had slipped over his face as easily as if he donned a hat. "I was cleaning my pistols, my dear. You remember, the ones your brother, Devin, acquired for me in America?"

Meaghan nodded as she continued to clean his wound. "I remember. I could never understand what you wanted with them. Deadly looking things."

"Yes, indeed. You're quite right, my dear. I shouldn't have started cleaning them when I was tired. Definitely a mistake, and I know better. Mrs. O'Brien will no doubt take me to task for this." He sighed as though a stern talking to from his wife were the worst punishment he could envision.

Nick couldn't help admiring the easy aplomb with which he told his tale. No wonder O'Brien had acquired such a reputation in the Limerick courts.

"So you shot yourself in the shoulder?" Meaghan questioned as she began to apply a clean linen pad to the wound.

"Aye, lass, I did. And if you tell your da or your brothers, I'll never forgive you."

Thirteen

O'Brien tried for a chuckle after delivering his tale, but ruined it by groaning.

"Whiskey." Meaghan tossed the word over her shoulder.

Randall and Mrs. McFee both moved to do her bidding at the same time.

"I'm sorry, Uncle. I am almost through."

The housekeeper won out, returning with a generous portion of amber liquid in a crystal tumbler, which she handed to the barrister.

"Ah, thank you both." He sipped it gratefully as Meaghan finished binding his wound with strips of linen. Color began to return to his face.

Mrs. McFee used one of the damp cloths to sponge the blood from his deep gray jacket. Two small, jagged holes appeared from the mess in front and back of the shoulder. Randall caught Nick's eye as he raised a brow. Most likely his thoughts mirrored Nick's own. A few inches down or over and O'Brien would indeed be dead on his office floor.

"You're lucky this passed where it did, but you'll have to have the wound cleaned thoroughly again tomorrow. And you must promise to be more careful. Now you should rest. Mrs. McFee, we need to ready—"

"Oh, no, my dear. I cannot stay. My poor Edna would be beside herself. Moreover, the two of you are too newly wed to have me underfoot. That's the reason young Jamie is to dine with us most nights this week."

The barrister's face paled again. "Dear heaven, tonight's supper. I completely forgot. I'm in for it now. Ashton, could you have your man fetch a hackney? I need to get home."

"Indeed."

"You're in no shape for entertaining—" Meaghan's wide green gaze flew to Nick, filled with appeal.

"Meaghan, you know your aunt when there is a supper party planned," O'Brien interrupted. "If I put in an appearance and then cry off because of a headache, she will be less vexed than if I fail to appear at all."

"But—"

"Randall, see to the hackney and escort Mr. O'Brien home," Nick ordered before she could complete her protest. "I believe he's had enough excitement for one night."

"Aye, sir." Randall exited the room. Mrs. McFee gathered the bloody linens and washbowl and followed on his heels, claiming she would make certain he found the way.

"Nicholas?" Meaghan kept her gleaming gaze fixed on him, her brow knit with confusion. He couldn't blame her. They were dancing around her as fast as they could, given the barrister's injury.

"In a moment, my dear wife." He stroked his fingers across her cheek. "Could you make certain Mrs. McFee doesn't do more harm than good on her way to help Randall?"

Without another word she turned from him and swept out of the dining room, the graceful folds of her deep green dress fairly simmering with outraged impatience.

"You'll pay for that one, Lord Ashton. I've seen that gait before. When a woman's skirts snap like a flag in a sharp wind, beware, as her own da describes it." O'Brien's chuckle ended on another groan and he swallowed the rest of the whiskey in his tumbler before releasing a grateful sigh.

"Indeed." Nick turned his attention back to his guest. "Be that as it may, we need to discuss what we will do next."

"The point is well taken." The barrister tapped a finger to his chin. "We have that fool party planned for tomorrow night. It was originally planned as a formal introduction to society for Meaghan. Now it is to introduce the two of you as a married couple. I suppose we should cancel the gala and keep everyone close to home for the foreseeable future."

"No."

"No?" Despite his pain, the barrister's gaze was quite keen when he fixed it on Nick.

"Whoever is behind this seems to have an uncanny knack for figuring out exactly where we will be and when we are most vulnerable. Aside from your court days, there is no rhyme or reason to your late nights. Today you were not in court, so your staff left early."

O'Brien raised his brows at the summation of his routine. "You know quite a bit about my days."

"A necessity." Nick offered him a rueful grin. "I suspected you, remember."

"Indeed." The barrister frowned at him. "Then what do you propose?"

"If this person or persons knows as much, it may very well be we have someone introduced into our households who is feeding them information."

"Gads, I hadn't thought of that. You'd make a good solicitor."

Nick had the distinct impression he had just risen a notch in O'Brien's opinions.

"So you think our comings and goings are common knowledge? That is a most unsettling notion."

"Indeed," Nick agreed. "If I am right in this supposition, we would do ourselves a disservice by tipping our hand. We need to let the party and all its preparations continue as planned."

"And walk ourselves neatly into a possible trap?"

Nick shook his head. "We prepare ourselves and walk our common enemy into his own trap once we compare notes and determine who he or they may be."

"I like the way you think, my boy. Err, Lord Ashton."

"Nick will do."

O'Brien bobbed his head in deference to the new lack of title. "Nick, then. How do you propose to accomplish this turning of the tables?"

"Through Randall. In case you haven't suspected, he is more than a personal valet."

"I thought there might be more to it when he dispatched me to you so efficiently."

"He is a former soldier, a sergeant, with battlefield experience and a nose for trouble. I hired him after my own series of accidents began."

"The trust."

"Yes. Our common holding. This puts my cousin at risk as well, although so far he has not been subject to accidents."

"If I didn't know better, I would suspect Neville Chase of being behind the entire thing. But that embezzling cheat died almost twenty years ago. He was a rum touch, deeply deceptive. Gave quite an appearance of being a gentleman. Fooled us all. And fooling Gerald Mansfield was no easy task."

Deep regret snared Nick at the mention of his father. Guilt. He'd allowed his suspicions of O'Brien to overshadow the deep ties the barrister had shared with his father. Relief that he was not the enemy surged. "I traveled that path myself, but are you certain of his demise? My inquiries have come back rather vague where he is concerned. It's as if he just vanished."

"Oh, yes, quite certain. Your father was not one to leave things to chance, nor was your uncle. We had the entire matter thoroughly investigated at the time of the accident. Prison barge sank in the middle of the river. Terrible tragedy. All were lost."

O'Brien reached for his jacket and winced. Nick helped him slide his uninjured arm into his sleeve. "If it makes your mind easier, I'll have someone hunt up that old report and bring it round to you in the morning."

"Thank you." Nick hung the damaged fabric over O'Brien's wound. He'd not be poking his head into the dining room this evening. Edna

O'Brien's vexation or not, but he'd rest better in his own bed. Nick hoped he wouldn't develop a fever. He had a feeling the barrister would prove a valuable ally.

"If you and I are not to blame and Chase is dead, we are left with the unknown. Unless Chase had relatives? Someone who might yet benefit from his portion?"

"None. He was an orphan with no kith or kin. A bitter, secretive man. His parents long dead."

"Then I confess, I am perplexed." Nick raked a hand through his hair. "Who would benefit from murdering the remaining members of the trust?"

"None but our families, the barrister stated with finality. "And mine have no knowledge of it. Yours?"

"There is no one save Jamie. I would trust him with my life a thousand times over."

Randall returned to the dining room. "The hackney is here, my lord."

"Very good, Randall. Where is Lady Ashton?"

"Here, Nicholas." She entered behind the ex-soldier, and Nick couldn't help wondering how much she might have overheard.

The idea of Meaghan being exposed to danger sliced him with a dagger of fear. Now that she was his wife, and a beneficiary of the trust as well, her life could be in the very same peril as his own and Jamie's.

He held out his hand to her and she crossed to him, placing her hand in his without question. The feel of her soft skin against his fingers eased his worries for the moment, but he would have to come up with a plan, and quickly. He couldn't have her in danger and he couldn't bring himself to confess what his inability to control his lust might mean for her. This marriage may have delivered her a death sentence.

"Make sure all is well at the O'Brien household, Randall." He had every confidence the valet knew that included informing Jamie and his escort of the night's revelations. "Once Mr. O'Brien is safely ensconced in his bed, report back to me."

"Aye, my lord." Randall helped O'Brien to his feet.

"Good evening, Meaghan. I shall look forward to seeing you tomorrow under better circumstances."

"Rest well, Uncle." She pressed a kiss to his cheek. "Please take care."

The door closed behind the two of them.

"Now, where were we, my wife, before we were so summarily interrupted?" Nick stepped behind her and looped his arms around her slender waist. For the time being he wanted to forget all the threats, all the dark future, and bury himself in the moment, in his wife.

The scent of skin-warmed honeysuckle and meadowsweet drifted up to him. Despite this latest disturbing interlude, his desire for her tightened immediately.

"No, Nicholas." She pushed out of his arms and turned to face him.

"No?" He owed her the explanation she was about to demand. The rigid set of her shoulders and upturned chin told him she was serious. But all he could think about was how the green of her dress matched the fire of determination in her eyes.

"There was more going on here than what any

of you were willing to tell me. I want to know the whole tale."

"There is no tale, sweet Meaghan." He took a step toward her and she retreated, holding her hands up in front of her as if to shield herself from his touch. He reached for one hand and slid his fingers between her own.

"Please, Nicholas." Her eyes darkened as he touched her. She pulled her hand away, but not before he had seen the shudder ripple over her.

"You said earlier you . . . wanted something." He stepped closer still.

"I did, but not at the expense of my self-respect."

Her statement brought him to a halt. "Your self-respect?"

"Aye."

"What does that mean?"

"It means there is more here than you are telling me and sidetracking me with the uncontrollable . . . things I feel for you is unfair."

"Meaghan—"

"You sent me from the room, Nicholas," she told him softly, sorrow edging the corners of her mouth. "You cannot placate me with a few kisses. I left only because I could see you needed me to go. You wanted to discuss whatever occurred with Uncle Gill in private. You trusted Randall more than your wife. We may only have been married a day, but I know trust is essential to married life."

She was right. He could not fault her logic. She was an intelligent woman. Smart. Beautiful. His.

"I will tell you what I can when I can," he told her as truthfully as he could.

Chagrin passed over her brow. "But—"

"Don't ask me for more than I can give you, Meaghan," he told her, wishing he could offer her more than he could. She locked her gaze with his for a long moment and then offered him silent, shuddering acceptance for his troubles.

"Very well, Nicholas." She released a shaky sigh, letting him know exactly how much her acceptance cost her. "I will bend on this because there must be a beginning to the trust we build between us. But I intend to hold you to that promise."

He breathed a silent sigh of relief. "I have no doubt you will. Now come to me, Wife."

She lifted her chin a notch higher and met his gaze full on, her own dark and turbulent with struggle. "If you want me, Husband, you will need to come to me."

Challenge underscored her words. She would bend for him, but in return she expected something from him as well. There was far more to the depths of his fiery Irish lass than he had suspected, but then, from the very beginning she had been a far cry from the milk-and-water misses he was used to.

For the span of several heartbeats their gazes held, hers the stormy green of a tempestuous, untamable sea.

He was a man used to getting what he wanted when he wanted it. He crossed the small distance separating them, allowing her the small victory. She arched one dark brow.

"You are mine, Meaghan," he told her.

"Aye." Her tone held the same challenge.

He caught her stubborn little chin in his fingers and tipped her head farther back. "What have you earned with this play?"

"Does it matter?" she asked him, her breath warm against his lips.

He slid his arm around her waist and pulled her slender form against him. "Aye." He mocked her lilting tones. "It does."

"I've earned this, my lord husband." She reached up on her tiptoes and pressed herself more fully against him, making the hot blood race through his veins once more.

"And this." She coaxed his head down to hers and pressed her lips against his, bolder this time, as though she were more sure of herself.

Something had changed very subtly in the last hour. And he realized with something of a start that she had not answered his question.

He pulled away from the mesmerizing taste of her lips. "Touché."

Color ran high over her fair cheeks.

"I'll not play games with you, Meaghan."

"I'm not playing a game, Nicholas."

He tightened one arm about her hips and used the other hand to massage the tight muscles at her back. Her eyes slitted. She was passionate, something he had only just begun to taste last night.

"We shall see." He reached behind her and threw the bolt on the double doors to the room.

"What are you doing?"

"Testing your resolve." *And my own.*

"What do you mean?"

"I'm going to show you." *If she wished to test his limits, he was more than willing to see how far her show of feminine power went. He would test her as well, his passionate little virgin bride.*

He drew her along with him toward the settee that had only a short time ago held her uncle's injured form, standing her in front of it with her back to him.

He pulled the pins from her hair until the shining mass of it spilled in magnificent splendor down her back.

"Nicholas—"

"Hush." He placed a finger over her lips. "No more questions. Not now."

He tilted her head to the side and drew the hair from her neck with the slow stroke of his fingers. She sighed. He bent his head and nipped the tender skin below her ear, then laved it with his tongue. She tasted sweet and all too tempting.

With slow deliberateness he ran the palms of his hands over her shoulders and down the sides of her gown, just skimming the outer swells of her breasts. He stroked down over the inner curve of her arms, placing them straight down at her sides.

He laced his fingers through hers and rubbed her palms with his thumbs in a slow circular motion as he continued to kiss and lick her neck in the same slow circles.

"Nicholas." She sighed his name and leaned back against him.

"Yes?" He released her and reached for the buttons of her gown.

"I—"

"No questions," he reminded her, parting the buttons one by one. He sucked the lower lobe of her ear into his mouth and nibbled it as he parted the bodice of her gown.

Beneath the sheer fabric of her chemise her

nipples were tight, thrusting against the silk. He slid the bodice jacket from her shoulders and let it droop down her arms, but only partway. With her arms behind her, between the two of them, the full swell of her breasts pressed against the thin silk, inviting his touch. Her breathing quickened.

He released her earlobe, nipping it slightly.

She shivered.

He massaged her shoulders, easing the tension from her and letting her wonder what he would do next. Where he would touch her next. A sweet torture of waiting.

He traced the slender line of her bared arms, slow and light and then lower, pressing his palms over her hips, her stomach, her abdomen. He pressed long, slow circles into her flesh.

She squirmed against him. He could almost taste her rising anticipation.

"Be still, beloved," he whispered, letting his breath stir the fine hairs at the back of her neck. She shivered in response.

He let his fingers trace the edge of her skirt until he reached the fastenings. He released them and the heavy taffeta sighed to the floor, leaving her in naught but petticoats, stays, and chemise. He dropped two layers of petticoats in rapid succession and then two more, leaving only one thin layer of gentility.

Beneath her layers, she'd chosen pure silk pantaloons alone to grace her slender legs on their night at home. He could see a hint of the dark thatch of curls at the apex of her thighs. Desire swelled painfully. His erection throbbed at the confinement of his trousers, but he was not done tormenting her yet. Not nearly done.

He pulled her tight against him. The softness of her womanly bottom settled enticingly sweet against his rigid arousal. He stroked her stomach and then slowly stroked up over her corset until the backs of his hands brushed the undersides of her breasts, so soft and full against the stiffness of her stays. She moaned at the contact.

Her hands, still caught between them in her bodice, sought purchase on his thighs. Her questing fingers nearly drove him to distraction with the whorls of passion they set off in him.

He slid his hands up over her breasts, cupping them boldly, gratifying them both for an instant as he savored the soft resilience in his palms.

"Nicholas." His name formed a plea on her lips, but the lesson had only just begun for the two of them.

"Shh," he soothed her again and released her breasts.

She tilted her head back against his shoulder. He indulged them both in a hot kiss, licking her lips with his tongue and teasing her own.

Then he continued his torment, sliding his hands back down over her stomach and lower still to her thighs. Slowly he bunched the fabric of her one remaining petticoat with his fingers, lifting it higher and higher. Then he slid his hands beneath, echoing her moan as he touched her stomach, her thighs and flirted with the dark thatch of hair shielded from him by the fabric of her pantaloons.

He caught his fingers in the drawstring at her waist and released it. The silk sighed to the floor, baring the long line of her legs. His engorged flesh leaped against her. Who was he tormenting more?

"Step out of them slowly." He barely recognized the husky rasp as his own. By God he wanted her. Badly. The lesson he had intended solely for her was rapidly becoming his own.

She stepped out of the pantaloons. First one foot and then the other. In between, as she raised her leg, he traced her inner thigh with his fingers, close, so close, to her womanly folds, but not quite touching.

She shivered against him in abject surrender. "Nicholas."

He turned her in his arms.

Heat rushed over Meaghan. She stood in her husband's arms, practically naked, in her brother's dining room. And she was enjoying every single moment.

Nicholas kissed her, his tongue melding with hers in a slow dance of passion. Her knees felt weak with desire and her very skin felt on fire. She longed for him to touch her more. Everywhere. And yet his slow, deliberate seduction burned every inch of her body.

He released her lips. Cool air rushed over her hot skin as he lifted her petticoat. "Sit down, Meaghan."

She sat on the raw silk of the settee. The cool fabric sliding against her hot flesh seemed wildly decadent. She had never considered what it might feel like to have her naked buttocks against a stately piece of furniture. She shivered.

Nicholas knelt in front of her. He settled the fabric of her petticoat around her, high against her thighs. Then he reached for her feet, lifting them off the floor after divesting her of her slippers. He rubbed the bottoms of her soles with the same slow circular motion he had already used too successfully on the rest of her body. Languid heat licked her still further. Hot skin on the cool silk.

She moaned again. His touch felt too good.

After a moment, he released her feet and slid his fingers along her ankles, up her calves, to the backs of her knees. Her hands dug into the silk upholstery as he skimmed higher and sent showers of sparks along her skin. He traced the pads of his fingers along the inner curve of her thighs. She would surely go mad from anticipation.

"Open for me," he commanded.

She parted her legs, feeling raw heat wash over her face. No one had ever looked at her so intimately. He slid his fingers higher, kneading the inner muscles of her thighs and coaxing her legs farther and farther apart. Her heartbeat thudded in her ears as she waited for him to touch her.

"Nicholas." His name exploded from her. She bit her lip and shivered from the sweet torture of expectation.

Higher and higher he stroked, watching her with his blazing blue gaze.

"What do you want, Wife?" he teased her, barely brushing his fingers against her.

Even so, the contact shot straight through her like a thousand tiny lightning bolts. She shuddered and leaned forward to grip his shoulders.

"Please," she panted and could get nothing else out. He knew full well what she wanted, what he did to her with his touch.

"Yes, sweet Meaghan. And that is what you shall have. A pleasuring such as you have never imagined."

He slid his hands along her outer thighs to

cup her buttocks beneath her petticoat. She could have moaned with disappointment. What was he doing to her?

He tugged her forward to sit at the very edge of the settee. Every inch of her quivered. She had never felt so very alive. He kissed her again, long, slow and maddeningly, tugging her chemise as he did so.

Cool air kissed her breasts for an instant; then Nicholas caressed her—laving her aching nipples with his tongue, biting with his teeth, sucking her into his mouth, and leaving her nipples glistening in the candlelight when he released them.

Then he dipped his head lower still. She panted as his breath touched her intimately, hot and teasing. And then his tongue flicked over her. Back and forth. Back and forth. Tasting her just as surely as he had tasted her lips and tongue. Just as he had feasted at her breast.

He cupped her bottom and arched her to better accommodate the invasion of his mouth against her most private areas. He dipped his tongue into her with long, slow strokes. She moaned, watching as his head dipped and he licked her again and again.

He found the nub of flesh that was plump and aching for his touch. Sensual shivers racked her as he sucked it into his hot mouth.

"Oh. Oh." All words, all thought, fled as he suckled her. First gentle, then hard, his tongue darting against her. Pressure built inside her. Exquisite pleasure and pain begging release. All wrapped up in the touch of her husband's lips against her body, his hands kneading her bottom.

"Nicholas. Please."

His hands captured her breasts, rubbing her

wet nipples between his thumbs and forefingers. Pulling and rolling them, sending blinding heat and desire flooding through her.

"Oh." And then there was no control, no help for the things he made her feel as the pressure broke over her in long hot waves. Rushing through her over and over again. He did not stop. Did not release her from his tender torment until she was limp and moaning. Mindless and satiated.

She could only blink in wonder at the satisfied blaze in her husband's blue eyes and the triumphant smile curving his mouth.

"There, my wife, did that—"

"Lord Ashton?" The double doors to the foyer rattled as someone tried to open them.

He tensed and the smile evaporated as he swung on his heels to look at them.

"Nicholas." She struggled to sit up. Her body tingled from head to foot. Her clothes scattered the floor in front of the settee like so much flotsam on the ocean. Married or not, mortification washed through her at having anyone guess the marvels she had just experienced.

"It's Randall. Stay put." Nicholas crossed to the doorway and threw back the bolt, opened it the slightest crack, shielding her from sight with his body.

The low hum of Randall's report reached her from the doorway, but she couldn't understand what he said. And it didn't seem to matter, either. At the moment, her thoughts were scattered to the four winds. So much for finding out the full story by using her womanly wiles on her husband.

Nicholas nodded. "Very good, Randall. You may retire."

"Thank you, my lord."

Nicholas shut the door and turned to her. She suddenly felt even more naked as his gaze swept her disheveled hair and bared breasts. She hadn't even pushed down her petticoat.

The decidedly masculine smile of triumph lit his face again. "And now, my dear wife, where were we?"

Fourteen

Meaghan stayed half reclined against the settee, feeling drained and disheveled, and anything but ladylike. Not that Nicholas appeared to notice. The smile he favored her with as he walked across the room told her he thought she looked more than beautiful. The word ravishing drifted through her mind.

It seemed hardly fair. How could Nicholas stand there looking so handsome and aristocratic after he had just wrung everything out of her? Only the stray lock of golden hair drooping over his forehead made him look the slightest bit mussed.

"I . . ." She pushed her one flimsy petticoat down. "I believe we were . . . finished, were we not?"

Heat stung her cheeks, despite the lingering pleasure drugging her limbs. Did being married make the things they were doing together proper behavior? At the moment the very idea seemed ludicrous. But Aunt Edna had said married couples found pleasure in many ways.

She shied away from thoughts of her aunt and

uncle or her parents—even her brothers thusly engaged.

What might the Ladies Guild think if they could see her at the moment and what effect would that have on her work with the Nightingale Society? She shoved those concerns aside as her husband advanced toward her.

"No, beautiful Meaghan. We are far from finished." His deep, husky tone shivered over her.

"Oh?" She glanced about for something to cover herself with as Nicholas moved closer still.

He reached for her bare shoulders and plucked her off the settee as if she weighed less than a down feather.

Her one remaining petticoat, loosened from their recent endeavors atop the settee, slipped to her ankles, leaving her in naught but her stays and the glow of the passion and pleasure her husband had given her a few short minutes before.

The blue of his eyes darkened and a muscle ticked in his cheek. He reached under her breasts and made short work of her corset ties, pulling her remaining garment from her and flinging it aside.

He sucked his breath in over his teeth as he swept his gaze over her. "You are beautiful, Meaghan Reilly. You know that, don't you?"

She shivered again and made an attempt to sound prim despite her nudity. "That's Lady Ashton, now."

"Indeed." He smiled. "As much as I would like to continue right here against your brother's mahogany dinner table, I think we should seek the privacy of our bedchamber. Two interruptions are two too many."

He undid the remaining buttons on his shirt and doffed it quickly before draping it over her shoulders. The shirttails fell to her knees.

"My clothes—"

"We'll worry about them later." He gathered her up into his arms, kicked the doors aside, and strode from the room.

"Nicholas," she gasped as he started for the stairs and she saw their reflection in the dining room windows, "the shades weren't drawn."

"No." A rueful grin twisted his firm lips. "I believe the shrubbery in the garden may be blushing even now."

"But—"

"I'm sorry, Meaghan. You made me forget myself. Thank goodness there are bushes in front of the window."

Warmth pervaded her limbs. *You made me forget myself.* The idea that he had been equally as overcome by the things they felt for each other pleased her enormously, despite the chance they'd taken of being discovered.

Emboldened, she looped her hands around his neck and kissed his cheek. "You are forgiven," she whispered against his neck.

He took the stairs two at a time, crossed the landing to their chamber in two strides, and kicked the bedroom door shut behind them.

Neville stood silent in the shadowy philodendrons foresting the small side garden of the proper town house long after the occupants of the room he viewed had quit the scene. His grip on the windowsill threatened to snap the wood in half.

He shook—every inch of his body, shaking and quivering. Worse, the interlude he had just witnessed had unmanned him there amidst the damp earthy redolence of green growing things with spasms of pleasure so violent he had never experienced their like before.

He shuddered again and forced himself to relax his tight grip.

The spectacle of Nicholas Mansfield making love to his luscious young bride had not drawn him to this window. Indeed, the idea that the two of them might engage in such activity outside their bedchamber would not have occurred to him had he not witnessed the incident firsthand.

He had followed O'Brien and the lout who had rushed into the barrister's office so unexpectedly, intent on determining just how far astray of the mark he had thrown himself by giving into impulse and confronting Gill O'Brien on his own.

The impulse may have united his enemies, but at least he had heard them reiterate the story that had cost him so dear over the years. Through bribery and stolen records, false testimony and witnesses struck down, Neville Chase was dead.

That satisfaction he hoarded. Let them chase their tails a few days more while he devised a master stroke. Soon it would be they who occupied graves while he resurrected his clean slate with no one living to dispute his story. Or his claim to the benefits from the investments he had established.

He lingered when the passion leapt to life between Mansfield and the woman, finding it impossible to tear himself away. She looked so fresh, so appealing. The kind of woman his mother would have approved.

When Mansfield stood her, all prim and proper in the midst of the empty dining room, then stripped her of her clothing until she turned from fine lady into fiery strumpet, Neville had been transfixed and inflamed beyond all bounds.

Even now, with his feet cold and wet and sinking into the wormy earth, he could still hear the echo of her husky cries—feel the rippling paroxysms of his own pleasure spurting out of him in perfect rhythm with her shamelessness.

He felt soiled for having enjoyed the spectacle. And even dirtier for contemplating which window on the second floor might afford him the best view of the next stage they might be taking their indecency toward.

Voyeurism. He tasted the concept against his tongue and almost laughed aloud, despite the pain threatening his temples.

Damnation, but he hated Mansfield. Seed of his vile father, even now pouring his seed into the dark-haired wanton upstairs. The deep and righteous hatred nearly strangled him, but could not prevent him from wanting to watch each thrust of his enemy as he enjoyed the woman he'd married.

Lust rippled through Neville again and he shuddered, quite certain more depravity was exactly what Mansfield intended when he swept her up in his arms and kicked his way out of the dining room.

The image of him replacing his enemy, pushing himself between her fair legs, pumping and straining to gain his release within her tender sweetness, her breasts peaking for him and her head rolling as she cried out, "Neville, Neville," rose to taunt him.

And tempt him.

The perfect act of vengeance. He sprang to life again with the notion.

Pain exploded behind Neville's eyes. He crept away from his earthy post. The inky abyss rose up to greet him with all its lustrous allure. He paused, swaying in the darkness. Fresh from his pleasures, the abyss didn't seem quite so frightening, not even the pain rampaging his temples dampened the magnetic attraction coursing through him.

Ah, the dark charisma of power. He could sink into the abyss and know peace at last.

Maybe, just maybe.

"No." His hoarse denial shuddered out of him, strident and forced.

He'd be damned if he'd give in before he finished. Maybe madness was his destiny. Maybe he'd been wrong to struggle so hard to stay away through all the years it called to him. Maybe. But the dark temptation could not negate his promise and it wouldn't provide the righteous vengeance he sought.

He had a duty to complete—a calling higher and more noble than the darkness entreating him.

He pushed away from the temptation lurking deep inside his soul with the dawning certainty that he would not be able to avoid it for very much longer. His gaze drifted back to the windows on the second floor of the town house.

It couldn't hurt to keep an eye on Mansfield through the night, could it? Couldn't hurt surely to see exactly what depths of depravity he and his tasty little whore might indulge.

Neville hurried toward the back of the house next door and the drain pipe that would afford him a means of gaining a second-floor perch and the view he sought.

Nick spilled his tender burden onto the velvet-cloaked bed where he had taken her virginity only the night before.

Moonlight cut a slender swath through the window to kiss her body, shadowing the dips and hollows of her pale skin between the parted folds of his shirt. He had told her she was beautiful and she was. Ever more so.

He pulled off his boots and prepared to claim her.

Balanced on her elbows, she looked up at him. Anticipation shone in her eyes. Eager for him. Offering herself to him. Pride swelled his chest and hitched his breath in his throat. Meaghan proved a prize too valuable to be wagered in this deadly game in which he found himself.

He needed to find a way to protect her. Whatever the cost. If he should lose her . . . Pain tightened his chest, hard and fast, so strong it took his breath away.

He shoved aside the worry. He would come up with a plan to protect her even if it meant sending her away. In the morning.

But for now, in the moonlight, she belonged with him, to him. And that was all that mattered.

She arched her back and her breasts thrust high, parting the shirt still further as the fabric hung suspended at the tips of her breasts. His mouth went dry. The sight held him mesmerized, unable to move as he waited for the linen to part the rest of the way and display the bounty within.

"Meaghan."

She sighed, her eyes a smoky dark green. "Aye?"

"No one woman should make a man feel this way."

"What way?"

She raised herself up further on her elbows and the shirt parted below, giving him a glimpse of the shadowy dark curls between her thighs. A smile creased her lips.

Her cries of pleasure when he had feasted on her in the dining room still echoed in his ears. His erection pulsed, a painful pressure that need not be denied any longer. He unbuttoned his trousers, drawing her gaze as his fingers went about their task.

"As though heaven and hell are to be found in her arms." He watched her face as the buttons came free and his trousers gaped open.

"Oh?" Her mouth parted, her gaze fastened to the opening. The tip of her tongue peeked out between her lips. How could she make him harder still just with the look on her face? Amazing, but then the sweet and so properly improper *Lady Ashton* had made his pulses pound from the moment he met her.

Now that she was his wife, she seemed to have increased her powers a hundredfold.

"As though"—he began sliding his trousers downward—"he cannot get enough of her. No matter how many times he takes her to his bed."

He inched them further down, her avid expression nearly unmanning him where he stood. "As though he can never get enough of making love to her."

His flesh sprang free of his trousers and he quickly shed the garment, kicking it away.

Her gaze widened and the tiniest gasp came from her. "Oh, Nicholas, I don't think I shall ever get used to the size of you."

He gritted his teeth, shuddering with his need for her. "Then perhaps we'd best work at that." He managed to grind out the words as he walked toward her, his desire jutting in the moonlight.

"Aye." One soft syllable that brought him to a halt at the edge of the bed.

She sat up and scooted toward him. His shirt parted the rest of the way to reveal her full breasts, bobbing with her movements.

"I want to." She darted a shy glance up at him as she made her bold admission. "I want to touch you."

He sucked in a breath. "By all means."

She reached toward him. An eternity passed through him as he awaited her touch.

Her fingers, cool and soft, slid over his aching flesh. He groaned, low and guttural.

She stopped instantly and looked up. "Have I hurt you?"

"No, Wife, you have not." He barely got out the words. The feel of her fingers wrapped around him would drive him mad.

"But—"

"You hear my pleasure, not pain."

"Oh." A smile played on her lips and she looked down again.

He groaned a second time as her fingers slid over his length, testing him, probing as she explored.

"You are so hard, and yet smooth like hot velvet here. More like satin or even silk there."

Next she weighed his laden testes in her palm, considering them.

Dear heaven, he would lose himself in her hands if she continued to torture him.

"Meaghan." Despite the warning edge he put in his tone, she continued her soft stroking movements.

"I want . . ." She halted and glanced up at him. Fire smoldered in her eyes.

"What?" His mind blazed, needing her answer more than he needed his next breath.

"I want to . . . taste you"—her words burned a sizzling path through his blood—"as you . . . tasted me."

Hot waves surged through him, blinding him to all but the image of her lips on him, surrounding him. His breath hung suspended in his throat until his chest burned, his entire body flamed.

"Yes." All the answer he could manage to choke out, raw and rough.

Her gaze darted back to his, just a flicker of hesitation, then she moved closer, her luscious breasts swaying with her movements. Her ebony hair rippled over her shoulders. He died a thousand deaths while her head bent toward him.

Waiting.

Waiting.

And then her lips were against him. Soft. Light. Warm. Experimental.

Her breath fanned him intimately, sending shivers of lust straight to his core.

Air rushed out of him and he released a groan that welled from the depths of his soul.

"Meaghan, you will drive me—"

He couldn't speak, couldn't think. Her mouth moved over his straining erection. Warm, wet heat slid in slippery pleasure over his flesh as she tasted him. Her tongue flicked his sensitive head.

"Mmm." The sound vibrated from her lips against him as she massaged her tongue down his length, her lips closing around his shaft.

Heaven and hell.

He slid his fingers in the dark wealth of her silky hair. As soft as the feel of her mouth around him. Her tongue stroked up his length, up and down. He inched forward and retreated while she laved him. He coaxed her, cupping her head with his hands, and she caught his rhythm. Back and forth, back and forth, her lips and tongue moved over him, stroking, teasing, burning him to a cinder with the pleasure she evoked.

He bent his head and watched her. Her lips sliding over him, his engorged flesh wet from her mouth as she tasted him, swelled him to the point of bursting. Pain and pleasure, so intense he almost could not bear it, rippled along his nerve endings.

"Meaghan." His voice seethed, hoarse with desire and the needs she built to a fever pitch in him. "You will get more than you bargained for if you do not stop."

She continued her attentions for a timeless moment as he stood entranced by her touch and the view of his engorged flesh being sucked deep into her mouth only to appear again, slippery and wet, glistening as she enjoyed him.

He was completely incapable of stopping her, unable to do anything but succumb to the things she made him feel. Back and forth, over and under. Again and again while his body screamed for release and he was certain he had lost all control.

Finally, she released him from the torment. Cool air shivered over his wet flesh.

"Did you like that?" Her voice quivered over him. Such an innocent, unknowing question after nearly driving him out of his skull.

"More than you know, Wife." He ground out the words, his hands already reaching for the shirt he had put on her. He tore it from her and slid his hands over her bare flesh. Her shoulders, her back, her arms—all his. All of her, his.

"More than you know."

"Heaven and hell?"

"And more." He slid his fingers beneath her chin and tipped her head back, bending to take her mouth with his.

He kissed her deeply, melding together all the fiery, exquisite tastes of each other they had shared. It no longer mattered for what reason she was his. Why he had married her. Or she him. No right or wrong. All that mattered was that he needed her more than he had ever needed any woman. And that he wanted her so badly she was a fire in his soul.

"Meaghan, I want you," he told her, unable to find better words to say everything raging through him.

"Aye." Her face glowed in the pale moonlight. "Make love to me, Nicholas."

"Gladly." He kissed her again, gathering her to him. Her breasts pressed against his chest as he tumbled with her onto the bed. He pulled her to him and twisted onto his back. His hands swept the slender length of her back under the dark curtain of her hair, cupping her buttocks as he drew her atop him.

He groaned, awash in desire so strong his head spun. Her softness pressed against him. He kneaded the resilient swells of her buttocks with his hands, rubbing her against him with his movements.

Her fingers slid into his hair and suddenly she was kissing him. His fiery bride had taken control, her tongue delving into his mouth, echoing the rhythm of the lovemaking he intended.

He stilled beneath her, allowing her the control she sought as she kissed him thoroughly, sucking his tongue into her mouth to lave with her own. He slid his hands up her sides and traced the outer curves of her breasts.

She sighed into his mouth.

He cupped her breasts fully and rubbed at her tight nipples with his thumbs. She groaned.

"Nicholas."

She sat atop him, her legs sliding to either side of his torso. The warm, wet heat of her pressing intimately against him, teased yet again.

She was so very beautiful in the moonlight. He caressed her breasts, weighing them with his palms, stroking her passion-tight nipples. She sighed and tilted her head back. Her hair brushed his thighs. The pale column of her throat beckoned. God, how he wanted her.

He drew her down toward him again and fastened his lips to her breast, drawing one tight nipple into his mouth.

She gasped, squirming atop him as he teased and tortured her nipple with his tongue, nipping with his teeth and suckling her thoroughly.

"Nicholas, I—"

He cupped her bottom, urging her closer against him. Her slick wet heat slid against his flesh.

Twin groans of pleasure echoed in the air.

"Nicholas." His name became a plea for the pleasure she knew he could give her.

Satisfaction tightened inside him. His fiery little bride wanted him as much as he wanted her.

In answer to her plea, he released the one succulent nipple to transfer his attentions to the other. He offered this one the same torment as the first, laving and nipping and suckling.

She tasted so good, felt so good in his arms. As though she had never belonged anywhere else but right here.

With him.

She squirmed and groaned and squirmed, sliding her wet seductive heat over him again and again, delivering her own brand of torment with her movements.

He gripped her hips, unable to stand the waiting any longer. Poising her over his flesh, he urged her downward. Wordlessly she thrust her hips down.

He slid into her hot velvety heat in a single stroke as she impaled herself atop him.

Again, their twin groans of pleasure echoed in the air around them. She clung to him—so hot, so tight, so wet. He buried himself so deep inside her, sheathed to the hilt.

"Nicholas." She looked down at him, her eyes wide and dazed.

"Yes, beloved." He drew her to him for a tender kiss. The movement slid him out of her, just slightly. With a murmur of denial that didn't even part their lips, she slid down again, sheathing him fully.

He groaned his approval into her mouth.

Catching his meaning, she lifted her hips without further urging, sliding him out and then pushing back down again, accepting his full length into her sweet body.

Wild heat raced through his body, pooling in blazing urgency low in his belly as he held himself still and allowed her to make love to him of her own accord.

Up. Down. Up. Down.

In slow, slick rhythm she moved her hips.

It was heaven.

It was hell.

He had never known such pleasure. He could not take much more.

Finally, he could no longer restrain the primal instincts burning inside him, demanding he take her completely.

He gripped her hips and thrust into her, turning in one smooth motion to place her beneath him. Her hips cradled him as he ground himself against her.

"Oh, Nicholas, oh." She arched her neck and he kissed her there, nibbling her soft flesh as he gave in to the desires he'd been restraining.

He moved inside her, pulling back and then thrusting himself into her. Oh, yes. Heaven and hell, indeed. He burned for this woman alone.

"Aye, *laoch grian*. Aye."

But it was not enough.

The burning demand inside him to move and move and move, pumping his hips and driving himself into her, took over. Thought became a thing long forgotten. He possessed naught but passion and desire. And a need so strong it blotted out everything else.

He increased his rhythm as she clung to him. Driving himself faster, harder.

She cried out again and again. His name. Words he didn't understand. It didn't matter.

He cupped her buttocks, tilting her to accept him deeper and then deeper still. She slid her legs up over his hips.

"Yes." The word ground out of him as he increased his thrusts still further. Mindless now to all but the need to mate with her—as deeply and as completely as humanly possible.

Her cries punctuated each thrust—faster and faster, harder and harder. She shuddered in his arms, again and again and again. He took her mouth with his, swallowing her passionate cries as she experienced her pleasure.

"Mine."

He managed the one word; then his own release ripped through him in a blaze of blinding heat. His seed exploded into her and he shuddered inside her as the echo of his passion for her rippled through him over and over.

Finally, there was naught but the mingled sounds of their harsh breathing to break the cool silence of the darkened bedroom. Lethargy crawled his limbs and drugged his mind. He had never experienced anything such as he just shared with his tender little bride.

The hidden depths and untold rewards within her more than made up for their irregular beginning. He'd a feeling he had only begun to know this, a feeling that sent ripples of warmth through him to snake straight into his heart.

He levered himself up onto his elbows, managing to keep himself still deep inside her. She lay beneath him, damp and replete. Her muscles tightened, urging stray reverberations of pleasure through him.

Satisfaction curved his lips into a smile.

She tilted her head a little to the side. "And just what are you smiling about, Lord Ashton? If I may be so bold as to ask."

"Indeed." He smiled wider. "I was just thinking about what you said downstairs in the dining room. And I have an answer for you, even though it wasn't really a question."

"Oh?" Soft pink color washed her cheeks.

With her hair spread across the pillows in resplendent disarray and her cheeks aglow, he'd never seen her look more lovely. He realized with something of a start and a certainty that rocked him to his depths that he would remember this image of her for the rest of his life.

Tenderness ached through him and tightened his throat.

"Yes." He bent and kissed her very, very softly on her parted lips. "And the answer is—now."

Puzzlement wrinkled her brow. "Now?"

"Indeed." He kissed her again. "You were wondering if we were finished."

"Oh." Her arms slid up around his neck to draw him down for a further kiss.

"Mmm, maybe not." Laughter edged her suggestion and he joined her.

She proved right. They weren't done.

Not yet.

Fifteen

"Blasted oaf."

Neville restrained his growing desire to kick the incompetent Muldoons from Limerick to Dublin, but only with tremendous effort. They were hardly worth the exertion.

His head still blazed with pain. The remorseless misery almost made him regret giving in to his desire to stay and watch Mansfield take his wife. The things they had done to each other. Their pleasure. His own.

He felt as despoiled and violated as the young woman Mansfield had so thoroughly sullied. The Irish strumpet's willing participation made it clear she would never make a fit lady, no matter her pretensions to the title through her brief union with her English husband. He had stripped both father and son of their own claims long ago in his mind, refusing to use their exalted designations unless absolutely necessary.

The misery in his head pounded afresh. Hours now and still no relief. It didn't seem to matter how many times he listed his logical arguments. Or how loudly he proclaimed them until they bounced from the crude walls of his room. The fact that he had begun to talk to himself aloud, where others could hear, showed but another of the many strains littering his life. And all of them could be laid rightfully at Mansfield's door.

"Mister Chase, I tried. They said they'd no need of any extra help. They only took Cullen 'cause he were there the last time."

Neville fixed his gaze on Rory Muldoon. He felt as if he viewed the man at the end of a long tunnel. The spiral of his dark thoughts pulled him further away, but he fought back.

"No help? How can they not need help when they're hosting a party large enough to supply the entire continent of Australia with food for a week?" Neville rubbed at his temples. It did no good. The pain didn't budge, darting beneath his fingers, just out of reach.

He sighed, his breath harsh in his ears. "That damned O'Brien. He always hires extra help for his entertainments. Always. I paid the receipts for enough of his parties to know."

The injustice of this change in habit brought to mind, in color so vivid it hurt his eyes, the long-ago time he had been a trusted employee. More than an employee, a confidant to the powerful men who had encouraged him to raise his life to the heights, only to dash him to the rocks like so much wasted filth when they were through with him.

The Muldoon skulking in front of him cast him a wary glance and Neville realized his mistake. A cold thrill etched his spine. That made twice now in the space of only a few minutes. Twice he had spoken aloud thoughts that should have been safely locked behind the confines of his mind. His mind appeared to be splitting at the seams.

He shivered, reminded all too clearly of his father and the promises his mother had begged, no demanded, of him on her deathbed.

Protect your father's good name.

So far the abyss had made no appearance, despite the agony splintering in upon itself in his mind. But he was quite certain the darkness lurked nearby.

And when the time came?

He shivered again and couldn't finish the thought. Not now. Not yet. He wasn't finished yet. Tightening his lips, he forced himself to concentrate on the orders he wanted carried out.

"I don't care how many times you have been rebuffed. O'Brien will pay no heed to who serves him once they are hired. Make yourself useful around the house or yard. Dress like the others and blend in. The livery I supplied you both the other day should stand you in good stead."

He rubbed his temple for a moment. Surely fate would smile on him and allow him his victory soon enough to beat the abyss. Time was slipping away, however. The time he needed to enjoy his restoration to society. If only his assistants would bring him the information he needed.

Anger sliced Neville anew—anger for their ineptitude and for his own lack of means to hire more thorough assassins. If the pain would only abate, even just a tiny bit, he could think more clearly.

He blew out a long shaky breath and gritted his teeth.

"Find out the timing for the party. Get a list of the attendees if you can. Tell Cullen to keep

his ears open in the stable. I can make no plans
without the information. Report back to me as
swiftly as you can. There isn't much time."

"Aye, sir." Rory bobbed his dark head and
backed out of the room. He crossed the bare
wood floors like a wiry, black-haired rat before
scuttling off into the darkness to do Neville's bidding. Neville almost laughed at the image his
thoughts drew to mind. Perhaps he would do
away with them as well. And leave even less witnesses to tell the tale when all was said and done.

It couldn't hurt to squash a few rats.

Could it?

Something is going on.

Meaghan wasn't quite sure what that something was, but there was a definite difference,
almost palpable, in the air. She hadn't lived with
her father's worsening health and the troubles
that had plagued Reilly Ship Works at one time,
not to notice the undercurrents of strain swirling
around her.

There had been hints of tension between her
uncle and Nicholas from the moment he arrived
at the O'Brien household, but this was different
from that as well. At least the men were united
now, almost conspiratorial in their worrying.
That made things worse, not better, though. She
could almost taste the troubled expectations
pouring from the men downstairs in the study.

Added to that, the entire household seemed
aswarm with extra footmen. She'd been party to
O'Brien gatherings before. They always hired extra servants— kitchen assistants for Mrs. Kelly,
grooms for the horses and carriages, maids to

attend the female guests or assist the footmen and Jacobs with refreshments—but this multitude was more than she had ever seen before. Big, burly footmen who seemed all thumbs from the amount of *tsk-tsking* coming from Aunt Edna and Mrs. McKeever.

She paced across the hallway, watching the emerald flash as she twisted her rings on her fingers. Too many accidents. Her thoughts kept circling through the number of accidents in such a short amount of time.

The whole household had talked of Nicholas's arrival, soaking wet from a dunking in the harbor. Then there was the runaway wagon in front of O'Brien and Mallory, the shot that sent her horse out of control and ended with Nick prostrate on the ground, and finally, Uncle Gill being carried into Bryan's dining room last night.

She should just confront the three of them with her questions and be done with it.

I will tell you what I can, when I can.

Her husband's words last night echoed back to her. She had agreed to wait, to trust him. But the light in Jamie's eyes matched the look in Nicholas's. Uncle Gill completed the triad when she had arrived this afternoon.

Her thoughts returned again to the previous night and Uncle Gill's injury. She really should go and demand that they tell her what was going on. She hated this feeling of vulnerability from not knowing. But she had promised Nicholas.

She sighed and paced back in the other direction.

"Meaghan, come in here at once and get dressed or you'll never be ready in time." Sheila stood in naught but chemise and petticoats. She motioned to Meaghan from the doorway of her bedchamber.

With reluctance, Meaghan gave up her struggle in the hallway and joined her cousin.

"Whatever will my mother think?" Sheila scolded, though her eyes twinkled. "You out there dawdling in the hall like a nervous bride when you are already an old married woman."

Meaghan couldn't help but laugh at Sheila's teasing. "Hardly that. I've been married barely two days."

"Well, how long does it take to become an old married woman?"

"I have no idea." A broad grin spread over Meaghan's lips and lifted some of the tension she'd been shouldering.

"Perhaps my mother knows."

"I'll have to remember to ask her. *After* the party."

Sheila gave Meaghan a hug. Comfort oozed from her and Meaghan almost cried with relief. A loud sigh escaped her, welling from the depths of her worry over too many things.

"Are you happy?" Sheila's quiet question tugged at Meaghan unexpectedly. "Do you like married life?"

Meaghan caught back another sigh and hugged Sheila tighter. "It's too soon to tell, I think. Things have happened so very quickly between Nicholas and me."

"Aye." Sheila heaved one of her more dramatic sighs. "Why, one day you greeted him with a passionate kiss in our drawing room and practically the very next you were his wife."

"She." Meaghan nudged her cousin, uncomfortable still with reminders of that first encounter and the lingering essence of the Reilly Blessing she had yet to unravel. Another mystery.

Sheila dissolved into laughter. "I just want you to be happy, Meggy. I want to know if it is possible to meet someone on such short acquaintance and discover the one person who will give you a lifetime of happiness. Of love."

"I know. You want to believe in happily-ever-after, just like in the novels you sneak under your mattress." Meaghan stepped back from her cousin and friend.

Sheila clearly wanted to believe what was growing between herself and Jamie Mansfield could lead to her own future happiness. If Meaghan and Nicholas could make their marriage work in such a short time, so could they.

"Suffice it to say I've been . . . Blessed."

Sheila frowned for a moment. "Blessed?"

"Aye." Meaghan nodded and offered a smile. "And leave it at that."

Blessing or Curse, for all time. She still was not quite certain which hers had become.

"All right. Blessed it is." Sheila smiled, undaunted by Meaghan's lack of responsiveness. "Did you see the envelope on my dresser? It came for you yesterday and I held on to it, knowing you would be here today."

"Envelope?"

"Aye." With a rustle of petticoats Sheila disappeared into the dressing room. "Oh, where is Triona? She was supposed to have my gown ready by now. It's on the top by the mirror." She continued muttering to herself as Meaghan scanned the dresser.

A crisp vellum envelope graced the top, the

handwriting bold and flowing. *Miss Meaghan Reilly*, it read, marked *from Mrs. Jeremiah Sullivan*.

Meaghan's heart sank to her toes. Elmira Sullivan, the widow she had visited the week before last. The day of the incident in front of Uncle Gill's office. The woman had sat in her front parlor, dressed completely in black, and questioned her stone-faced for well over an hour before ending the interview with only a cryptic, "You'll hear from me after I consider the matter further."

Somehow she couldn't face opening the envelope. With all that had happened in the intervening weeks, she had surely lost whatever chance she had possessed of garnering financing for the Limerick Nightingale Society. Even Nicholas smearing varnish across her reputation by marrying her almost instantly could not repair everything.

"Did you see who it's from?"

Meaghan jumped as Sheila's question came from right behind her.

"Aye."

"Well, aren't you going to open it? You were absolutely driving me mad waiting to hear from her. Maybe she's decided to offer you a wedding gift."

"Somehow I doubt that. Mrs. Sullivan is about as proper as proper can be, Sheila. And I . . . well, I have shown myself to be anything but proper almost from the moment I came to stay with you." Meaghan tapped the letter with her fingernails, anxious to know the answer and yet torn with the desire to leave things be.

"Well, give it to me then and I'll open it." Sheila reached for the envelope and Meaghan let it slip from her fingers.

"Oh, miss." Triona shuffled into the room. "I'm that sorry. I meant to be up here ta help ye both some time ago. But first Mrs. Kelly needed me and then it was Agnes with the linens. Some of the men Mr. O'Brien hired ta help this time don't seem to have the least notion of how to go on. Yer mother is beside herself."

"It's all right, Triona. Don't fret." Sheila winked at Meaghan and dropped the envelope back to the dresser unopened. "We still have plenty of time to get ready."

"Oh, thank ye, miss. Agnes said ye'd understand." The little maid sighed and then bobbed a quick curtsy to Meaghan. "Hullo, yer ladyship. 'Tis good ta see ye again."

"Thank you, Triona." How long would it take before "your ladyship" became a form of address she recognized without a start?

"Yer gown should be up straight away. Agnes still had to press out the flounce. She promised to bring it right up."

"That's fine." Meaghan eyed the envelope again, then sighed.

"Is Jamie downstairs with Nicholas?" The question she knew Sheila had been bursting to ask since she'd opened the door and dragged her in from the hall finally popped out.

"Aye, of course he is."

"Oh, good." Sheila's brown eyes twinkled. "I so like him, Meaghan."

Meaghan raised her eyebrows. *That* was an understatement.

"Aye, and he likes ye too, miss," Triona murmured from her position behind Sheila. "Ye can see it in his eyes when he looks at ye. My mum

always said a man shows his feelin's in his eyes.
And Mum's right most of the time."

"Do you really think so?" Color touched
Sheila's cheeks and a quick smile of satisfaction
lit her face.

"Well, he talks about you often enough,"
Meaghan offered, settling herself on the edge of
Sheila's bed as Triona helped her cousin into a
shimmering peach satin gown shot through with
gold threads.

"He does?" Enthusiasm echoed from the
depths of the gown. "Oh, Triona, help!"

The little maid laughed as she tugged the
gown down into place and set to work on the
tiny row of buttons up the back.

"Of course he does."

"Oh, Meaghan." Sheila's eyes sparkled. "Does
he really? What does he say? What do you talk
about? Oh, I have a thousand questions."

"Well, still your questions for later, my girl."
Aunt Edna swept into the room, resplendent in
deep indigo velvet that highlighted her fair coloring and brought out the soft blue of her eyes.
She closed the door behind her with an impatient snap. "Our guests will be gathering below
very shortly and you are not even finished dressing."

Despite her artful hair and the diamonds sparkling in her ears and around her neck, her face
looked decidedly washed. The worry of the men
must have transferred to her, too. Or maybe Uncle Gill had trusted his wife of many years when
Nicholas could not bring himself to trust his wife
of but a few days. Guess that would put paid to
Sheila's query about what might make one an
old married woman—your husband's trust.

The confirmation that her husband did not trust her plummeted through Meaghan.

Aunt Edna stopped her progress into the room and looked sharply at Meaghan on the bed. "Meaghan, why are you still sitting there in your day dress? Triona, what is the delay?"

"Downstairs, Aunt. Agnes should deliver it shortly."

"I'm sorry, missus. I was delayed in my duties." Triona looked very contrite as she turned Aunt Edna's attention to herself.

"No excuses, Triona. You know how little tolerance I have for lateness. We cannot be late to our own affair."

"Aye, Missus." Triona bobbed quickly, hustling Sheila toward the dressing mirror to finish her hair.

"We'll be ready. Don't worry," Sheila offered as she tilted her head to allow Triona better access to her long brown curls.

The door popped open and Meaghan's dress ushered itself into the room. A dark cranberry-colored brushed satin, suspended in the air, atop two dark boots. The women in the room froze for an instant.

"What on earth?" Aunt Edna marched over to the offending garment and the temporary footman holding it aloft. "Don't you know better than to enter a room without knocking? Without being given leave! This is my daughter's bedchamber."

"Beg pardon, mum. I was asked ta bring it up. Took me a bit. This is the sixth door. No one answered at the last five."

"Knock on all the doors the next time. Now, place the dress on the bed and get back below.

I'm sure they've a use for you downstairs." Aunt Edna gripped her hands together.

The footman bowed briefly and exited the room.

Aunt Edna released a heavy sigh. "Why I must make do during an affair of this caliber without our usual help is beyond me. Your father would not give me the slightest inclination, and yet he insisted we use these ill-trained people instead of the ones from our usual agency. I have never been so upset. And after the condition he came home in last night. So inebriated, Lord Ashton's man nearly carried him up the stairs."

Edna fanned herself; high color dotted her smooth cheeks. So Uncle Gill hadn't enlightened her over his accident. Surprise rippled through Meaghan. How out of character. They shared everything.

Sheila sprang up from the dressing table as Triona finished tucking the last curl into place. "I haven't been much help, either. As soon as Meaghan is dressed, we will do whatever you ask. We can arrange flowers, fold napkins, upbraid the lot of these new footmen—whatever you want."

She wrapped her arms around her mother and offered a soothing hug as Triona motioned hurriedly to Meaghan.

Sheila continued, as Aunt Edna's color returned more to normal. "I'm sure Father has his reasons for insisting things be as they are. You know he always gives over all the preparations to you."

"Yes, he does. And he's never been disappointed."

"Never," Sheila soothed again. "Don't worry.

I'm certain he'll explain himself. Maybe he has a surprise for you."

"I do hope he has a plausible explanation for all of this." Edna pulled back from her daughter and her look softened. "Oh, Sheila, you look wonderful."

As Triona settled the satin gown around Meaghan's waist, Meaghan had to agree. With her dark brown hair swept up atop her head, her eyes sparkling with anticipation and set off to perfection by the peach coloring in her gown, Sheila O'Brien was beautiful.

"Thank you, Mums." This long-ago endearment brought a smile to Edna's lips.

"You are incorrigible, my darling daughter. But that is only one of the many reasons I love you."

"And you, Meaghan." Soothed by her daughter's attentions, Edna was once more back on an even keel. "I just knew the cranberry hue would highlight your black hair to perfection, and it does. Don't you agree, Sheila?"

"Indeed." Sheila twinkled. "Even her husband will be spellbound tonight."

A swirl of pleasure whirled through Meaghan at the thought of Nicholas being spellbound by the sight of her. She couldn't quash the hope it would be so. Triona settled Meaghan in front of the dressing mirror and went to work on her long black hair, brushing it to a high shine before twisting the mass of it into a fine chignon. The girl glowing back at Meaghan from the mirror looked pale and refined in her cranberry gown. White skin showed in abundance above the gown's daring decolletage; even her shoulders were bare.

"Jewelry, my lady?" Triona's question broke into Meaghan's thoughts.

"She'll appear more stunning without any," Aunt Edna answered before Meaghan could reply. "Meaghan looks dramatic enough in her ensemble to need no other jewelry, but Sheila will wear my pearls tonight."

"Your pearls?" Sheila gasped, and her eyebrows shot up to her hairline.

"You've earned them, darling." Edna patted her daughter's cheek. "I'll be right back."

Meaghan escaped the dressing table and her own all-too-ladylike reflection as Edna swept from the room. She fastened the fine gold chain of her granny's elegant pearl cross behind her neck. The truth of Aunt Edna's summation aside, the simplicity of the necklace did not detract from her ensemble and wearing this piece of home helped her face the rigors of her first night at a major social event as Lady Ashton.

Feeling it between her breasts would help keep her rooted in her own identity, her heritage.

"I need to check something with Nicholas."

"But we promised to help Mother."

"I won't be long. If I'm not back before you need to leave, go on down without me. I'll find you." Meaghan closed the door behind her and hurried toward the steps.

Her aunt's concerns about the servants only served to tie in with her own certainty that something was wrong. Uncle Gill hiding things from his wife only heightened the mess. Nicholas knew the source of all this contention, and so did Jamie and Uncle Gill. She needed to get to the heart of her suspicions and put an end to the fears running wild through her mind.

Satin whispered and shushed around her as she made her way down the long staircase in her soft leather dancing slippers. Servants scurried back and forth through the marbled hallway below. Voices sounded from the direction of Uncle Gill's study. She went toward them. She stopped with her hand on the doorknob as their conversation seeped through the thick oak portal.

"If we could just put our hands on the culprit and be done with it, the entire night would sit far better with me." Uncle Gill sounded almost as agitated as Aunt Edna had been only a few moments before. "Mrs. O'Brien is ready to ream my skull out in order to get answers to her questions. She was already at fever pitch over last night. I ended up just putting my foot down, but I don't know how long that will last. I've never interfered in her running of the household before."

"She'll just have to wait with the rest of us." Nicholas sounded distant and unconcerned.

Meaghan tightened her grip on the brass doorknob, took a deep breath, and started to twist it.

"Have you considered what you're going to do with your wife going forward?" Her uncle's question stilled her in her tracks.

"My wife?" Nicholas asked, his tone wary.

Meaghan's heart sank, twisting deep inside her. He was going to do something with her? That did not sound at all good. She had become a problem to him. A problem that needed resolution in the form of a discussion with her uncle. How mortifying.

"Yes, man. Have you not thought where you might send her?"

He was sending her away.

Pain clogged her throat and tears blurred her vision. Painful bands tightened around her chest, robbing her of breath.

Her mother said those who listened at closed doors heard nothing they liked. How right she was. How right she had always been. Right in every note of caution she ever sounded. Suddenly, Meaghan longed for nothing so much as to be enfolded in her mother's loving and understanding arms.

"Yes, my plans are set."

The pain wrenched again, and it was all she could do to stay where she was. Part of her longed to throw open the doors and demand the answers to the questions that had dragged her downstairs in the first place. The other wanted to scream in frustration that he could make such tender ardent love to her and only hours later be considering how best to set her aside. She gripped the door frame.

Neither action would accomplish what she most wanted. For Nicholas to trust her. To want her. Not because society dictated it. And not just for the hot pleasures they shared. But by his own choice. Losing all hope made her true desires crystal clear.

She had heard of such things, tales of forgotten wives set aside by husbands who found them unsuitable, but she had never dreamed it would happen to her. Not with Nicholas. Not after . . .

A sob welled up inside her and she held it back with an effort.

"I'm sending her home. To her island. I've already sent a message to her brother, informing him fully of my reasons. We just have to get through this evening."

So she was being sent home to Beannacht in disgrace, and Quin would know the full scope of her humiliation. That just completed the circle of despair whirling wildly through her heart.

She had heard enough to last her a lifetime. How would she ever get through this interminable social affair? Her heart lay in ruins, her future in rags. Her feet fairly flew over the marble foyer as she made her way to the staircase.

Tears burned down her cheeks as she hurried up the steps. Memories of the last time she had made this rushed flight haunted each step she took. She had come from the study that night, too. The night Nicholas had kissed her so passionately and burned a place into her heart.

She stopped at the top of the stairs, her heart thumping painfully. She placed her hand tight over her mouth to keep the telltale sobs locked away inside her. She had run from him then, but it had already been too late. Nicholas Mansfield, Lord Ashton of Suffolk, had already done harm far more irreparable than tarnishing her reputation.

He had made her love him.

Pain wrenched again. She loved him. All this time and she hadn't even realized it. More fool her to succumb to The Blessing and love a man plotting how best to cut free of her.

Perhaps that was The Curse. Her Curse. To love a man who could never love her.

All the times she had insisted, demanded, her own Blessing tumbled back through her mind. In each and every one of them she had been determined it was her right as a Reilly to have what had been promised. Now all she could think of were the gloomier parts of The Blessing, the dark undertones she'd always ignored despite her brothers's teasing. *That won't happen to me. I won't be Cursed,* she told them.

A dreadful promise.

Wasn't that part of it?

A fearsome gratitude.

Hysterical laughter bubbled in her chest. The darkness of the thoughts locked in her heart burst. She gave in to a horrible mingling of laughter and tears that left her drained and breathless and clutching the newel post for support.

"Oh, Granny Reilly, if only I had listened to the whole story and not been in such a terrible hurry to claim something I'm no longer certain I want."

Her voice came out shaky and clogged with tears. In the distance she could almost smell a faint hint of lavender and feel the salty breeze drifting over Beannacht Harbor.

She straightened and forced herself to take several long, deep breaths. If this was her fate, she would face it. She would manage to live through whatever needed to be. She loved Nicholas. That was a fact. She would always remember his touch, the twin scents of oranges and mint that seemed to be his alone, and the taste of his mouth against hers.

Pride as ancient and honor bound as her heritage tugged her shoulders taut. She was Reilly born and Reilly bred.

She would survive this.

Sixteen

Concern tugged at Nick, worrying the edges of his composure as surely as a hound worrying a fox. "I don't like the idea of sending my wife anywhere."

He downed the contents of his cut-crystal tumbler in one long swallow. He set the glass down on Gill O'Brien's marble mantel with a loud clink.

The brandy's burn couldn't begin to touch the knot in his stomach, a knot formed in the early hours of the morning. The city of Limerick stirred to teeming life around them while Meaghan slept in his arms. He'd realized then how much her safety meant to him. Keeping her with him in the face of escalating danger was selfish. O'Brien had actually been shot last night!

Everything inside Nick screamed to get Meaghan as far away as possible, and as quickly as possible. Instead, he stood there discussing it as though they had more than enough time at his disposal. "I would prefer to keep her close by, where I can see to her security myself."

"I understand, Nick, truly." Gill O'Brien paced the length of his study, his strides punchy with his own tension, his black velvet coat and white lace cravat and cuffs bobbed with each step. "But I think you are right to send her to Quin. He's a good man. The islanders look after their own."

He stopped at the window behind his desk and looked out over his front lawns as he ran a thoughtful finger over his mustache. "Edna and Sheila will accompany her. No one will get to them there."

He looked over at Nick, who nodded his agreement. Having her aunt and cousin with her to bear her company might make the separation easier for Meaghan. If only they didn't have to traverse the River Shannon to reach Beannacht. Something had the hairs on the back of his neck prickling as they had done before almost every calamity.

Perhaps he should reconsider and send them to Bryan. But an overland route posed even more danger in his estimation. And so the hound went, worrying at the fox.

"Sending our womenfolk out of harm's way will allow us to turn our entire attentions toward figuring out who is behind this debacle." The barrister finished the contents in his tumbler as well and let loose a gusty sigh. "And at least Edna would not be here to ask me what is going on at every possible moment. Although how I'll gain her cooperation on this without alarming her further I am at a loss to say."

"I think you must persevere, sir." Jamie straightened from his nonchalant pose by the hearth. "I certainly would feel much more comfortable if I knew Sheila was not anywhere she might come to harm."

"Indeed?" O'Brien snapped back into his barrister's suspicion without even dusting his trousers. "And why might that be?"

"I . . . I . . ." Jamie looked to Nick for support.

Quite obviously, he had not planned on his voicing his concern for O'Brien's chit in such a proprietary manner. Nick smothered a smile. "I believe my ward . . . er, my cousin, is trying to tell you that his feelings for your daughter go beyond those of mere friendship."

Jamie colored, managing to look both relieved and chagrined by Nick's description at one and the same time. The urge to smile deepened. Those very same feelings should make it easier on the pup to swallow Nick's plan for him to accompany the ladies as they sought refuge with Quintin Reilly. He hoped to put it to the boy that he'd be seeing to their safety during the voyage.

"The devil you say." O'Brien frowned at Jamie as though he had just discovered a new form of judicial infraction. He placed his tumbler back on the desk with a slight thump, wincing slightly at the pain that surely reverberated up his arm.

Nick's shoulder twinged in sympathy. The poor man had already told him the length of trouble he had to go to in order to hide his injury from his all-too-inquisitive wife. He'd gone so far as to allow her to think he'd come home too inebriated to attend her supper party last night.

O'Brien settled himself against the edge of his desk, his piercing gaze never shifting from Jamie. He lifted one brow. Very slowly. "And when did all this come about, young Mansfield?"

Jamie lifted his chin, despite the fresh stain of

bright red color climbing his cheeks above the cool ivory of his cravat.

"I care very much for her, sir. I don't know how it came about, to tell you the truth. Some time during that ride to seek help when Nick was injured, when she kept going despite the rain and lightning, and the problems we had locating you in the ruins, I found myself unwilling to consider spending a lifetime without her to share it with me."

Jamie looked over at Nick just then, his gaze begging for understanding. "Though I have not had the chance to discuss this with Nick yet, I would like you to consider agreeing to my proposal of marriage for Sheila."

Too much. Your timing is definitely off, stripling.

Nick managed to bite back the words. Now did not seem the time to remonstrate the boy. The man, he corrected himself. For despite the blushes coming and going across Jamie's all-too-serious features, resolve and maturity showed in the way he held himself as he awaited Gill O'Brien's answer.

"Brandy?" Nick leaned forward and reached for the decanter, pouring healthy refills into all three empty tumblers. The activity offered only slight distraction from O'Brien's silence.

The barrister accepted the libation gratefully and all but drained the glass in one swallow. He sighed and rubbed at his shoulder when he had finished.

Jamie's grip on his own glass had tightened to the point that his fingertips showed a dull white against the crystal, but his determined expression did not change.

A swell of pride tightened Nick's chest. He

sipped his brandy and waited to see who would speak first.

"Sir?" Jamie prompted.

O'Brien closed his eyes for a moment, sighed again and fixed his stern gaze on Jamie once more. "You have not picked the most opportune time to discuss this with me. You know that, don't you?"

"Yes, sir." Jamie nodded but held his stance. "I apologize, but you see, I . . . I love Sheila. And I want to be able to tell her."

Not the slightest twitch changed Gill O'Brien's expression as Jamie revealed his love for the Irish barrister's daughter. Nick wondered for a moment if the man had even heard what Jamie had said. Then Nick noted just the tiniest glimmer of moisture gathering at the corner of the father's eye. Silence held as the moments ticked past on the mantelpiece clock.

"I can think of far worse fates for my daughter," O'Brien said finally.

"Sir?" Jamie's brows knit together.

"You may tell her, though heaven help you if Mrs. O'Brien isn't happy over this development. There will be no living with her then, whatever the outcome of our current situation."

"Thank you, sir." Jamie beamed with mingled relief and pride.

The barrister nodded.

"Speaking of our current situation," Nick said, determined to bring them back to the subject at hand. "Have you any further insight to provide?"

"None so far." Gill shook his head. "I looked through my files from the inception of the trust right through the first decade when your father began to suspect everything was not as it should be with the investments. My records appear incomplete from that period until right before your father's death."

"The records of the embezzlement are not in your possession?" The hair on the back of Nick's neck prickled again.

"Lost?" Jamie shot him a puzzled look.

"Misplaced over the years, most likely."

"Tell me again the details of the incident. I only remember a sketchy bit from my childhood visit to the courthouse."

O'Brien looked puzzled, but nodded."You father caught him in the act. I remember how surprised he was. How surprised we all were. We trusted Chase with far more than was wise, considering the circumstances. Later we found out his father had been mad. I'd always suspected Neville was foraging his way down the same road, poor devil."

"I thought he was dead." This from Jamie, who seemed to have recovered some of his equilibrium.

"Yes. I worked the case myself. He received a sentence of life in the prison colony in Australia. Not a pretty thing to face for a man like Neville Chase."

"You are certain he couldn't have gotten free?" Nick asked.

"Quite certain. He died in transport. Ship exploded, killing everyone on board."

Ship exploded. The description burned in Nick's brain with a dull and painful heat. Strange, his father had lost his life in the same way as the man he had helped sentence. Strange and all too coincidental.

He shivered, caught for a moment in the cold wash of old memories.

There had been a time when his aunt and uncle had presumed him lost as well, when his parents died. The first reports had stated all were lost. Only after Nick came back to himself enough to make his way to the authorities did they learn he lived.

It was Gill O'Brien who had taken him in, sheltering him until Jamie's parents arrived for him. It was O'Brien who had identified his parents' bodies and had them taken care of prior to transport home to England. Through the veil of his suspicions he'd forgotten how much he owed the barrister.

"—Then who could it be? Other than the trust, there is nothing to tie the three of us together." Jamie's question made Nick realize he'd lost track of the conversation.

"I'm not so certain." Even as he said the words, a cold, hard surety grabbed the pit of his stomach.

"What do you mean, Nick?"

"Everything indicated Chase died in an explosion?"

"Yes. Those were the reports that came back to us. You can see for yourself. Once I locate them. Your father insisted they be extremely thorough. He spent some time talking with the man after his arrest. It was more than any of us cared to do, but you know your father. Gerald Mansfield always stood ready to listen to the other man's side of a story. He wanted to give Neville the chance to explain."

Gill rubbed a hand over his chin. "Something Chase said to him must have bothered him though, because he never went back after the first time. And he seemed quite determined to find proof of his death. When the proof arrived, he seemed relieved. He never wanted to discuss Chase after that."

Cold certainty squeezed Nick. "He must be our culprit."

"Chase?" O'Brien's eyebrows shot up to his nonexistent hairline. "That can't be. Too many years have passed."

"I think it is. How tasty his final vengeance will seem, served on a silver platter. If we are eliminated and all the records lost, he alone can gain the proceeds of the investment trust." Nick tightened his lips. Dread curled itself around his heart.

He pressed on. "I think Neville Chase escaped that prison-ship explosion. If so, he could be responsible for the explosion that killed my parents, and the fire that took Jamie's. Accidents of murder so like the ones you and I have both escaped of late."

Varying degrees of denial, concern, and understanding flitted across the faces of Jamie and the barrister. Silence reigned for a moment, broken only by the sounds of the household readying for the party and the solemn ticking of the mantelpiece clock.

Finally, agreement echoed back to him from their gazes, deepening his dread.

"Then we'd best get the women off to Beannacht as quickly as possible."

Meaghan slipped into the bedroom next to Sheila's, hers only a few short days ago. She dashed cool water over her cheeks to wash away the signs of her tears. No matter what Nicholas might be planning, she wouldn't ruin Sheila's or Aunt Edna's evenings by letting them see her distress.

"There will be plenty of time for feeling sorry for yourself later," she promised herself. After she'd been banished.

After she was alone. On Beannacht.

She glanced toward the mirror. The same cool ladylike reflection stared back at her, pale and refined in her dark satin gown. If only . . .

She shook her head, unwilling to torture herself over dreams of what might have been between herself and Nicholas. When he touched her and she lost all sense of herself, when she could think of naught but him, she had been willing to believe they could make a life for themselves together. But in the cold light of reality, what future could there be for a lord and the daughter of a shipbuilder?

Despite The Blessing.

Because of The Curse?

She blew out a deep breath. There was no time for dwelling on this now. She'd promised to help and help she would. She didn't want Nicholas to have any inkling that she had heard his plans. Her Reilly pride forbade it. She would hold her pain tight in her heart this night. Opening the connecting door between the two bedrooms she crossed through into Sheila's room.

They'd gone on ahead.

Relief tingled through her. She'd gained a few more minutes to pull herself together.

The envelope Meaghan had been unwilling to investigate earlier lay on the bed, the top torn open by a hasty hand. A smile curved Meaghan's lips despite her distress. Sheila had been determined to get the answer for her.

Meaghan scooped up the envelope and crossed toward the windows. With the last waning light spilling in she would read the letter and find out for herself just how much damage she had done to her efforts to garner funding for the Nightingale Society.

She glanced out the window as she pulled the sheaves of fine vellum from the envelope. Below in the gardens, movement drew her attention. It was Sheila. Aunt Edna was a shrewd woman with her fashion choices. The shimmering gold-shot peach satin would have set Sheila apart from the crowd anywhere.

It was awfully late for Aunt Edna to send Sheila out for flowers to augment her arrangements. What could she be doing there?

Behind Sheila in the deep shadows, deepening still further as Meaghan watched, other movement showed.

Someone was out there with Sheila. Behind her. Too big to be Triona. Too small for Jamie.

Meaghan put her hand on the latch as a face peered out of the shrubbery, highlighted by the last streaks of sunlight. A shiver traced Meaghan's spine as she recognized that face. It was the groomsman present on the day of the picnic. The one who had made her flesh crawl just by looking at her.

Her stomach clenched. *He shouldn't be here.* Certainty as sure as the sunset hitched her breath. And he shouldn't be in the gardens with Sheila. She needed the groomsman to know he was being observed. She tapped on the window.

"Sheila!"

"No, my dear." A wiry arm snaked around Meaghan's waist and pulled her away from the window.

She stumbled backward and her breath whooshed out of her. Her envelope fluttered to the floor along with its papers.

"I don't think we'll be alerting the young lady in the gardens just yet." Fetid breath fanned her cheeks. "I've a need for her. For both of you."

She drew in breath to scream only to have it cut off by a hand pressed over her mouth.

"I truly do not wish to hurt you." The arm around her waist tightened, pulling her further backward until he held her tight against his hard body. Below in the gardens there was a flash of movement and then Sheila disappeared from sight.

"No!" Meaghan screamed against his hand. The sound went nowhere.

The man held her even tighter, pressing her with cruel intimacy against him. She tried to break free of his hand, but he clamped harder, until his fingers bruised her jaw and his stiff collar scraped against her neck.

"I've been watching you. I know what he's made you do." Hot breath harassed her cheek. She could feel the stubble of an unshaven cheek on her ear. What was he talking about? What did he intend to do next?

"No man should treat his wife in such a fashion."

Nicholas. He had watched her and Nicholas? When? How? What was happening? She fought the panic and tried to listen, to figure things out.

"Especially not him. I have come to stop him. To help you."

The sensation of lips pressed ever so briefly against the back of her hair chilled her blood. She struggled, kicking against the man's legs. Hampered by her voluminous skirts her slipper-clad heels made little impact.

The arm about her tightened just a bit further. Pain edged her ribs. She could barely breathe between the vise of his grip and the hand on her mouth.

"I don't *want* to hurt you. But if you endanger your own rescue, it may become necessary." His tone carried a strange mingling of concern and threat. She felt dizzy from the lack of air.

"We've got the one, sir." A whisper hissed out of the darkened hallway. "We'd best go quickly."

"Ready the horses." A sharp retort. Hot breath stirred the fine hairs at the back of her neck and poured over her bare shoulders. Something brushed briefly against her breast. She shuddered. Darkness closed around her. She needed to breathe. To think.

"We must go, my dear. We've a ways to travel before we are ready to await your husband."

What on earth did he mean? What plans did this nameless, faceless foe have for Nicholas? And what did any of this have to do with Sheila? Fear sliced Meaghan as he moved her easily through the bedroom toward the doorway. No matter her struggles he half pulled, half carried her along, as though she weighed very little. Her efforts otherwise mattered not one whit.

He couldn't possibly get her out of a house peopled with servants and family members. Her mind raced, and she remembered her childhood

and all the boisterous and very unladylike games
she had played with her brothers. What would
Quin have done in a situation like this? Or
Devin?

The light dawned. Preparing herself to fall, she
went limp in his arms, making herself a dead
weight.

She had the minor satisfaction of hearing her
captor curse and then the arms about her tightened still further. Pain twinged sharper this time.

"Don't make me hurt you, I don't *want* to hurt
you." Venom hissed in her ear, grating along her
nerve endings.

He removed his hand long enough for a quick
gulp of air before he stuffed a cloth in her
mouth. She gagged on the vile scrap. And then,
"Help me. Grab her legs. We must hurry before
we are discovered."

A second pair of arms clamped around her
legs and she was airborne, carried quickly down
the back steps and whisked out into the open
air. She remained limp but managed a good look
at the second of her abductors. The footman
who had delivered her dress. Somehow she was
not surprised.

Oh, Nicholas.

The scent of roses surrounded her as the two
men bore her into the darkness bordering the
gardens. Her heart sank as her gaze found
Sheila, neatly trussed up and gagged, her shimmering peach satin ball gown stained with grass
and mud from her obvious struggles to avoid
capture.

She sat huddled on the grass, the groomsman
who had snatched her looming nearby. Tears

sparkled on Sheila's cheeks and her hair hung in damp ringlets over her shoulders.

"At least you accomplished one task correctly." The sharp voice of her captor gloated. "Help me with Lady Ashton."

"Aye, sir." There was a scuffle of sound as the other two did his bidding. Harsh rope bit into her wrists after they were jerked behind her. They looped the rope about her chest several times, pulling tight to press her arms into her sides.

"Gently now," her captor scolded. "I told you I wanted no harm to come to this one."

What about Sheila? Surely he meant no harm must come to either of them.

"I'm sorry to do this, my dear," he told her, his soft voice almost begging her forgiveness. His hand stroked her bare shoulder in a short, hesitant contact. "I would much prefer to have you both ride upright, but until you hear me out it is best we take precautions."

His breath fanned the side of her neck for a moment. She feared he would try to kiss her. She squirmed.

"My lady." His hand trailed down her arm as though he were loath to release her.

Revulsion rolled deep in her stomach.

Strong arms hoisted her high and tossed her atop the back of a waiting horse. She struggled and almost succeeded in spilling herself from the back. Then pain slammed against the side of her head and darkness spilled over her mind.

"Rodents." Neville spat the word in disgust. As soon as he broke free of his need for these Muldoons he would right some of the wrongs they had perpetrated against himself and against these two ladies.

The sight of Mansfield's innocent young bride slung unconscious across the nags they'd brought with them, like a sack of potatoes, churned his gut. With an effort, he contained his need to beat the Muldoons senseless in retaliation and swung up into the saddle.

He took a deep breath and closed his eyes, letting the raw night sounds move over him as the sun finished its descent and poured cool darkness over his thoughts.

Even the air tasted fine and sweet tonight, like the choicest nectar against his tongue. He could smell his victory. And it carried the same fresh floral scent that wafted from Lady Ashton's silken skin. Laughter swelled in his chest and he caught it back. Now was not the time.

His bumbling buffoons rode along behind him, each in charge of the precious cargo they had stolen right from beneath the very noses of Mansfield and O'Brien. Neville had always suspected O'Brien was not the master intellect, not the man he proclaimed himself to be. And here was the proof.

What better protection could he provide for his father's name than to clear it of the stinking stain Mansfield's father and O'Brien had placed there so long ago? The final evidence that might reverse his hard work would vanish with Mansfield and O'Brien.

Oh, that would be the sweetest taste yet. Just the anticipation of it proved intoxicating.

Moonlight spilled over the inky purple landscape, lighting their way. Very soon now, his enemies would realize that their women were gone.

Then they would realize there was righteous
vengeance afoot. They would begin to tremble.
But it was already too late.

He laughed finally as the road dipped downward, leaving the O'Brien household behind
them. Even his headache abated, leaving behind
a unique and piquant kind of peace such as he
had never known before.

Setting his final vengeance into motion had
freed him of the pain that had been his frequent
companion for far too long.

Perhaps it wasn't the abyss he needed to fear
after all.

He laughed again, listening to the sound of
mirth echo like the chink of fine crystal. Such
was the sound of a free and righteous man. A
man avenged. A man who would finally take his
rightful place among the society that had
damned him to the hell that had been his life
for too long.

But very soon, oh yes, all too soon that would
end. He would never again have to look back in
shame. Never have to hear his mother's voice,
shaking with disappointment and quivering with
the despair his father had wrought for her.

It would all end.

And that made even hell worthwhile.

He rode with the moonlight streaming down
at him like blessings from above, like his
mother's approval, his father's relief, stroking
him through the darkness. He felt light. He felt
powerful. Nothing could stop him now.

They crossed the land in silence, broken only
by Neville's occasional bursts of laughter and the
pounding of the horses' hooves as they churned
the dark green pastures. The inn he'd chosen

for his final revenge would be a ride, but as he savored the night he was comfortable with that.

As they got closer, he motioned for one of the hulking Muldoons to take the lead. No use in taking the chance one of their lack-witted relatives would mistake him for a criminal and shoot him from the saddle.

Their hoofbeats clattered in sharp staccato over the worn cobbles in the dark inn yard. The windows stood as yawning pitch-black mauls and the door was locked and barred. Not many made their way to the *Thie Oast Awiney,* The Riverside Inn. Especially since the River Shannon still lay further to the east.

Ramshackle and forgotten, the place was perfect for what he had in mind, however. Pleasure rippled through him.

One Muldoon slid from the back of his horse and beat a rapid tattoo against the inn door.

Silence held for a moment and then the door creaked inward.

"That you?" a hushed voice called out into the darkness.

"Aye, 'tis me and Rory and that fellow we been workin' fer. Let us in."

The door opened wider and light spilled out over the cobbles.

"Ye can go in, Mr. Chase. Me and Rory will bring yer guests in fer ye."

"See that you do," Neville told them, sliding easily from his horse's back. His gut tightened. Oh, it was a glorious night. And there would be more glory still to come. He threw back his shoulders and strutted into the inn like a man about to regain his life.

"Innkeep? I'll have ale, if you please. And I

need two rooms immediately for my companions. Something comfortable, but restrained. Locks on the doors are a must."

The girl in the peach-colored satin squeaked a protest as Rory Muldoon heaved her over his shoulder and awaited the innkeep's reply.

"We've yer rooms ready. Where's yer money?"

Ill-mannered dog. Another Muldoon, no doubt. Neville forced himself to hide his disgust. Just another rat to join the dirty pack he had surrounded himself with. But not for much longer.

"Your money is here, my good man." He placed a small bag of silver on the table. "And there is more if you demonstrate your ability to cooperate."

The man didn't bother to open his bounty, only weighing it in his hand while his narrow little eyes assessed Neville in silence. This Muldoon seemed a tad sharper than the others. Money alone did not prod him. Good. He would have need of such a man before morning.

"Ye'll get yer cooperation." He nodded to Neville and then motioned to his two relatives. "If'n the price is right.

"Take 'em upstairs and to the left. There's rooms and they both 'ave locks on 'em."

"Put them together for the moment," Neville called after them.

His gaze caught on the sight of Mansfield's bride tossed over the back of his minion with her white petticoats glowing in the firelight and a smooth expanse of calf exposed. Pressure swelled in his groin.

The distant echo of his headache twinged at his temples and he looked away.

"Here's yer ale." The innkeeper clunked a

chipped mug before Neville, slopping ale onto the table as he did so.

Neville's lip itched to curl, but he suppressed it. Cur. They were all so slovenly and commonplace. He forced his features to a bland smile. Everything was going his way; he could afford to be magnanimous for one night.

"Thank you, my good man. You have been very helpful." He leaned forward, gesturing for his new companion to sit. "Now, here is what else I require."

Seventeen

Meaghan's heartbeat drummed in her ears as she twisted her hands, fighting the knots. Her fingers stretched and strained, the hemp biting her skin raw for her efforts. How long had she been at this?

Blasted knots. They were far too tight. But she had years of picking at seamen's knots to guide her. She couldn't give up.

Sheila had mercifully lost consciousness after spending her fury and hysteria in a storm of tears when they had first been dumped onto the floor and the door locked behind them.

How long ago had that been? How long until someone noticed their absence and rode after them? How long before their captor sought this revenge he craved on her husband?

The stench of stale ale and staler men permeated the air. Meaghan could see next to nothing in the darkened room. The only light available was a thin stream of moonlight piercing the cracked boards across the windows and a ribbon from the door's warped edge.

Small feet scurried by in the darkness. *Rats.* She was almost certain.

She swallowed hard and choked on the gag in her mouth. Forcing herself to concentrate on the knots, she blotted out everything else. If she could manage to pick them and free Sheila as well, they would at least have a chance to defend themselves.

If not—her mind shuddered away from the alternative. She could still feel their captor's hot breath in her hair and his fingers against her skin.

Sweat dampened her fingers and they slid against the knots. She groaned, a fear-laced frustration that stretched into the darkness.

Oh, Nicholas. Your enemy is going to try to use me to trap you somehow. She couldn't bear it. Not if he were killed. Not if he were killed because of her. She had to get free.

The door opened, loosing a wide swatch of light and shadows across the floor. She tensed. Perhaps she should feign a swoon herself so that her captors might ease either her bonds or the gag.

"That one, eh?"

"Aye, the one in the red. He'd wanted 'er moved." The errant footman and the grooms-man sauntered into the room, bold and loose hipped.

"Well, what about that one, eh? I wouldn't mind takin' a go at her." The taller one scratched himself, a lewd smile twisting his features.

"Not now. We haven't time," his shorter companion complained. "And ye'd best not settle yerself on the wrong side of Chase. He don't appear to be the kind that'd take well ta ye takin' somethin' he wanted fer himself."

"He don't want that one." The taller one

jerked a thumb toward Sheila's prone form. "It's
this one he wants." His thumb twitched in
Meaghan's direction. "Ye can tell from the way
he looks at her. Like a hound in heat."

"I'm not about ta take chances over a bit of
skirt. If that's what ye want ta do, then help
yerself."

"Ah, hell. I'll wait till later. He can't keep 'em
both busy." The taller one snorted at his own
jest. Both pairs of booted feet came toward
Meaghan. She swallowed hard as fear rolled
through her in dizzying waves.

They jerked her to her feet, their hands tight
against her arms. Pain arched through her shoulders and she groaned again.

"Sorry darlin'. We don't see too many fine ladies," the taller one told her, his leer going
straight down the front of her bodice. She kicked
at him and missed. He clamped a callused hand
on her bare shoulder and rubbed his thumb
along her collar bone.

"Leave 'er be," the shorter one told him.
"Chase is going ta wonder what's takin' us so
long."

"Yer no fun anymore, Rory."

The two men dragged Meaghan out of the
room and locked it behind them. Meaghan
prayed Sheila would not awaken and find herself
alone in the dark anytime soon. The scurvies
opened the door to another room. There was
light in this room. One foul-smelling oil lamp
was sitting atop a crooked table. They deposited
her on a bed with a sagging mattress and ragged
gray coverlet.

"Ye won't be lonely long, missus." The taller
one patted her cheek, and she could only stare

her outrage at him. "Mr. Chase is anxious ta lay his hands on ye."

He chuckled at his own humor once again.

"Leave us." Icy tones spilled from the doorway, stopping her current tormentor's taunts.

"Aye, sir."

"You know what I expect. Do you think you can carry this last out without flummoxing the entire thing?"

"Aye, sir." Again their heads bobbed in unison. Their master rubbed at his temples.

"Get out. And don't come back until you can give me the proper report." They hurried away, and he slapped the door shut behind them, turning the key in the lock before pocketing it.

Meaghan eyed him warily. He was tall and slender. Older than she had expected, with a jutting chin, weathered face, and dark, glittering eyes. His clothes seemed out of place given this rough place. His jacket was far from the first fashion. Clean and neat, but showing signs of frequent mending. What kind of thug worried about holes in his clothing?

"I apologize, my dear lady." He walked toward her. The dull oil lamp flickered over his sharp features and lackluster brown-and-gray hair as he advanced to the bed. "It has never been my intention to do you harm, nor even to frighten you."

He shook his head, and a look of anger streaked over his face. "Your current predicament can be laid squarely at your husband's doorstep."

The anger subsided from his eyes, leaving his face a bland mask. "You and I are alike in that respect. For, you see, I have been wronged as well. I recognize you as a . . . kindred spirit. Another beleaguered soul taken advantage of without so much as a by-your-leave."

Meaghan watched him warily, wishing she could tell him exactly what she thought of a man who stole women against their will. But the gag still held firm, and she could do little beyond glare her outrage.

"Ah, I see you still do not understand. You are angry with me." He frowned, his gaze traveling her face and then downward over her body. He rubbed at his temples again. "I suppose you have a right to be. I have yet to explain myself. But when I have, when you have seen the rightness of what I am doing, then you will understand. You will applaud what I am about to accomplish."

He leaned toward her, and she shrank back from him as far as the wall would allow. He reeked of ale. His fingers, slender and bony, slipped around her neck. An icy chill shivered over her. She closed her eyes and offered up a quick prayer, certain she would never leave there alive. In her mind she could see Nicholas's face, and her heart wrenched with sorrow.

The gag fell away and she could breathe easier. She blinked in surprise.

"My intention has never been to harm you, my dear. I apologize for the unnecessary roughness with which you have been treated."

"The best apology you could offer would be our freedom." Her voice was dry and hoarse. If she screamed, would anyone in the tap downstairs take pity on her?

Her captor drew a lopsided chair from its pose by the table and settled it beside the bed. He sat in it, arranging his coat carefully at his sides be-

fore folding his hands in his lap to peer at her.
Dull light flicked against the side of his face,
throwing one half in deep shadow.

"We are in a rather desolate area where your
voice will not be heard by anyone save myself
and those in my employ." He answered her as if
he had heard her questioning thoughts.

She licked her lips. "Who are you? Why do
you wish to harm my husband?"

"Neville Chase." He nodded slightly and
spread his hands wide before resuming his former careful pose. "I have no desire to harm your
husband. I only wish him dead."

The flatness to his tone frightened her more
than his anger earlier.

"I am . . . or I was, employed by your husband's family and also by one Gill O'Brien. At
one time, I dared to consider them not just my
employers, but my friends. That was quite some
time ago. In the course of carrying out my duties, there were decisions to be made and choices
to be carried out. I made those choices. Your
husband's father, and his brother, and with the
inordinately enthusiastic help of Mr. O'Brien,
had me condemned as an embezzler and banished to a penal colony."

Who was this man? Kidnapper? Embezzler?
The fact that he had come back from a penal
colony settled a cold fear in her stomach.

"What do you want?"

"Ah, directly to the heart of the matter. No
nonsense or hysterics. You are as intelligent as
you are beautiful." Approval sharpened his features and gleamed in the depths of his black
eyes.

"I want justice served. That has been my life's

pursuit for the past two decades." His gaze clouded for a moment, and he tilted his head to one side as though listening to something she could not hear. Then he focused on her again. "Long enough to plan everything to the last detail."

"To plan what?" She couldn't stop the question, even though she was already quite certain she did not want to hear his answer.

"His death, my dear. And my vengeance." All said in a reasonable tone, as though this were the only thing he could do.

"But Nicholas had no—"

"Please, my dear." He waved his hand and leaned close again. "Do not start down a path that will only lead to frustration."

He gave her an indulgent look. "It does not matter that your Mansfield was not the root of the problem. He is guilty as his father was guilty. The sins of the fathers visited against the sons. He came to court. He witnessed my disgrace."

A frown flitted across his features before he continued. "He escaped me once, long ago, when I took care of his parents. But tonight, thanks in part to you, his time has come."

Horror crawled Meaghan's spine. Nicholas's recounting of the night his parents died, the explosion, the sinking, all those poor people, flooded her mind. "You . . . murdered them?"

"Murder." He made a face and flicked an invisible piece of lint from his worn jacket. "That is an ugly word. I prefer to think of it as retribution."

And now he was going to use her to get to Nicholas. Would her husband even try to rescue the wife he wished to shed? She knew he would.

That he probably even now rode to his death. The world tilted around Meaghan. Chase was mad. He had to be. "You killed innocent people."

"Indeed. I carry that with me every day. A dark blot against my soul. But I did only what I had to do." He nodded to himself.

Fear shuddered through Meaghan again.

He straightened his jacket and smoothed his limp hair before resuming his reasonable tone. "They arranged my transport on a ship destined to sink. There was no concern for the hundreds that went down in that explosion. Your husband's high-and-mighty father and his friends cared not one whit for the men who went down aboard that ship, screaming for their lives, shackled together with no hope of release."

"But you survived."

A corner of his mouth turned up in a smile. "The luck of the righteous placed me near the explosion. My bonds tore apart with the percussion. I was tossed, bleeding, into the dark sea. My leg was broken. It is only through the grace of heaven that I made shore at all. The grace of heaven, my dear."

He took a deep breath and favored her with a full grin that sent chills straight through her heart. His was the grin of utter madness. "Only I survived. All else was lost. That's when I knew I was right to plan my revenge. It was meant to be a sign."

He sighed. "Ashton's family got exactly what they deserved. I but applied their plan to their own lives."

Something dark and evil glittered in his eyes. "The satisfaction of watching them die is some-

thing I will never forget. I saw them, Ashton and
his wife, bobbing in the water, shouting to their
son to swim to safety."

He'd been there. Been there the night that
haunted Nicholas. Watching his handiwork bear
fruit as he murdered all those innocents, including Nicholas's parents. She could have wept, but
she needed to hang on. To try to get him to tell
her his plans for Nicholas.

Laughter, sharp and high-pitched, bubbled out
of him. "I whacked them good. Both of them.
There is nothing quite like the sound of an oar
cracking a man's skull." He rubbed his hands
together, relishing his murderous actions. "They
went under after that. The authorities fished
their bloated bodies from the water two days
later and a mile downstream."

She gagged at his delight in the events he described. She daren't let him see the horror she
felt.

Chase sighed again, a long sound of satisfaction.

She shivered, nausea whirling in her stomach.
"What are you planning to do with Nicholas?"

"Are you sure you wish to know?"

No. No, she didn't want to know at all. She
wanted someone to wake her from this terrible
nightmare and assure her that this madman did
not truly exist.

"Yes, I want to know. You told me I would understand and I do." She forced the words out
and tried to smile wide-eyed at him, the way
she'd seen Triona look at Seamus, the coachman.
"I want to hear the full measure of your vengeance so I can appreciate that, too."

"Indeed?" Chase studied her for a moment.

Her answer must have hit the right note. "Very well. For my lady's pleasure. Your Nicholas should have died that night with his parents. Drowned in the dank depths of the Shannon. But instead he got away. After I'd finished his parents he was too close to the shore and other people. I allowed the boy to live. And then I went off about my business. I raised funds. I paid dearly for the evidence brought against me."

"What of Nicholas now? What will you do to him?" she prodded when Chase drifted off in his reverie and fell silent.

"I have all but cleared my name. All that is left is disposing of the few people left alive who have firsthand knowledge of the original charges and the means to cause me further injury. Tonight, your husband will drown as he should have almost fifteen years ago. O'Brien with him. Then you and I will both be free." The finality of his tone tightened the cold writhing in the pit of her stomach.

"How? How will you get him there?" Meaghan's throat was tight. She already knew. The planking of the walls bit into her shoulders and scraped her knuckles raw. And terror for her husband rasped her soul.

"You are the key." His madness answered her. The simplicity of his plan tied into his twisted, circular logic.

"You should be pleased I am about to set you free of him. He abused your good name before he married you and he continues to abuse you."

"Nicholas has never hurt me." The denial burst from her.

"Of course he has." Something dark sizzled in the look Chase passed over her. "I know what he has done to you. I have seen what he forced you to do as his wife. In his bed."

His tongue flicked over his lips. With a hot rush of shock she realized exactly what he was trying to say. Somehow he knew what had passed between her and Nicholas in the privacy of their marriage.

"Yes, my dear." His gaze bore into hers. "I know all that he has done to you. I would never treat my wife so . . . harshly. I would never have you perform the acts of a whore with me."

Again his tongue flicked his lips. His gaze traveled to her breasts. Her blood ran cold. "I do understand. He enticed you. He overwhelmed your innocence with his depraved appetites. He even made you enjoy being stripped and ravaged in the dining room."

A spark of annoyance flared in the depths of the glittering gaze he kept fixed on her breasts.

Gooseflesh pebbled every inch of her skin. Revulsion twisted inside her. He had watched them in their most private moments. She shuddered. He was taking the only thing she had with Nicholas and making it ugly.

He reached out a hand and slid his cold fingers over her cheek. "Before you thank me for the years of shame my actions tonight will spare you at his hand, I want to assure you that I will be a tender, considerate lover."

She recoiled. He had seen her with Nicholas and now he wanted to take his turn. Tears gathered in her eyes. "Please don't," she whispered.

He ignored her and stroked down her cheek, to her throat and then over her bare shoulders and along the neckline of her gown. And back again in a circuit of torment. "Such fair skin, so pale and soft. You are almost an angel."

Chase rose from the lopsided chair and eased himself onto the bed beside her. The mattress sagged under his weight and he shifted her up against him. "He should not dress you in a harlot's red. It will give other men . . . ideas."

His fingers slid inside the neckline of her gown, following the chain that held her granny's cross. A knock rattled the door behind him.

"Mr. Chase?"

"What is it?" His voice rasped sharp with irritation. His fingers tightened on her bodice. "I am busy."

"Ye wanted ta know when they were comin'. Signal says they'll be here within the hour."

Chase's hands stilled against her skin. He closed his eyes and stretched his head back, pulling her hard against his body. She could feel the shudders running through him. She almost wretched.

"Now. Now is the time to claim my victory." His hands rubbed over her shoulders and her back almost spastically.

"Stop. Stop." She tried to break through to him, to no avail, as she squirmed in his mad embrace.

He stroked his hand along her shoulder, then down to her bodice to grope her breast. "Thus a man is freed from the shackles too long binding his heart and mind."

Meaghan twisted in his hold.

He bent over her. The sparkle of evil shimmering in his black eyes made her frightened heartbeat thump loudly in her ears. Gone was the veneer of civility with which he first greeted her.

Something fearful looked out at her from the shell of Neville Chase.

"And thus is all brought to sweet vengeance." He mashed his mouth down over hers, smothering the scream welling up inside her.

Hot and wet, his kiss went on interminably as he licked at her lips, moaning and grunting. Her tears spilled down her cheeks, but he paid them and her struggles no mind.

His hands gripped her tight to his body as he rubbed himself against her, thrusting obscenely against her gown and driving her hands and head back into the wall. Then he shuddered, quivering against her over and over again.

He released a gusty sigh of pleasure and flung her from his grasp. She fell back against the mattress with a thud. He stepped away from the bed, his breathing harsh. A dark stain blotched the front of his trousers.

He looked down at himself and laughed—a sharp sound, like broken crystal.

"Mr. Chase?" The door rattled again.

"I'll be there directly. Make the preparations I told you."

He looked back at her. His features once again arranged into a polite, bland mask. "And so the dance begins. You will be uncomfortable in the hours to come, madam. Prepare yourself. But in the end you will be free."

He walked away from her, slamming the door behind him and turning the key in the lock.

Meaghan shook with the sobs she could no longer hold back. This madman was going to kill Nicholas and Uncle Gill. Then probably Sheila and her, for good measure. She renewed her efforts with the knots binding her hands. If there was any way to stop Chase, she had to find it before Nicholas met the horror planned for him.

She must.

Jamie grasped his arm. "I've got to come with you."

"No." Nick shook him off and reached for the reins to the roan gelding with his mind racing.

Meaghan was in danger and it was his fault. His. The fear roiling in his stomach burned like ice. "I'll not have you in danger as well."

Gill and Randall mounted beside him. The ex-sergeant handed Nick a pistol.

"Sheila is in danger as well. You can't make me stay."

Nick didn't stop to debate. He clocked Jamie squarely on the chin. His ward crumpled to the ground. "I'm sorry, stripling, but this is our fight. Not yours."

"Get him into the house," O'Brien told the waiting Seamus.

Nick kicked the gelding into motion and the other two men rode beside him. Fear and reprisals clashed together in his mind as the three of them rode in silence. The note they'd found from Neville Chase ran over and over in his mind. The man was pure poison and Nick had all but given Meaghan over to him. He should have put her on a boat for her island that morning.

On through the night the horses pounded. His heart pounded. His fear pounded. They didn't have much time. Chase had been all too thorough in his description of what he had in store for the two women he had kidnapped. The details the bastard listed with apparent relish chilled Nick to his core.

Adding the descriptions of what he had done to Nick's parents, and to Jamie's, proved his madness.

The ground flew by beneath the gelding's feet. Randall's and O'Brien's mounts kept pace. Conversation was impossible. Each man was left to the bleakness and horror of his own thoughts.

Cold moonlight sparkled over the darkened landscape. Each second that ticked by put Meaghan and her cousin in more and more danger. No matter how fast he urged the roan, it never felt fast enough. He felt caught in a waking nightmare.

But it was all too real. Chase had even provided them the exact location where they could find the two women. Randall's words echoed over and over in Nick's mind.

He wouldn't have told you that, if he thought you had any chance of rescuing them, my lord.

His heart wrenched. Fear twisted deeper and deeper inside him. Meaghan, his Meaghan. He had to be able to help her. He had to be able to save her. Why hadn't he kept her right by his side? Why hadn't he sent her far away? The horse pounding beneath him quickened in speed.

"Please, God, let me get there in time." The words fell from his lips over and over again. "I love her. Please let me get there in time."

Pain coursed through him. He could not fail her. Could not lose everyone he held dearest to the clutches of a madman.

Hours crawled like years.

And then over the brow of the hill, they saw it. The river sparkling like madness in the moonlight. The inn. Just as Chase had said. Coldness shrouded Nick's stomach.

"Now what?" Gill O'Brien sounded winded beside him.

"Now we free them."

"My lord."

"I know what you said, Randall. I know you are most likely right. "Nick locked his gaze with the ex-soldier turned valet. "Know this. I must save her. There can be no other option."

Hold on Meaghan. I'm coming.

Don't come Nicholas. Don't come. Meaghan said the prayer over and over as the water crept ever upward. She prayed he'd be delayed just a little longer. She shivered in the cold water and tested her bonds for the hundredth time.

The water crawled higher and higher, lapping at her chin. Cold racked her again, icy death. She knew Chase waited in the rocks somewhere nearby. In the dark. He had disappeared from sight long before the water reached her hips, laughing his strange off-key laugh. And now he waited for Nicholas to come to her aid so he could be murdered just like his parents.

Fear tightened inside her with each numbing inch the current brought. Chase's men had bound her tight and set her in this tidal pool deep in the banks of the river maybe hours, maybe minutes ago. She couldn't tell. All she could think about was Nicholas.

The river water flowed in as the tide of the estuary pushed on to Limerick. Great boulders rimmed the pool on three sides, and the river took the fourth. She was in the open, a lamb leading her husband to slaughter. Heavy rocks weighted her feet. She could not move, let alone get free.

She gave up hope for herself.

The only hope left in her was for Nicholas. If only he arrived here too late. If only he saved Sheila first. The madman had some horrible scheme in store for her as well, meant to lure her father to his death next.

The water lapped still higher. She tasted the river's earthy tang. She fought the urge to scream by thinking of the special moments in her life. Cricket with her brothers, reading with Da, baking with Mama. And sharing a garden bench and her first kiss, her Blessing, with Nicholas. The certainty that Nick had been the boy who had comforted her so long ago surprised her with the clarity of the memory of that day and its portent for their future.

Tears stung her, flowing to mingle with the river her family had plied for countless generations. She cried for all she and Nicholas would never experience together. For the children they would never see and the love she would never be able to give him.

"Oh, Nicholas." Her teeth chattered. "I love you."

"And I you," his voice whispered out of the darkness. Not from the riverbank, but from the current itself. A small splash sounded behind her.

He was here. He had come for her.

Meaghan's spine tingled with the sudden sweep of anticipation and fear.

"Nicholas?"

"Aye, beloved. I will have you free in just a

moment." His hands touched her shoulders and slid down her arms to her wrists.

"A man named Neville Chase is here. He will kill you. He killed your parents." She tried to remain still and speak her warning as quietly as possible, knowing how easily sound carried over water. Terror that even now she might betray Nicholas to his enemy ripped through her. "You must go."

"Not without you."

The water slapped at her mouth and she tilted her chin. "Please, Nicholas."

"Ever the stubborn one." He kissed her on the nape of her neck. His mouth had never felt so warm. In a moment her hands finally came free of the bonds. She waved them just under the surface of the water, willing them to help keep the water from her face. To make her buoyant.

"My feet," she told him, unwilling to argue further.

He disappeared beneath the surface. She could feel his hands on her legs. Her heart pounded as she waited for Chase to make his move.

They were terribly vulnerable here in the tidal pool, especially when the man realized she was free. She struggled to remain still enough to fool him into thinking she was still bound.

The silence stretched ominously as she felt Nick working her free of the rocks. She took a breath as the water crested her nose. In a swoop of water the level rose over her head. Fear knifed her. She could no longer hear or see. Her feet came free at last. Breath tasted sweet as she kicked to the surface.

Chase was there at the edge of the pool. Waiting.

Panic iced Meaghan's veins. Nick bobbed to the surface beside her.

The choice once made cannot be altered. She flung herself in front of her husband as a shot splintered the cool night air.

"Meaghan, no!" Nick caught her in his arms and turned his back toward his enemy, shielding her with his body.

"No. This can't be." Chase's voice sounded full of confusion. "I must succeed . . . Not ready . . ."

He coughed, the sound wet and hoarse.

Meaghan turned in Nick's arms. A dark stain spread across Neville Chase's chest.

"For . . . the . . . abyss . . ." He fell into the water with a loud splash and sank below the dark surface.

"Randall? O'Brien?" Nick hoisted Meaghan toward the edge of the pool. A hand reached out for hers and pulled her to safety.

"Told you I needed to come, Nick." Jamie helped her to her feet and then offered his hand to Nicholas. A dark purple bruise dotted the younger man's chin.

"Stripling?"

Jamie pulled him to safety as well. "Yes."

"A bit the worse for wear."

"Yes, to that as well." A smile twisted Jamie's lips. "But I had to find Sheila."

"But where is Randall? And O'Brien?" Nick pulled Meaghan to him. It didn't matter that she was wet and shivering. She was safe in his arms. She was alive and she was his. That was all that mattered in the entire world.

"Randall ran into a bit of trouble with Chase's hired thugs. They got away, according to the innkeeper. I left Randall stretched out in the inn. He'll be sporting a few of these himself by dawn." He pointed to his chin.

"Shhh . . . She . . ." Meaghan shivered too violently to get her words out. Nick rubbed her arms to warm her.

"Sheila is a little worse for wear, but with her father. He told me you planned to swim in behind Chase's designation."

"And the pistol?"

"I took that from Randall. Thought it might come in handy." Jamie smiled.

"I'm sorry I punched you, Stripling. Turns out I did need you."

"Indeed." Jamie quirked a brow at him. "You'll get no argument from me on that score."

Hours later, dry and warmed beyond measure by her husband's loving attentions, Meaghan lay back against the pillows, snuggled against Nick's shoulder.

"I love you, Lord Ashton," she told him softly.

"And I you, sweet Meaghan." He kissed her, soft and slow, spinning her world in long circles. She would never get enough of the feel of his skin against hers and their lips locked together. "Are you happy?"

"I have only one regret now."

"And what is that?"

"I did not get all the funding for the Nightingale Society. The building of a nurses training school will be delayed."

"Ahh, that reminds me." He stretched across

the bed to retrieve a packet of papers from the nightstand. "Sheila gave me this before we left the O'Briens'. She said you might want to read it."

Meaghan recognized the envelope she had opened just as Chase came up behind her. She shivered. The man might be dead and gone, but she could still remember the sound of his voice and his twisted determination that he was right. That his plans were righteous.

. Poor deluded soul. At least he could harm no more of Nick's family. Her family.

She opened the envelope as Nick pulled her back against him, spilling the vellum sheets against the coverlet.

"What does it say?" He whispered the question against her neck, sending little whorls of heat along her spine.

She read quickly and tears sprang to her eyes as she did.

"What does it say?" This time Nick sounded more insistent.

"Oh, she is going to give us so much. She says that her son served in the Crimea. That the war cost her both her men. Her son died from his wounds and her husband died of a broken heart. It's so sad."

"Indeed?" He relaxed a little and ran his fingers along her arm in the way that drove her wild.

Meaghan nodded and read on. "Then she thanks me for giving her a means to prevent other wives and mothers from losing their sons and husbands. And she ends it by telling me she admires the way I spoke to her and answered all her questions without quibbling. And that I

mustn't mind what others say. That if I continue
to speak and act from my heart everything will
turn out in the end."

"Oh, Nicholas, I didn't fail after all." Meaghan
turned in his arms and kissed him squarely on
the mouth, her excitement over her success
transferring quickly to passion.

"Mmm, my dear." Nicholas rolled her onto
her back, the vellumed sheets fluttering to the
floor. "I'd hardly call you a failure. It is my distinct understanding from your brothers, your uncle, and anyone else who knows your family, that
Reillys rarely fail at anything they set their minds
to. You may be Lady Ashton to all and sundry,
but at heart you will always be a Reilly."

She laughed and tightened her arms about his
neck. "Is that what they told you? Nicholas, there
is so much to tell you. So much you do not
know."

"And a lifetime to tell it in, my wife." He
kissed her again, slower and even more thoroughly than the last.

"Aye." She sighed and caressed his cheek. "A
lifetime to tell you all the tales you need to hear.
But mostly there is one thing I want you know."

"And what is that, my lady?"

"You are my Blessing, Lord Ashton. And you
have been since the moment of our very first
kiss."

"Indeed?" He nibbled the corner of her
mouth. "You've known since that first day barely
a fortnight ago?"

"Oh, it was much longer than that," she told
him softly as the passion building between them
burned brighter.

"Really? You must enlighten me."

"I will," she told him as she gave herself over to loving him.

"Later."

There would be time to tell him all the tales he needed to hear. Beginning with their first kiss, when she was only five years old.

She sighed against his lips and their kisses blended one unto the other as laughter pure and joyous echoed through her and a rainbow of colored stars chased through her heart.

AUTHORS' NOTE

Florence Nightingale (1820-1910) organized a unit of women in 1854 to nurse wounded British soldiers during the Crimean War. Also known as the Lady with the lamp, her efforts were chronicled in the *Times*. In 1860 she founded a nursing school and home at St. Thomas Hospital, London, implementing the practices she espoused in her first book, *Notes on Nursing*, published that year.

Although the Limerick Nightingale Society referred to in this novel is fictional, the reforms sparked by Miss Nightingale spread around the world and her work is still honored today.

ABOUT THE AUTHORS

Elizabeth Keys is the pseudonym for the multi award-winning writing team, Mary Lou Frank and Susan C. Stevenson, lifelong friends and residents of southern New Jersey.

This Irish Blessing historical illustrates the authors' belief in achieving your heart's desire through love's special magic.

They love hearing from readers either through e-mail: mail@elizabethkeys.com or by writing: Elizabeth Keys P.O. Box 243 Alloway, NJ 08001.

Discover your KEYS to romance . . . www.elizabethkeys.com.

Look for the other books in the Irish Blessing series: *Reilly's Law, Reilly's Gold, Reilly's Pride.*

COMING IN JANUARY 2002
FROM ZEBRA BALLAD ROMANCES

__THE BRIDE WORE BLUE: The Brides of Bath__
 by Cheryl Bolen   0-8217-7247-3 $5.99US/$7.99CAN
Felicity came to the aid of Thomas Moreland after a band of highwaymen left him for dead. Now he's determined to convince her that there's more to life than assembly rooms, matrons, and matchmaking. But what Felicity doesn't know yet is that her greatest desire of all is to spend the rest of her life in Thomas's arms . . .

__PROMISE THE MOON: The Vaudrys__
 by Linda Lea Castle   0-8217-7266-X $5.99US/$7.99CAN
Held captive by Thomas Le Revenant, and betrothed against her will to his son, Rowanne Vaudry is doomed to a life of misery. Then fate—in the form of Brandt Le Revenant—steps in, rescuing her as she journeys to meet her fiancé. How can Rowanne know that Brandt, a knight newly returned from the Crusades, has his own reasons for helping her?

__NATE: The Rock Creek Six__
 by Lori Handeland   0-8217-7275-9 $5.99US/$7.99CAN
When Josephine Clancy met Nate Lang, she couldn't help but offer her friendship. Haunted by the War Between the States, Nate was the kind of man who needed someone. But Jo hadn't counted on falling in love with the hurting, secretive stranger—or the lengths she would travel to rescue him from the melancholy that threatened to destroy him.

__REUNION: Men of Honor__
 by Kathryn Fox   0-8217-7242-2 $5.99US/$7.99CAN
Lauren often thought of the hardships she would face as the wife of a Canadian Mountie. But she never imagined that her first challenge would be her own betrothed, for Adam McPhail now seems distant and cautious. Lauren wonders if the marriage she's dreamed of has ended before it has begun.
